Praise for *Fire and Thorns*:

'Elisa is a wonderful, believable hero, the kind that every reader can imagine as herself. I charged through the book in two days, savouring Elisa's realness and her unique, wonderful world! Engrossing'

New York Times bestselling author Tamora Pierce

'I LOVED this book! It's a transformation story that both teens and adults can believe in. Rae Carson has delivered a unique magical system and built a world with strong series potential'

New York Times bestselling author Cinda Williams Chima

'A delicious debut'   Paolo Bacigalupi

'A smart, complex fantasy with stellar characters . . . Carson's mature writing style, thoughtful storytelling, appealing characters and surprising twists add up to a page-turner with broad appeal'   *Publishers Weekly*

THE
CROWN of
EMBERS

RAE CARSON

The right of Rae Carson to be identified as the author
of this work has been asserted by her in accordance
with the Copyright, Designs and Patents Act 1988.

First published in Great Britain in 2012
by Gollancz
An imprint of the Orion Publishing Group
Orion House, 5 Upper St Martin's Lane,
London WC2H 9EA
An Hachette UK Company

This edition published in Great Britain in 2013
by Gollancz

1 3 5 7 9 10 8 6 4 2

A CIP catalogue record for this book
is available from the British Library

ISBN 978 0 575 09920 3

Printed in Great Britain by Clays Ltd, St Ives plc

The Orion Publishing Group's policy is to use papers
that are natural, renewable and recyclable products and
made from wood grown in sustainable forests. The logging
and manufacturing processes are expected to conform to
the environmental regulations of the country of origin.

www.raecarson.com
www.orionbooks.co.uk
www.gollancz.co.uk

1

MY entourage of guards struggles to keep pace as I fly down the corridors of my palace. Servants in starched frocks and shined shoes line the way, bowing like dominoes as I pass. From far away comes a low thrum, filtering even through walls of stone and mortar, steady as falling water, hollow as distant thunder. It's the crowd outside, chanting my name.

I barrel around a corner and collide with a gleaming breast-plate. Firm hands grasp my shoulders, saving me from tumbling backward. My crown is not so lucky. The monstrous thing clatters to the ground, yanking strands of hair painfully with it.

He releases my shoulders and rubs at red spot on his neck. "That crown of yours is a mighty weapon," says Lord-Commander Hector of the Royal Guard.

"Sorry," I say, blinking up at him. He and the other guards shaved their mustaches to mark our recent victory, and I've yet to adjust to this new, younger-looking Hector.

Ximena, my gray-haired nurse, bends to retrieve the crown and brushes it off. It's thick with gold and inlaid with a single cabochon ruby. No dainty queen's diadem for me. By tradition, I wear the crown of a fully empowered monarch.

"I expected you an hour ago," he says as I take his offered arm. We travel the corridor at a bruising pace.

"General Luz-Manuel kept me. He wanted to change the parade route again."

He stops cold, and I nearly trip. "Again?"

"He wants to avoid the bottleneck where the Avenida de la Serpiente crosses the merchant's alley. He says a stranger in the crowd could spear me too easily."

Ximena takes advantage of our stillness to reposition the crown on my head. I grimace as she shoves hairpins through the velvet loops to hold it in place.

Hector is shaking his head. "But the rooftops are low in that area. You'll be safer from arrows, which is the greater danger."

"Exactly what I said. He was . . . displeased." I tug on his arm to keep us moving.

"He should know better."

"I may have told him as much."

"I'm sure he appreciated that," he says dryly.

"I've no idea what advantage he thought to gain by it," I say. "Whatever it was, I was not going to give it to him."

Hector glances around at the people lining the corridors, then adds in a lowered voice, "Elisa, as your personal defender, I must beg you one last time to reconsider. The whole world knows you bear the Godstone."

I sigh against the truth of his words. Yes, I'm now the target of religious fanatics, Invierne spies, even black market gem traders. But my birthday parade is the one day each year when everyone—from laundress to stable boy to weather-worn sailor—can glimpse their ruling monarch. It's a national holiday, one they've been looking forward to for months. I won't deny them the opportunity.

And I refuse to be governed by fear. The life stretching before me is that of a queen. It's a life I chose. Fought for, even. I cannot—will not—squander it on dread.

"Hector, I won't hide in the sand like a frightened jerboa."

"Sometimes," Ximena cuts in, with her soft but deliberate voice, "protecting Elisa means protecting her interests. Elisa must show herself publicly. These early months are important as she consolidates her power. We'll keep her safe, you and I. And God. She has a great destiny. . . ."

I turn a deaf ear to her words. So much has happened in the last year, but I feel no closer to my appointment with destiny than I did when God first lodged his stone in my navel seventeen years ago. It still pulses with power, warms in response to my prayers, reminds me that I have not done *enough*, that God has plans for me yet.

And I am sick to death of hearing about it.

"I understand, my lady," Hector is saying. "But it would be safer—"

"Hector!" I snap. "I've made up my mind."

He stiffens. "Yes, Your Majesty."

Shame tightens my throat. Why did I snap at Hector? Ximena is the one I'm frustrated with.

Moments later we reach the carriage house, which reeks

of steaming manure and moldy straw on this especially hot day. My open carriage awaits, a marvel of polished mahogany and swirling bronze scrollwork. Banners of royal blue stream from the posts. The door panels display my royal crest—a ruby crown resting on a bed of sacrament roses.

Fernando, my best archer, stands on the rear platform, bow slung over his shoulder. He bows from the waist, his face grave. Four horses flick their tails and dance in their jeweled traces. I eye them warily while Hector helps me up.

Then he offers a hand to Ximena, and in spite of their recent disagreement, a look of fierce understanding passes between them. They are a formidable team, my guard and my guardian. Sometimes it's as though they plot my safety behind my back.

Hector gives the order, my driver whips the reins, and the carriage lurches forward. My Royal Guard, in its gleaming ceremonial armor, falls in around us. They march a deep one-two-one-two as we leave the shade of the carriage house for desert sunshine.

The moment we turn onto the Colonnade, the air erupts with cheering.

Thousands line the way, packed shoulder to shoulder, waving their hands, flags, tattered linens. Children sit on shoulders, tossing birdseed and rose petals into the air. A banner stretches the length of six people and reads, HAPPY BIRTHDAY TO HER MAJESTY QUEEN LUCERO-ELISA!

"Oh," I breathe.

Ximena grasps my hand and squeezes. "You're a war hero, remember?"

But I'm also a foreigner queen, ruling by an accident of marriage and war. Warmth and pride blossom in my chest, to see my people accepting me with their whole hearts.

Then Ximena's face sobers, and she leans over and whispers, "Remember this moment and treasure it, my sky. No sovereign remains popular forever."

I nod from respectful habit, but I can't keep the frown from creeping onto my face. My people are giving me a gift, and she takes it away so soon.

The steep Colonnade is lined on either side by decadent three-story townhomes. Their sculpted sandstone cornices sparkle in the sun, and silk standards swing from flat garden rooftops. But as we descend from the height of the city, cheered all the way, the townhomes gradually become less stately, until finally we reach the city's outer circle, where only a few humble buildings rise from the war rubble.

I ignore the destruction as long as I can, gazing instead at the city's great wall. It rises the height of several men, protecting us from the swirling desert beyond. I crane my neck and glimpse the soldiers posted between the wall's crenellations, bows held at the ready.

The main gate stands open for daytime commerce. Framed by the barbed portcullis is our cobbled highway. Beyond it are the sweeping dunes of my beautiful desert, wind smoothed and deceptively soft in the yellow light of midday. My gaze lingers too long on the sand as we turn onto the Avenida de la Serpiente.

When I can avoid it no longer, I finally take in the view that twists my heart. For Brisadulce's outer circle is a scar on the face of the world, blackened and crumbled and reeking of wet char. This is where the Invierne army broke through our gate, where their sorcerous animagi burned everything in sight with the blue-hot fire of their Godstone amulets.

A ceiling beam catches my eye, toppled across a pile of adobe rubble. At one end the wood grain shows pristine, but it blackens along its length, shrinking and shriveling until it ends in a ragged stump glowing red with embers. A wisp of smoke curls into the air.

The outer ring is rife with these glowing reminders of the war we won at such a cost. Months later, we still cannot wholly quench their fire. Father Nicandro, my head priest, says that since magic caused these fires, only magic can cool them. Either magic or time.

My city may burn for a hundred years.

So I smile and wave. I do it with ferocity, like my life depends on it, as if a whole glorious future lies before us and these sorcerous embers are not worth a passing irritation.

The crowd loves me for it. They scream and cheer, and it is like magic, a good magic, how after a while *they* win *me* over to hope, and my smile becomes genuine.

The street narrows, and the crowd presses in as we push forward. Hector's hand goes to his scabbard as he inches nearer to the carriage. I tell myself that I don't mind their proximity, that I love their smiling faces, their unrestrained energy.

But as we approach the massive amphitheater with its stone columns, I sense a subtle shift, a dampening of spirits—as if everyone has become distracted. The guards scan the crowd with suspicion.

"Something isn't right," Ximena whispers.

I glance at her with alarm. From long habit, my fingertips find the Godstone, seeking a clue; it heats up around friends and becomes ice when my life is in peril. Do I imagine that it is cooler than usual?

The theater is shaped like a giant horseshoe, its massive ends running perpendicular to the avenida. As we near it, movement draws my gaze upward. High above the crowd stands a man in a white wind-whipped robe.

My Godstone freezes—unhelpfully—and ice shoots through my limbs as I note his hair: lightest yellow, almost white, streaming to his waist. Sunlight catches on something embedded in the top of his wooden staff. *Oh, God.*

I'm too shocked to cry out, and by the time Hector notices the white figure, it's too late: My carriage is within range. The crowd is eerily silent, as if all the air has gotten sucked away, for everyone has heard descriptions of the animagi, Invierne's sorcerers.

The top of the animagus' staff begins to glow Godstone blue.

My terror is like the thick muck of a dream as I struggle to find my voice. "Fernando!" I yell. "Shoot him! Shoot to kill!"

An arrow whizzes toward the animagus in blurred relief against the crystal sky.

The animagus whips his staff toward it. A stream of blue-hot fire erupts from the tip, collides with the arrow, explodes it into a shower of splinters and sparks.

People scream. Hector gestures at the guards, barking orders. Half tighten formation around me; the rest sprint away to flank the sorcerer. But the crowd is panicked and thrashing, and my guards are trapped in a mill of bodies.

"Archers!" Hector yells. "Fire!"

Hundreds of arrows let fly in a giant *whoosh*.

The animagus spins in a circle, staff outstretched. The air around him bends to his will, and I catch the barest glimpse of a barrier forming—like glass, like a wavering desert mirage—before Ximena leaps across the bench and covers me with her own body.

"To the queen!" comes Hector's voice. "We must retreat!" But the carriage doesn't budge, for the milling crowd has hemmed us in.

"Queen Lucero-Elisa," comes a sibilant voice, magnified by the peculiar nature of the amphitheater. "Bearer of the only living Godstone, you belong to us, to us, to us."

He's coming down the stairway. I know he is. He's coming for *me*. He'll blaze a path through my people and—

"You think you've beaten us back, but we are as numerous as the desert sands. Next time we'll come at you like ghosts in a dream. And you will know the gate of your enemy!"

In the corner of my eye I catch the gleam of Hector's sword as he raises it high, and my stomach thuds with the realization that he'll cut through our own people if that's what it takes to whisk me away.

"Ximena!" I gasp. "Get off. Hector . . . he'll do anything. We can't let him—"

She understands instantly. "Stay down," she orders as she launches against the door and tumbles into the street.

Heart pounding, I peek over the edge of the carriage. The animagus stares at me hungrily as he descends the great stair, like I am a juicy mouse caught in his trap. My Godstone's icy warning is relentless.

He could have killed me by now if he wanted to; we've no way to stop his fire. So why doesn't he? Eyeing him carefully, I stand up in the carriage.

"Elisa, no!" cries Hector. Ximena has trapped his sword arm, but he flings her off and rushes toward me. He jerks to a stop midstride, and his face puckers with strain: The animagus has frozen him with magic.

But Hector is the strongest man I know. *Fight it, Hector.*

Shivering with bone-deep cold, I force myself to step from the carriage. *I* am what the sorcerer wants, so maybe I can distract him, buy enough time for my guards to flank him, give Hector a chance to break free.

Sun glints off a bit of armor creeping up on the animagus from above, so I keep my gaze steady, and my voice is steel when I say, "I burned your brothers to dust. I will do the same to you." The lie weighs heavy on my tongue. I've harnessed the power of my stone only once, and I'm not sure how.

The animagus' answering grin is feral and slick. "Surrender yourself. If you do, we will spare your people."

A guard is within range now. The animagus has not noticed him. The solider quietly feeds an arrow into his bow, aims.

Look strong, Elisa. Do not flinch. Hold his gaze.

The arrow zings through the air. The sorcerer whirls at the sound, but it is too late; the arrowhead buries itself in his ribs.

The animagus wobbles. He turns back to me, eyes flared with pain or zeal, one shoulder hanging lower than the other. Crimson spreads like spilled ink across his robe. "Watch closely, my queen," he says, and his voice is liquid with drowning. "This is what will happen to everyone in Joya d'Arena if you do not present yourself as a *willing sacrifice*."

Hector reaches me at last, grabs my shoulders, and starts to pull me away, even as the guards rush the animagus. But his Godstone already glows like a tiny sun; they will not capture him in time. I expect fire to shoot toward us, to turn my people into craters of melt and char, and suddenly I'm grappling for purchase at the joints of Hector's armor, at his sword belt, pushing him along, for I can't bear to see another friend burn.

But the animagus turns the fire on himself.

He screams, "It is God's will!" He raises his arms to the sky, and his lips move as if in prayer while the conflagration melts his skin, blackens his hair, turns him into a living torch for the whole city to see.

The scent of burning flesh fills the air as the remaining crowd scatters. The horses rear and plunge away, trampling everyone in their path, the carriage rattling behind.

"To the queen!" Hector yells above my head.

A wind gusts through the amphitheater, extinguishing the biggest flames and flinging bits of hair and robe into the sky. The animagus' charred body topples off the stair and plunges to the ground, trailing smoke and sparks.

I turn to rest my forehead against Hector's breastplate and close my eyes as the chaos around us gradually dissipates. The chill of my Godstone fades, and I breathe deep of warm desert air and of relief.

Hector says, "We must get you back to the palace."

"Yes, of course," I say, pulling away from him and standing tall. "Let's go." Maybe if I pretend hard enough, I will feel strong in truth.

My guards form a wedge of clanking armor and drawn swords. As we begin the long, steep trek home, a bit of white robe, edged with glowing cinders, flutters to the ground at my feet.

2

I pray during the walk back, thanking God for my life and the lives of my guards, asking him to keep us safe just a little while longer. But as we approach the palace, Hector holds up a fist to halt our procession.

The portcullis is dropped and barred. Hundreds gather outside. Some yell and stomp, rattling the iron bars. Others stand quietly, carrying blankets, packs, small children. Their number swells as others trickle in from the adjoining streets and alleys.

"They think we're being attacked," I say, my voice catching. "They want protection within the palace walls."

"Maybe we are," Ximena says quietly. "Maybe it's war all over again."

"Back away quickly," Hector says. "But no sudden moves." I hear what he's not saying—if the desperate throng discovers me, I could be mobbed.

We crowd into a narrow alley between two townhomes. Hector whips off the bright red cloak marking him as a Royal Guard and turns it inside out so the softer, paler side shows.

"Put this on. That gown is much too noticeable."

The cloak smells of Hector—oiled steel and worn leather and spiced wine. After I fasten the claps at my neck, I gesture to the others. "All of you. Turn your cloaks inside out. Ximena, can you hide my crown?" I lift it from my head, and she untangles my hair from the various pins keeping it in place.

She holds it out for a moment, considering. She slips behind me, out of sight of the guards, and when she reveals herself again, the front of her skirt is lumpy and distended. "At least it doesn't look like a crown," she says with an apologetic shrug.

"Now what?" I say. "If the portcullis is barred, the stables are surely closed off as well."

"The kitchens?" a guard suggests.

"Or the receiving hall," says another.

Hector shakes his head. "The garrison is trained to lock down all entrances during drills."

Any member of the Royal Guard would be allowed admittance without question. There is a reason he's not sending someone to the palace to fetch a larger escort and a window-less carriage. "You think it's no accident," I say, "that someone ordered the palace locked down before I was safely inside. You think the crowd may not be the greater danger."

His gaze on me is solemn. "I'll take no chances with you."

"The escape tunnel!" I say. "Leading from the king's suite to the merchants' alley. Alejandro said only a few know of it." I swallow against the memory of long days spent in my husband's suite as he lay dying. I paid close attention to his every word, storing them up in my heart so I could someday pass them along to his son, Rosario.

Hector rubs at his jaw. "It's in disrepair. I haven't been inside since Alejandro and I were boys."

It will have to do. "Let's go," I order.

We leave the shadow of the brick alley and step into sunshine. From habit, the guards fall into perfect formation.

"No, no." I motion vaguely. "Relax. Don't look so . . . guardlike."

They drop formation at once, glancing at one another shamefaced. Hector drapes an arm around my shoulder as if we are out for a companionable stroll. He leans down and says, "So. Horrible heat we've had lately."

I can't help grinning, even as I note the tenseness of his shoulders, the way his eyes roam the street and his free hand wraps around the hilt of his sword. I say, "I'd prefer to discuss the latest fashion craze of jeweled stoles."

He laughs. "No, you wouldn't."

We reach the merchants' alley without incident. It's eerily silent, the booths vacant, the cobblestone street empty of rumbling carts. It's a national holiday. This place should be filled with shoppers, acrobats, and beggars, with coconut scones and sticky date pops and meat pies.

The news must have whipped through the city with the destructive force of a sandstorm. *The Inviernos are back! And they threatened the queen!*

All this emptiness makes us nothing if not noticeable. My neck prickles as I glance at the surrounding buildings, expecting furtive heads to appear in windowsills. But I see no one.

Quietly I say, "Alejandro said the entrance was through a blacksmith's home."

"Yes. Just around the corner . . . there." He indicates a large awning outside a two-story adobe building. The bellows beneath it is cold, and the traces dangle empty chains.

Hector's hand on my shoulder tightens as he peers under the awning. "Ho, blacksmith!" he calls.

The door creaks open. A bald man with a sooty leather apron and forearms like corded tree trunks steps over the threshold. His eyes widen.

"Goodman Rialto!" the blacksmith exclaims, and his cheer is a little too forced. "Your cauldron is ready. A beauty, I must say. Had some extra bronze sheeting lying around, which will reduce your total cost. Please come in!"

I look up at Hector for confirmation, and he nods, almost imperceptibly. We follow the blacksmith inside.

Every space of wall is used to display his work—swords, grates, animal traps, spoons, candlesticks, gauntlets. The scent of the place is biting, like copper gone sour. A low cooking fire crackles in a clay hearth. Only a blacksmith could stand to have a fire going on a day as hot as this. After we filter in, he closes the door behind us and drops the latch.

"This way, Your Majesty," he says, all trace of brightness evaporated. "Quickly." He pulls up the corner of a thick rug and reveals a trapdoor. With a grunt, he heaves on the brass ring. The trapdoor swings open to show rickety wooden stairs descending into darkness.

"We'll need light," I say.

He grabs a candle and a brass holder from a nearby table, reaches toward the hearth to light the wick, and hands it to me. "Be wary," he says. "The tunnel is reinforced with wooden beams. They're very old and very dry."

"I'll go first," Hector says, and the stair creaks under his weight.

I start to follow but hesitate. "Ximena, take the rest of the guards and return to the palace through the main entrance. They'll let you in. People should be seen leaving here, just in case they saw us coming."

She frowns. "My place is by your side."

"I'm safe with Hector." Before she can protest, I turn and address the blacksmith. "Your name, sir?"

"Mandrano," he says proudly. "Formerly of His Majesty King Nicolao's Royal Guard, now retired."

I clasp his shoulder; it's as hard and round as a boulder. "Thank you, Mandrano. You have done your queen a great service today."

He bows low. I don't wait for him to rise, and I don't bother to see that Ximena and the guards have followed my orders. I step down quickly after Hector, holding my candle low to light my way.

His fingers reach out of the gloom, offering support, and I grab them. Just as my feet reach dry earth, the trapdoor bangs closed, making the darkness complete but for our puddle of candlelight.

I move close enough for the candle to illuminate us both. The flame casts strange shadows on his skin—blurring the scar on his cheek, softening his eyes, and rounding his features—and I am reminded how very young he is.

"Hector, who besides you and me has the authority to lock down—"

"Conde Eduardo, General Luz-Manuel, and the mayordomo." He rattles off the list so quickly that I realize he's been rehearsing it in his mind.

"You think someone *intended* to lock us out?"

Ximena would offer a kind inanity about it being an unfortunate misunderstanding. But Hector has nothing of dissembling in him. "Even after you're safely returned, we must tread strategically," he says.

I pass him the candle, nodding agreement. He leads the way, and I follow close enough that I can grab his sword belt if necessary. The tunnel is so tight that my shoulders brush the wood beams propping up the ceiling. I fight the urge to sneeze against the dust we kick up.

Something scuttles over my foot, glowing Godstone blue, and I squeal.

Hector whirls, but then he says, "Just a cave scorpion. They glow when frightened. Nearly harmless."

Nearly harmless is not harmless, and I open my mouth to point out as much, but I decide I'd rather be brave in front of him. "It startled me," I say calmly. "Please, continue."

He turns back around, but not before I catch the amused quirk of his lips. "Be glad it wasn't a Death Stalker," he says, pushing aside a thick cobweb.

"Oh?"

"They're much larger scorpions. Very poisonous. They live in the scrub desert around Basajuan. I'm surprised you didn't encounter them when you were leading the rebellion."

"I wish I *had* encountered Death Stalkers. They would have been marvelous weapons."

"What?" He stops short, and I nearly collide with him.

"One of the village boys kept vipers. I ordered him to toss them into an Invierno camp. He didn't stick around to see if anyone died, but he did report a lot of screaming. Scorpions would have been even better."

He is silent for so long that I'm worried I've offended him somehow. "Hector?"

"You always surprise me." And he moves off into the darkness.

We reach a crooked stair. The bottom step has collapsed with rot.

"This winds through the walls of the palace," Hector whispers. "We must go quietly."

He waits until I nod, then ventures upward. The wood-reinforced earthen walls cede to stone and mortar as the steps bend and creak with our weight. I notice signs of life—footsteps, muted voices, wash water running through pipes to the sewer below.

The stair dead-ends. Hector holds up the candle, exposing a wall too smooth for stone. He runs a finger across it, which leaves a rivulet of darkness in the dust-gray surface. Something clicks. The door slides soundlessly aside, revealing a slightly brighter gloom.

"The wardrobe," he whispers, stepping inside. "Stay here while I check the room."

Light floods our passageway as he pushes the double doors open, but then he closes them again, leaving me alone in the dull murk. My heart twists to sense the empty space around me. My husband's clothes used to hang here. I wonder what became of them all?

I wait the space of several heartbeats, listening hard for the sounds of a scuffle, wishing Hector had at least left me the candle.

Then he opens the doors, and I blink against the onslaught of brightness. "All clear," he says. I take his offered hand and step into the king's suite.

My late husband's bedchamber is huge and decadent, with marble floors and polished mahogany furniture. Tapestries the height of two men hang from gilded crown molding. An enormous bed looms in the room's center like a squat tower, its red silk canopy rising to a point.

I could live here if I wanted—it's my right, as monarch. But I hate this room. It feels garish and ridiculous. And because I've only ever been here to hold the hand of a wasted man and ease his passing, it also feels like death.

Just ahead is a smaller door that leads to my own chambers— and home. "I checked. No one there but Mara," Hector says when he sees me eyeing it with longing. "You're safe for now."

For now. *We must tread strategically*, he said in the tunnel. I clench my hands into fists, preparing for something, though I'm not sure what. "Let's go then."

We have returned ahead of Ximena and the guards. I pace in the bedchamber while Hector stands at the entrance, arms crossed, chin set.

"I have to *do* something," I say. "I can't just wait here."

Mara, my lady-in-waiting, beckons me toward the sun-drenched atrium. "But we need to change your gown," she says hurriedly. "It's covered in dust. And I should repowder your face and smooth your hair and . . . and . . ."

The soft desperation in her voice makes me study her carefully. She's as tall and slender as a palm—seventeen years old, like me. She won't look me in the eye as she adds, "And I just had the atrium pool cleaned! Wouldn't you like a bath?"

"Later. I have to figure out . . ." My protest dies when I see her trembling lip. I stride toward her and wrap her in a hug.

She draws in a surprised breath, then wraps her arms around me, squeezing tight.

"I'm fine, Mara," I say into her hair. "Truly."

"The animagus could have killed you," she whispers.

"But he didn't."

She's the first to pull away. When she straightens, her lips are pressed into a resolved line.

"Hector," I say.

He uncrosses his arms and stands at attention, but he regards me warily.

"I can't leave all those people out there. They'll work themselves into a terrified mob."

He frowns. "You want to open the gates."

"They should know that their queen will protect them, no matter what."

"To reverse the order of a Quorum lord, you must give the command in person." He puts up a hand to keep me from rushing out the door. "But you need a proper escort. We should wait until Lady Ximena and the other guards return."

"People are mobbing the gate *now*."

He considers a moment, then nods reluctantly.

To Mara, I say, "Will you check on Prince Rosario?" Treading strategically means protecting my heir.

She reaches for my hand and gives it a squeeze. "Of course. Please be careful." She doesn't let go until I squeeze back.

Hector and I hurry into the hallway and immediately stop short. Soldiers pour from an adjoining corridor and run off ahead of us, a cacophony of clanking armor and creaking leather. They wear the plain cloaks of palace garrison—General Luz-Manuel's men. "Hector? What—"

"I have no idea." But he draws his sword.

Another group approaches from behind, and we step aside to let them pass. They move with such haste that they fail to notice their queen staring at them as they go by.

The soldier bringing up the rear is a little younger, a little shorter than the others. I grab him by the collar and yank him backward. He whips his sword around to defend himself, but Hector blocks him neatly. My ears ring from the clash of steel on steel, but I manage not to flinch.

The soldier's face blanches when he recognizes me. "Your Majesty! I'm so sorry. I didn't see . . ." He drops to his knee and bows his head. Hector does not lower his sword.

"Where are you going?" I demand.

"The main gate, Your Majesty."

"Why?"

"We are under siege."

Hector and I exchange a startled glance. It must be the Inviernos. How did they sneak into the city unnoticed? How could so many—

"The citizens of Brisadulce are rioting," the soldier adds.

Oh, God. "You mean we're defending the palace against *our own people*? Tell me who gave the order to lock down the palace."

He folds in on himself a little. "It—it was Lord-Conde Eduardo."

"By sealed message or in person?" Hector asks, and it takes me a moment to understand: If it was a sealed message, the parchment might still exist.

"His adviser, Franco, relayed the message."

Franco. I've made it a point to memorize the names and positions of every person in my court, but I don't recognize this one.

"I require your escort to the palace gate," I tell him as Hector nods approval. "Quickly." I gesture for him to lead the way, preferring Hector at my back, and lift my skirts to keep pace.

The dusty yard teems with palace garrison—archers up along the palace wall, light infantry in a row, ten paces back from the gate. Spearmen stand at the portcullis, swatting at grappling hands with their spear points, barking warnings to the people on the other side. From the swelling noise, the crowd has at least tripled.

"Thank you," I tell the young soldier. "You may join your company." He bows and flees.

Hector points to the wall above the gate, to a space between crenellations. "It's Conde Eduardo."

Sure enough, a figure stands tall, hands on hips, observing the crowd beyond.

"Let's go."

Hector bellows, "Make way for the queen!"

Soldiers scurry out of the way as we rush forward and take the stairs to the top of the wall two at a time.

The conde's eyes widen slightly as I approach, but a blanket of composure drops across his features quickly. He's an almost-handsome man with broad shoulders, sharp eyes, and a black close-cropped beard that cedes to gray along his temples. "You shouldn't be here, Your Majesty," he says. "It isn't safe for you."

"Did you order the palace lockdown?" I ask, breathless from the quick climb.

"No. The mayordomo did."

I peer into the conde's face, trying to read any deception or nervousness there, but he is as preternaturally calm as always.

"I want the gate opened," I tell him.

"I'm not sure that's a good—"

"They're *our* people. Not our enemies."

"They're panicked. Panicked people do horrible things."

"Like dropping the gate against those we're supposed to protect?"

His nostrils flare as he takes a deep breath. He leans forward, eyes narrowed, and I resist the urge to flinch away. *Do not back down, Elisa.* Below, the mob has quieted. They have no doubt spotted me. They're waiting to see what I'll do.

Finally the conde straightens. "As Your Majesty wishes," he says.

I lift my chin to address the command toward the crowd. "The citizens of Brisadulce are most welcome. Raise the gate!"

The cry echoes throughout the yard. Gears shriek as the portcullis grinds upward. The garrison soldiers make way as the people of my city rush into the yard. But the initial panic blows itself out quickly, and after a moment, everyone filters through with orderly haste. My shoulders sag with relief. Until this moment, I was only *mostly* sure of my decision.

If the conde has a reaction to the quieting crowd, he does not show it, "There is much to discuss regarding today's events," he says.

"Indeed," I agree with equal calm. "I'm calling an emergency meeting of the Quorum."

He bows from the waist, then turns on his heel and strides away along the wall.

I watch him go, wondering about the flicker on his face when he first saw me, at his hesitation to follow my orders. Then I turn my back on him and the crowd gathering in the courtyard to look out over my city. I need to feel wide-open space, cleaner air.

I sense Hector beside me. He leans his elbows onto the wall so that our shoulders almost touch, and he says, "This is your first major crisis as sole monarch. You are weathering it well."

"Thank you." But I clutch the wall's edge with misgiving. I gaze out across the flat rooftops of Brisadulce. They hug the downslope like massive adobe stairs, lush with garden plants and trellises. Beyond them, the ocean horizon stretches and curves, as though someone has thumb-smeared the bottom of the sky with indigo paint. "Hector, you know how when clouds roll across the sky, everyone turns an eye toward the docks to see if the water will leap over them and flood the streets? To see if the coming storm is actually a hurricane?"

"Yes."

"I fear that's what this is. Merely the heralding surge."

3

I hate Quorum meetings.

Calling one is the right thing to do; we must deal with this incident decisively. But the lord-general and the lord-conde have been in power for decades. I'm the upstart—a seventeen-year-old queen reigning by royal decree rather than inheritance. On a good day, they talk over me as if I'm not there. On a bad one, I feel like a pesky sand chigger in danger of a swift swatting.

I'm the last to arrive. My entourage of ladies and guards stops at the threshold, for only Quorum members are allowed inside. Mara forces an encouraging smile as I swing the huge double doors shut and slide the bolt home to lock us in.

The Quorum chamber is low ceilinged and windowless, like a tomb. Candles flicker from sconces set in dusty mortar between gray stones. A squat oak table fills the center, surrounded by red cushions. The air is thick with unyielding silence, and I feel as though the ghosts of weighty decisions and secret councils press in around me, telling me to hush.

Hector is already seated on his cushion, looking stern. We always arrive separately, for it would be gauche to flaunt our close association. He lifts his chin in cold greeting, giving no hint that there is any warmth between us.

General Luz-Manuel, commander of my army, rises to welcome me, but his smile does not reach his eyes. He's a small, hunched man, unimposing enough that his rise to military prominence seems puzzling. Because of this, I know better than to underestimate him.

"You were right to call this meeting, Your Majesty," he says.

Beside him sits Lady Jada, who clasps her hands together and smiles as if in raptures. "Oh, Your Majesty, I'm so delighted the lord-general invited me again!"

I blink at her, marveling at her seeming unawareness of the moment's gravity. Jada is wife to Brisadulce's mayor and a temporary addition to the Quorum. We have been minus a member since I allowed the eastern holdings to secede, but we dare not meet with fewer than five, the holy number of perfection. Lady Jada is neither clever nor interesting, and therefore an unintimidating choice until we decide on a permanent replacement.

"I'm delighted you accepted," I tell her sincerely.

Conde Eduardo bows his head in greeting, then calls the meeting to order by quoting God's own words from the *Scriptura Sancta*: "Wherever five are gathered, there am I in their midst."

I settle onto a cushion at the head of the table.

The conde continues, his voice grave. "It concerns me deeply that an animagus could creep into our city unnoticed, much less climb to the top of the amphitheater. And his demand that we give the queen over to Invierne—"

"Is an empty threat," Hector says. "They were beaten badly. Her Majesty destroyed nine of their sorcerers that day."

"And yet one remained," says General Luz-Manuel. "Who knows how many others lurk in our city? How many more in their mountains? He claimed their population to be more numerous than the desert sands. Could they launch another army at us, even bigger than the last? We would not survive another such onslaught."

Hector frowns. "You don't actually believe we should give in to their demand, do you?"

I shift on my cushion, dreading the general's response.

After an awkward hesitation, he says, "Of course not."

"We should attempt some kind of diplomacy," Eduardo says. "Our greatest weakness has ever been that we know so little about them. And I'm sure our queen could charm them—"

"Their ambassadors were never forthcoming." I jump in, mostly because I'm already sick of being talked over as if I'm not here. "Short of sending a delegation to Invierne, I don't know how we'll find out what we need to know. But they always refused offers of a return delegation from my father."

"It was the same here," Hector says. "King Alejandro offered delegations several times, only to be rebuffed."

I know what my sister, Crown Princess Alodia, would counsel. "We need spies," I say.

General Luz-Manuel shakes his head. "We can't outfit spies over such a long distance. There's nothing left in the coffers.

And we'd have no way of communicating with them. It's too far, even for pigeons."

The helpless expression on everyone's face makes the chamber feel even tighter, even hotter. I wish I'd brought a fan with me.

"We have a more immediate problem," Conde Eduardo says. "Five months after the Battle of Brisadulce, our nation was finally beginning to heal. This is a terrible blow. Several people were killed today in the ensuing chaos."

My heart drops into my stomach. I remember the panic, the crowd, the runaway carriage. I hadn't realized people were dying around me. Maybe that was the Inviernos' plan all along, to frighten us into hurting ourselves.

Conde Eduardo adds, "Some misguided souls may even call for the queen's head."

"Surely not!" Lady Jada protests.

The conde shrugs. "If they believe giving Her Majesty over to Invierne will save their brothers and sons and wives, they will demand it be done. You saw how they nearly stormed the palace this morning."

The same people who cheered me along the parade, who chanted my name and hailed me as a hero. Ximena was right.

Lady Jada turns to me. "Can't you just"—she makes an obscure gesture with one hand—"do something with your Godstone? Defeat them like last time?"

I wilt a little on my cushion. "If only I could, my lady. I had an amulet then, and several old stones from long-dead bearers. Now I've only my own. Father Nicandro and I are working together to figure out how to channel its power." I choose not to mention that, aside from bringing a warm glow to the stone, I've accomplished nothing.

General Luz-Manuel leans forward, eyes gleaming. "I have an idea." He is a consummate politician, and he allows an exactly perfect stretch of silence before adding, "Your Majesty, we must discuss the issue of your regency."

I wipe my suddenly sweating palms on my knees. "I am not the prince's regent," I tell him, pretending to misunderstand. "It is wholly my choice whether or not to hand the throne over to Rosario when he comes of age. The king named me his unequivocal heir and Queen *Regnant*." I'm proud of my steady voice.

"The king was on his deathbed and suffering tremendously, perhaps not in his right mind. You are so young, Your Majesty; not yet come of age yourself. And foreign. Many doubt your worthiness to rule. Add to that today's terrifying incident, and you must consider that *you* need a regent. It would go a long way toward assuring the populace."

I do my best not to gape at him. "I fought for this nation as one born to it!"

He nods solemnly. "What you did was an important part of the whole effort." I curl my hands into fists against the condescension in his voice. "But you have difficult decisions coming up, like raising taxes to support rebuilding efforts. You will find that when people are tightening their belts, your heroics won't matter. They will blame you, Your Majesty, and you alone. They'll demand we hand you over to our enemy."

I knew my Quorum held little respect for me. But I didn't anticipate this. And his words cut hard because he is right. I am a child, and an inexperienced one. Leading a small desert rebellion, defeating Invierne's animagi with my Godstone— these things were impressive, certainly. But they were nothing like ruling.

Lady Jada's gaze shifts between the general and me, her eyes large and eager. She is a keen gossip, and I wonder if Luz-Manuel invited her specifically in the hope that she would spread the idea of my regency. Or the *reason* for my proposed regency—that I can't rule on my own.

Conde Eduardo stares into the distance, rubbing at his close-cropped beard. Finally he says, "There is another way." He leans his elbows onto the table and stares at each Quorum member in turn, settling finally on me. "My dear queen, it is time for you to choose a husband."

Ah, so that's it. The regency discussion was simply meant to introduce marriage as the more palatable alternative. They probably worked it out between themselves ahead of time.

"Oh, yes!" says Jada. "Someone whose counsel is widely respected. Everyone would accept your queenship with a strong prince consort at your side, even given today's events."

Softly Hector says, "The king has only been dead five months."

"The queen is beyond the ceremonial mourning period," Conde Eduardo says with a shrug. He turns to me. "I don't mean to speak ill of the dead, but our nation suffered weak rule under Alejandro and Nicolao. We were coming apart at the seams even before the war. Your Majesty, I beg you to put your people first. Please choose either a regent or a strong husband, and bring the stability we so desperately need."

"You would gain the most political advantage by choosing someone from the northern holdings," the general adds. "The north bore the brunt of the war."

"I'll compile an eligibility list," Lady Jada says. "We can look over it at our next meeting. Lord Liano of Altapalma comes to mind. And of course Conde Tristán of Selvarica, who is a southern lord but should not be discounted. Also . . ."

I can't bear to pay attention as Jada prattles on about every lordling in the entire kingdom. I've known for a while that I would marry for the good of Joya d'Arena. But now, faced with the prospect, I don't want to. I want to love someone again, the way I loved Humberto, or at the very least share a friendship, as Alejandro and I did in the end.

And I want to be queen of this great country not because someone is holding my hand, but because *I* can do it. Me. Elisa.

But I agree to look at Lady Jada's list at our next meeting, because I don't know what else to do or say. If nothing else, it buys me time to consider my options.

Our conversation moves to reconstruction. Whole villages along the desert caravan route still lie in ruins after the enemy's march. The cost to clean and rebuild is becoming enormous. The highway through Puerto Verde is near impassable after several years of unusually bad weather. The tanners' and weavers' guilds are close to rioting over the shortage of hide and wool, now that the seceded country of

Basajuan is no longer forced to trade sheep with the capital.

The nation is in shambles. Though we won the war, our coffers are drained, our army weakened, our people dispirited. Today's birthday parade was supposed to inspire hope, to demonstrate the safe normalcy our lives were returning to.

My ridiculous crown grows unbearable as I ponder the centuries of rulers who came before me and sat in this same room, at this same table. Did any of them inherit a mess this big? Were any of them mere children, like me?

I can't mask my relief when our meeting is over. I rise stiffly and thank everyone for coming; then Hector releases the bolt and opens the door. I bask in the fresher air that hits my face.

Once outside, my ladies press close. I yank off my crown and fling it at Ximena. Mara mops sweat along my hairline with a cloth and fluffs my skirt.

I say, "I need to walk." Mostly, I need to *think*, away from watchful eyes and weighty problems.

They clear a path, and Hector steps up to accompany me.

I shake my head. "I need to go alone."

"I'd rather you didn't."

"I'll just be a few minutes," I assure him. "I'm going to the catacombs to pray. I'll only walk where our own guards patrol. Come looking for me if I'm not back when the monastery bells ring the hour."

He reaches up as if to grasp my arm, but then changes his mind and lowers his hand. "Be wary, my queen."

I smile assurance, and then I'm off, away from the crowd.

The cobblestones beneath my feet are worn smooth, for

Brisadulce was built almost two thousand years ago, after God scooped up our ancestors from the dying world with his righteous right hand and deposited them onto this one.

As I walk, I run a finger along the rough stone wall, taking comfort in its solidness. I imagine the palace and its ancient capital, sprawling across its peninsula of limestone, surrounded by ocean on three sides and desert on one. My new home is such a determined place, unchanging despite being hemmed in by things that pound it with deadly sandstorms and hurricanes for a season each year, and the rest of the time are merely fluid and forceful.

The city's salvation is its underbelly. My old tutor used to tell me that long ago, before people arrived, our great sand desert was an inland sea. Something cataclysmic happened to drive all that water deep underground. Now it rushes out to meet the ocean in the caverns beneath my feet, providing plenty of fresh water for the beautiful oasis that is my capital city.

The catacombs, which were built to take advantage of the natural water-formed caverns, are my favorite place to find solitude.

The guard at the entrance is not surprised to see me. He greets me with a bow and a smile. "Glad to see you back safely, Your Majesty," he says. "I heard what happened."

"Thank you, Martín." But I don't want to talk about that. "How is your wife?"

He is one of the youngest among the Royal Guard, and it's hard to believe that someone barely older than me could be married and expecting a child already. "Approaching her ninth month of pregnancy. And cursing the desert heat every day." He lifts a torch from a wall sconce and hands it over. Martín's grin turns sheepish. "If it's a girl, she wants to name her Elisa."

I nearly drop the torch. "Oh. Well ... er, I would be honored, of course. Either way, you must promise to introduce the child to me when it comes."

He knocks his chest with the flat of his fist—the gesture of a true oath. "I swear it, Your Majesty."

It's a strange thing to be a queen, to have one's every word given such import. I am a bit discomfited as I hold the torch high and descend the cool, tight stair. My gown drags on the steps behind me, but I don't care. I pray as I go, asking God's blessing for Martín's baby-who-might-be-Elisa, that she grow up to be charming and slender and beautiful.

An orange glow suffuses my path ahead. I duck through a low archway and enter the vast Hall of Skulls.

It's a cathedral of bones. Skulls layer like bricks, reach toward an arched ceiling so high as to be lost in shadow. A row of larger skulls juts out at the wall's midline, their gaping jaws plastered open and inset with glowing votive candles. Curving rib bones frame dark openings at regular intervals along the wall.

I am weary of death. When I close my eyes, I see blood leaching into the sand, flesh melting like wax beneath an anima-gus' fire, gangrenous wounds, lifeless eyes. But these beautiful skulls are free of their rotting flesh, preserved and smiling. I love this reminder that death is an important foundation of my great city, that something of the dead can remain forever.

I pass through the third entrance on the right and enter the tomb of King Alejandro de Vega. His chamber still smells of roses and incense. I sconce my torch in a brass holder and wait as my eyes adjust to the dim light. In the echoing distance, the underground river pounds through the caverns. It's near enough to stir the moist air, and my torch wavers.

Five stone caskets rest on giant pedestals, but the meager torchlight illuminates only the nearest three. One holds the remains of Alejandro's father. The second contains my husband's first wife, who died giving birth to our little prince, Rosario.

In the third is my husband.

A silk banner covers the casket, and I trace its smooth length with my forefinger. Banners cover the other caskets too, but they are tattered with time, or maybe with the moisture that pricks at my nostrils.

"Hello, Alejandro." My whisper echoes around me.

Talking to a dead man is likely foolish. Do those who cross the barrier into the next life see or hear what happens to those stuck in this one? The *Scriptura Sancta* is unclear on the point. But I talk to him anyway, because even foolish comfort is something.

"I watched a man set himself on fire today. I thought of you, the way they burned you." I place my palm against the casket, and for a crazy moment, I imagine Alejandro's heartbeat thrumming beneath the stone. I wrench my hand away.

"The Quorum wants me to remarry, and I think I must do as they ask. *Our* marriage was a jest, I know. Still, we started to become friends in the end. You even said we could have loved each other, given time. Or were those words simply your final kindness to me?"

I came close to death myself today; I embrace it fully, let the truth of it wash over me. The animagus could have turned his fire on me. I would have died young, like most of the bearers before me.

And once the idea has settled into my bones, I'm suddenly eager to say to Alejandro what I never could when he was alive.

"You were a good man but an awful king. Indecisive, frightened, unwise." I swallow hard against the still-unfamiliar sensation of missing him. "Oh, but now I wonder if I judged you too harshly. I must tell you, because I must tell someone, that I am . . . anxious. About being queen. I'm not sure I'm doing a good job of it so far. Ximena tells me I'm the only monarch in history who is also a bearer. But I'm only six . . . seventeen. What if I'm even worse than you were? Maybe—"

The Godstone freezes. I gasp as icy shards shoot through my blood, numbing my fingers and toes. I spin, seeking the source of danger.

Wind whips through the tomb. My torch winks out, leaving me in darkness.

Instinctively, I pray hard and fast, begging God to protect me from whatever lies ahead. The Godstone responds by easing warmth into my abdomen, just enough for my breath to come easier, to let me *think*.

I consider a strategic scream. But screaming would give away my exact location to whatever lies in ambush.

I need a weapon. I search frantically for something, anything. A silk banner flutters in the breeze. I grab the tassels and whisk the banner from its casket. Dust puffs into the air, and my chest lurches with the need to cough. The banner is long, nearly twice my height. Praying warmth into my limbs, I fold it in half, then once more.

I have no idea what to do with it. Venturing from the crypt armed with a silk banner is a ridiculous idea. And during my time in the desert, I learned it is stupid to fight when you can run and hide.

Two of the caskets are empty, awaiting their permanent residents. I have a sudden urge to crawl inside one, cross my arms over my chest, and close my eyes to the world. Instead, I creep behind the nearest and squat down so I can't be seen from the doorway. I only need to be invisible long enough for Hector to come looking for me.

A shape moves in the dark.

My stomach drops into my toes. Someone is here, has been in the crypt the whole time.

I lurch away, but I am too cold, too slow.

Light winks against a steel edge. I raise my banner against the wicked glimmer.

Something rams the silk, slides off, ricochets against my forearm. My skin parts; pain sluices up to my shoulder.

I drop the banner, scurry backward in a crab crawl, but I collide with a pedestal. The blade plunges again.

I scream as it glances off my Godstone, slips into my stomach as if I am made of butter.

The pain is like nothing I've experienced. I know I will burst from it.

Warmth glides across my belly, down my thighs. The blade is ripped from my body, and I crumple to the stone. My cheek splats into a pool of my own blood.

My last thought is of Alejandro, and how surprised he'll be to see me.

4

I awaken as if into a dream—a dream of light and heat and pain.

I should open my eyes, but I can't seem to find them in my head. I ought to cry out, but I'm too distant from my flesh to figure out how. I'm lost in the desert of my own mind, in a wilderness of sand and light.

. . . *dead soon*, I imagine the general's voice saying, distantly, as if from another world. . . . *the priest . . . final sacrament.* He wants me to die. I know it with surety, even from this bright, lost place.

But I refuse.

And later, maybe much later: *Elisa? . . . Hector. . . hand moved!* Rosario's high voice this time—someone who very much wants me to live. I focus hard on his words, cling to them as to a lifeline.

Warmth. Pressure. My hand! Someone squeezes it.

I make my hand my whole world. *Hand hand hand hand.* I push through the sand and light and heat, and with every bit of strength I have in me, I squeeze back.

My next awakening is more real, my perception sharper, my pain so much more exquisite. My eyes are crusted closed, and I give up trying to open them.

My head is heavy and huge, like it has swollen to twice its normal size. The worst pain, though, is in my abdomen, just left of the Godstone.

I remember, and my breath comes in short gasps. The darkness, the gleaming steel edge, the dagger plummeting . . .

No. All this pain means that I am *alive.* I will think about that instead.

Even with my eyes closed, I know I'm in my bed. A cool night breeze caresses my fevered skin, bringing a sweet concoction of freesia and hibiscus. My balcony curtains whisper as they move; my bathing pool gurgles with a fresh infusion of water.

Someone found me, brought me here. Someone saved my life.

I sense movement against my shoulder. My stomach muscles clench involuntarily, which sends a wave of pain all the way to my breastbone. I force myself to relax, to breathe.

Then I turn my head to discover what rests at my shoulder. I get a noseful of soft, freshly washed hair, a blast of warm, sleeping breath.

I'd recognize his scent anywhere. It's Rosario, my little prince. I wonder if he's here by design or if he slipped his nurse again.

It makes my head swim to lift my neck, but I do it anyway,

just enough for my lips to find his forehead. He snuggles closer, which helps me focus. I'm awake a long time. In pain. Glad to be alive.

When I stir again, my eyes open easily. I start to sit up but abandon the effort. Pain aside, my stomach muscles simply do not cooperate. What if the assassin's dagger broke something inside me?

Rosario is gone, but I am surrounded by guards. One stands at the foot of my bed, two at my balcony, two at the entry door, one at the opening to my atrium.

I take a deep breath. "Morning," I say with enormous effort. My voice is that of a stranger, all cracked and dry.

They snap to attention.

One steps forward. My vision wavers with heat and dizziness, but I recognize Lord Hector by the broad set of his shoulders.

He whispers, "Elisa?"

Questions tumble in my mind, competing for attention. Who rescued me? Did they find the assassin? How badly am I hurt? Where are Mara and Ximena? Did I imagine Rosario cuddled beside me in the dead of night?

Bringing all this to my lips is impossible. I open my mouth, but nothing comes out.

"Your Majesty?" he says. "Are you able to tell me how you feel?"

My bedroom is taut with silence as everyone awaits my response. They *need* me to respond. They're afraid I can't.

So I try again. "Sandstorm," I manage.

It's not coming out right. The guards exchange worried glances.

I take an excruciating breath. "Sandstorm," I repeat. "Like I've been lost. And flayed alive."

Lord Hector wilts with relief. "You look it too."

The others gasp at his audacity, but I laugh. It sounds like a wheeze.

Hector turns to one of the guards. "Get word to General Luz-Manuel and Conde Eduardo *at once*. Tell them Her Majesty is awake and of sound mind."

Hearing his name, I'm tickled by a darkly distant memory of the general sitting my deathwatch. Or did I imagine it?

"I'll fetch Ximena and Mara," Hector says. "I forced them to eat and rest."

"Thank you." Already my vision clouds, and I want more than anything to close my eyes. "Wait! How long was I—"

"Three days."

It's like a punch to my already-aching gut. "And the assassin?" Words, at least, are coming more easily.

"Disappeared. We've searched everywhere."

I feared as much. Why else would I require so many sentries? "Was Invierne behind it? Was it related to the animagus' threat?"

"The other Quorum members think so. The people think so. Conde Eduardo posted notices throughout the city advising that no one go anywhere alone. Several districts have requested a stronger guard presence."

My mouth opens to ask if anyone has suggested giving me over to Invierne, but I can't bring myself to do it. Instead, I say, "Did you find me down there? Are you the person who saved my life?"

He freezes, and I wish my vision were clearer, for I would dearly love to read his face.

"I'll send your ladies," he says, and he strides away before I can respond.

I'm drifting in almost-sleep when Nurse Ximena and Lady Mara bustle inside, followed by a lanky man I recognize as the royal physician. Hector does not accompany them.

Ximena showers my face with kisses. "Oh, my sky," she says. "We thought . . . we were worried that . . . it's good to see you awake."

Mara fluffs my pillows. She doesn't meet my gaze, but I notice a tear in the corner of her eye, which she quickly scrapes away. "You remember Doctor Enzo?" she says.

"Of course. He took wonderful care of the king . . ." I almost say, *as he lay dying*. "After he was injured."

The ladies step aside, and Doctor Enzo leans forward to peer at me. He has a beakish nose and a razor-thin mustache that twitches with excitement as he absorbs information about my look and bearing. "I'm surprised to see you awake so soon. Your vision must be disastrous. Can you see at all?" Doctor Enzo was never one for niceties.

"It seems to be getting better."

"Nauseated?"

"Mostly dizzy. Doctor, please tell me—"

"Right here." He makes a stabbing gesture left of the

Godstone. My stomach clenches painfully in response. "Fortunately, the assassin missed. The knife slid in sideways. Didn't hit the important bits. There's a muscle here"—with his forefinger, he indicates an imaginary line alongside my navel— "that was nearly severed. If you remain very still for a couple of weeks, it may heal properly. As it is, you'll have a tremendous scar. May I document your recovery? It's such a *devastating* and *fascinating* injury."

"He didn't miss," I whisper.

"What was that?"

"The assassin didn't miss. The blade was deflected by my Godstone."

Someone gasps. The guards exchange looks of wonder, and I almost laugh. No sorcery was involved in the Godstone's interference, nothing divine. It was random luck.

"There's a slice across your forearm also," Doctor Enzo continues. "Bled a good bit, but stitched up beautifully. Some of my finest work. In a few years, you'll have only a faint scar."

"Why am I so dizzy?"

"You hit the back of your head. Your skull is intact, but your face swelled magnificently. You may have permanent damage."

I'm as taken aback by his emotionless delivery as the words themselves: *Permanent damage.* My heart squeezes at the thought. I am not beautiful. I am not a devotee of court politics. I'm not particularly queenly in bearing. What I *am* is well-studied and intelligent. My mind is my single advantage, the one thing I've allowed myself to take pride in. Any kind of damage is unacceptable.

"When will I know?" I ask in a shaky voice. "If there is . . . damage?" This conversation may be better had in private, away from the guards. Perhaps it is unwise to offer even the barest hint that the new queen is compromised.

Doctor Enzo pats my shoulder awkwardly. "The fact that you are awake and alert is a good sign."

I am not reassured. But I am too tired to think about it a moment more. Of their own volition, my eyes drift closed.

No. I snap them open. I've been asleep long enough. "Doctor, send someone to fetch my mayordomo." I need his report on the state of things immediately. Conde Eduardo and General Luz-Manuel have no doubt been ruling in my absence, and if they are willing to contest my worthiness in a face-to-face meeting, how much more will they undermine me while I am indisposed?

My mayordomo arrives within minutes. He is a decadent man prone to egregious ruffles and bright colors, but I admire his quiet dignity as my guards search him for weapons. It's probably the first time in his tenure as ranking palace official that he's been treated so abominably.

"Thank you for coming so quickly," I say in a warm voice, hoping to lessen some of the sting.

He has hardly risen from his bow when he blurts, "Your Majesty, the city garrison just put down another riot. They made several arrests."

I start to lurch to a sitting position, but the tearing at my abdomen sends me crashing back against my pillow. "*Another* riot?" I say weakly. "Why?"

"There have been three in protest of the tax increase. All were quickly put down by the garrison, but each riot has been progressively larger. . . ."

My head swims. Riots? Tax increase? How could I forget about a tax increase? Maybe this is what Doctor Enzo meant by "permanent damage."

"Remind me," I say carefully, "about the details of this tax increase."

"The Quorum pushed it through while you were indisposed."

I gape at him. "Can they do that?"

"According to article 67 of the *Concordancia*, when the monarch is physically unable to perform his duties, the longest-sitting member of the Quorum must vote on his behalf."

"So the general had two votes."

"Yes."

I clutch at my sheets until they are balled into my fists, but sharp pain darts up my forearm, so I force myself to unclench. *Maybe I would have voted for a tax increase*, I tell myself. *Maybe it's for the best.* We're desperate to refill the coffers for reconstruction. To rebuild our army before Invierne can mount another attack.

"And how did Hector vote?" I ask in a small voice.

"He abstained."

I sink into my bedcovers with relief, though I'm not sure why it's so important. "Thank you for your report," I tell him.

He turns to go.

"Wait!"

He spins and drops into a courtier's bow. "Your Majesty?"

"That day. When the animagus burned himself. Did you order the palace lockdown?"

"No, Your Majesty."

"Who did?"

"It was General Luz-Manuel."

The soldier told me it was the conde. The conde told me it was the mayordomo. What am I missing?

"Did you speak to the general in person?"

His eyebrows knit together thoughtfully. "I received word through His Grace the conde's emissary, Lord Franco. He is a much trusted adviser. Did I do wrong?"

Franco again. I must meet this person, and soon. "No, you did well. I assume the city has been searched thoroughly?"

"No other Inviernos have been discovered, though I'm sure the mere possibility of another attack contributed to this sudden spate of riots."

My city is splintering apart. I sense it as surely as if I still stood on the palace wall with Hector, watching it happen. "Thank you. You may go."

Doctor Enzo insists I'm in no shape to hold appointments or even make decisions, so the mayordomo clears my schedule. But I hate being useless. I lie awake for hours each day, trying to figure out how to rule effectively from my bed. First I summon Lord Franco, the man who reportedly ordered the palace lockdown, but I'm told that he has left for Conde Eduardo's southern holdings to oversee rebuilding projects.

I demand an accounting from General Luz-Manuel for

the tax increase. He insists that he couldn't wait. His queen was not expected to survive, and can he be blamed for acting quickly when so many of Brisadulce's unemployed citizens are desperate for the construction work the increase would provide?

Though I'm unable to find fault with his arguments, I can't shake the phantom memory of the general looming over my unconscious body, eager for my death. Something else is taking shape beneath his placid surface of diplomatic politeness. I'm sure of it.

Prince Rosario visits often at first, sneaking out of the nursery to be with me while the guards pretend not to notice. But once the boy has assured himself that I'm no longer in danger of dying like his father, his visits grow less frequent. I don't mind. It's hard to have him at my bedside without the freedom to ruffle his hair or play a quick game of cards.

Word has spread like wildfire that I seek a husband—even though I've made no official announcement. Gifts pour in from the nobility—especially potential suitors—and there's a disconcerting intimacy about them. "Sapphire earrings to match the blue of your Godstone," one note reads. "Since you are a scholar of holy scripture, here is a centuries-old copy of the *Belleza Guerra*," says another. So many strangers know so much about me, and they shower me with priceless gifts, just on the chance of catching my attention.

No one is sure what to do with the gifts, so Ximena shoves them into a corner of my atrium for later sorting.

I also get notes that are unnerving. A journeyman tanner

blames me for not having enough hide to practice his craft and calls for my abdication. A young widow with four children begs for a job. An acolyte from the Monastery-at-Puerto Verde sends a withered black rose, saying that the Godstone's blasphemous sorcery blackens my soul and makes a mockery of our most precious sacrament.

Several letters claim that because I allowed the eastern holdings to secede and form their own nation, I should do the same with the southern holdings. One letter boldly declares the south to be an independent nation.

General Luz-Manuel promises that each letter will be investigated for sedition and any true threat to my person will be dealt with. But even his assurances fill me with misgiving.

Every night, I dream of my assassin. In my nightmares, the catacombs are a huge black emptiness. I'm moving forward, arms outstretched against the dark, when I see a wicked glimmer. I have a flash of horrified understanding before the assassin becomes an inferno, and his flaming blade is plunging into my stomach, tearing me in half, and I scream and scream. . . .

Someone is always at my bedside when I wake. My ladies calm me with gentle words and cool, soothing hands, whispering that I'll heal faster if I don't try to leave the bed, that I'm safe now. But I can't return to sleep until Ximena has read to me from the *Scriptura Sancta*, or Mara has plied me with a cup of spiced wine, or Hector has checked the balcony for intruders.

One afternoon I'm startled by a commotion outside. I hear shouting, the ring of steel, tromping boots.

Beside me, Ximena continues to loop and pull with her

embroidery needle, but she meets my gaze with her own puzzled look.

Lord Hector bursts through the door. "Elisa! I need your help."

"What is it?" Fear shoots through me. The last time I saw him so wide-eyed and breathless, the animagi were burning down the city gate.

"It's an execution. I tried to stop it, but General Luz-Manuel—"

"Whose execution?" I demand. "Why?"

"Martín. General Luz-Manuel found him guilty of conspiring with Invierne to assassinate you. He sentenced him to death by beheading." He leans over and places his hands on the foot of my bed. "Elisa, he's one of my own men. I trained him myself. He would never harm you."

I try to rise from the bed. "Martín would never . . . he was going to name his baby—"

Ximena pushes me back down. "You're supposed to rest!"

I struggle against her. "Hector, help me up. Take me out there if you have to carry me yourself." The blood pumping through my veins makes my thoughts spin faster, and I revel in the clarity of it.

I could try to stop the execution with a missive, but there might not be time to authenticate the message. And Martín would forever be known as the man who *may* have allowed an assassin to attack the queen—unless I declare my belief in his innocence before the entire city.

Ximena steps out of the way, her face carved in stone, as

Hector reaches beneath my shoulders and knees and lifts me to his chest as if I am a small child. My boundless nightgown tangles at his knees.

My nightgown! I can't barrel into the courtyard dressed like this.

"Ximena, please bring my robe." I wrap my good arm around Hector's neck. "Hurry!"

He maneuvers me through the door and into the hallway, gesturing with a lift of his chin for the other guards to accompany us. Ximena trails behind, my robe in her hands.

"The assassin was already there when I arrived," I say as we rush through the palace corridors and down a flight of stairs. "I have no idea how long he was lying in wait. Maybe days. He could have sneaked down during anyone's shift."

His brisk pace brings knife pain to my abdomen. "I know," he says. "But the general outranks me, and when I scheduled a Quorum meeting to discuss it, he pushed up the date of the execution without telling—"

"Just get me there quickly."

We reach the entrance to the courtyard. Framed by the archway, a crowd gathers on the green, surrounding a wooden platform. On it, the hooded executioner stands tall and bare chested. Sun glints off the huge ax blade resting at his shoulder. My own crown-seal banner snaps in the wind above him.

"Put me down."

"Can you stand?"

"I must. Ximena, my robe."

Hector sets me down, so gently. My legs barely support my

weight, and I lean into the archway to keep my balance. The newly healed skin on my stitched stomach feels too tight, too thin. Ximena wraps the robe around my shoulders, ties it at my neck. It will have to do.

I whisper, "Catch me if I fall?" And I take a wobbly step into the sunshine.

My breath is ragged, my heart a drum in my head, as I look around for Martín. Surely the prison guards will make an entrance with him soon. But then the executioner raises the ax, and I know that beyond the wall of spectators, Martín must already be in place, his head on the block.

"No!" I shout as loud as I can, and a handful of people turn toward me, but it is not enough.

The executioner's voice booms, "In the name of Her Majesty, Queen Lucero-Elisa de—"

"Stop!" yells Lord Hector. "By order of the queen!"

The executioner's head comes up in surprise, but it is too late to stop the ax's descent. It whistles downward, disappears behind the crowd, and thwacks wetly into the wooden block below.

5

IT takes a moment for the crowd to register what has happened. As one, they turn a stunned gaze on me and my escort.

I am as still and silent as a stone. Ximena hurriedly adjusts my robe to cover more of my nightgown, but all I can think about is how an innocent man is dead in my name, beneath the waving emblem of my reign.

A few collect themselves enough to drop to their knees. The rest of the crowd follows, like an ocean wave, until finally the wooden stage and its broken body are revealed. It has fallen to the side, and the neck is a meaty, bloody stump. I can't see where the head rolled off to. And then I'm woozy with the understanding that I'm looking for the disembodied head of a man I considered a friend.

"Send General Luz-Manuel to my suite immediately," I say, in as cutting a voice as I can muster. I turn, intending to depart in dramatic fashion before everyone notices the tears streaming down my face, but my legs crumble. Ximena and Hector knock heads catching me. They half drag, half support me through the archway and into the shady corridor. Hector abandons all pretense of allowing me to walk and sweeps me up.

"I think I ripped my stitches," I say, as wet warmth blossoms beneath my bandages. I'm glad because it gives me something to think about other than the hole that seems to have opened up in my chest.

"Oh, my sky," Ximena says. "Oh, Elisa."

Doctor Enzo is already in my suite when we return. He glares at me.

Mara gives me an apologetic look. "I fetched him," she says.

After Hector lays me on the bed, he turns away so Enzo can lift my nightgown and examine my bandages. I hiss with pain as he peels them back.

Enzo says, "Surely nothing was so important that you couldn't—"

"I don't want to hear it."

He mumbles insincere apologies while pressing his fingertips against my abdomen. It hurts, but not terribly. "Fascinating. I must know, have you been gravely injured before?"

I once tried to cut the Godstone out of my stomach, but I don't want to talk about that. "I broke a couple of ribs," I say. "Ripped off a fingernail. Had a badly infected cut from the nails of an Invierno. They poison their nails, you know."

He squeezes the skin around the stitches and mops up the resulting ooze with a dry cloth. "How long after you broke your ribs until you could walk easily?"

I have to think about it. Humberto was the one who took care of me. I sigh at the memory of him slipping duerma leaf into my soup so I would be forced to sleep instead of travel. "A day. It hurt, but I could do it."

Enzo lifts his head to meet my gaze dead-on. "And how long until the pain went away?"

"Less than a week."

His nose twitches with excitement. He is like a hunting hound on the scent of his prey.

He stares at my abdomen, and I realize he's not looking at the wound, but at my Godstone. Tentatively, he reaches out with his forefinger, lets it hover above my navel.

"It's all right. You can touch it."

He does, reverently, drawing little circles with his forefinger against the topmost facet.

I sense the pressure of his finger, but the Godstone does not respond, just continues its usual mild pulsing. It's odd to feel someone else touching it. No one does that. Even Ximena and Mara barely brush it when they are dressing me.

"It's like a heartbeat," Enzo breathes in wonder.

Hector continues to face politely away, but he reaches for his sword. He grips the pommel, ready to unsheathe at a moment's need.

I'm growing uncomfortable. "What's this about, Enzo?"

He yanks back his finger as if stung. "Your Majesty, I believe, that is, I think, though I can't be sure, but it seems . . ." He takes a deep breath. "I mean to say that you heal too fast."

I frown. Though I have the benefit of a royal education, I am the least studied in the healing arts. I have to take his word for it. "And it has something to do with the Godstone?"

"I have no other explanation for why you show no sign of infection, how you were able to stand at all after having your abdominal wall severed, or for the fact that, even after your ill-conceived outing, I will only replace two stitches."

I'll have to think about it more later, when the blessed darkness of nighttime feels something like privacy. I grit my teeth against the pain as he stitches me up. Then Ximena ushers him out and pulls the covers up to my shoulders just in time to receive General Luz-Manuel.

"Your Majesty." He bows low but rises before I release him.

I inhale through my nose and tell myself to relax. The general is so slender and stooped, his hair thinning at the top, and once again I marvel that this insubstantial person commands my entire army. "General," I say in a cold voice. "I am displeased at the execution of someone I believed a loyal subject and ally." Displeased is an understatement, but I'm leery of being too forceful until I hear what he has to say.

"Indeed, Your Majesty, this has been unpleasant and disappointing for all of us."

I stare at him. Is he being deliberately obtuse? *Careful, Elisa. He is cleverer than he appears.*

"Forgive me for misspeaking, Lord-General. I did not mean to remark on the general unpleasantness so much as my specific disappointment with *your* decision to execute this man."

His gaze holds such concern. "You've been through so much, Your Majesty. First the animagus, and now this. It must be overwhelming. But I can assure you that the matter was thoroughly looked into."

"Not that thoroughly."

"My queen, we investigated every—"

"You never bothered to get details from the one witness to this crime."

He looks charmingly confused.

"You do realize, don't you, that *I* was present during the assassination attempt?" I snap.

Ximena gives me a warning look. Mocking the general may not be my best strategy, especially in front of the guards, who I am certain are intent on every word in spite of their carefully bland faces.

I force softness into my voice. "I don't mean to be curt, Lord-General, but I'm exhausted and deeply saddened. What's done is done, but do promise me that no one else will be punished in connection with the attempt on my life without my knowledge and consent. I'm sure you understand my wish to be personally involved?"

"Of course, Your Majesty," he says, bowing his head. "Anything to put your mind at rest and aid in your recovery."

I clench my jaw. He won't do as I ask because my input is valuable, or even because I am his queen. He'll only agree to consult me because it will make me *feel better*?

The general turns to go.

"Wait."

He whirls, and it's possible I imagine his flitting look of impatience.

God, what do I say to this man? How can I convey that I am the sovereign and he is not? That even though I come from a foreign land, these are my *people?*

The Godstone leaps in response to my prayer, and an answer floats to me gently on the afternoon breeze.

Sorrow comes easily to my voice when I say, "I lost so many people I loved in the war with Invierne. We all did. But the only reason we survive to mourn is because our army fought bravely and selflessly. And no one fought harder than my own Royal Guard, who held off the invaders at tremendous cost so I could have time to work the Godstone's magic." I hope he hears what I'm not saying: *Yes, General, we won the day because of* me, *remember?* "I'll not see them doubted or disrespected. In fact, I'll defend each one of them with my dying breath if I must, as they defended me. Am I clear?"

He stares at me as if deciding whether to protest further. But I know I've said the right thing because Hector and the guards stand a little straighter, and their eyes glow with pride. I hope they take this back to the barracks, the sure knowledge that their queen would die for them.

Finally the general bows, a little lower this time, and excuses himself.

The moment the door closes behind him, all the fight melts from my body. I cannot fathom why the general would do such a thing. Was he trying to discredit me on purpose? Is this his way of taking power for himself while I am unwell? Was he looking for a scapegoat to assuage the fear of palace residents? Or did he genuinely think Martín deserved to die? A single tear slides from the corner of my left eye. *Oh, Martín, I'm so sorry I couldn't save you.*

I am about to close my eyes and meet oblivion when Hector says, "My queen?"

I force myself to raise my head and meet his eye.

"I would like to inquire about Martín's wife and family. Make sure they are provided for." Emotion tinges his voice, and his face is gaunt with weariness.

Very few members of the Royal Guard are as young as their commander, were selected and trained by him the way Martín was. I've no doubt that Hector grieves deeply for him.

"Thank you. I would take it as a personal favor."

"I'll return as soon as I'm able," he says.

"Take your time. You deserve a respite from being at my side. Oh, speaking of being at my side . . . please tell me, did General Luz-Manuel visit when I was . . . indisposed?"

"Many times. He brought prayer candles and held vigil for hours."

I don't believe for a moment that the general wished for my recovery.

"I never left him alone with you," Hector adds softly, his face unreadable. "Not once."

I'm not sure what to say, so I just nod gratefully.

Tonight my dream changes. This time I carry a torch, and its warmth and light wrap around me. I think that I am *safe*.

The breeze is gentle at first, lifting strands of my hair, bringing a hint of brine. But the wind grows stronger; the gust becomes a gale. The torch dies, plunging me into darkness. The Godstone turns to ice.

I sob from sudden terror, knowing what comes next, waiting for it. The blade glimmers hot and cruel as it strikes. . . .

My own scream wakes me.

"Elisa?"

I grasp blindly for Hector. He clasps my hand in both of his, trying to squeeze the panic from my body by the force of his grip.

Gradually the pounding in my chest softens, my breathing slows. The high slant of sun through my balcony's glass doors indicates that I slept well into the morning.

When I can manage it, I say, "Did you find Martín's family?" I need to talk about something real and solid to shake the dream from my head.

"The Guard took up a collection. I delivered it this evening. In spite of everything, she was . . ." He swallows hard, then says with a touch of wonder, "She was *grateful*."

"I'm sorry I couldn't save him for you."

"Thank you for trying."

He gives my hand one last squeeze before letting it go. I snake it under my blankets, feeling vaguely disappointed. He has been stiff and uneasy with me since my brush with death. Ximena or Mara would have held my hand as long as I needed.

He leans back in his chair and crosses his arms, as if putting a wall between us. "It's very common for soldiers to experience nightmares after combat," he says. "Especially if they were injured."

My chest lurches just to think about it. "Oh?"

"And sometimes it helps to talk about them."

"Do you have nightmares?"

"Yes." His voice is hardly more than a whisper.

"And do you talk about them?"

He turns his head to avoid me. "No."

I study his profile. He usually looks so regal, even with the crisscross of scars on his left cheek. But the light pouring in from my balcony softens his features and makes him seem almost boyish. I say, "But you'd like me to talk about mine."

"Only if you want to."

"We could trade. A nightmare for a nightmare."

His gaze turns inward while he considers. When he finally looks at me, I catch the barest shift of his eyes as he studies every part of my face.

He opens his mouth. Closes it. At last he says, "I think it would be best if you discussed your dreams with Ximena or Mara."

The hurt that wells up my throat is unexpected and inexplicable. "Maybe I will," I whisper. "Thank you for your counsel."

During the next couple of days, I think hard about what Hector said. I try, twice, to talk to Ximena about my dreams. But the words clot in my mouth. It's not fear so much as shame that stills my tongue. I can't bear to be weak and frightened in front of everyone. I am queen now. I should be so much braver, so much stronger.

But then comes the night when the knife is so real, so cold and sharp against my skin for the barest instant before it is an exploding fire in my belly. Then the nightmare flashes to a different place, a different knife, a different terror. I am helpless, my limbs leaden, as the dagger pricks at Humberto's precious throat. "You could have stopped this, Elisa," he tells me, just before the blade whisks across his neck and Humberto's hot blood spurts all over my crown, which is suddenly in my hands.

This time, my waking screams are cut off by vomit spewing from my mouth.

Mara and Ximena rush to help me clean up. I try to rise, and they hold me down, insisting they will have me set to rights in no time. But I thrust them back with more strength than I ought to have. Clutching the bedpost, I drag myself over the side and gain my feet.

My legs quiver with disuse, but they do not betray me. "Find Hector," I order to no one in particular. The vomit is already a cold plaster gluing my nightgown to my skin, and my nose stings from the rotten-spice scent. "I'm going to wash," I tell them. "And then . . . and then . . ." I have no choice. I have to face this black monster of terror before it eats me from the inside out. "And then, I must return to the catacombs. Tonight."

I bathe quickly, with Mara's help. Ximena plies me with a gown, but I refuse. "Pants," I say. "And my linen blouse." I'll not be hampered by a skirt—it's all I can do to remain steady as it is—and I know I'll feel more comfortable, more capable, in my desert garb.

Hector arrives as Ximena finishes lacing my camel-hair boots, and I rise to greet him. "Sorry to rouse you," I say. I feel guilty that I've decided on an excursion during the one night he allows himself to rest.

"A queen needn't ever apologize to her guard. Where are we going?"

"The catacombs. I need to . . . to see the place again."

"We scoured it a dozen times. We found nothing."

Ximena weaves my hair into one long braid down my back. I have so much hair that she usually weaves two, one atop the other, but she senses my urgency. "*We* found nothing? Or the general?" I ask. "Forgive me if I don't trust him to be thorough."

Hector opens his mouth as if to say something, but changes his mind.

I wave off the question. "Also . . . there's something else. Like a memory that's almost there but not."

My nurse ties the end of my braid and gives my back a gentle pat. Hector says, "Then we go. But do let me carry you if you tire."

"Of course. Thank you." I turn away to hide my flushing face, remembering how he carried me in our failed rush to save Martín. It would be easy to let him do it again. For a moment, I consider pretending to be weaker than I am.

But I shake it off. I'm already in danger of being thought a feeble queen, and I will not pretend weakness. Not ever, not for anyone.

I hold my head high as my entourage—Hector, Ximena, Mara, and a handful of guards—array themselves in a protective circle around me. In careful formation, we exit the suite and hurry to the ground floor.

A sentry I've never met before stands in Martín's place. Anger at him boils up inside me, but I recognize the feeling as unfair and manage a nod as he bows low. Hector insists on leading us into the stairwell, and I let him. The steps are tricky, and my legs feel like date jelly, but I put a hand on Hector's shoulder and use him as a crutch as I descend.

The yawning jaws of the Hall of Skulls seem to pulse in the flickering candle flames. Mara is rigid beside me, and I find strange comfort in the fact that someone is as frightened as I am.

But the fear dissipates as we enter Alejandro's tomb. It's so different than in my nightmares, crowded with my companions this time, several bearing torches. It's bright and warm, the air still. I feel everyone's eyes on me as I wander through the caskets, my fingers brushing the silk banners. I'm not sure what I'm hoping to find, how this excursion will help. When the toes of my boots encounter a large dark stain on the stone floor, I freeze.

My blood.

My fingertips find the wound at my side, then the bump on my skull. I fell and hit my head, Doctor Enzo told me. But that's not right. I fell onto my side. Now that I'm staring at the exact spot, I remember my cheek splatting in my own blood. How, then, did I get such a terrible knot on the back of my head? What really happened here?

I mutter, "Something isn't . . . I don't remember . . ." I'm not sure what I'm trying to say. That I didn't hit my head? I obviously did. Maybe I tried to get up and then fell a second time. I lost so much blood, it's a wonder I remember as much as I do.

"Elisa?" Hector says.

I look up, startled by his voice. The torchlight makes

hollows of his cheeks. "I'm not sure. I . . ." Something about the light. The way it's moving. So different from my dream. My gaze moves to the torch he carries. "Your torch."

He waits for me to puzzle it out, familiar by now with the way my mind works.

Think, Elisa! And then I have it. "Your torch flame isn't moving."

"No," he agrees. "It's very still."

Everyone is watching us, watching me. Perhaps they're worried that my injuries have addled my mind, that, as Doctor Enzo suggested, there is permanent damage. But my thoughts are clearer than ever.

"In my dream—no, in my *memory*—there was a breeze." I close my eyes, listen to the underground river wash through the caverns. I remember the brush of air against my face before the torch winked out. "It was more than a breeze. It *gusted*. My torch was sconced in the wall. And when the wind blew, it died." I open my eyes.

It's such a small thing, the slightest sliver of strangeness, but I am queen and they must take me seriously.

"Maybe someone opened the entrance upstairs," Ximena suggests.

"Or what if someone walked by?" says one of the guards. "In a hurry."

"Her Majesty said it *gusted*," Mara says. "Walking by would not cause a torch to go out."

"Maybe he had bad gas," says another. "Have you seen what they feed us in the barracks?"

"Fernando!" Hector snaps, but I chuckle. It's not particularly funny, but everyone joins me, and I allow myself to keep at it because in spite of the pain, it also feels really nice.

Finally I catch my breath and say what everyone is surely thinking: "I suppose we ought to consider that there is a hidden entrance to this chamber."

6

THINKING of the escape tunnel Hector and I used to reenter the palace, I realize that of course my new home would have other secrets, many of them forgotten, perhaps lost to centuries of restorations and additions.

Ximena brushes past me and begins searching the stone wall with her fingertips. "If there is another way in, we *must* find it," she mutters. She's right; we dare not leave any entrance to the palace unguarded.

Everyone jumps to help in the search, and my nurse directs them with strategic efficiency. Within moments, each section of wall and floor suffers the scrutiny of prying fingers. I itch to join them, but it's all I can do to prop myself upright against an empty casket.

"Search quietly," Ximena says. "Tell me if you hear something or feel air movement." It comes as no surprise that my guardian knows something of secret passageways. She probably knows as many ways to exit a fortress as she does to kill a man.

Mara is crawling on the floor when she says, "I feel something. A breeze maybe."

I start forward too quickly, and pain shoots down my side. Hector is at my elbow instantly. I lean into him.

"Which direction?" Ximena asks.

"Not sure." Mara looks up. "I felt it against my left cheek."

One of the guards crouches beside her with a torch.

"Watch the banner," Ximena says as the flame comes dangerously close to the casket's silk covering.

Mara and the guard run their fingers along the cobblestones, searching for cracks.

"Try pressing on them?" the guard suggests. "In my father's library, one of the hearthstones triggers a door."

So they press on all the nearest stones, from every different angle. Still nothing.

I say, "Try the pedestal." The casket resting upon it is empty, patiently awaiting a permanent resident, maybe me.

Everyone crowds around, torches held high, blocking my view. I loose an exasperated breath.

Hector whispers into my ear, "Everything all right?"

"Just frustrated. I hate being weak. And I may have dragged everyone down here in the middle of the night for noth—"

"A latch!" Ximena says. "Tucked under the base. Let me see if I can . . ."

The casket rises a finger's breadth. Several guards jump out of the way as the pedestal and its coffin pivot soundlessly to the side. Fresh air blasts the room, and a torch winks out. The others waver but hold.

Holding Hector's arm to steady myself, I peer over Mara's shoulder and almost sneeze from the cool, briny air pricking my nostrils. Where the pedestal stood is a gaping hole. Stone steps, edged with green moss, spiral into darkness. The guard shifts his torch, the light glints off the green stuff, and I see that it's actually a viscous mold.

"Ugh," says Mara.

"Ugh," Ximena agrees.

Hector says, "You were right, Majesty," and I get the feeling he's speaking for everyone else's benefit. "You were right to trust your instincts, and you were right to trust Martín."

His words warm me. Hector has always been my greatest ally. I catch his eye and nod slightly, hoping he understands how grateful I am to him right now.

"Well," I say. "Let's exonerate him by finding out where this leads."

The guards press toward the secret stairway, eager to step into the dangerous unknown.

"Wait a moment," I say. "Mara, return to my suite. Make excuses to any visitors. On your way, tell the sentry that I wish to be undisturbed as I pray."

She nods with obvious relief, and Hector gestures for two guards to accompany her.

As they depart, he turns to me. "Are you sure you're ready for this?"

"Doing something active is the best thing for my recovery."

"I knew you'd say that." The slightest smile curves his lips. "A walk in the monastery garden is something active. This is—"

"This is what I'm going to do."

He sighs, resigned. "Times like this, I miss Alejandro. He was malleable."

I choke back a startled laugh.

"Hold on to my shoulder. And if you change your mind—"

"Yes, let's *go*."

I glance over at Ximena, expecting her to protest, but she just stares at Hector, her face unreadable.

Fernando steps into the hole first, holding the torch aloft, and Hector follows. When my turn comes, I'm careful to land squarely on the balls of my feet to avoid slipping on the green slime. Moist air tickles my face, lifting strands of hair from my temples. We are sure to encounter water on this expedition, for the underground river is nearby, its rushing steady and monstrous, so ever-present that it is almost like silence.

The stair spirals—tight and steep. The close-in walls are covered with the slime, and I'm reluctant to touch them, even for balance. I find it's easier to leave my hand at the crook of Hector's shoulder and trust him to keep us both upright.

"There are scuffs in the slime," Fernando says, and his voice echoes around us. "Someone passed this way."

"There were no footprints in the tomb," Hector asks.

"Did the floor look *too* clean, by chance?" I ask. "Who was first to investigate?"

Hector pauses on the step, and my knees bump the backs of his thighs. But he continues without answering. Maybe he doesn't want to name the general within hearing of his men.

My wounded abdomen throbs with strain by the time the

stair ends at a low tunnel. The sand floor is smoothly rippled, like a beach after the waves have retreated.

"It's flooded at high tide," Hector says as I'm drawing the same conclusion. "There's the water line." He points to the wall, where a wainscoting of barnacles reaches knee-high.

I swallow against disappointment. All trace of those who passed before will have washed away, and we are unlikely to find a clue here about my would-be assassin.

Fernando squeals, and we all jump. "Sorry," he says, breathless. "Crab." I'm suddenly very glad for my desert boots, which are impervious to slime and sand and scuttling creatures.

Something on the wall catches my eye—a carved rivulet in the stone. "What's that?" I point.

Fernando lifts his torch to reveal a line of script, each letter the height of my pinky finger. My Godstone warms with recognition.

"It's in the Lengua Classica," Ximena says, her voice breathy with wonder. "From the *Scriptura Sancta.*"

I translate. "The gate that leads to life is narrow and small so that few find it."

Ximena reaches out to trace the letters with her fingers. She was a scribe at the Monastery-at-Amalur before she became my nurse, and like me, she has a reverent interest in ancient texts and holy writings.

"Look at this loop here," she says. "And the flip at the end of the accent mark. This style of script hasn't been used for centuries."

"But is it meant for those coming or going?" I muse. "Which direction 'leads to life'?"

"Only one way to find out," Hector says, and it warms me to hear the anticipation in his voice.

The limestone squeezes tighter until the corridor is barely wide enough for the guards' armored shoulders. Though it's cool and breezy, I'm too aware of the weight of rock above. So huge, so heavy. A whole city goes about its business up there. I'm becoming very nervous when Fernando announces, "Another stair."

This one leads upward, straight instead of spiraled, and rough-hewn as if carved by a giant clumsy ax. I'm glad to note dry, mold-free steps.

"Fernando," says Hector. "Aim your torch away."

The guard puts the torch behind his back. Ximena does the same with hers, and it becomes apparent that a separate glow, faint but true, illuminates the stairway.

"Do you think it leads outside?" I ask.

"We've descended too far," Hector says. "Unless I've gotten turned around, I think we're beneath the Wallows."

The Wallows. The most dangerous quarter of my city, where I'm not to travel even with an armed escort. The place each monarch before me has vowed to improve, with mixed— mostly poor—results. Where prostitutes and beggars and black-market merchants band together to form a society within a society, outside of my rule.

Hector turns to me, his gaze fierce. "Majesty, if I sense danger, I'll hustle you away, against your will if necessary."

"And if that happens, I promise to be only temporarily enraged." It comes out more sharply than I intend, mostly out of pique that he has reverted to calling me Majesty even among friends. "Let's go."

Climbing yanks at my sore stomach, and I slow everyone down. The passage is so tight and steep that hanging on to Hector is more trouble than it's worth. The sound of rushing water gets louder, and the glow brightens. Soon we don't need the torches at all. I can't imagine what would cause such light so deep underground.

The stairway levels off. Fernando gasps, and I'm about to ask him what he sees, but speech leaves me when I step into brightness.

The stair has ended at a high ledge overlooking the most enormous cavern I've ever seen. The river curves against the sheer wall opposite our ledge. The water is as smooth and clear as glass, though a constant sound like rushing wind attests to rapids nearby. To our left, the wall is riddled with smaller caves, all connected to one another by swinging ladders and scalloping rope bridges. On the floor of the cavern are several large huts, cobbled together from driftwood and shipwreck scavenge.

People are everywhere, going about their lives as if this were any ordinary place. A woman sits framed in the entrance to one of the small caves, stirring something over a cook fire. Outside the largest hut, two bearded, wind-chapped men work together repairing a fishing net. Near the river, a group of barefoot children plays a game with sticks and a leather ball.

Light streams through cracks in the ceiling. These sunlit crevices are lush with plants: broad-leafed creepers, a few ferns, and hundreds of hanging vines that don't quite brush the tops of the huts.

"It's a whole village," I whisper, "right beneath our feet all this time."

"I've not even heard of this place," Hector whispers back.

But the peculiar nature of the cavern amplifies our voices, carries them to the huts below. Everyone freezes and looks up. I see my own shock mirrored in their faces.

Hector's hand flies to his scabbard. He and Fernando step up to shield me from view. But it is too late, for someone bellows, "It's the queen!"

I hear gasps of surprise, utensils clattering, running footsteps.

Hector whirls on me. "We need to get you out of here."

"Not yet! They're more afraid of us than we are of them, see?"

Fernando swings his bow over his shoulder and fits an arrow. He and Hector exchange a look, and Hector nods. The guard steps forward, draws the bow, aims toward the milieu below.

"Halt!" Hector booms. "In the name of the queen."

The sounds of humanity fade, leaving only the wind whistling above and the water rushing below. Now that everyone has stilled, I note bandages, a sling, a splinted leg, a head wrap stained brownish red.

"We have their attention, Your Majesty," Hector says. "Would you like to address them? Or do you wish to retreat? I recommend ret—"

"Hector, these people are wounded," I whisper.

"They were most likely involved in the riots," he says matter-of-factly.

They all stare up at me, half in terror, half in hope, and the sight is so familiar that my heart aches. Who would hurt these people? "They look like they've been to war."

"Riots *are* war."

Oh. My stomach thuds with the understanding that they were probably injured in my name. I am at war again. A nebulous, aimless kind, but a war nevertheless. These are my people. But maybe they're my enemy too.

"Do they have weapons?" I ask. "Can they reach us from down there?"

"I see none. We have the high ground and the advantage for now."

Maybe I should burn the place to the ground, force everyone to the surface. But the *Belleza Guerra* rings in my head. *Always cultivate allies. When that fails, cultivate fear in your enemies.*

I step forward. Hector moves aside to let me pass, but I know from the whisper of steel on steel that he has drawn his sword. Fernando's eyes roam the crowd, ready to shift his sights in the space of an instant.

My confidence grows, which seems strange until I realize that this secret cavern reminds me of the hidden desert camp where I spent months plotting our war against Invierne. Like my desert rebels, these people are ragged but clean, wounded but proud. I probably should not allow myself this feeling of kinship.

"This is a surprise," I say, and my voice echoes around me. I smile, hoping to put them at ease, but I see only fear reflected back. One woman reaches down and hooks a young boy with her arm, pulling him against her.

I decide honesty is the best approach. "I could send a company of soldiers to empty this place." Eyes widen, feet shift. "It's clear you've already caused some trouble, but I might be convinced to overlook that. If you're hiding here just to avoid the tax increase or to do some honest commerce away from the guilds' prying eyes, then I'm sure we can come to an arrangement."

Their collective wariness does not ebb in the slightest.

I try a different tack. "Do you have a leader I can speak with? If not, you must appoint a representative right away." I step back from the edge.

Ximena gives me a quick nod of approval, even as she bends over to pull a dagger from the inside of her boot. I watched her kill a man with a long hairpin once, in my defense. She slipped it under his jaw and into his brain with the ease of long practice and training.

A voice rings from below. "Your Majesty!"

Fernando trains his bow on an old man who has limped forward. He is weathered by wind chap, his hair thin and gray. A long piece of driftwood serves as his cane; it's polished smooth by waves but as gnarled as the hand clutching it.

"You lead these people?" I ask.

"No, Your Majesty. Lo Chato leads us, but he is not here. I expect him to return this evening."

The ground beneath me sways, and I grasp for Hector's arm to steady myself.

I've heard the name once before. Lo Chato was the animagus who interrogated me when I was a prisoner in the enemy's camp. Even months later I can imagine him with perfect clarity—his baby-smooth skin, Godstone-blue eyes, flowing white hair. I shudder to think of the preternatural grace of his movement, the way his sibilant voice managed to bury itself inside me. I thought I had killed him.

What are the chances of encountering the name of an old enemy only weeks after one of his brethren martyred himself in my city?

I ask the old man, "How long has this village been here?"

"Almost as long as Brisadulce itself. But we live and do business above ground too, in the Wallows. We are Your Majesty's loyal subjects."

"I'm glad to know it." I have so many questions. But my legs begin to tremble, and my breath comes too hard. I need to make an exit before my weakened state is too apparent. "When Lo Chato returns, tell him I require his presence in the palace. He will not be harmed. I wish only to speak with him. I'll leave word with my mayordomo that he is to be received at once."

The old man inclines his head in what I presume is the only kind of bow his body will manage. "You should know that he is a private, reclusive person. He will be wary of your summons."

"Then you must convince him. I would be *very* disappointed if he did not come." I pause long enough to see understanding in the faces below. Then I bid them good day and gesture for my entourage to retreat.

"Tyrant!" someone yells at my back, and I whirl.

The people shift uncomfortably, avoiding my gaze, and I can't tell who the heckler is. "Fernando," I say, clenching my fists. "Fire a warning shot."

He looses the arrow at once. It thuds into the ground at the old man's feet. Its fletched tail vibrates with impact, as the crowd recoils.

"Do *not*," I say, "add sedition to your transgressions."

I turn away and head into the tunnel, Hector and Ximena at my back. During our return journey, I nearly trip over myself more than once, so lost am I in thought. It was a small group— maybe sixty people. Why so few? Is the secret of the village so well guarded? Have they climbed the ledge and traveled this path to reach the catacombs? Was the heckler expressing the feelings of the whole group? Maybe the whole city?

Most disturbing of all is the mysterious man called Lo Chato. He could be my assassin. And I have invited him to my threshold. But the *Belleza Guerra* devotes a whole chapter to the art of keeping one's enemies close, and so long as I am cautious, I know I am doing the right thing.

By the time we reach Alejandro's tomb, my breath comes in gasps and pain shoots through my side. I want nothing more than a mug of spiced wine and a day of sleep.

Fernando asks permission to stay behind. "I'd like to experiment with this opening a bit," he says, gesturing toward the gaping hole we just climbed out of. "I want to see how it opens from beneath, determine how often it is used."

"Please do. We must keep it guarded from now on."

"I'll take care of it."

"I'll have breakfast sent to you. *Not* from the barracks."

He bows formally, but his lips twitch.

When we reach my suite, I don't bother changing into my nightgown. Ximena helps me shuck my boots, then I loosen the ties of my pants and collapse into bed, which is made up with freshly laundered sheets, thanks to Mara. They're still warm, and I burrow into my pillows, catching the faint scent of rosewater. Truly, my bed is the greatest place in the world.

I am drifting away when an idea startles me awake. "Hector?" I blink to fight off sleep.

"Here," he says from the foot of my bed.

"Do we have contacts in the Wallows? I'd like to pinpoint the cave's location from the surface, find out all we can about it."

"I'll look into it, Majesty."

"And please stop calling me Majesty in private. It makes me grit my teeth."

He nods with exaggerated solemnity. "I'd hate for you to ruin your teeth on my behalf."

"If that happened, I'd have no choice but to follow the general's lead and order your execution." I make a vague gesture and say, "Off with his head!" And then my face burns with my own crass inappropriateness.

But Hector chuckles deep in his throat, and I feel it all the way down to my toes. Softly he says, "My life has ever been yours, Elisa."

My limbs tingle and heat fills my cheeks as we stare at each other.

I snap back to myself. He's talking about his *duty*. Of course his life is mine. He is Queen's Guard, after all, sworn to jump in front of a crossbow bolt if that's what it takes to save me.

Carefully I say, "You're a good friend, Hector. And I'm grateful to have you at my side."

His gaze drops to the ground, and his chest rises and falls with a breath. "Always."

7

It's late evening, and sunset glows warmly through my balcony windows. Ximena and I sit cross-legged on my bed, surrounded by faded parchment and musty scrolls—old palace architectural plans, retrieved from the monastery archive by my request. We've been studying them for hours.

One shows the restoration of the throne room, another the monastery addition, but none give clues about secret tunnels or underground villages. I push them away with frustration.

Something slips from one of the scrolls—a tighter coil of vellum, blackening along its tips. Curious, I break the wax seal with my thumbnail, and my fingers smear with something dark—rot or mold?—as I unroll it onto my thigh.

It's a map of Joya d'Arena. My native county of Orovalle is unmarked—the beautiful valley that lies north of the Hinders was undiscovered when this map was drawn. Which means it is probably five hundred years old, a priceless treasure that I have now exposed to light and air. I should send it back to the archive immediately for treatment and safekeeping. But I can't make myself look away.

The eastern holdings beyond the desert—now the country of Basajuan, ruled by my friend Cosmé—are referred to as "territories." Only the northern and southern holdings are clearly defined. Much like my country appears now, I realize with a start. The arable land of Joya d'Arena is once again a crooked sort of hourglass—fat on the top and bottom, thin and fragile in the center where the desert and ocean push together right here at my capital.

But Joya d'Arena is not alone anymore. I have allies now, protecting my borders on two sides—my father and sister to the north, Cosmé to the east. It makes me feel a little safer.

"My sky, there's something I must tell you," Ximena says.

I look up at my nurse. Dust smudges her right cheek, and wisps of gray hair dangle from her usually neat bun.

She takes a deep breath, as if steeling herself. "I've been doing some research on the Godstone. Since you fell into a coma."

I straighten too fast, and several scrolls topple off my bed. "Oh?"

She runs a reverent forefinger across the parchment in her lap. "You know the prophecy in Homer's Afflatus, the one that says, 'He could not know what awaited at the gate of the enemy, and he was led, like a pig to the slaughter, into the realm of sorcery'?"

"Father Alentín thinks I fulfilled that prophecy when I was captured by Inviernos." I keep my tone and expression bland, afraid she'll change her mind about talking to me. Ximena spent years cultivating my ignorance on matters pertaining to the stone I bear. She believed it was the will of God. I know how much it costs her to turn her back on this tenet of a deeply personal faith.

"I'm not so sure you did."

I swallow hard. "Oh." I've been clinging to the hope that I am done with 'the realm of sorcery,' that being queen will be my great service to God.

She dumps the parchment off her lap and stands. "It's the word 'gate' that gave me pause," she says as she begins pacing at the foot of my bed. "In the Lengua Classica, it's an archaic usage that also sometimes translates to 'path.' As in, 'narrow is the path that restores the soul,' from the *Scriptura Sancta.*"

"Go on."

"It's the same word we just found etched into the tunnel below the catacombs."

I whisper, "'The gate that leads to life is narrow and small so that few find it.'" I wrap my arms around myself. "I'm not sure what you're getting at," I say, but my heart patters and my limbs tingle. There is something to what she's saying. Something important.

"I made a study of that word when I was a scribe. I went through all four of the holy scriptures looking for usages. It occurs exactly ten times. Five times, it refers to the gate—or path—of the enemy. But the other five times, it refers to something positive. Like life, or restoration, or healing." Ximena pauses and grabs one of my bedposts. We lock gazes, and she says, "What are the chances of each reference occurring exactly five times?"

I shrug. "It's the holy number of perfection. Something will occur exactly five times if God wills it."

"Exactly. He must will it so. Such things do not happen by chance." She resumes pacing, and her face grows distant. "I always thought those verses were metaphorical. I thought the path that restores the soul was a way to live one's life. The way of faith, maybe. But what if . . ." She takes a deep breath. "What if it's a real place? What if they are both *real places*?"

The Godstone buzzes with affirmation, sending prickles up my spine. "Both of them, real places," I murmur. "The gate of the enemy, and the gate that leads to life."

"I don't know, my sky. But I'm looking into it."

"Father Nicandro might be able to help. He has provided quiet aid to me in the past. Also, he is fluent in the Lengua Classica, and I trust him with my life."

She nods. "I'll discuss it with him. I'm at the point where I need access to the restricted areas of the monastery archive anyway."

"Ximena," I whisper. "What if it *is* a real place? What if I still have to go there?"

A year ago, she would have offered meaningless platitudes—or maybe a pastry—in an attempt to brush away my fears. But now she just gazes at me, her small black eyes full of determination, maybe even excitement. I shiver.

Glass shatters. Something thumps to the ground.

Ximena rushes into the atrium. I follow as quickly as I can.

Mara is doubled over beside the bathing pool, hands clutching her stomach. Several items from the vanity lie strewn about the floor. The moist air is too thick and sweet with my freesia perfume.

"What's wrong?" I demand. "What happened?"

"I . . . shaking out your gown . . . my . . ."

"Her scar," Ximena says. "It split open again."

Her scar. From when the animagi burned her. Mara threw herself into the path of Invierne's sorcerers to allow me time to work the magic of my Godstone. She barely survived. I have hardly given a thought to her injuries since that day.

I yell for one of the guards to fetch Doctor Enzo.

Mara slips to the ground, legs stretched out. Ximena unlaces her bodice to reveal a white chemise dotted with bright blood. Then she gingerly peels the chemise from Mara's midriff.

I can't control the gasp that escapes me. A ropy scar, about four fingers wide, stretches across her stomach, ridged with peaks and valleys of skin where her navel ought to be. Blood wells along a line of split skin.

"It's deep this time," Ximena says, blotting gently with the edge of Mara's ruined chemise. "But it's clean and straight. Easily stitched."

"This time?" I ask. "It happens often?"

"I've been forgetting," Mara says between breaths, "to put salve on it."

"What salve? Where?" I demand.

"Small pot on the shelf by her bed," says Ximena, continuing to blot.

"I'll be right back." I hurry through the atrium to the maids' room.

It's much smaller than my own chamber, with one high window, four bunked beds, and a shelf next to each bed for personal items. A few simple gowns hang from pegs on the wall below the window, and beside them is a writing desk with several half-melted candles. Such a tiny place to live. I can't imagine how crowded it will feel when I finally acquiesce to my mayordomo's request to take on more attendants.

I spot the round clay pot on the shelf beside Mara's bed and grab it. Even without lifting the lid, I catch the strong scent of eucalyptus.

I'm hurrying back through the atrium when I step on something sharp. I nearly drop the pot as I lurch sideways to shift the weight from my foot. The effort tears at my abdomen, but I keep my balance. I peer down at the floor to see what nearly tripped me.

It's one of my ancient Godstones, detached from its long-dead bearer. After using it to magnify the power of my own living Godstone and defeating the animagi, I tossed it along with its used-up brothers into a jewelry box on my dressing table. Mara must have knocked it over.

I lift it up between thumb and forefinger. It's as blue-black as a bruise and jagged from its final devastating act. But in the wash of atrium light, I catch the hint of a spark, a tiny mote of untouched perfection deep inside the shattered jewel.

I hand the pot to Ximena, set the cracked Godstone on the vanity table, and crouch to face my lady-in-waiting.

"It's doesn't hurt that badly," Mara assures me. "It just caught me by surprise."

"She's being brave," Ximena says. "The rip is deep, and she shouldn't be moved until Doctor Enzo gets here. The salve will help keep the skin moist."

Someone pounds at my door, and with an apologetic shrug to Ximena and Mara, I hurry back to the bedchamber. A guard is peering through the peephole. "It's the mayordomo, on some urgency," he says.

His timing could not be worse. "Show him in." I smooth my rumpled pants, wishing I'd taken the time to bathe and change today.

The mayordomo has made a gallant attempt at elegance, with a velvet vest over a blouse with flared lace cuffs. But as always, his clothes are a size too small, and his belly strains the buttons near to popping. He dips into a courtier's bow.

"Rise."

"Forgive the intrusion, Your Majesty." He eyes the manuscripts strewn across my unmade bed. "I know you said to clear your schedule, but a delegation from Queen Cosmé of Basajuan has just arrived. I've assigned them to the dignitaries' suite. They expressed a strong desire to see you as soon as possible."

A delegation from Cosmé! I hope she sent friends, dear people I have not seen since my time in the desert. "You were right to inform me. See if they require food and drink. I'll be there as soon as I can."

Ximena appears in the doorway to the atrium, Mara's pot still clutched in her hand.

The mayordomo bows again. "Yes, Your Majesty. If you're ready to receive guests, does that mean we may discuss your schedule? Several noblewomen have applied for the open attendant positions—a queen needs more than two ladies! And I'm afraid you've acquired a long list of suitors; His Grace the conde Tristán of Selvarica has been relentless in trying to schedule an audience with you. There was a riot in the merchants' alley yesterday over the wheat shortage, so the mayor would like to discuss increasing the guard presence there and in the Wallows—"

I wave him silent. "Later. See to our guests."

He flees without another word. I frown at his back, unease curling in my stomach. *Another riot.* I resolve to call him back the moment I'm finished with the delegation.

"You'll need a quick bath and a change of clothes," Ximena says.

"No time for a bath," I say, heading toward her.

"You can't dress yourself with that injury!"

I grab the pot from her hands. "I'll apply the salve while you shake out my dress and undo the bodice." The stuff inside is thick and brown, with the consistency of something between wax and date jelly.

Ximena squeezes my shoulder and grabs my gown from the floor where Mara dropped it.

I crouch beside Mara and dip two fingers in the pot.

"It's not right, Elisa," Mara protests. "You're my queen. You shouldn't—"

"Oh, shut up. Should I avoid the tear itself?"

"No. It's also a disinfectant. It will sting, but . . . I'll be fine if you want to wait—"

I hush her by touching a blob of the stuff directly to the tear. She hisses.

Her skin feels strange beneath my fingertips, so lumpy and stiff, hardly like skin at all. But it's as warm as normal flesh and bleeds just as easily. Gently I massage the salve along the edges of the wound, pretending not to notice when it mixes with seeping blood. I refuse to let myself feel revulsion, all the while thinking, *Mara is this way because of me. She did it for* me.

Mara makes no sound, but her head falls back against the wall as she squeezes her eyes closed.

"Your gown is ready," Ximena says.

I give Mara's arm a squeeze, then rinse my hands. Ximena dresses me with quick efficiency and then directs me to the edge of my bed. I'm not quite healed enough to bend over and reach my feet, so Ximena slides my stockings on. While she works, I pull out the pin holding up my braids and unravel my hair.

Thinking of Mara sitting alone on the floor of the atrium, I say, "The mayordomo is right, isn't he? I need more than two attendants."

"Serving you is an easy privilege, my sky. But once in a while, when we must hurry or when something goes a little wrong, like today, then yes, it would be nice to have one more person. Maybe two." She slips on a pair of soft leather slippers.

My world is already so crowded with guards and constant visitors. It's been nice to have a smidge of privacy in the atrium with only my two ladies, who are dear friends besides. I cannot imagine adding a stranger to the mix. But as Ximena sweeps up a layer of my hair and pins it with a mother-of-pearl comb, I say, "I'll speak to the mayordomo about it soon."

She plants a kiss on my cheek. "You'll do what is best." She helps me to my feet.

"Will you stay here with Mara?"

"I'm sure she'll be fine without me."

I open my mouth to snap that it's a command, not a question. But at the last moment, I decide on a softer tack. "It will bring me comfort to know you are with her." And I turn away, signaling the guards to accompany me.

We step into the corridor, and they center me in a tight formation of creaking leather and swinging swords.

Lord Hector hurries up as we round the first corner. The guards shift formation so he can walk beside me. "I just heard about the delegation," he says. "How are you feeling?"

"Healthy and hearty and eager to see old friends." We descend a wide stairway, and I gladly take his offered arm.

"It's strange to think of Cosmé as queen," he says. "I still picture her in her maid's cap."

Thinking of my friend brings an easy smile. "And I still see her in leather boots and a desert cloak, tending to the wounded and teaching the little ones to use their slings."

"She has always been exceedingly capable," he says.

"Indeed." Many times I have wished I were half so capable as Cosmé.

When we reach the dignitaries' suite, my guards clear a path so I can knock on the door myself. An older boy answers, and I don't recognize him until his face lights up upon seeing me. "It's Queen Elisa," he hollers over his shoulder.

I clasp his upper arm. "You've grown tall, Matteo."

His eyes are wide as he steps aside, and we have passed beyond him when he adds hurriedly, "I'll be fourteen next month!"

The suite is about the size of my own, with two large beds instead of one. The bathing area is partly blocked by a velvet curtain, but I see the edge of a garderobe and a large wooden tub with carrying handles.

A familiar voice says, "Hello, Elisa," as a figure pushes the curtain aside.

My breath catches as I look into the grinning face of Father Alentín, the one-armed rebel priest who became my mentor in the desert. He wears a traditional rough-woven tunic and robe, and as usual, his empty sleeve is tucked in at the shoulder.

Alentín wraps me in a hug. "Oh, my dear girl," he says. "It has been too long." He embraces me with such easy spontaneity, as if I'm merely a girl instead of a queen, and I melt into it.

I let myself cling to him, inhaling the dusty cook-fire scent of his woolen robe. I have to squeeze my eyes tight and swallow hard. "It's good to see you too," I manage.

He murmurs, "I have been praying for you every day."

I step back and hold him at arm's length. "And I you! How is Cosmé?"

"Struggling with limited funds to establish a stable government and build a garrison on the Invierne border. Growling at anyone who gets in her way. Putting nobles in their places."

"So, the usual."

"She sends her love. Actually, she said 'regards,' which amounts to the same thing."

I smile. There was a time when Cosmé held me in very low regard indeed.

Alentín's expression turns serious. "Elisa, there is something else. Something you should know."

"Oh?"

He turns toward the bathing area and hollers, "Come on out now."

"What?" I say. "Who are you—"

A young man steps from behind the curtain, and my throat squeezes. He is impossibly tall and reed thin, with a sharp jaw and hooked nose that make him austerely handsome. He wears a black leather patch over one eye.

It is Belén.

The betrayer. The boy who sold me to the Invierne army. He nearly ruined everything we had fought for, in his mistaken belief that he was doing God's will.

Softly he says, "Hello, Elisa."

I'm not sure what to say. It aches a little to see him, because before he betrayed me, he was my friend. And once he realized his mistake, he risked his own life to warn me of the animagi's plans.

But I can't force warmth into my voice when I say, "Why are you here, Belén?"

He opens his mouth but changes his mind about whatever he was going to say. Instead he hangs his head.

Alentín reaches out and gives Belén's shoulder a squeeze.

"This boy is quite reformed. But he remains unpopular in Basajuan, as you can imagine. The court demands his execution, but Cosmé can't bear to see him killed. She thought to make use of his scouting ability, sending him on forays into enemy territory. Alas, his reporting visits to the city have become increasingly challenging. There was a scuffle in the stables—"

"But why send him here? Why to me?"

"Because I asked her to," Belén says. He dares to hold my gaze. I catch myself looking back and forth between his eye and his patch before focusing determinedly on the bridge of his nose. "The *Scriptura Sancta* says that making amends is a holy and cleansing fire unto the soul. And that's what I want to do: to make amends, to pledge my life to your service."

I stare at him.

He whispers, "Please, Elisa."

"I'll think about it."

He hides his disappointment quickly. "Thank you."

I have a sudden urge to strike out at something, or maybe someone. Cosmé should not have sent Belén to me without regard for my wishes. Alentín should have known better than to support the plan. And yet I am forced to accept Belén's presence here, since he travels in a delegation.

I have trouble enough holding my own at court. How much worse is it to be manipulated by my allies and friends? To have them foist off their own problems on me? I glare coldly as I address them both. "From this point forward, you shall address us as Your Majesty."

They bow. "Of course, Your Majesty," the traitor says.

To Alentín I say, "Are you here in an official ambassadorial role?" Though I know the answer; it's the only way to ensure Belén's safety.

"I am," he says, and his bearing is suddenly stiff. "Queen Cosmé wishes you to know of an incident that occurred in her public marketplace and would like your view on it. In short, an animagus appeared, demanded that you give yourself over to Invierne as a willing sacrifice, and then burned himself alive."

I gape at him. "It was the same here!"

He nods gravely. "I was in your city not two minutes before I learned of the event."

But I hardly hear him for the pounding in my ears. Two similar occurrences in succession speak of planning, of deadly seriousness. What is so important as to be worth two martyrs? What could they possibly want with *me*?

You will know the gate of your enemy.

Frowning, I say, "Belén?"

"Yes, Your Majesty."

"Delegation or no, if I sense you are out to harm me or any of my people, I will have you imprisoned and tried for treason. If Hector does not kill you first."

If he has a response, I do not know or care, for I spin on my heel and head toward the door. My guards fall in around me.

I pause in the threshold and say to Alentín, "Weekly services will be held tomorrow in the monastery. You and Belén and Matteo should attend."

His eyes are wide. "Yes, Eli—Your Majesty."

They all regard me as if I am a stranger, and a creeping emptiness worms through my chest. I am nearly returned to my suite before I recognize the feeling as loneliness.

8

MARA is stretched out on my bed, Doctor Enzo hovering over her as he tucks in the edges of a bandage. The guards have turned politely away, as they do when I am dressing.

I grab her hand. "How do you feel?"

"Rather like I just split in half."

Enzo snorts. "Well short of half. Although stitching scar tissue is a complicated and delicate process. I used seven stitches this time, all quite small thanks to a new needle I commissioned."

Seven? This time? I'm about to ask about the other times when Ximena hurries in from the atrium. "I have everything set to rights. Mara made quite a mess when she fell."

Mara squeezes my hand. "Who was it? Anyone from Father Alentín's camp? I was so hoping—"

"Alentín himself is here." I hush her startled exclamation. "But there is more, which I will tell you in a moment."

Her eyes narrow, and she nods.

Doctor Enzo pulls Mara's chemise down over the bandage

and straightens. "Light work only for the girl," he tells me. "For a week. Bandages must be changed daily, the salve applied each time. Would you like me to look at you too, since I'm here?" He stares toward my abdomen, and his fingers twitch with eagerness. "I hear you've been up and about against my recommendation. I predict you have continued to heal anyway. I consulted some records in the archive of previous bearers, and—"

"Later, Enzo. You are dismissed."

He mutters disjointed grumblings as he exits the suite.

Mara struggles to sit up. I give her arm a gentle pull, and she slides from the bed onto her feet.

I relate my meeting with Alentín. Ximena's eyes narrow at the news that another animagus burned himself alive. And when Mara learns that Belén is in the palace, she collapses back onto the bed, looking dazed.

Ximena paces. "I don't like this," she murmurs. "Just how many animagi must there be for Invierne to sacrifice them so easily? And Belén. He needs to be watched. Which means we must assign some of the Royal Guard to their quarters. After the lockdown, I'm not sure we can trust the palace garrison."

"Which means," Hector says, "using some of the men who are assigned to your own protection."

Fernando, from his post at the door, clears his throat and says to Hector, "My lord?"

"Yes?"

"There is not one among us who would balk at a double watch." I gape at him, realizing he must have come straight here after poking around in the catacombs. Do my guards ever rest?

But they are all nodding agreement.

"I'm glad to know it," Hector says. "It may come to that."

In the silence that follows, I know what everyone is thinking: Before the war, the Royal Guard was a full garrison of sixty. Now, only thirty-two remain. No, I correct myself. Thirty-one, with the loss of Martín.

Determining the right size for a Royal Guard is a delicate balance. Too many, and my court would distrust me, fearing what I could do with my own personal army. But right now I don't have nearly enough. It makes me weak, vulnerable. And everyone knows it.

I tell my mayordomo that I'm ready to ease back into a schedule. The first thing I want to do is address the recent spate of riots, but he insists I begin by interviewing suitors, starting with Conde Tristán of Selvarica. The conde is here for next week's Deliverance Gala and has taken to accosting the mayordomo in the halls with regular requests for an audience.

I agree to see him first thing in the morning, telling myself that everything else can wait another day, and the mayordomo wilts with relief.

So I rise early, and while Mara sleeps in, I sit on my vanity stool while Ximena sculpts my hair into an elaborate coif of loops and curls. I'm holding up my neck curls so she can work the clasp of a sapphire-drop necklace—a piece I inherited from Queen Rosaura—when she says, "You're very nervous and fidgety this morning."

I hadn't noticed the fidgeting, but my stomach is indeed in knots. "Yes," I admit. She finishes clasping the necklace, and I drop the curls. Our eyes meet in the mirror. "Oh, Ximena, the appearance of the animagus, the assassination attempt—they have weakened my position greatly."

"Yes," she agrees solemnly.

"The way I see it, I have two bargaining chips right now: the vacant spot on the Quorum, which every noble house in the country is vying for, and my own marriage. My country is splintering apart. I *must* acquire strong allies with my choices. I can't make the wrong decisions!"

"Three bargaining chips," she says.

"Three? What do you mean?"

She gazes at me a moment, her eyes full of sympathy. "Hector, as second-highest ranking officer in the kingdom, has an automatic Quorum seat. He is young and handsome. He has the friendship of the queen. He is of modest but noble birth. He is, in short, the most eligible bachelor in your kingdom. You could marry him off to tremendous advantage."

"Oh." I blink at her, vaguely stunned. "Yes, of course." Why has this never occurred to me?

A knock sounds at the door to my bedroom, and moments later, a guard announces the presence of Lord-Conde Eduardo.

I fix a smile on my face as he enters the atrium. At least it's not the general.

"Ah, Your Majesty, I'm delighted to see you looking so well!"

My nose twitches against his sharp myrrh musk as I take

his outstretched hands and kiss his cheek. "It feels good to get back to a regular schedule," I say.

"Yes, I heard you would begin interviewing suitors today. I cleared my schedule so I could come and offer my support to you during your meetings."

My grin is so hard and stiff that my teeth ache. "Oh, you shouldn't have, Your Grace. I hate to think I'm keeping you from important matters."

He waves off my protest. "Our kingdom is desperate for stability. This might be the most important decision you make during your entire reign. Of *course* I will be there for you." He grasps my shoulder and squeezes tight, looking like a concerned father with his furrowed brow.

But every instinct screams against allowing him to accompany me. *Think, Elisa!*

I duck my head respectfully. "In that case, I am grateful for your presence and your counsel." He brightens visibly. "But I have a few more private preparations to make. Will you meet me in my office?"

"Of course, Your Majesty." His eyes sweep over me, taking note of my gown, my hair, my necklace. "You'll wear your crown, won't you?"

"I wasn't planning—"

"It's important you go into these interviews appropriately accessorized by the symbols of your office, don't you think?"

I groan inwardly, thinking of the headache I'll have by the time we break for the noon meal. "Of course you're right, Your Grace."

He smiles indulgently. "I'll see you soon." He bows and exits my bedchamber.

As soon as the door closes at his back, I say to no one in particular, "I want Conde Eduardo out of my office as soon as possible."

"I'll take care of it, my sky," Ximena says, and her soft voice has such a weight of authority that I have no doubt she can do as she promises. "I need some time—you'll have to suffer his company at first. But I'll have him away as soon as possible."

"Thank you."

When she places the crown on my head, it feels like a millstone. I fantasize about commissioning a new one, something delicate and feminine and light. But my coffers are drained, and a new crown would be an insulting extravagance when I can't even afford to hire and train more Royal Guards.

She pushes hairpins through the loops in the lining, but it doesn't matter—the crown lists to the right until the heavy edge presses against the top of my ear.

"I feel like I've grown an extra brow," I say, wrinkling my forehead experimentally. Sure enough, the crown slips even farther, and the cartilage of my ear starts to fold over. Ximena does some rearranging until the crown wobbles but stays put. *No sudden head movements,* I tell myself as she pronounces me ready to receive suitors.

I've hardly used my office since Alejandro's death. It's a bright room, with wood-paneled walls and two long windows whose deep ledges are lush with potted ferns. But I'm not yet at home here. Sitting at the desk, I feel like an imposter, like I'm playing at ruling. Still, it's better than my vast, echoing audience hall with its backache-inducing throne.

Hector takes his position at my right shoulder, Conde Eduardo at my left. Guards stand sentry at the windows and doorway. My secretary sits in a corner at a small desk, his quill poised to take notes. I can only see the top of his head because a small tower of documents sits at the edge of his desk, blocking my view. I'm supposed to review and sign them all. I force myself to ignore the stack; I can't think about it now.

My heart pounds with nervousness as we wait. How does a queen handle a suitor? When I was a princess of Orovalle, I was overweight and solitary, with an unnatural attraction to musty scrolls. Anyone who wished to court me did so behind the scenes, in negotiation with my father.

As queen, I must do my own negotiating. Everyone will want something—a new title, better trading opportunities, or maybe just power. Though they'll pretend otherwise, none will want *me*.

I don't know how I'll bear the polite dance of flirtation and innuendo that always precedes these agreements. Or even how to navigate the maze that is a royal marriage treaty. I certainly don't want to make any missteps that would cause Eduardo to feel he must jump in and help.

"He arrives," says a guard.

I straighten in my chair, trying to look regal.

A barrel-shaped man with thinning hair enters. His eyes are wide, his expression serious. Droplets of sweat collect on his protruding upper lip. He bows low.

"Your Majesty," says Conde Eduardo at my ear. "May I present Lord Liano of Altapalma?"

I look up at him sharply. I was expecting Conde Tristán.

"I took the liberty of making some slight changes to your receiving schedule so we could accommodate my good friend here," Eduardo explains. "I know how eager you are to make the acquaintance of some of the northern lords."

I'm not sure whether to protest or pretend gratitude. Is it a common practice here in Joya for everyone else to manage the monarch's schedule?

I force blandness to my face and say, "Welcome, Lord Liano. Thank you for coming."

He rises from his bow but says nothing. Am I supposed to direct our conversation?

"Lord Liano is heir to the countship of Altapalma until his older brother produces a son." Eduardo jumps in. "He's a devout observer of the holy sacraments and an accomplished hunter."

"Wild javelinas," Liano blurts out. "I've won the annual tournament three years in a row."

I can't stop staring at his wet upper lip. "Oh. That's . . . impressive," I manage.

His whole body shifts forward with eagerness. "And I tan javelina hides! My hides are soft enough to make riding garb for even the finest ladies. I make all my own hunting weapons. And . . ." He draws himself to full height. "I am Grand Master of the Society for the Advocacy of Javelinas as Livestock."

"So accomplished," I murmur, more than a little stunned. I

could not marry this man. Not ever. Not even to save my country. I'd rather abdicate.

Someone pounds on the door, and Lord Liano jumps.

A guard answers. After a muted conversation, he says, "Pardon me, Lord-Conde Eduardo, but Your Grace is summoned on a very urgent matter. Something about a letter from home?"

Eduardo's face blanches. He makes quick apologies and hurries out the door. I suddenly breathe easier. *Thank you, Ximena*.

I turn back to Lord Liano. "I am forced to cut our appointment short, my lord. I'm afraid my dear friend the conde was overly eager in scheduling you, as I have another appointment in moments."

His expression turns tragic, like that of a child who just had his favorite sweet taken away, and I hastily add, "But I'd love to discuss . . . javelina hunting further at some point. Are you in town awhile for the Deliverance Gala?"

He bows. "Of course, Your Majesty."

"Then I look forward to seeing you."

Once he is gone, I turn to Hector, who is trying very hard not to laugh.

"I can't, Hector. Not him."

"You can do better," he agrees.

Another knock, another murmured conversation, and my guard swings the door wide to receive Conde Tristán.

A small, foppish man with puffed sleeves and a plumed hat sweeps in and bows with a flourish. I am about to greet him, but he intones, "I present to you His Grace Conde Tristán, master equestrian, fighting man, and the pride of Selvarica."

Ah, just a herald then.

He steps aside as a second man strides through the door. He's of average height and lanky, and he moves with a dancer's purposed grace. His features are a touch too delicate for true handsomeness, the black hair gently curling at his nape a little too beautiful, but his eyes shine with warmth and intelligence. He looks younger than I imagined. I'm surprised to find myself returning his shy smile with one of my own.

He bows, straightens, stares.

"Um, hello," I say lamely. "Welcome."

"Thank you. Er, Your Majesty. It is . . . You are . . ." He shakes his head ruefully. "I'm sorry. I'm usually more articulate than this. It's just that you are so much more beautiful than I remember."

My eyes narrow as I try to discern his level of sincerity. In my peripheral vision, I notice Hector shift on his feet and cross his arms over his chest.

I decide to be frank. "Don't be ridiculous, Your Grace. You and I both know my court has pronounced me unlovely."

He decides to be frank right back. "True. Gossip has you pegged as portly, prone to uncouth wardrobe choices, and alarmingly blunt." His smile reveals straight white teeth. "I concur that you are blunt."

"I assure you they are correct about my fashion sense too. Were it not for my devoted attendants, I would be dressed in sand chaps and a goat-hair tunic."

"I'm certain you would be stunning in them."

I wait for him to make placating noises about the gossip regarding my reputed corpulence, and I'm a little disappointed, a little relieved, when he does not.

I'm not sure what to say next. From the corner comes the *scrape-scrape* of quill against parchment as the secretary feverishly records our meeting. I imagine him writing: . . . *goat-hair tunic.*

My head is now pounding from the relentless weight of my crown. Frustration boils over, and I say, "Conde Tristán, why are you here?"

He has the grace to seem flustered. He says, "I was hoping we could get to know each other. It is no secret that my people would benefit greatly if I were to . . . ally myself . . . with Your Majesty. But there is no hurry. I simply propose that we meet once in a while and see if we enjoy each other's company."

"That's it for now? No requests, no favors?"

"Well, there is one thing."

Of course there is. "What?"

"At the upcoming Deliverance Gala, would you be so kind as to honor me with two dances?"

Oh, God, I will have to dance. It hadn't occurred to me. I'm a terrible dancer.

The horror on my face must be apparent, for Conde Tristán takes a step backward, eyes wide with alarm. "I apologize, Your Majesty. Perhaps I am too forward—"

"Yes, you may have two dances. But it is my plan to test your devotion by stepping on your feet."

His eyes crinkle with genuine mirth. "I shall look forward

to it. You may find, though, that I am not so easy to step on."

I force myself to resist his smile, even as I admit to myself that I like him a little. I gesture to one of the guards and say, "Please escort the conde and his . . ." Herald? Assistant? ". . . and his man back to their rooms and make sure they have everything they need."

If the conde is discouraged by the dismissal, he doesn't show it. "Until the festival, Your Majesty." He executes a polished bow. His attendant does the same, and they leave with the guard.

After the door shuts, Hector says, "He thought you were joking about stepping on his feet," and we exchange a quick smile.

The secretary scribbles last-minute notations about the meeting. Will he record every single word spoken in this room?

"Mr. Secretary," I say.

He looks up, mid–pen stroke. A smudge of ink mars the tip of his nose. "Your Majesty?"

"I'm thirsty. Fetch me a glass of water, please?"

He frowns with the understanding that I'm getting rid of him but schools his expression quickly. "Yes, Your Majesty."

Once he's gone, I lean back in my chair and look up at Hector. "What did you think of the conde? An improvement on Liano, at least, yes?" I rub at my temples. The weight of this stupid crown is making it hard to think.

Hector's gaze turns inward as he ponders. I have always liked this about him, the way he mulls ideas over in his head.

He never feels obliged to speak until he has exactly the right words.

He says, "Conde Tristán is at the top of Lady Jada's list, but I think it has more to do with his general popularity and charm than it does his suitability. Selvarica is a small southern holding, consisting mostly of islands. It's difficult to access, not heavily populated. I'm not sure what the conde feels he can offer the throne. I think you can do better. And Eduardo and Luz-Manuel have both expressed a preference that you choose someone from the north."

He says it all without emotion, as if quoting an academic text. I look down at my lap. "But what of *him*?" I say softly. "What kind of man is he, do you think?"

Seconds pass. I feel his eyes on me, but I can't bring myself to meet his gaze, so I focus hard on the hands resting atop my skirt. My dark skin lies in sharp contrast to the blue of my gown. My right thumbnail is uneven from my habit of biting it. I should have Mara file it for me.

At last he says, "He inherited young, when his father died in a riding accident. By reputation, he is intelligent and charming. The ladies of the court consider him quite dashing. That's all I know."

His voice is so tight that I look up to try to read his face. It's hard and determined. We stare at each other for a long moment.

I need to fill the silence, to explain, so I say, "I know I'll marry for the benefit of Joya d'Arena, and my own feelings will not be a consideration. So it's silly to hope . . . but I can't help it. . . . That is, I hope I marry a good man. Like Alejandro.

I know he didn't love me, but he *was* my friend." The sigh that escapes is almost like a sob.

His eyes flash with something—pity, maybe—and he reaches down, grabs my hand. His thumb sweeps across my knuckles as he says in a gruff whisper, "I can't imagine there is a man in all of Joya who is good enough for our queen. But if such a man exists, we will find him. I swear it."

I swallow hard. "Thank you."

The mayordomo rushes unannounced through the doorway. Hector drops my hand and lurches to attention.

"Your Majesty!" the mayordomo pants. "He's here. Lo Chato from the Wallows. Do you still wish to grant immediate audience? You're scheduled to see Lady Jada next. I could ask her to wait."

My startled reaction has dislodged my crown, and it slips down my brow. I pull it off, wincing when strands of hair are yanked out by the roots. "Did Lo Chato come alone?" Even saying the name gives me a shiver.

"Yes, Your Majesty."

I set the crown on the edge of my desk. I hate that I am not big enough, not strong enough, to wear it. "Then send him in," I whisper.

He bows and exits the office.

"Be ready," Hector says to the guards, and hands move to scabbards; eyes shift toward the door. With a metallic *whisk*, Hector draws his gauntlet daggers. A smart choice, since his position between my desk and the wall gives him little range of motion for a sword.

The mayordomo enters and says in a clipped, formal voice, "Your Majesty, I present Lo Chato of the Wallows."

A figure glides into the room. He is impossibly tall, and he wears a long black cloak with a deep cowl that shadows his face. He drops to one knee, bows his head, and waits silently.

"Rise," I say, hoping he doesn't notice the tremor in my voice. I place a fingertip to the Godstone, hoping for a tickle of warmth, or even a chill—anything to indicate whether the person before me is friend or foe. But I feel nothing.

The cowled man straightens.

"Remove your hood."

He raises his hands, and I already know, even as he slides the hood back from his head—by the pale peach of his hands, the preternatural grace of his movement—what will be revealed.

Eyes as green as moss, a face so sharply delicate as to be catlike, waist-long hair the syrupy gold of honey.

It takes only a split second for my guards to ring him with swords. Hector steps in front of me, daggers in defensive position.

The man before me carries himself like an animagus. My forearm throbs with the phantom memory of a sorcerer's claws lashing into my skin, and I stare at his hands, expecting to see clawlike points embedded in his nails.

His nails are cracked and encrusted with dirt, but they are free of barbs. And unlike the uncannily perfect animagi I encountered, he has faint lines across his forehead; a patch of dry, peeling skin across his nose; and weary, bloodshot eyes. Not blue, those eyes. And his hair is not white.

Not a sorcerer, then. I breathe deeply through my nose, savoring this feeling of relief.

Still, an Invierno has been secretly living in my city, leading a group of my own people.

The mayordomo stands just out of range of the guards' swords, gaping at the creature he escorted in. I say with a steadiness that surprises me, "The secretary will return soon from an errand. Please head him off. And tell no one, not even Lady Jada, the nature of my current appointment."

"Yes, Your Majesty." He departs gratefully.

I gesture to one of the guards to close and bar the door.

The Invierno regards me calmly.

I'm not sure how to proceed, so I say, "Thank you for coming."

"Your Majesty commanded it, and I obeyed." He speaks perfect Plebeya, without even a trace of the clipped impatience I've heard from animagi.

"Why would an Invierno feel compelled to obey me?"

"I am Your Majesty's loyal subject."

Not likely. "Is Lo Chato your name?"

"A title."

"Do many Inviernos carry the title of 'Lo Chato'?" I ask, too tentatively.

"We have more Chatos than you have condes," he says.

I don't want to call him that. Not ever. "And your name?"

"My name, in God's language, means 'He Who Wafts Gently with the Wind Becomes as Mighty as the Thunderstorm.'"

One of the guards snorts.

He shrugs. "It's a common name in Invierne. But the people of my village call me Storm when they are being familiar."

"Ah, yes. Please explain why you live in a cavern beneath the Wallows."

"I first came to serve as ambassador to Joya d'Arena. I was a member of King Alejandro's court for several years. As the war began, I found it necessary to go into hiding."

The first part is easy enough to prove. "Hector, do you recognize this man?"

Hector is studying him, eyes narrowed. "No. Well, maybe."

"Maybe?"

"It *could* be him. There are similarities. The man I remember had darker hair."

"I see." I purse my lips, thinking hard. I can't read the Invierno's face, much less separate truth from falsehood. "You call yourself my loyal subject. That sounds more like defection than hiding."

"You are correct, Your Majesty. I was not hiding from the people of Joya, but from my own."

"Why?"

His face is void of feeling as he says, "I had failed, you see. After years of campaigning for port rights, I had nothing to show for my efforts. My life was forfeit, and my choice was to either go home in disgrace and face execution, or find a new home here."

"A harsh sentence."

"My kind embrace honorable death. I am wretched in my unusual desire to live beyond the shame of my failure."

I shudder, remembering the zeal with which the animagus atop the amphitheater burned himself. And before that, how dozens of Inviernos submitted themselves to the animagi's knives, the way their blood poured into the sand and fueled the fire magic that nearly burned our city to the ground. Did they all believe they were embracing honorable death?

Hector asks, "Why didn't you seek asylum? The king would have granted it."

"Your king could not have protected me. I had to disappear completely." Storm smiles for the first time—a slow, edged grin that sends shivers down my back. "Surely you realize? Your city is crawling with Invierne spies."

The guards exchange a startled glance.

I breathe deeply through my nose to keep steady. Though my pulse races, I wave a hand nonchalantly and say, "Everyone spies on everyone else. My own father, King Hitzedar of Orovalle, has several spies in my court."

Storm says, "Your Majesty, there are hundreds. Living right here in the city."

"Inviernos like you? Or are Joya's own citizens turning against her?"

"Both."

Hector says, "We would recognize Inviernos among us."

He just shrugs and looks off in the distance as if bored.

I lean forward. "Would we, Storm? Would we recognize them?"

His expression turns smug. "All of you Joyans and Orovalleños look exactly alike, with your dirty skin and dark hair and wood-rot eyes. You are like black rats crawling across the sand. But we Inviernos are a colorful people, and as numerous as the stars in the sky. It is rare to find some among us who resemble you enough to pass, but found them we have. Enough to make spies."

"You claim to be my loyal subject, yet you speak as though you hold my people in contempt." I should be angrier, but I find myself fascinated with his complete disregard for propriety.

"You are a contemptible people. I am loyal out of necessity, not love."

Strange that he does not make even the barest attempt at flattery. "Hard to believe you were unable to make diplomatic headway in my husband's court, charming as you are."

He nods knowingly. "This is the *sarcasm* your people are so fond of. When you say one thing but mean another. Inviernos value honesty too much for it, in accordance with God's will."

I don't have the time or energy for a doctrinal debate, so I let that go. "The animagus who burned himself alive . . . surely you heard about it?"

He nods. "Everyone within two weeks' journey has heard by now."

"Did you know him? Did you know what would happen?"

"No, and no. I was not surprised, though. The animagi are fond of such demonstrations."

"Are you the person who tried to kill me?"

He doesn't even flinch. "No."

"If your life is in such great danger, why answer my summons?"

His lips twist into that cruel smile. "I came to warn you, my queen. It occurred to me that a warning would be taken more seriously if it came from me rather than from an ignorant, impoverished denizen of the Wallows."

He's probably right about that. "And what is your warning?"

"You are in grave peril, Your Majesty. I have seen the signs, and I know Invierne will make another play. Soon. But this time, there will be no army to defend against. This time, they will come at you like spirits in the night, and you won't recognize the danger until it's too late."

The animagus uttered similar words. I swallow the panic that rises in my throat. "Why? Why warn me?"

"I like my life. My secret village turns a nice profit on river scavenge. The people I lead are stupid and filthy, but they treat me with respect, even worship. All my needs are tended to. I would like things to stay exactly the way they are, and I know the city of Brisadulce has its best chance of remaining stable if you are in power and well aware of the Invierne threat."

Hector leans forward, nostrils flared, face hard. I have never seen him so angry. "The Inviernos will find that Elisa is very difficult to kill," he says, making the dagger dance in the air by some gymnastic of wrist and fingers.

Storm laughs, and the sound is as brittle as breaking glass. "Did I say kill? I don't believe I did. Invierne wants her very much alive. Though I assure you that if one of Invierne's innumerable spies gets hold of her, she will wish herself dead."

It's possible that I hate this man after all. "This audience is over," I snap. "Take him to the prison tower."

My guards pin his arms and turn him around.

"Arresting me will mean my death, Your Majesty," he calls over his shoulder. "And once Invierne finds me and kills me, you'll learn nothing more. I know you're curious. About us. About what we want with that thing in your belly."

"Wait!" I say, and the guards halt. "And if I let you return to your village?"

"Visit any time and ask all the questions you want. As I said, I am your loyal subject. You have nothing to fear from me."

I pretend to consider for a long moment. "You may go free. But Storm, in accordance with God's will, I must be *honest* and tell you that I hope you will give me an excuse to kill you."

Something flits across his face. I hope it's fear. He bows. "Until we meet again, Your Majesty. Remember to watch yourself." The guards step aside. He flips the cowl over his head and sweeps from the room.

I whisper to the guards, "Follow him."

They nod, wait a few beats, and then one slips out the door after him.

"Well," says Hector, sheathing his daggers. "I believe that really was the former ambassador, different hair color notwithstanding. I remember him being deeply unpleasant."

"Arrogant superiority must be a cultural obsession. The animagi I encountered were much the same."

He crosses his arms and leans a hip against the desk. "You could simply make it known that he's here. If what he said is true, his own people will take care of him."

Seeing Hector in such a relaxed pose helps me force the

tension from my own limbs. I take a cleansing breath and say, "I'm glad you were here, Hector. I admit that was terrifying."

His sloppy grin makes my stomach clench, not unpleasantly. "You faced him down like a seasoned warrior," he says.

"Only because I had your daggers at my back."

"Always."

"Do you think he was telling the truth? About the spies? About why he wanted to warn me?"

Hector shrugs. "Alejandro and I used to speculate that the Inviernos are incapable of falsehood. They tend to go silent and refuse to speak rather than lie. He was wrong about one thing, though. *Someone* wants you dead, as your wounds attest."

Reflexively, my fingers find my Godstone. Then they shift left, skim my bodice. It's thin enough for me to feel the ridges of my new scar. Another possibility occurs to me, and I gasp in surprise.

"What is it?"

"Hector, what if it *wasn't* an assassination attempt. Is that possible? Did someone mean to take me *alive*?"

His dark eyes seem to whirl as his considerable intelligence chews on the idea. Without breaking my gaze, he says to the remaining guard, "Lucás, step outside and watch the hallway."

"Yes, my lord," comes the voice. The door creaks open, bangs closed.

Hector and I are alone.

9

I'M suddenly aware of the silence; no creak of armor, no foot-steps, no quiet chatter. Just his breath and mine, steady and even. It's the first time I've been alone—truly alone—with anyone in weeks, and it feels as though we are sharing a secret.

He says, "I don't care to discuss what happened that day in front of my men."

"Why not?" Looking up at him is giving my neck and shoulders a crick, so I stand and stretch my arms to the ceiling, careful of my mending side. Softly, I say, "What *did* happen that day, Hector? Were you the one who found me?"

He turns, putting his back to me. "The general held me back after the Quorum meeting," he says. "I let myself get distracted. I didn't go after you right away." When he turns back around, his face is stricken. "Elisa, I'm so sorry."

"Just tell me."

He runs a hand through his hair. "You left, and I was about to go after you, but the general grabbed my arm. He wanted to discuss a new rotation near the amphitheater—a collaboration between the Royal Guard and his own soldiers. It was ten minutes or more before I followed you."

"I see."

"I let myself get distracted. It won't happen again."

"I'm not angry."

He sighs as if exasperated. "You're rarely angry. Even when you should be."

"I'm angry all the time!"

"Not at me."

"No, not at you. I told you I wanted to be alone that day, remember?"

"Yes."

"How can I be angry when I got my wish? I was the foolish one, not you. You warned me. And I'm sorry about that. I caused a lot of trouble, especially for you." He starts to protest, but I put up a hand and look him straight in the eye. "Do you think Luz-Manuel drew you away on purpose?"

"How could he know you would go to the catacombs?"

"Well, I *had* been making a regular habit of it. Maybe it was just a matter of waiting for the right opportunity."

He looks off into the distance, worrying the pommel of his sword with his fingertips. "A few weeks ago, I would never have considered it," he says. "I've always thought him a devoted Joyan who would give his life for his country."

"And now?"

"Now I'll make sure you are never unguarded, even in your own palace."

Again I touch my forefinger to my waist, to the scar there.

I shudder to remember the blade, how it felt plunging into my abdomen. "Were you the one who found me?"

He rubs the back of his head as if suddenly exhausted. "I called your name, but there was no response. Then I saw your foot, poking out from behind one of the pedestals. I ran over, and . . . God, Elisa, I thought you were dead."

I clasp my hands together to keep them steady.

"You had stopped bleeding," he continues. "I've seen it in battle; a wounded soldier often stops bleeding when he dies. But then . . . you breathed. A big, strong breath. So I gathered you up and got you to Doctor Enzo as quick as I could."

I whisper, "Thank you."

He stares at me, and I stare back. His lashes are short but thick, and he has a tiny freckle at the crease of his left eye. He has the deepest eyes I've ever seen on a person, like a whole world goes on inside his head.

He says, "I think the Godstone protected you. Or started to heal you. Enzo didn't realize how badly you'd been stabbed until he broke the scab and cleaned the wound. At first he thought it was just the bump to your head that had sent you into a coma."

Hearing his account, it seems as though I barely escaped death. But something about it feels strange. Something doesn't add up.

"Is it possible my assassin knew exactly how badly to wound me without killing me? Was there any indication that he didn't leave me for dead? That he planned to take me alive?"

"No. Wait. Maybe. There was blood all over your face, even

though your face wasn't anywhere near the pool of blood. And the floor was streaked. I thought you had managed to crawl away before collapsing. But what if—"

"What if I was dragged? What if by coming to look for me, you interrupted something?"

Hector moves to the windows, paces back and forth between them. "This might be a good thing," he says. "Kidnapping you requires planning. Finesse. Merely killing you is easy by comparison."

"Oh?" The last thing I want to hear is that killing me would be *easy*.

"An abduction requires getting very close to the victim," he muses. "Nothing long range. They'd have to draw you away from your protectors. . . ."

An idea slams me. I turn it over in my head, considering it from different angles.

"Elisa?"

I led a rebellion, defeated sorcerers, became queen. I can do this too. I push my shoulders back, raise my chin, and say in my best queen voice, "Teach me to defend myself." Before he can protest, I add, "I'm not saying make me into an elite soldier. Just teach me to survive a close-quarters encounter. Teach me to evade an attacker. I'm a *very* good student. I can learn anything if I study hard enough."

He nods. "I know you can. But what about your injury? Shouldn't you—"

"We'll start slow and easy."

He grasps the pommel of his sword. "If you had been raised

to the throne, you would have learned basic techniques anyway."

"We'll need space. Privacy." I don't want to be clumsy and awkward before my entire guard.

"Alejandro's suite?" he suggests. "It's quite large, especially if we moved the bed to the side."

"Good idea." I grin in anticipation.

His lips twitch as he fights very hard to not grin right back.

The next day, the guards rearrange everything in the king's suite to open up space, shoving the absurd tower bed against the wall. Several rugs cover the floor in an array of sunset colors and textures. The guards start to remove these, too, but Hector stops them.

"You're mostly likely to be assaulted in the palace," he says. "So we'll practice with the rugs underfoot at first. And it's not just assassins I'm worried about—a queen can just as easily be killed by a mob. So we're going to focus on close-quarters encounters."

Hector dismisses all the guards except for Fernando, telling them to take up their regular posts in my own rooms. He orders Fernando to guard the door outside the king's suite.

I've given Mara the hour off, but Ximena settles on the bed to watch. Hector eyes her warily but says nothing. I sense the tension between them, but it is right that Ximena be here.

Hector and I face each other. Nervousness patters in my chest. I know it's silly, but I'm afraid of looking like a fool in front of him.

He says, "If I were an enemy, and I started bearing down

on you like this"—he draws his sword, stretches the tip toward me, takes a single step in my direction—"what would you do?"

Possibilities race through my head. Should I look for a weapon? Dodge and come up behind his guard? Trip him? Insult his mother?

I decide to be honest. "I would run," I admit. "As fast as I could."

"Good! That's the right decision. Escaping should always be your first resort. Everything I teach you is a contingency, to be used only if your first resort fails. Clear?"

"Clear." I glance over at Ximena to find her nodding approval.

"So, to start, I'd like you to get accustomed to holding a knife." From a utility belt at his waist, he pulls a short, light dagger. It's plain, with a wooden handle, but the blade shimmers from constant polishing and sharpening.

The blade.

My mouth goes dry.

He flips it in the air so that the blade is pinched between his thumb and forefinger and holds it out to me, handle first. "Go ahead," he says. "Take it."

I wipe my hand on my breeches. Slowly, heart pounding, I grasp the handle. It feels cold in my palm.

"You should have a knife on you at all times," he says. "We may have to adjust your wardrobe to accommodate one. If you keep it hidden, you'll have the advantage of surprise in a close-quarters encounter."

I stare at the thing in my hand.

"I'll teach you where to stab someone to inflict maximum damage," he says.

I stabbed someone before. I hated it. So intimate, so destructive. Afterward, there was blood everywhere.

"You'll notice that the edge is slightly serrated." He points to a couple of indentions near the tip. "That way, the blade does damage when you withdraw it as well."

The dagger that slid across Humberto's throat had a serrated edge. I remember it as if a painter had captured the moment and stretched out the canvas before my eyes. I wonder if the blade that plunged into my own body was serrated. Is that why I required so many stitches? It certainly went in easily enough.

My stomach roils with nausea. I swallow hard against it even as my cheeks go clammy cold.

"And since you are not a large person, I'll teach you how to get maximum leverage and force for stabbing. There are a few tricks—"

I drop the knife. It bounces off a rug, clatters to the stone floor. I wipe my hand on my pants again, as if I can wipe away the sensation memory.

"Elisa? What—"

"I can't," I whisper, looking everywhere but at him. "I'm sorry."

"I don't understand. This was your idea. And a good one. You should learn—"

"I'm not sure I can use a knife." I stare at it on the floor. Maybe I could work up to it again. I just won't think about it plunging into my own stomach. I can do it. I can be strong.

"It's the best way to defend yourself," he insists.

I'm about to tell him I'll give it another try when Ximena says, "It's really not."

He turns on her, brow furrowed.

Ximena scoots off the bed and lands heavily on her feet. She lumbers toward us, and I marvel that this large older woman is capable of protecting me. I'm eager to see what she'll do.

She bends over to pick up the dagger and hands it to Hector, hilt first. "Attack me," she says calmly.

Hector's eyes narrow. "You're sure about this, my lady?"

She smiles. "Do be gentle on an old woman, though."

He shrugs. Then, with lightning speed, he feints left, but sweeps right with the blade, arching it toward her belly.

She shifts to avoid it, and her arm blurs in a flurry of ruffles. Hector grunts. The dagger clatters onto the floor again.

Their eyes lock. Ximena holds his wrist, pinching it in such a way that his grip has relaxed and his hand flops uselessly. The sleeve of her voluminous blouse is torn.

"The Royal Guard trains in hand-to-hand combat," she says, "so you know as well as I do how easy it is to disarm someone." She lets his wrist go and steps back. "It is especially easy to disarm someone who is not adept with knife work. Which means, in essence, that the enemy ends up holding an extra weapon."

Hector rubs his wrist, frowning. "I *did* go easy on you," he says.

"Thank you," she says solemnly, but her eyes twinkle.

He turns to me and says, "Your nurse has a good point. But

I insist on training you to defend against a knife attack, even if you don't choose to keep one."

It's a fair concession. "Agreed."

"I'd like to teach you to use some kind of weapon," he says. "Maybe a quarterstaff?"

"A quarterstaff is not very subtle," I say. "Or handy. If a kidnapper comes at me, what am I supposed to do? Say, 'Excuse me, my lord, while I pull my *enormous quarterstaff* out of my bodice?'"

Hector rubs his jaw. "You're right. I'll give it some thought. But for now, we'll start with the easiest escape maneuver." He gestures with his hand. "Come here and turn around."

Feeling suddenly unsure, I glance at Ximena, who gives a nod of approval.

I approach, turn around. He presses up behind me and wraps his left arm around my torso, across my breasts, trapping my own arms to my sides. My head fits snugly and perfectly beneath his chin. The mink-oil scent of his rawhide armor pricks at my nose.

"It's instinct," he says, his breath tickling my scalp, "for an attacker to think of your arms and hands as dangerous. He'll subdue them as soon as possible. And it's instinct for the victim thus subdued to feel powerless."

"I see." I don't feel powerless at all. Pulled tight against Hector, hearing his voice shift low, I feel safer than ever. "I could stomp on your foot," I tell him.

"That's exactly what you should do. The instep of the human foot is made up of hundreds of tiny bones. You can do immense damage with one good stomp. So try it. Gently, please."

I comply by halfheartedly sending my heel onto the top of his foot. The force can't possibly be enough to hurt him through his boot, but he releases me instantly.

I turn to find him grinning at me.

He says, "Now that you have momentarily incapacitated me, what do you do?"

"I run?"

"Like you're being chased by a sandstorm." I begin to think that maybe I should practice *running*. "Come back. Let's do it again."

This time, when his arm slides around me, it feels slower, more deliberate. "The trick," he says in my ear, "is to be wholly committed to your action. No hesitation." His arm tightens in a little jerk, and I catch my breath. "Do you understand, Elisa? You might have to stomp to *live*."

I swallow hard. "I understand."

"Lady Ximena, can you bring us a few pillows?"

My nurse rustles around on the bed. She must know exactly what Hector has in mind, for she strides into my field of vision and, without being asked, crouches down to cover Hector's right foot with cushions.

Hector says, "Now come down as hard as you can on my foot."

"No! I don't want to—"

"Do it."

I lift my knee high and slam my heel into his instep.

He gasps, releases me.

I spin to face him. He is bent over slightly, regarding me

with wide eyes. Then he says, "Well done!"

I wilt with relief. "It hurts," I admit, flexing my toes.

"That's why I had Ximena bring cushions. You must be willing to hurt yourself a little in the short term."

I laugh. "The cushions were for *your* protection. If not for them, I would have broken your foot."

He shrugs. "You'll have to stomp a lot harder than that."

My mouth opens in surprise. Then I realize he's trying to goad me. It's working.

Without breaking his gaze, I say, "Ximena, please fetch more pillows. Hector is going to need them."

As she hurries away, he says, "Think you can learn this faster than your seven-year-old heir did?"

"Watch me."

He grins.

We spend several more minutes stomping, with each foot, and then he teaches me to dislocate someone's kneecap. By the time Ximena calls a halt, my heels ache, the muscles in my calves and shins tremble, and the scar on my abdomen stings with overstretching.

I'm surprised to realize I enjoyed myself. I rotate my ankles experimentally, relishing the burn. I feel strong in spite of my fatigue. Powerful, even. And Hector has always been easy to be with, since that day more than a year ago when he took a lonely princess on a tour of the palace to help her feel at home. I hope we have our next lesson soon.

10

I'VE neglected Father Alentín and Queen Cosmé's delegation long enough to give offense. It's especially insulting given that he now quietly aids Ximena in researching the Godstone. So I decide to host a small dinner in my private dining room, hoping to relax in the company of friends, share stories, rediscover the ease of having close companions.

But the mayordomo insists I also invite Conde Tristán and his foppish attaché, along with Lady Jada, whose Quorum vote I may need if we do not find a permanent replacement soon. He's right—it's the strategic thing to do. But my anticipation is replaced by dread. I had so hoped to indulge in an evening of not being *queen*.

By design, I am the last to arrive, for I can't stomach the idea of making idle chatter while waiting to be served. As is tradition in Joya d'Arena, the table is low and surrounded by huge sitting cushions. Not for the first time, I consider drawing up a royal edict demanding the use of proper tables and chairs.

Hector and Ximena seat themselves on either side of me. I

frown to think that I can't even enjoy a small private dinner without their protective hedge.

I nod to Father Alentín and Belén, sitting at the other end. Lady Jada is directly across from me, and after greeting me warmly, she goes right back to gazing shamelessly at Conde Tristán sitting beside her. But the conde doesn't notice because *his* gaze fixed on me the moment I entered and now does not waver.

I sigh as I reach for my glass of rose-hip wine, anticipating a long and tedious evening. If it were just Alentín and Belén, I would know exactly what to say, exactly how to be. I find that my anger with them has faded, so eager am I for the familiar.

To my relief, Conde Tristán is the one to open conversation. "Lady Ximena, how goes the late-night studying in the monastery?"

Everyone freezes. Belén becomes as dark and coiled as a storm cloud.

The conde looks around at us in alarm. "I've said something, haven't I? Something wrong?"

Lady Jada says, "Oh, I'm sure it's nothing. We just need to get to know each other." She turns to me. "Isn't that right, Your Majesty?"

My voice is dead flat when I say, "Your Grace, do tell me how you came to know about Ximena's studies."

He and his herald exchange a confused glance. The conde says, "I often walk at night, after everyone has gone to sleep. Lately I've been going to the monastery to pray. Last night I saw Lady Ximena with the ambassador from Basajuan." He indicates Alentín with a lift of his chin. "I just thought . . . I know she used to be a scribe. . . . That is to say, I've started studying the scriptures myself lately, and I thought to chat about . . ."

I laugh the moment a good lie comes to mind. It's a forced sound that will fool no one who knows me, but the conde's face relaxes at once. "I didn't mean to alarm Your Grace," I say. "It's just that we've kept it quiet intentionally. You see, not many people know that Basajuan's monastery archive took some damage during the war. We've been working with them to restore what documents we can, even scribing new ones as necessary."

He nods. "I'm glad to hear it. Small gestures will go a long way toward building goodwill with Queen Cosmé. Which is vital now that her country stands between us and Invierne."

"Indeed." I raise my wineglass. "To continued goodwill between Basajuan and Joya d'Arena."

Everyone raises their glasses and echoes the sentiment with polite relief.

"Were I you, though," the conde muses, "I would be scouring the archive for clues about the Godstone."

I stare at him. Is he bringing up these things out of innocent coincidence? Or is there a purpose to his comments?

"Why is that?" Ximena asks, and I can't be the only one who recognizes the dangerous edge in her voice.

"Well, the animagus, for one. The one who martyred himself. Invierne still wants that stone desperately. I must confess that I am deeply curious as to why. And I'm not the only one.

The whole city is talking about it. Maybe the whole country."

"Maybe they're afraid of it?" Lady Jada offers. "Her Majesty destroyed several of their most powerful sorcerers with it."

Tristán shrugs. "There have been bearers, Godstones, every hundred years for two millennia. Why go to extremes only now?"

I feel I should interject something, though I don't know what. They're talking about me, the most important part of my life, as if I'm not even here. There are probably exchanges like this going on all over the country.

My Godstone. Me. A dinner-table conversation. I suppose that as queen, I belong to everyone a little.

"You know what I think?" Lady Jada says.

"I would love to know," I tell her sincerely.

She lifts her chin. "I think they want this land back."

"Oh?"

"I would be a poor mayor's wife if I didn't know my history," she says primly. "My tutor says that a few centuries after God dropped the first families onto this world, one family went mad with ambition, gobbling up land and resources through marriage and war. But the others united against them and drove them out. They fled into the wilderness, the curse of God upon them, and became the Inviernos.

"They were *driven* out," she continues. "Everyone knows Brisadulce is the most beautiful city in the world. I think the Inviernos want it back."

Her history is mostly right, but her assessment of our capital is not. Brisadulce is an isolated city, surrounded on all sides by natural disaster, forced to trade for the bulk of its supplies. It remains our capital from long tradition and history and maybe nostalgia. But the land itself is impractical, even useless. Why would the Inviernos want it when they could pursue Puerto Verde or the lush rolling hills of the southern holdings instead?

I say solemnly, "A well-conceived theory. Maybe you're right."

Ximena chokes on her wine.

The kitchen master enters, accompanied by wait staff carrying trays piled with shredded chicken, corn tortillas, and fresh fruit slices. My mouth waters to see honey-coconut scones, my favorite. They're still hot from the oven; the honey glaze melts down the sides.

Lady Jada claps her hands. "Pollo pibil! It was the king's favorite, I hear." She points to the plate of chicken.

"It was," Hector says. "He first encountered it in my father's hacienda." At my questioning look, he says, "One summer King Nicolao's ship got caught in a storm and ran onto the reef. He and Prince Alejandro took shelter with us while the hull was repaired. It's how we met."

I've never heard this story. I wonder how many other things I don't know about Hector.

Father Alentín says, "You must have impressed him greatly, to have been named his page. And later, to be appointed commander of the guard. You're the youngest in history."

Hector shrugs, looking sheepish. "It was mostly an accident."

"What do you mean?" the priest asks.

"I had two older brothers, and we used to spar with toy

swords in the courtyard. The morning Alejandro was there, one of them knocked me off my feet, and the other starting teasing me, poking at me with his sword. It was all good-natured, nothing that hadn't happened a hundred times before. But Alejandro observed the whole thing through his bedroom window, and he came barreling into the courtyard, yelling at them to back off, that he had just named me his personal page and *how dare they threaten the royal page?"*

"He thought he was saving you," I say.

Hector nods, his eyes warm with the memory. "I was only twelve years old at the time, so naturally I thought he was the most wonderful person who ever lived."

"But eventually the two of you became friends in truth," I say.

"Yes, quickly. He was lonely. An only child. It was good for him to have a younger boy around, someone he could easily whip in swordsmanship." He adds haughtily, "That only lasted a couple of years, of course."

I laugh. "Of course. He told me you were the most fearsome warrior he knew."

"He did?" A shield drops from his face, and I see its truer expression, as if he and sorrow are steady companions.

"He did," I say gently. "He spoke of you often while he lay in hospice. Becoming his page may have been an accident, but becoming lord-commander certainly was not. He said it was the easiest choice he ever made, even though you were so young."

Hector swallows hard, nodding, and turns away to hide his face.

"This is fabulous," says Lady Jada, and I jump. For a moment, it felt like Hector and I were alone. She adds, "The pollo pibil, I mean. Your kitchen master is to be commended."

I'd love to ignore her, to press Hector for more details about his childhood, but I invited Jada for a reason, so I force myself to pay attention to her. "Thank you." I glance around for the kitchen master, but he has already slipped away to put the finishing touches on dessert. "He makes pastries specially for me now, from a recipe I brought from Orovalle." I grab a corn tortilla and nibble on it.

"Yes, your love of pastries is well known."

I study her face, trying to determine if she insults me on purpose, but she chews blissfully on her pollo pibil.

It is the traitor Belén who says, "Her Majesty has an even greater passion for jerboa soup."

I almost choke on my tortilla. Jerboa soup was our daily repast when we traveled together through the deep desert. If I taste it again in this life, it will be too soon. I glance over to find his lips twitching with humor.

Jada says, "But jerboa soup is so . . . pedestrian."

"Sometimes." I swallow the lump of tortilla and say gravely, "Life's simpler foods have great poetry to them, don't you think?" I have no idea what that means, but she nods as if concurring with a profound truth.

Conde Tristán says, "The official dish of Selvarica is called the sendara de vida. It's made of starfruit soaked in honey and lime, then roasted over peppered coals. It's sublime. If any of you come for a visit, I'd be delighted to serve it."

Ximena and I exchange a startled look. Her face is white.

My nurse turns toward the conde and says, carefully, "The *sendara de vida.* That means 'the gate of life.'"

He nods. "Named after an old legend."

"Oh, do tell us!" I say, with what I hope is artless enthusiasm. "I'd love to hear more about Selvarica."

At the end of the table, Father Alentín leans forward, eyes narrowed. Beside me, Hector sets down his wineglass and places his hands casually on the table.

Conde Tristán looks around at his suddenly rapt audience, aware that once again he is on the outside of an ongoing conversation. But he proceeds gamely. "It's wholly apocryphal, but legend says God created two gates, one that leads to the enemy and one that leads to life. The gate that leads to life, *la sendara de vida,* is somewhere in Selvarica, and many a nobleman's younger son has set off in search of it, hoping to prove himself and make his fortune. No one has succeeded, of course. But many of my people believe in its existence. They say whoever finds it will find life eternal and perfect happiness."

Silence weighs like a heavy blanket over the dining room.

Finally Alentín says in a tight voice, "Strange that I have not heard of this legend."

The conde shrugs. "I barely knew of it growing up. But Iladro reminded me." He indicates the overdressed herald beside him. "Right, Iladro?"

The herald reddens at our sudden scrutiny. The plume of his hat wobbles as he nods. "Yes, Your Grace," he says in an understated tone that belies his announcing voice. "The legend remains popular in the remote island villages." He grabs a scone from the tray and shoves it into his mouth, possibly to discourage the conde from calling on him to speak further.

"Apocryphal," Ximena mutters to herself.

"An old manuscript or two alludes to it," the conde says. "But that's how we know there's no truth to the legend, right? None of the inspired holy scriptures mentions it once."

"Indeed," Ximena says, but I hear the doubt—or possibly wonder—in her voice.

"What is 'apocryphal'?" Lady Jada asks.

Hector says, "The Apocrypha is a group of documents that were put forward as being inspired by God, but were proved by scholars and priests to be merely legends. Nothing divine about them after all."

I look at him in surprise and delight. I had no idea he knew about such things.

He regards me sidelong, his eyes dancing. "But interesting as pseudohistorical documents," he says to Lady Jada. "They say much about the attitudes and customs of the time during which they were written."

"What about you, Lady Jada?" I say, still smiling. "As wife of the mayor, can you tell me about any spectacular dishes—or legends—from Brisadulce your queen should know of?"

Lady Jada throws her shoulders back and opens her mouth to launch into what I am certain will be a treatise of profound triviality. "Your Majesty should instruct the kitchen master to prepare—"

She freezes at the sound of retching.

"Iladro?" says Conde Tristán.

The herald bends over the table, his body convulsing. He looks up, his eyes oozing tears. His delicate face is a blotchy purple.

Ximena launches across the table, a blur of ruffled skirts. She grabs his fork with one hand, forces open his jaw with the other.

Hector yanks me to my feet. With his free hand, he whisks a dagger from his vambrace. "Elisa, spit out any food in your mouth. Now."

Poison. My skin goes clammy cold. "I . . . there's nothing."

Ximena shoves the handle of the fork down Iladro's throat, saying, "Let yourself vomit, my lord. It may save your life."

And he does, in great geysers of half-digested, red-tinged pollo pibil and pastry lumps, all over the table before me. Acid singes my nostrils.

"The scone!" Belén says. "He was the only person who had one."

The kitchen master bursts into the room, yelling, "Stop! Spit out your food! The taster just—" He sees the mess on the table, and his face drains of blood. "Too late."

"Lady Jada," I order. "Find Doctor Enzo at once." She launches to her feet and runs from the dining room.

"Will he—?" the conde asks in a wavery voice, stroking his herald's arm. "Oh, Iladro, what did you—"

Hector's arm wraps across my shoulders, pulling my back against his torso as he backs us away from the table. He still holds a dagger in his free hand, though I've no idea what he thinks he can do with it.

"Water!" Ximena yells to no one in particular, and a glass appears before her. She tips it down the herald's throat. He chokes, and water spews from his mouth, but she yells something at him and he starts to gulp it down like his life depends on it, which it might. And then she makes him throw up again.

"Let's go, Elisa," Hector says, and he starts to drag me from the dining room.

But I resist. "No."

"It's not safe! We need to—"

I whirl on him. "Your sword will *not* protect me from poison." To the rest, I say, "Ximena, stay with Iladro until Doctor Enzo comes. Everyone else, with me *now*." I stride through the door to the kitchen, and everyone tumbles after me.

The kitchen is chaos. People rush everywhere to dump food and clean bowls and utensils. I catch the acrid scents of vomit and of burning bread. On the stone floor beside the chopping table lies a man I've never seen before. He is clearly dead. His eyes bulge, frozen in terror and pain. Blood-tinged vomit leaks from the corner of his mouth and puddles beside him. A girl in a maid's frock stares at him from behind the roasting spit. Tears stream down her face. Belén and the guards move to block the entrances.

"Silence!" I yell. Quiet settles, even as eyes widen with dread. "Everyone against the wall, there." I gesture, but they do not move fast enough. "Now!"

They scramble all over one another in their hurry to comply, but manage to line up neatly.

I pace in front of them. "Who prepared the scones?" I ask.

Silence. Then a timid voice says, "I did, Your Majesty. Felipe and I."

I turn on the source of that voice. It's the crying maid. "Did you poison them?"

"Oh, no, Your Majesty, I would never—"

"Where is Felipe?"

"I don't know." She can't bring herself to meet my gaze, and her maid's cap has skewed forward. It bothers me that I can't see her expression to read it.

So I reach forward and tip up her chin with my fingers. "When did you last see him?"

She swallows hard and blinks wet eyes. "I'm not sure. Maybe . . . just before we served? He said he needed wine to . . . to soak the pears. But . . . oh, God."

"Oh, God, what?"

"Pears weren't on the menu. I didn't think . . . at the time . . . I was so busy. How could I know?" Her gaze is terrified and shaky but guileless. I find myself believing her.

Without breaking her gaze, I say, "Belén, please check the wine cellar."

"At once, Your Majesty."

I step back, clenching my hands into fists. This cannot go unpunished. What will happen when the city learns that poison entered my private dining room? They will see me as weak, unable to govern my own staff, much less a country. And they will be right.

I need a show of strength. Of wrath. Something memorable.

I pace, worrying my thumbnail with my teeth. I could dismiss them all, throw them out of the palace. That would certainly be memorable. But there can be no doubt that most of them—maybe all—are innocent. If had proof, I would not hesitate to have the poisoner beheaded.

I freeze in my tracks. Is this why General Luz-Manuel had Martín executed? Merely as a show of strength? Because it was politically prudent to cast the blame *somewhere*?

Belén appears in the stone archway leading to the cellar. "He is here," he says, and I know from his grave expression that the news is not good.

"No one is to leave this kitchen," I say, and receive a flurry of "Yes, Your Majesty"s in response. "Hector, Tristán, with me."

Together we enter the cellar stair. It's steep and cool and smells of wet wood and pitch. Alongside the stair is a smooth slope for rolling barrels.

Belén is at the bottom, standing over the body of another dead man. A boy, really. He lies on his side, his arm crooked beneath his torso in an unnatural position. Vomit soaks his shirt and puddles at the base of a wine barrel.

He clutches a scrap of leather.

Hector bends to pry it from his stiffening fingers. He spreads it open and says, "A note."

"Read it."

"'Death to tyrants.'" Hector looks up. "That's all it says."

"Oh, God."

With a cry of anguish, Tristán rushes forward and sends a hard kick into the boy's flank. The body lurches; a dead arm flops hard against the ground, and something inside it cracks.

"Tristán, control yourself," I say.

The conde whirls to face me, and for the first time, I notice the wet brownish stain on his linen blouse. "But . . . Iladro, my herald . . . he might . . . he could be . . ."

"I know. My own personal physician is attending him. We'll do all we can."

His shoulders shake with rage, but he nods. "Yes, Your Majesty. Thank you."

"I'm not convinced," Belén says in his quiet voice.

"What do you mean?"

"Did this Felipe know how to read and write? If so, is this his handwriting?"

"Belén is right," Hector says, and the two share a look of accord. "It's too convenient to find him with this note clutched in his hand."

I put my thumb and forefinger to the bridge of my nose. The note is not proof—not really. But maybe I have to pretend it is.

I say, "Hector, will you learn everything you can about this boy? Maybe his family knows something."

"Yes, of course."

"Thank you. I need a demonstration. A show of strength. Tristán, what counsel would you offer me?"

His eyes narrow with the understanding that I'm testing him. "I suggest you have the kitchen staff flogged for negligence," he says evenly. "I know it's harsh, but it will do no lasting harm. You must send a clear message that you are not weak, and that you can retaliate quickly and effectively."

I breathe deeply to steady myself. Yes, a flogging. It will be awful, but better than executions or dismissals. "Thank you, Your Grace. Why don't you attend to your man now?"

He bows quickly and flees.

Hector studies me. "*Can* you?" he says gently. "I'll give the order for you, if you like."

I smother the instant feeling of relief. "No. I should order it myself. It's a sign of strength, right?" Before I can change my mind, I hurry up the stairs, Hector and Belén following after.

My kitchen staff are still lined up against the wall, under the watch of my guards. Alentín sits on the edge of the hearth, praying. Lady Jada has returned from fetching Doctor Enzo. Her eyes are wide with excitement, no doubt anxious to relate these events to everyone she knows. I find I can't bear to look at her.

I address the staff. "Felipe is dead, by his own hand. I believe he was the poisoner. I don't know if any of you conspired with him. However, I do know that you were negligent in allowing the food to be served too soon after being tasted."

I wait a few beats for it to sink in. Hopefully, they will fear the worst, and my punishment will seem mild by comparison.

"And so, tomorrow morning, you will be brought to the palace green." Someone chokes out a sob. "There you will each be flogged, in sight of the entire court." I see flashes of terror, but a few exhale relief.

I clench my hands into fists so no one can see how badly they shake. I have just ordered that innocent people be hurt, for my own political advantage. What kind of person does that? Someone like General Luz-Manuel, I guess.

A guard clears his throat. "Your Majesty, how many lashes are you ordering?"

Oh, God, lashes. I don't know anything about that. I need to hurt, not harm. How many is too many? Too few, and the punishment lacks weight.

Hector jumps in. "I suggest ten each, Your Majesty," he says.

I could hug him. "Yes, of course. Ten each." I'll have to watch it happen. Display myself at the flogging. The space between my eyes stings with threatening tears.

I must leave this room before I lose control. I take another deep breath and lift my chin to address a guard. "Hold them in the prison tower until the flogging tomorrow. Everyone else is free to go." And with that I stride from the kitchen and into the hallway.

Hector hurries to catch up. "Please allow me to accompany you," he says.

"Of course," I say wearily. "I just had to get away."

"You did well."

I don't feel like I did well at all.

He says, "I'll send Doctor Enzo to you when he has a prognosis on the conde's man."

"Thank you."

Moments later, we arrive at the door to my suite. He looks down at me, not bothering to hide his concern. "Will you be all right?"

"I hate myself right now," I admit.

He reaches out as if to touch me, hesitates, lets his arm drop. He says, "I know. But I don't. Hate you, that is." And then he's gone.

11

I pace back and forth in my suite, awaiting word from Doctor Enzo. I pray as I pace, begging God to spare Iladro's life. The Godstone suffuses me with warmth, but I know from long experience that the warmth is only an acknowledgment of my prayers, not an answer.

Mara paces right along with me, wringing her hands. "This would not have happened if I hadn't injured myself," she mutters. "If I had been the one cooking—"

Ximena has been calmly watching us. But now she grabs Mara's shoulder and stops her midstride. "Injury aside, it isn't right that the queen's lady-in-waiting cooks for eight people. For the queen, occasionally. But you will *not* cook for state dinners. You're a lady now, Mara. A noblewoman."

I stare at my nurse. Why Ximena feels compelled to argue such a point at a time like this is beyond me.

Mara peers around her to give me a stricken look. "You could have died. The kitchen master's taster is *dead*."

"Yes," I whisper. I hate this. My taster in Orovalle died too, when I was just a princess. Hundreds of my Malficio—my desert rebels—died because of the hope I gave them. Then Humberto. King Alejandro. The guard Martín. Will my continued existence carve a bloody path through the lives around me? Will my life's greatest legacy be a wake of bodies?

I wish Hector were here. I need his solid presence, his sure-burning intelligence. Then I chide myself for weakness. My personal comfort is not as important as finding answers, and Hector is best where he is.

The rotten-pepper scent of vomit precedes Doctor Enzo, and I look up even as the guards announce his arrival.

"The herald?" I demand. "How is he?"

"He'll live."

My breath leaves me in a *whoosh* of relief as I collapse onto the bed.

"He may have stomach pain the rest of his life. He vomited blood, which means the poison ate into the lining—"

I hold up a hand to forestall further details. "What kind of poison?"

"Duerma berries, I think," he says, and I gasp. "He'll probably sleep a day or two."

"I poisoned an animagus with duerma berries once," I tell him. "It was nothing like what happened to Iladro. After digesting them, the animagus toppled over, passed out."

"You used raw berries?"

I nod.

"They're more toxic when dried and pounded into a powder. Mashed into flour, it would be almost tasteless. I suspect the powder mixed with alcohol is incredibly corrosive."

"We had wine with our meal." *All* of us.

"That would do it."

"That's why it didn't take effect on the taster as quickly. No wine."

"Rather ingenious, isn't it?"

I don't appreciate his admiring tone. "Thank you, Enzo. Good work tonight, as usual." I dismiss him with a wave of my hand.

I resume pacing. Unlike the first attempt on my life, this one was clumsy and unfocused. Ill planned. Anyone could have eaten those pastries. Everyone in the dining room could have been poisoned. There is a clue here somewhere. *Think, Elisa!*

Crickets begin their nightly serenade, and the sun disappears behind the distant palace wall so that only the faintest glow seeps through my balcony doors. Ximena lights the candles on my bedside table. Mara retrieves my nightgown and lays it out on the bed, then fetches a brush to start working on my hair.

But I'm not ready for our nightly routine. I'm about to assign them useless tasks, just to keep them occupied and out of my pacing range, when Hector returns. His face is grave.

"The assassin's employer?" I ask.

"No sign. The family knew nothing."

Disappointment is like a rock in my gut. I am desperate for answers.

"A stranger gave them gold yesterday," he continues. "Tall, young, hair slicked back with olive oil. Said he owed Felipe a debt. They gave it up eagerly once they learned what had happened."

My sweaty hands grip my skirt. "He was paid to do it!"

Hector nods. "The note was meant to scare you—if you survived."

I force my hands to release the fabric, to relax. Without meeting his eye, I say, "Maybe the poison wasn't meant for me. Maybe it was meant for someone else. The conde. Or even Alentín. He's an ambassador now, you know."

"*Honey-coconut scones*, Elisa. Distilled duerma poison, according to Enzo. It's hard to come by in Brisadulce. You have to cross the desert to find it. Someone was making a statement."

I rub at the headache forming at the bridge of my nose. "Someone who knew I poisoned the animagus with duerma plant."

"You also poisoned half the Invierne army, remember?"

"Hector, if that poison was meant for me, then someone truly wants me dead. Not taken alive, like the Inviernos do."

"That has occurred to me."

"Which means I have more than one enemy."

He says nothing, just presses his lips into a firm line. For the first time, I notice a shadow of stubble along his jaw. He is always clean shaven, as befits the commander of the Royal Guard. Either he hasn't had time today, or he forgot. It makes him look darker, fiercer.

I jump when Ximena's hand settles on my shoulder. "I wish we could get you away," she mutters. "There are too many people in Brisadulce. Too many agendas, too many dark corners."

I round on her. "No!"

She recoils, black eyes wide.

"I won't run away again. You and Papá and Alodia sent me away to keep me safe, remember?" Anger I barely knew I was holding in check rises in my throat like bile. "You forced me to marry a man who didn't love me, who hardly even acknowledged me. It didn't work out very well, did it? He's dead. And I've had more brushes with death than I can count. Running away just made . . ." I hesitate, realizing how shrill my voice is, how awful I sound. Like maybe I hate this place and this life.

She regards me with endless calm.

"I don't regret anything," I tell her.

"I know."

"But I won't run away again."

She crosses her arms and leans against the bedpost, which creaks in response. "Would you consider running *to* something?"

"What do you mean?"

She glances around at the room. Besides Mara and Hector, three guards stand watch, and as usual, their faces betray nothing of the conversation they are overhearing. They are so still and silent as to be nearly—but not quite—invisible. Ximena says, "There is something to the, er, line of research I'm engaged in that might require a long outing." She forces cheer to her face. "Maybe we can incorporate it into that tour of the country the Quorum would like you to go on."

She's talking about the gate. The one that "leads to life." And she doesn't want to discuss details in front of the guards.

Hector says, "I thought the conde's conversation grew particularly interesting tonight at dinner, before his man took ill."

"Indeed," Ximena agrees.

In the silence that ensues, I know we are thinking the same thing. The words used by the conde to describe his legend were uncannily similar to the verse carved into the rock beneath my city. *The gate that leads to life is narrow and small so that few find it.*

I say, "Our friend in the Wallows might know something."

Ximena nods. "He also might have insight into this latest attack."

The thought of seeing Storm again gives me a shudder. I imagine his too-perfect face with such clarity, dread the arrogance in his sibilant voice. But I need to take him up on his offer for information as soon as possible.

With no small amount of reluctance, I say, "I'll pay him a visit tomorrow morning."

Hector looses an exasperated breath. "Please don't. I don't know the territory. I wouldn't know how to place the guards. And the way that cavern echoes . . . there's no way you could have a private conversation."

I open my mouth to protest, to remind him that I refuse to be governed by fear, but I pause. Ignoring his advice has gotten me nearly killed.

"You're about to insist, aren't you?" he says, looking pained.

"No. I was thinking I ought to let you do your job for a change."

He gapes at me for a split second before recovering his

usual poise. "In that case, I'll send my men to fetch him tomorrow morning."

"Thank you. And if he doesn't come willingly and immediately, arrest him and bring him anyway."

He smiles. "With pleasure."

Mara steps toward me, and her face is bright and fierce. "I didn't understand any of that, and I don't care." She brandishes my brush at me. "All I know is that I am going to make breakfast for you tomorrow, and you will eat every bite."

The next morning, after eating Mara's goat-cheese omelet with diced scallions and red peppers, I must face the punishment I ordered. It's a small consolation that with everyone on the green, Hector may be able to slip the Invierno into the tower unnoticed.

With my entourage of guards and ladies, I parade through the inner courtyard to the beat of a slow marching drum. A huge crowd has assembled, and they part to make way for me. I wear a gown with wine-red brocade and gold embroidery, and I regret the choice as sweat pools under my arms and between my breasts. I hold my head high, in spite of the weight of my crown.

It's the same place where Martín was killed, the same dais, the same large crowd. But this time, I am a willing participant.

The kitchen staff are already in place. They face inward in a circle, their hands tied above their heads to a thick pillory made from the massive trunk of a banyan tree. All twelve fit around it easily. They are naked from the waist up, even the maids.

I clench my jaw to keep it from trembling as I mount the dais and sit in its makeshift wooden throne. Ximena and Mara stand at either shoulder. From here, I have a perfect view of the accused and the sea of spectators beyond. Some jostle for a better look. A young boy sits on his father's shoulders. Everyone is wide-eyed with fear, or maybe excitement.

A man approaches, carrying a long red cushion, and kneels at my feet. Is he the same man who beheaded Martín?

Like the prisoners, he's naked from the waist up. A black shawl covers his head and sweeps around to shield his mouth and nose. Ridged white scars slash across his tautly muscled torso and shoulders. He holds out the cushion. On it are various flogging instruments: a rod, a willow switch, a cat-o'-nine-tails, and a leather whip coiled like a snake except for the jagged bit of steel tied to the end.

Tears prick at the back of my throat.

The executioner whispers, in a voice as scarred and used-up as his skin, "Your Majesty, you must choose the instrument of punishment."

It takes a moment for his words to sink in, and when they do, despair settles over me like a hot heavy blanket. Of course I must.

They are arranged in order of potential damage. I don't want these people harmed. But I also cannot choose the mildest punishment.

I say, in my best queen voice, "Use the switch."

The scarred man faces the audience and lifts the switch high; it bends slightly under its own weight. The crowd roars approval.

And then I force myself to watch unflinchingly as, slowly and methodically, he flogs my kitchen staff. The switch slaps wetly against bare skin, sending tears stinging to my eyes. Welts rise up on their backs, and they arch away from the blows, but the pillory leaves them nowhere to go. The scarred man is very thorough, his aim precise. He varies the switch's landing so that every part of their flesh suffers its brutality.

A few refuse to cry out, but not most, and their raw, anguished voices arrow straight into my heart. One boy, the youngest by far, weeps openly, his cheek pressed against the pillory.

I am a stone. I am ice. I feel nothing.

Only the kitchen master remains standing after the tenth lash. The others sag on their feet, held in place by the manacles at their wrists.

The scarred man returns to me and bows. The switch in his huge hand drips blood. "It is done, Your Majesty."

"Thank you," I choke out.

"Do you wish to address the people?" he asks.

No, of course not. I can't wait to get away, to toss off my crown and bury my head in my pillows.

But then the small boy at the edge of the crowd, the one on his father's shoulders, spits on the maid who prepared the scones with Felipe. A viscous wad slips down her sweaty cheek and plops onto her bared breast.

I launch to my feet and stride to the edge of the dais. The crowd hushes.

"We consider their crime of negligence to be paid in full," I call out. "There will be no more recriminations. Anyone who seeks to do them physical harm, or harass them, or even"—I look pointedly at the little boy—"spit on them, will be dealt with severely."

I whirl away from the crowd and move toward Ximena, whispering, "I am shaking quite a lot and could use your arm to aid my dramatic exit." I suddenly wish Hector were here. I always feel so much safer, stronger, when he is at my side.

But she offers it at once, and together we float down the dais in what I dare hope is a show of regal righteousness. We depart the green far more quickly than we came, which is good now that I'm tasting a more acrid version of Mara's omelet in the back of my throat.

12

Hector returns to my suite with the unsurprising news that the Invierno was reluctant to answer my summons and had to be arrested. I take just enough time to lose my crown and change into a simpler gown before rushing out again. I'm glad for the haste—it gives me little opportunity to dwell on the flogging.

I've never been inside the prison tower. It's the highest point of the palace, and I expect that from its topmost chamber, I could see everything from the great sand desert and the walls of Brisadulce, across the merchant's circle and the Wallows, to the docks and the blue horizon beyond.

The tower is made of gray limestone, a dull and dirty contrast to the coral sandstone of its shorter brothers. It rises like a blight on the sky, and I see how impossible it would be to escape such a place. There is only one way up or down, and that is the stairway inside its walls.

It's an odd group that accompanies me to interrogate our prisoner: a one-armed priest, an aging nurse, a Quorum lord, and, unexpectedly, a seven-year-old prince. Hector had to cancel their daily swordsmanship lesson, and little Rosario was determined to come from the moment he learned the reason.

Our group is nothing if not memorable, and I curse myself for thoughtlessness. The news that someone of vast import is being kept here will be palacewide by evening.

Before we step through the arched entryway, I bend down and grasp Rosario's shoulder. "You're sure you want to come, Highness? There's an Invierno up there. He looks a lot like . . ." *Like the animagi who killed your papa.* "Er, like those other Inviernos we saw."

He puts his hand to the wooden practice sword at his belt. He glares at me, saying, "I'm not afraid."

I know better than to smile. "Well, *I* am. Just a little."

"I'll protect you. Like Hector does."

The boy has always idolized my guard, but even more so since his father's death. "That does make me feel better. Thank you."

As I straighten, Hector catches my eye and shrugs. I nod in response. If Rosario thinks he is ready to face an Invierno again, it would feel cruel to forbid it.

The moment we leave the sunny courtyard for the shade of the tower, I am hit full in the face by the scents of sweat and urine and moldy straw. The tower guards lurch up from a rough table strewn with playing cards and snap to attention. They are Luz-Manuel's soldiers, not Royal Guard, and they eye us warily as we pass. I hope they will do as ordered and keep quiet about their latest prisoner.

Hector leads us to the creaking stair that zigzags up one side of the stone wall. The inner structure consists of a series of wooden platforms, with huge beams and smaller wooden trusses to hold each platform in place. The stairway opens up to the platforms at regular intervals, and in the dim light provided by long slits in the wall, I see people, ten or so to a platform. They are barely clothed, scrawny, filthy, hairy. I can't begin to guess their ages. Each is manacled to the wall, out of reach of the stairway.

One, a woman with wild hair, strains against her bonds and spits at me. The glob lands on the planking near my feet. Ximena moves toward her, but I put a hand to her forearm.

"She suffers enough," I say.

Another prisoner, a man with a gray beard that swallows his face, gives the spitting woman a swift kick to the ankle. "Some of us remember," he says to me, and his voice has the harsh accent of the dockworkers. "We remember what you did for us, Your Majesty."

As Hector hustles me away, I wish I'd had the presence of mind to thank the man, to let him know how much his words of support mean to me.

I can't help but wonder what they all did to wind up in this awful place. Surely something terrible. By the time we reach the top, I am breathless, nauseated, and wracked by uncertainty. Maybe I shouldn't have had the Invierno brought here. All he did was refuse a royal summons.

The final, highest platform is the least squalid, with several extra slits for light and air, a small cot, and a slop bucket instead of rushes. But Storm obviously does not appreciate the distinction. He paces back and forth like a restless cat, all lithe grace and hunting fury. Ankle manacles are hidden by his long black cloak, but they rattle with every step.

When he sees us, he growls deep inside his chest, which sends shivers across the back of my shoulders. It's not a sound I've heard a human make before.

A tiny hand slips into mine, and I glance down to make sure Rosario is all right. But the hand gripping mine is the only indication Rosario is frightened. He leans forward, eyes narrowed, glaring at his enemy. I give him a light squeeze.

"Hello, Storm," I say in an even voice.

He whirls, and his moss-green eyes snap to mine. "You rank cow," he spits, and Hector's sword whisks from its scabbard. "We had a bargain."

Without breaking the Invierno's gaze, I put my free hand to Hector's chest to forestall anything hasty. "And you broke it. You refused audience."

"I would have gladly accepted audience in my village."

I laugh, genuinely amused at his audacity. "Surely you realize my predicament? There have been two attempts on my life. One not far from the underground village you call home. Of course I couldn't risk it."

"And yet you would risk my life by bringing me here. I'll be dead within two days. You have surely killed me."

I decide to give him the honesty he claims his people value so much. "Given a choice between my life and yours, I will choose mine. Every time. Without hesitation."

Some of the fight fades from his eyes. "I would do the same," he concedes.

"I plan either to let you go or move you to a different location. I haven't decided yet."

With a lift of his sharp chin, he indicates my companions. "Who are these people? The cripple and the old woman? I recognize only the commander and the prince."

"The 'cripple' is my friend Alentín; the 'old woman' is my friend Ximena."

"They must be important for you to bring them." When he realizes I'm not going to tell him, he shrugs and says, "What must I do to be let go?"

"Tell us about the gate that leads to life."

His eyes widen. He uses hooked forefingers to tuck his honey-gold hair behind his ears, and the motion startles me for its normalcy, its humanity. He turns his back to us. I wish I could see his face.

Still facing the wall, he says, "Take me with you."

"What? Take you where?"

"South. When you go in search of it."

"Of what? We haven't decided to go any—"

He whirls, and his green eyes spark. "You'll go. Make no mistake. It is the will of God."

It's utterly infuriating, the number of people I've encountered in my life who claimed to be the authority on God's will.

"I'm losing patience, Storm. Tell me everything you know about it, or you will never leave this tower on your feet."

His lips purse as he weighs the options. Then: "The gate

that leads to life is a place of mystery and power across the sea. But it is impossible to navigate there. Only those chosen by God can find it, much less pass through."

"And why would anyone pass through?"

"Because it leads to the *zafira*."

The Godstone leaps. I double over with the intensity, gasping for breath, as the stone pounds wave after wave of heat through my body.

"Elisa!" Hector's arm wraps around my waist. "Ximena, help me—"

"I'm all right," I gasp out. "Just give me a moment." It reacted this way once before—when I destroyed the animagi with my Godstone amulet. *What is it, God? What are you trying to tell me?*

Hector loosens his hold with slow reluctance and steps away. I force breath into my body until I can straighten again. The Godstone continues to pulse, though with less power, and my bodice sticks, sweat soaked, to my skin. Rosario's hand now grips mine so tightly that I can hardly feel my fingers.

The Invierno regards me through the lidded eyes of a smug, well-fed kitten. "Oh, yes, you will go."

Ximena demands, "What is this *zafira*?"

He regards her contemptuously.

She repeats her question in the Lengua Classica, adding, "If you don't tell us, we will leave you here to rot or be assassinated, whichever comes first."

If he is surprised that she speaks his language, he doesn't show it, but he says, "The *zafira* is the soul of the world, the magic crawling beneath our feet. The animagi use it to power their amulets. But those who pass through the gate can harness the power of the *zafira* directly, without the barrier of the world's skin. And it is power beyond imagining."

My body tingles with the Godstone's heat, and maybe with curiosity. *Power beyond imagining.* "How do you know about this?" I demand. "Is it in a scripture? Is it legend?"

"My people have always known. But we have been cut off from it. For more than a thousand years, we have had to grasp at the *zafira* through the world's shell, our power a fraction of what it once was."

"So that's it," Hector says. "That's what the Inviernos want."

I look up to see his eyes narrowed and distant. "Hector?"

"They've been campaigning for port rights for years. They want to search for it."

"Is that true?" I ask Storm.

"It is."

"So why reveal it now?"

"It is as I told you. I am Your Majesty's loyal subject."

"It must be terrible to subject yourself to a rank cow."

He nods in solemn agreement. "Indeed."

I consider him a moment. He is too valuable to risk. "I'm going to let you go. I'll send guards to escort you in secrecy. But next time you *must* answer my summons."

He opens his mouth as if to protest, then snaps it closed. Instead, he bows. "Yes, Your Majesty."

I turn to go, and my companions follow my lead. I'm sure Alentín and Ximena are itching to get back to the archive and scour it for references to the *zafira*. But Rosario yanks on my hand, stopping me. I look down into pleading eyes and a trembling lower lip. "What is it, Highness?"

He gathers himself up, blinks a few times, turns to face the Invierno.

Rosario says, "You are a very, *very* bad man." And he releases my hand and flees down the stairs ahead of us.

Hector and I exchange a puzzled look. He says, "I think Rosario just needed to . . . say something?"

"I'm not, you know," says Storm. "A bad man. I've always tried to do right, to follow the path of God."

I shrug. *"From the mouths of innocents flows truth."* I head for the stairs, not bothering to gauge his response. We hurry down, past the startled soldiers at their card table, and after our prince.

We find him alone in the courtyard. The sun glints off tears streaming down his cheeks. He wipes at them furiously, and we all slow down to give him time to compose himself.

In the most casual tone I can muster, I say, "I have a lesson now with Hector, but Father Alentín might have a moment to take you to the kitchens for some coconut pie."

He nods, gulping. Then he wraps my waist in a quick hug. He lets me ruffle his hair for just a moment before pushing off and finding Alentín's hand. The priest winks at me over his shoulder, and I watch them saunter off together toward the kitchens.

"He's a remarkable boy," Ximena says.

"He is. I just worry sometimes that he is . . . damaged. He watched his father burn."

"Alejandro was damaged too," Hector says, his brow furrowed. He rubs the pommel of his sword with his thumb. "Perhaps it is the price of ruling."

As I head back to my suite, flanked by my guard and my guardian, I wonder at his words, afraid to ask if he thinks I am damaged too.

As I anticipated, instead of staying to observe my self-defense lesson with Hector, Ximena hurries off to the monastery archive. Fernando steps outside to guard the door to the king's suite. The rest take up their posts in my own chambers. Like last time, I am dressed in my desert garb: soft breeches, a loose blouse, leather boots.

Hector's brow is still furrowed, and he paces back and forth like a restless cat. I search for a way to break the silence. "Er . . . will I stomp on your foot again today?"

"No," he snaps, and I almost take an involuntary step back. "Today, you'll learn which body parts should be sacrificed in defense of others." His words are clipped and harsh, his gaze dark with intensity.

"For instance," he continues, "it's better to block a sword with your forearm and let the bones shatter than allow someone access to your throat. And I'll show you which part of your forearm to use so that you're less likely to bleed out. After that, I'll demonstrate some pressure points, places on the body where you can inflict great pain with very little effort. And then—"

"Hector."

"—we'll do some stretching exercises to give you better

range of motion, especially in your arms and shoulders. It's easier to slip from someone's grasp without injury if—"

"Hector!"

"—the muscles are already limber and flexible. We need to get you thinking of your elbows, the crown of your head, even your chin, as potential weapons at your disposal. After that—"

"HECTOR! Stop."

His mouth snaps closed.

"You can't possibly teach me all of that in one afternoon."

He resumes pacing. "In that case, we'll get as far as we can. I think it's best we start with pressure points and then move—"

Swiftly I close the distance between us and cup his face with my hands.

He freezes, inhaling sharply.

We regard each other for a long moment. His jaw is warm in my palms. My right ring finger trails into his soft hairline. I watch carefully as the mania fades from his eyes.

"I need you to be clear-headed, Hector. I need that from you more than anyone."

He whispers, "I can't fail to protect you too." With gentle fingers, he peels my hands from his face. They're so much bigger, rough with calluses. "He was my best friend. I let him die. I dream . . ." His voice trails off.

"That's your nightmare, isn't it? The one you wouldn't tell me about? You dream of Alejandro's death."

"No. Not him."

I expect him to drop my hands, to put distance between us the way he always does. But he merely changes the subject.

"Elisa, you take too many risks. Every day. Like just now, interviewing the Invierno yourself. The animagus who burned himself alive could have hurt you if he wanted to. We were helpless to stop him. You almost died in the catacombs. And the poison . . ."

"You saved my life in the catacombs."

"I shouldn't have had to."

No, he shouldn't have. My face grows hot with shame. Hector is the most honorable man I know, devoted to his country, to his duty, to me. And I have prevented him from doing what is most important to him. "You advised me to cancel the birthday parade. You advised me not to go to the catacombs alone. You can't be blamed for my stubbornness."

He looks down at our entwined hands and mumbles, "And yet I like your stubbornness."

And abruptly, he releases them. I let them fall to my sides, where they ache coldly.

He says, "Dismiss me."

"No."

"I've failed to protect you. Someone else should—"

"I don't want anyone else." My own words echo in the air around me, hammering me with their truth, and I can't contain my slight gasp. *I don't want anyone else.*

He runs a hand through his hair, looks everywhere but at me. Silence stretches between us.

"I've been a fool," I admit finally. "I've been so afraid of seeming weak. Of being like . . . like Alejandro. I've made bad decisions. Hector, you are the person I trust most in the world.

I would do better to heed your counsel. And from now on, I will. But I promise you . . ." I force a smile. "If I die? You are definitely dismissed." I hold my breath and await his response. I know the morbid joke will either infuriate him or put him at ease.

After a moment he shakes his head ruefully. He returns my forced smile with his own feeble attempt and says, "In that case, today I will teach you nothing more than the warm-up series practiced by the Royal Guard. In addition to strengthening and stretching your muscles, I think you'll find it meditative and calming."

I exhale my relief. "Good. I could use 'meditative and calming' right now."

"Turn around." From behind, he reaches for my right arm and gently lifts it to shoulder level. "I'll guide your movements."

But something in the air has changed. I am too deeply aware of the warmth of his nearness, the scents of mink oil and aloe shaving gel, the touch of his callused but gentle fingers. And I am forced to conclude that doing the slow, dancelike warm-up exercises of the Royal Guard with Hector as my partner is not calming at all.

13

That evening, I send Mara to bed early for some healing rest. Ximena helps me don my nightgown, then leaves for a late night of poring over musty documents with Fathers Nicandro and Alentín.

In spite of everything that has happened, in spite of my doubts about God and his will and his words, I still find the *Scriptura Sancta* to be a soothing balm to the day's stresses, and I look forward to reading each night by candlelight before sleeping.

But I am too restless tonight. The words blur on the page. After I've read the same sentence several times without comprehending, I toss the manuscript onto the quilt and swing my legs over the edge of my bed. I grab the candle and its brass holder from my bedside table and carry it toward the atrium.

In the archway, I say to the guards, "I would like some privacy, please." They oblige by turning their backs as I enter.

The water in my ever-circulating bathing pool shimmers blue, and I don't have to look up at the skylight to know that the moon is full or near to it. As I approach with my candle, shards of reflected flame-light dance on the surface.

I set the candle on the tiled edge of the pool.

Before me is my vanity mirror—and my own reflection. I wear a silk nightgown of pale lavender edged in delicate lace. The looseness of the gown drapes pleasantly, flatteringly, and my thick sleeping braid snakes around one shoulder almost to my waist. My skin glows in the candlelight. I feel almost beautiful.

I light the oil lamp on my vanity so I can see better.

The outline of my Godstone is sharp against the thin material. I slip the nightgown's straps from my shoulders and let it fall to the ground.

I study my naked reflection, curious. I try to see myself through someone else's eyes. Would someone else look past the welted red scar, the faceted blue of my Godstone to notice the slight softness in my lower belly? The way my inner thighs just brush when I stand? My legs will never be willowy and elegant like my older sister's, but they're straight and strong.

Finally I allow my gaze to drift toward my breasts. They are the softest part of me, heavy enough that during the day, it is more comfortable to have them bound in a bodice. Unbound, they swoop low and full, enough to balance my hips nicely. Staring at them, I become acutely aware of cool air against their dark tips.

Ximena always told me men would notice my breasts. I've never noticed anyone noticing. But maybe I wouldn't. Mara says I'm pathetically ignorant in matters of love.

Slowly, face flushing, I lift my right hand to cup my left breast. I squeeze gently, and it is a tiny battle to decide what I want to understand most: the feel of a hand on my breast or a breast in my hand.

"Elisa?"

I whirl, hand dropping.

It's Mara. She stands in the doorway to the attendants' quarters, her hair mussed, her eyes heavy with sleep.

"I thought I heard something. Are you all right?"

She's seen me naked a hundred times, but I have a vague sensation that I've been caught at something shameful. "I'm fine. Couldn't sleep."

She regards me a moment as if considering. Then she beckons with one hand. "Why don't you come sit with me awhile?"

I crouch to grab the puddle of silk at my feet and hurriedly slip my arms through the straps. I stand and follow Mara into her room.

Mindful of her wounded stomach, she lowers herself onto one of the bottom bunks and pats the mattress beside her. "Sit," she says, as if she were the queen and I the maid.

I sit.

"You can tell me anything, you know," she says.

"I know."

A shaft of moonlight edges through the high window and hits the opposite wall above our heads, leaving us in shadow. It is the darkness and her patient silence that give me the courage to ask, "Mara, have you ever had a lover?"

She doesn't hesitate. "Yes. Two."

"Oh." How can someone so young have had two lovers already? I'm desperate to ask about them, about what it was like, if either of them broke her heart. But I can't make my mouth say the words.

"I'll tell you about them, if you like," she says.

Oh, thank God. "All right. Yes."

"The first was when I was barely fifteen. He was two years older, a virgin like me. We flirted for a week or two. He was the handsomest boy I'd ever seen. One day I took my father's sheep to a high canyon to graze. He followed, and I thought it was the most romantic thing in the world. We started kissing, and then we were taking each other's clothes off, and then I realized that the rocky ground was poking into my back, and it was very cold outside, and the sheep started drifting away. . . . I changed my mind about what we were doing. But I didn't say anything. I just endured. It was over after a few painful seconds. The next day in the village, he ignored me. We hardly spoke to each other during the next year."

I stare at her shadowy outline in horror. "That . . . I'm so sorry. It sounds . . . terrifying."

She shrugs. "It wasn't so bad. You know, my father was the priest of our village. Very strict. He used to say he could tell when a girl had lost her virginity by the way she walked. And I walked around very carefully for days after, terrified that he would know. But he never did. I was exactly the same person after as I was before. Just, maybe, a little wiser."

My heart is pounding. "Was it awful afterward?" I ask. "To be ignored like that?"

"Yes. I wish I'd waited, had the courage to say no or push him away. But the awfulness didn't last. We both met someone else."

"Oh?"

She takes a deep breath, releases it. "Julio was a little older. Not as handsome, but so much kinder. I used to make a goat-milk scone with pine nuts that I smeared with honeyed apricots. I sold it at market every week. He always bought several, and he always lingered to talk. It was months before he kissed me. Months more before we made love, which by the way was wonderful. We made love a lot. As often as possible. He was going to ask my father for my hand."

Softly I ask, "What happened to him?" Though I think I know.

"He was killed when Inviernos burned our village. Just before I met you in Father Alentín's rebel camp."

I remember. She was so sad at first. Meeting God's chosen one seemed to bring her comfort. "Oh, Mara."

"I still miss him. But I also know how lucky I am. I could have been pregnant when he died, for we were careless. My father could have found out and beaten me for it." She points to the scar above her eyelid. "I have another scar like this one between my shoulder blades. But Julio saw past the scars and found me beautiful."

Her voice catches a little on the word "beautiful," so I reach an arm around her shoulder and give her a squeeze. "You *are* beautiful."

She laughs. "I know! Even with these awful scars. Julio

always said he loved my smile. And my nose! Admit it, my nose is perfect."

"Your nose is perfect."

She leans into me. Her soft hair smells of honeysuckle. Her voice trembles a little when she says, "I do worry sometimes, since being burned by the animagi, that maybe I'm *too* scarred now. And burn scars have a particular awfulness, all ridged and warped and oddly colored. I may never take a lover again. I couldn't bear for someone I cared about to . . . to be repulsed."

It's a feeling I understand well. I used to dread the moment when Alejandro would turn away from me in disgust. But he died before I found the courage—or maybe the desire—to be naked before him.

"And I worry that what I shared with Julio is something that only happens once to a person," Mara says. "Maybe I've used up my love luck." She shrugs.

"I worry about that too."

She sighs. "I liked Humberto. He was always smiling, always cheerful. I didn't realize you were lovers until you told me about him."

"We weren't."

"You never . . . ?"

"Never."

And somehow she understands that by saying "never," I'm not just talking about Humberto, for she says, "You will. As queen, it's inevitable. You will marry, and everyone will pressure you to have a child so that there is more than one heir to the throne."

"You make it sound so calculating."

"Oh, it often is. But after marrying you could take a lover. Most of the royals do, or so I've heard."

I'm glad the darkness hides my flushed face. "I couldn't. When I married Alejandro, he had a lover already. It was . . . hurtful. Even though there was no intimacy between us."

"I see." And I know she does. I grab her hand and squeeze tight. I could never say it aloud, but I hope she understands how glad I am that she is here with me tonight instead of Ximena.

Her voice turns mischievous. "Well, maybe you'll get lucky. Maybe you'll marry a man who is rich and powerful and wise *and* wonderful to be naked with."

I can't help the giggle that bubbles from my mouth.

"Maybe," she says, "you should ask all your suitors to drop their breeches so you can inspect the merchandise."

"Mara!"

"You could make it a royal command."

I toss a pillow at her.

She just laughs at my discomfort. But then she sobers and says, "You're beautiful too, you know. When you get intense, you *spark*. And you have the kind of hair any man would want to get tangled in."

Of its own accord, my hand goes to my braid, strokes it. I've always liked my hair. Would a man really notice it?

Mara adds, "You don't have to settle for a first time like mine."

I shift the subject. "Well, if I ever meet that young man, I'll . . . er . . . speak sternly to him."

"Oh, you have already. It was Belén."

I am stunned. "I thought . . . he and Cosmé . . ."

"Yes. But that was after."

I had no idea the two knew each other before we formed the Malficio. What must it be like for Mara to have him show up here in the palace? I say, "I can make sure you never encounter him while he is here."

"No need. I'm quite over it. We even got to be friends again when we stayed in Father Alentín's camp." She stands. "And *you*, my queen, need to get some rest. Full schedule tomorrow."

I stand. On impulse, I wrap my arms around her. She freezes for a split second, but then she returns my embrace. "Thank you," I whisper.

After I creep back to bed and blow out my candle, my thoughts are still too busy, my skin too warm, for easy sleep. It's terrifying to consider that I might someday share a bed with a man who is a stranger, a calculated alliance, someone who might not care for me at all.

The next evening, escorted by Hector and several guards, I am hurrying toward my office for appointments with a few more suitors when Conde Eduardo intercepts us.

"May I walk with you, Your Majesty?" he asks.

Ugh. "Please." Hector moves aside to give him room. I hope the conde is not planning to intrude on my meetings again.

Eduardo is formally dressed as always, with gold epaulets that mark him as both a high conde and a Quorum lord. My nose stings at the sharp mix of tallow and palm oil, which means his close-cropped black beard has suffered a recent repair.

"I hear you visited the prison tower yesterday," he says.

"Hmm," I say noncommittally.

"And that the young prince accompanied you."

Once again, I curse myself for thoughtlessness. I should not have sent Storm to the tower, no matter how much I wanted to put him in his place. Now I must give an account or raise further suspicions. And I must say something that satisfies Eduardo enough that he won't pursue little Rosario with his questions.

In response to my silence, he adds, "The prison guards say it was a man. Tall, cowled. He only stayed for a few hours before being escorted away by the Royal Guard."

"Yes, that's an accurate description." My mind races. What to tell him? The truth will only lead to more questions about where the Invierno came from and what I want with him. I'm not ready to reveal the cavern beneath the Wallows or the fact that I'm using Storm to learn more about the Godstone.

Which leads me to the disconcerting realization that I do not trust Conde Eduardo, that my distrust goes well beyond that of mere political machinations. He is my own Quorum lord, a man who was a great ally during our war with Invierne. But my every instinct screams caution.

"Your Majesty—"

"Eduardo, obviously there are things we must discuss, but I'm afraid a quick jaunt through the hallway will not do justice to all I have to tell you." I give him my winningest smile.

"Do you think we could call a special Quorum meeting soon? Maybe two days hence?"

He frowns. "That's the day of the Deliverance Gala."

I feign surprised disappointment. "Of course. Thank you for reminding me. And everyone will be exhausted from the festivities the day after. So perhaps four days from now?"

I've trapped him neatly. He can't push without seeming desperate or impolitic. Still frowning, he nods and says, "I'll let everyone know and make arrangements."

"Thank you, Your Grace."

"One last thing before I leave you to your errands."

"Oh?" *What now?* I slow down, realizing I had unconsciously increased my pace as if to get away.

"Lord Liano has expressed a strong desire to see you again. I would take it as a personal favor if you would grant him a dance or two at the gala."

I school my features into perfect pleasantness and say, "I would be happy to."

He bows. "Until the gala, Your Majesty."

I incline my head, and he strides away.

All my breath leaves me. I hadn't known I was holding it.

"That was well done," Hector whispers once we are a safe distance away.

Strange how I can brush off Ximena's praise as the ravings of a madly affectionate nurse, but kind words from Hector feel like drops of water in the desert. "Thank you. But Hector, *four days*. That's how long we have to come up with something plausible."

"We'll do it. Somehow."

"You and I should meet with—" My Godstone turns to ice. "Elisa?"

"Hector! Something—"

He whirls with lightning speed, placing himself in my path, as an arrow meant for me impales the back of his shoulder.

He gasps. The blood drains from his face.

Heedless of the shaft sticking from his flesh, he grabs me, pushes me against the wall. "To the queen!" he yells, and my guards hem me in on all sides in a smooth maneuver that comes only from long practice.

Hector turns to face whatever is coming, sword drawn, and now I see that the arrow is lower than I thought. Below his shoulder blade. In his ribs. Bright blood spreads across his tunic. *Oh, God.*

An arrow whistles down the corridor and clatters harmlessly against a forearm shield. Another *thunks* into a guard's calf muscle. He cries out but does not break formation.

More arrows spear down the corridor from the opposite direction. We are trapped.

"Should I pursue?" a guard asks. "See if I can break through?"

"No!" Hector says. "They're trying to lure us into doing exactly that. Stay tight. They may not attack openly."

So we wait. Hector's back is to me, and I am lodged between him and the wall. Sweat breaks out at the nape of his neck. His skin is as white as an Invierno's.

Please, God, I pray furiously, my fingertips to my navel.

Not Hector. Keep him safe. Keep all my guards safe.

A crazy thought occurs to me. "Hector, shouldn't we yell for help?"

He actually laughs. "Yes, yes of course!"

So we do, every single one of us, and my voice soars over them all.

In moments, I hear running footsteps, the clang of steel on steel. Someone comes to our rescue.

The blood from Hector's wound drips to the floor now. My head swims at the sight. *Don't you dare faint, Elisa.*

Then something about the smell, metallic and hot, snaps me back to myself. It's familiar.

It's war.

I know exactly what Cosmé would do. "Hector, I need to break off the arrow shaft."

"Wait . . . what?" His voice is breathy with pain. I hope the arrowhead has not embedded itself in bone.

"You may need to use that arm. Can't risk the shaft getting knocked around. Please."

He twists to give me an easy grip. "Hurry."

Though I watched Cosmé do this a few times in our rebel camp, I never did it myself. My teeth are chattering and my hands shake, from the icy Godstone or from fear I cannot tell as I wrap both hands around it. Cosmé always braced the body part, snapped hard and fast.

He hisses from pain. "Snap lower," he says. "As close to my ribs as possible."

I move my hands until one rests against his back. The

sounds of fighting come closer. *Don't think, Elisa. Just do.*

With a grunt, I snap the shaft in two. The jagged end snags my palm, drawing blood. I toss the shaft to the ground and wipe my hand on my skirt.

Hector sways on his feet. Instinctively I wrap my arms around his waist to hold him up. He leans against me a moment, then straightens, breathing hard. "It's all right. I'm all right." But I'm not so sure. I know he can handle the pain, but his body could go into shock.

A flurry of bodies approaches. I see glinting blades, swinging limbs, a wooden shield. "To the queen!" calls a voice I recognize.

It's Conde Tristán. He works his way toward us, accompanied by men dressed in the sky blue and ivory of Selvarica. The assailants are no one I recognize. I count five, but in the chaos I can't be sure. They're dirty and unshaven and clothed in little more than rags, but they wield quality blades and bows.

Tristán cuts through attackers with astonishing speed, a short sword in one hand, a dagger in the other. His fighting style is beautiful, almost like a dance. He and his companions give no quarter, and the attackers cannot draw their bows.

Now that we have reinforcements, Hector gestures for three guards to investigate the opposite end of the corridor, and they take off running. The wounded guard is swaying on his feet, and Hector yanks him back toward me, saying, "Don't engage. Defend the queen."

Only two attackers remain. Hector lunges at one and pierces him cleanly through the breast. Tristán leaps, whipping his sword around toward the other as I yell, "I need him alive!"

The conde adjusts midair, lands easily, sends the hilt into the attacker's temple. The filthy man crumples to the ground. The Godstone's ice fades and is replaced by soft warmth.

My guards, Hector, Tristán, the men from Selvarica all look around at one another, in that shared moment of relief and triumph I've seen a dozen times before. Bodies litter the corridor. Tristán nudges one with the toe of his boot and watches for movement. Nothing.

"Mercenaries?" Tristán says.

Hector nods. "They fought poorly, and their attack was ill conceived. They might not even know their employer."

I point out, "There's no way men dressed like that can afford weapons like those."

"We'll need to question the one His Grace conked on the head," says Hector. "But he may not be able to tell us . . ." He sways.

I jump forward, lodge myself under his armpit, and wrap his arm around my shoulder. Blood soaks his shirt. It smears all over the skin of my neck, seeps into my bodice.

"Find Doctor Enzo!" I say to no one in particular. "Tell him to meet us in the commander's quarters."

Hector is almost limp in my arms. Fear stabs at my gut.

"Conde Tristán, can you escort us to the barracks?"

"Of course." He gestures to one of his own men. "Stay with the unconscious one. Tie his ankles and wrists. Roll him onto his side in case he vomits."

And we're off, down the corridor toward the barracks. Hector sags hard against my shoulder, and his feet drag. My thighs burn with effort as each step pounds a prayerful rhythm through my head: *Not Hector, not Hector, not Hector.*

14

HE is passed out by the time we reach his quarters, and Conde Tristán supports most of his weight as we drag him inside. The other guards help us lay him gently on his bed.

Doctor Enzo rushes in, followed by two assistants in gray frocks. "Too much blood," he murmurs. "Roll him onto his side and cut off his shirt," he orders one assistant. "And you," he says to a guard, "get me hot water and clean rags, as many as you can find. We need to clean him up so I can see exactly where he's bleeding from once I push the arrow through. Your Majesty, please step back."

I realize I'm hovering, but I don't move. "Is he . . . will he . . . ?"

He whirls and pushes me back by the shoulders until I hit the wall. "I suggest you start praying," he says.

Staring at Hector's pale form, I slide down the wall to the floor and pull my knees to my chest. Tristán settles beside me. He grabs my hand and says, "You care about him very much."

I nod. "Hector is . . . he's one of my dearest friends."

"Then I'll stay here and pray with you for a while."

"Thank you," I whisper. It's no use telling him I've prayed for people I care about before, that it didn't help.

Doctor Enzo yells at an assistant to light a fire in the hearth and heat the poker.

As Tristán murmurs a prayer beside me, my hand clasped in his, I can hardly focus on the words. I can only stare, horrified, as Doctor Enzo takes what looks like a man's razor with a long handle and begins to cut around the arrowhead.

"Interesting," the doctor says. "Very interesting."

"What?" I demand, interrupting Tristán's prayer.

"It almost split the rib," he says. "Right on the lung, so I can't push through. I'll have to pull it, but the arrowhead is scored. It will do some damage coming out."

But Hector's skin is too blanched, his breathing too shallow. Sweat sheens his cheeks. I don't know that he can survive more injury.

I find myself praying anyway; I don't know what else to do. I close my eyes, lean my forehead against Tristán's, and pray in earnest, letting the Godstone radiate its deceptive calm throughout my body. I refuse to cease praying, to open my eyes, even when Hector's unconscious grunt tells me Enzo has yanked the arrow out. Even when a hot poker hisses against flesh and the scent of burned blood fills the room.

The doctor and his assistants are cleaning up, removing blood-soaked rags and mopping the floor near Hector's bed when Tristán shakes my shoulder gently. "I must see to the man I knocked on the head," he says. "Find out what he knows."

I had forgotten about him. "Oh, yes, please do." He rises and heads for the door. "Tristán?" He turns back around. "Thank you. For coming to our rescue. For staying with me."

He bows low. "Is it all right to leave you here?"

"I'm safe in the barracks of my own Royal Guard."

"Of course. By your leave." And he exits Hector's quarters.

Hector's quarters. I've never been here before. I look around, unsurprised to find it austerely beautiful. His bed, his wardrobe, even the undyed woolen rug at my feet speak of elegant simplicity with their clean lines and subdued colors and perfect craftsmanship. On one wall hangs a painting, the only splash of true color in the place. It's of a vineyard, and rows of grapevines heavy with bloated grapes scallop over golden hills, fading into the sunset. Several manuscripts, even a few books, are piled haphazardly on his nightstand beside a half-melted candle—the only bit of disorderliness.

This is where Hector sleeps. And judging by the manuscripts, where he spends what little free time I allow him. I breathe deep. The place even smells of him—leather oil and aloe shaving jelly and a hint of sweat.

The doctor and his assistants head toward the door, arms laden with bloody rags. "Your Majesty, I need to see to the other guard. I hear he has a leg wound?"

"Wait. Tell me about Hector."

"He lost too much blood, and the arrow nicked his lungs. I couldn't keep him from going into shock. He is unlikely to survive, even with my considerable skill."

My vision tunnels and my bodice is suddenly too tight and hot.

"Are you staying awhile, Your Majesty?" he asks in an uncharacteristically soft voice.

"Yes," I hear myself say.

"In that case, I've left devil's nettle tea on the hearth. Make him drink it, in the unlikely event that he wakes. It will help the blood clot and relieve pain. I'm leaving orders for no one else to enter this room—he needs perfect rest. If you must leave, ask the guard outside to sit in here quietly to mark his . . . health. I'll return later to check the stitches and bandages."

I hardly notice when he closes the door behind him. I'm staring at Hector's face, at the eyelashes curling against his cheeks, his slightly open mouth, the dark stubble along his jawline.

My skin is flushed, from the still-glowing hearth, from the Godstone's responses to my prayers, from fear. *He is unlikely to survive.* I crawl to his bedside and kneel there. I reach for his hand and clasp it tight. He does not stir.

A great hollow has opened in my chest where my heart and lungs ought to be, and oh, it hurts. It's like the breath-stealing pain beneath my breastbone that comes of days walking the desert without enough to drink. It's like a dagger to the gut. It's like dying.

I rest my forehead on his knuckles. *Please, God, help him get better. Don't let him die.* My Godstone throbs, but I know it's not enough. How many times have I prayed for a life, only for God to turn away?

I will do anything. I'd give him my own life and health if I could.

He's a good man, the best man. He deserves to live. Please.

I imagine pouring my own life force out of my body, through our clasped hands, filling Hector, knitting his wound.

The Godstone becomes a fire. I cry out as white-hot pain zings up my spine.

After a moment the pain lessens. Something else takes its place, something like water or light or desert wind, leaching up from the ground, pouring into my Godstone. My body shivers with it until I feel like I will burst.

Hope dares to spark inside me, for I have felt this once before—when I killed the animagi with my Godstone amulet.

I don't know where the power came from or how I've managed to channel it again, but my body hums with possibility, with potential, as if the power building inside me is a huge boulder about to tumble off a cliff.

God, what do I do?

Hector's fingers twitch. I grip tighter, press my lips to the back of his hand, concentrating on the power inside me.

Live. Please live.

Nothing happens.

Think, Elisa! Last time, I quoted God's own words from holy scripture. It became a conduit for the power of my Godstone, focusing it where I needed.

Aloud, I say, "The gate that leads to life is narrow and small so that few find it." My Godstone lurches, and the force inside me begins a slow spin. Encouraged, I add, "For the righteous right hand of God is a healing hand; blessed is he who seeks renewal, for he shall be restored."

Power trickles out of me, from my hand into Hector's. My heart pounds with excitement, with hope. I wrack my mind for more.

The "Prayer of Service"! "Take my life, O God, as a consecrated offering, holy and pleasing. Make me your vessel of service . . ." The power begins to fade. "No! God, please no."

I gaze at Hector's face, memorizing every detail—his pale lips, the line of his jaw, the crisscross of scars on one cheek. And suddenly I have it. The perfect verse.

My heart swells with knowledge as certain as the tides. I whisper, "For love is more beautiful than rubies, sweeter than honey, finer than the king's wine. And no one has greater love than he who gives his own life for a friend. My love is like perfume poured out—"

The floodgates open. Power rushes out of me, into Hector. He arches his back, and his eyes fly open, showing nothing but bloodshot white. Then he crashes back to the bed.

I have just enough time to notice that his breathing is easier, that color returns to his face, before my vision blurs with exhaustion and dizziness. My heart slows to a single thunderous beat every few seconds. Too slow. Am I dying? Have I given my own life for Hector's?

A good trade, I think, as I collapse against the bed, my cheek thudding against his forearm.

I wake to a hand on my head, fingers tangling in my unraveling braid. A man's fingers, rough and thick. They trail down my cheek, stroke my jawline, brush my lips.

I raise my head and blink to clear my eyes. Hector is awake, staring at me with a strange expression. He does not move his hand from my face but lets it linger, his thumb gently tracing my chin.

My relief is so huge it feels like I can breathe again.

"You stayed," he says, and his voice is hoarse.

"And I'm not dead!" I say wonderingly. At the confusion on his face, I hastily add, "How do you feel?"

"Like I got punched in the back with Captain Lucio's gauntlet. Which is odd. I should feel worse."

"It worked!" His hand has still not left my face, and I have the urge to lean into it, kiss his fingers, maybe.

"What do you mean?"

"My Godstone. I knew it had healing properties, but I didn't know if it would work on someone else."

His hand drops, and he sits straight up, wincing. "You thought you were giving your life to me."

I open my mouth to deny it, but then I decide it's best to say nothing.

He swings his legs over to the side so that he faces me. "There's dried blood all over you," he whispers. "My blood, isn't it?"

I'm about to tell him that it's nothing that won't wash away, but speech leaves me when he cups my face with his hands. "Please, Elisa," he says, "don't ever, ever give *your* life for *mine*."

"I couldn't let you die. I'd rather—"

A knock sounds at the door, and we spring away from each other.

"Come in!" Hector calls, though he continues to hammer me with that unreadable stare.

Doctor Enzo bustles in, but he stops short, his mouth agape. "This is most unexpected."

After an awkward silence, I say, "Perhaps your skills are even more considerable than you realized?"

He looks back and forth between Hector and me, frowning. "I admit to a certain well-earned reputation," he says thoughtfully. "But this is not the result of my ministrations."

"A miracle?" I say weakly.

His gaze drifts to the general direction of my navel. "You healed him," he accuses. "Somehow."

I shrug, not wanting to talk about it. I do need to tell someone what happened. Father Alentín or Ximena. But not Enzo. "I fell asleep. Something happened before I woke up." Hector's eyes flash with understanding; he knows I'm not telling the whole truth. Before I can be pressed on the matter, I say, "I need to get back to my suite. I'm scheduled to be in preparations for the gala in the morning. Enzo, please make sure your patient rests. I'll find guards to escort me."

At my back, I hear Enzo say, "May I record this incident? The *Journal of Medical Anomalies* would be fascinated—"

As I close the door behind me, God's holy scripture echoes in my head. *My love is like perfume poured out . . .*

I bend over, hugging myself with relief, with unshed tears, with exhaustion, and with an understanding as bone-wrenching as it is pure: I am wholly and irreversibly in love with the commander of my Royal Guard.

Thank you, God. Thank you for saving him.

I straighten to find several guards staring at me. One is Fernando, who regards me with the helpless gaze of a frightened pup. "Lord Hector . . . ?" he says in a wavering voice.

"Will be fine," I say. "I require an escort to my rooms."

Fernando orders the others to accompany me, then takes up watch, his arms crossed, his face determined. I am not the only one who loves their commander.

Night has fallen, and I consider going to bed, but I know I won't manage any kind of sleep. "To the monastery," I say, and they fall into formation around me.

The corridors are empty and silent. Light from sconced torches shimmers against the glazed-tile pattern in the wall, but it also casts shadows over our cobbled path. I imagine assassins hiding in patches of darkness, behind corners. Every scuff of sound, every whisper, is an arrow flying through the air, a dagger whipped from its sheath.

I think of Hector, wishing he were here. And then I'm glad he isn't, for I have much to think about before I see him next.

We round a bend and enter the monastery, a place that never quite sleeps. Scattered petitioners kneel on prayer benches, and an acolyte in a gray robe quietly tends the candles on the altar. I breathe in the perfume of sacrament roses as comfort. Surely I am safe here, in this place of worship.

I open the door to the archive and find Ximena, Alentín, and Nicandro sitting on stools at the scribing table, bent over a piece of vellum so old that its edges are curled and black.

I thank the guards and ask them to watch the entrance, then I close the door behind me.

They look up, startled, and Ximena's face freezes with shock. "Elisa? Is that *blood* all over you?"

I had forgotten. "Yes. Hector's. We were attacked in the hallway outside my office. Hired mercenaries. Tristán came to our aid. But everyone is fine now." I came to tell her all about it, about healing him, but suddenly I don't want to. I need to think about something else for a bit, before I think on that.

"And the mercenaries?" she demands. "Do you know who hired them? Were they captured or killed? There may be more—"

I hold up a hand. "Later. Please distract me with moldy vellum and impenetrable wisdom. *Please.*"

The three of them exchange a glance, then Nicandro says, "I'll show you what we've found." He pats the stool next to him, then moves an oil lamp to the side to make a space for me at the table.

I hop up onto the stool, uneasy with the memory pricking at my thoughts. The last time I sat here late into the night with Father Nicandro, he revealed that I had been kept in ignorance of bearer lore, that a prophecy destined me to encounter the gate of my enemy.

And I thought I *had* encountered it, when I was captured by Inviernos and nearly tortured by an animagus. But maybe not. Maybe the worst is yet to come.

"This here," he says, pounding the vellum with a forefinger, "is the *Blasphemy of Lucero.*"

I gasp. "Lucero is my name."

He nods. "This document was presented for canonization as official scripture almost a century ago, but it was rejected by a council of priests."

"Not just rejected," Father Alentín cuts in. "It was *banned*."

"Wait. A century? That means . . ."

"He was your predecessor," Alentín confirms.

Lucero. The bearer before me. Though he lived a hundred years ago, I suddenly feel closer to him than anyone. My voice is shaky as I ask, "So why was this document banned?"

Ximena says, "The structure is atrocious, for one. It was penned by an uneducated hand; the original is rife with spelling and grammar errors. The council believed God would never allow his holy words to be anything less than pristine."

I stare down at the vellum. The script is faded with age, but the lines are even and precise, perfectly scribed. "So this is a copy."

Nicandro nods, "Of a copy of a copy, no doubt. The original is lost to us forever. No one felt it important to preserve it."

"And now you think the priests were wrong? Maybe it isn't blasphemy, but actual scripture?"

"No," Ximena says, even as Alentín says, "Definitely."

They exchange a friendly glare. Then Ximena sighs and says, "Adding to the cannon is no light matter. It could alter centuries of traditions. Of beliefs. I would have to be absolutely certain before I accepted it as God's own words."

Alentín says, "But you concede the possibility. We have compelling evidence."

"I concede the possibility."

"Aha!" he says, as if he's won a great victory, and then I'm shocked when Ximena rolls her eyes at him. I've never seen her resort to such impropriety.

"Tell me, then," I say. "Why you think it ought to be considered scripture? What does it say?"

Nicandro clears his throat. "Master Lucero was a poor village boy. He could neither read nor write. According to the introduction, he dictated his vision to a friend, who scribed it hastily on a sheep's hide. The friend, as it turned out, was also not very good at reading and writing. The manuscript, if you can call it that, was delivered to the nearest monastery, but the story was never verified. The boy disappeared. The monastery searched for him for years, to no avail."

"So the priests declared it blasphemy." I can see why. They would think it odd that God would speak through someone so poor and backward as to be totally illiterate. But I warm to the idea. It's nice to consider that God may not count imperfection as an obstacle to working out his will in the world.

"Seems a little convenient that he would disappear," Ximena grumbles. "Not available to answer questions or have his Godstone verified by the monastery."

Alentín leans forward, eyes bright. "But it's not unusual for a bearer to disappear. Three hundred years ago, for example. Another boy evaporated right out of the Monastery-at-Altapalma, his service undone. No one knows what happened."

I imagine that they fled—from expectations, from terror, from the constant barrage of others deciding the best way to accomplish God's will. Or maybe they died young, suddenly and unexpectedly, as most bearers seem to do. It's something I came to terms with when I lived in the desert—that I would likely die young in service to God.

I say, "Why do *you* think we should take the boy's message seriously?"

"Lucero knew things," Nicandro says. "Things an illiterate boy from a remote village could never know. I won't go into detail, but it was enough to give me pause. Enough to keep me reading eagerly. And then I reached this right here." He scrolls down with his finger until he finds the pertinent passage. "Go ahead, Your Majesty. Read it."

I lean forward, tingling with anticipation, with the possibility of discovery. "'The gate that leads to life is narrow and small so that few find it.'" I look up, puzzled. "Nothing new here. It says the same in the *Scriptura Sancta*."

"Keep reading," Ximena says.

"'The champion alone shall traverse it and find the *zafira*, for this wellspring of his power shall beckon him. And all the power of this world shall come into him and he shall have life eternal in accordance with God's will. None shall stand against him, and his enemies shall crumble, verily a thousand shall fall before his might.'"

All the power of this world. My Godstone thrums in recognition, sending shivers of warmth up my spine.

"The *zafira*," Ximena says.

"Just like the Invierno said," Alentín points out.

"How would an uneducated village boy know that word?"

Nicandro asks, his voice soft with awe. "It hasn't been in use since the first families came to this world. It's older even than the Lengua Classica."

Darkness edges my vision, whether from dread or excitement or residual exhaustion from healing Hector I can't tell. I ask, "What, exactly, is the *zafira*?"

Alentín says, "The *Afflatus* says that magic crawls beneath the skin of this world and that once in every four generations, God raises up a champion to bear his mark and fight magic with magic." I love the way his voice falls into rhythm whenever he quotes scripture. It takes me right back to our desert cavern and our lessons together while sitting on gritty shale and drawing letters in the dust.

After a pause, he adds, "Scripture supports the Invierno's claim that the *zafira* is the magic of the world."

I narrow my eyes, thinking hard. "The animagi can call the magic to them from anywhere. All they have to do is feed the earth a bit of blood. But Storm made the *zafira* sound like a specific place."

He nods. "Storm also made it sound as though calling this magic takes no small effort. But Lucero's *Blasphemy* describes a crack in the world, where the wellspring of power bubbles to the surface. I think it refers to a place where the world's magic is more accessible, or maybe more concentrated."

They all regard me with expectation as I mull their words.

I say, "The champion alone shall find the *zafira* . . ." And as soon as the words leave my mouth, I know I want to. More than anything.

But how would I manage such a thing? A queen does not have the luxury of leaving everything behind in pursuit of a nebulous quest.

"You *are* the champion," Nicandro says. "It goes on to say that your determination will be tested. That you must prove your worth. But it also says that he who bears God's own stone shall pass through the gate." He shrugs, sighing. "Frankly, I think it sounds dangerous."

Prophecy is a tricky thing, I have learned, full of edges and secret meanings and mischief. Prophecy can feel like the betrayal of a dear friend, the disappointment of a lifetime, the hope of a nation.

"This could be it, Elisa," Ximena says, and her black eyes spark with something fierce. "What you need to rule. To finally grasp the destiny I know God has prepared for you."

I'm not sure why, but her words make me uncomfortable—even though she's a little bit right. With that kind of power, I would be able to discourage the machinations of the Quorum. Keep my enemies at bay. Make my kingdom whole again.

"And Elisa . . ." Nicandro's voice is dark with gravity. "It's best that you tell no one about the *Blasphemy*. It's a forbidden text, after all."

"And yet you had a copy lying around in the monastery."

He shifts on his stool. "Er . . . no. Father Alentín did."

A laugh bubbles in my throat, and Alentín flashes me a mischievous grin. This is the man who stole the oldest known copy of Homer's *Afflatus* when he fled the Monastery-at-Basajuan. *Of course* he has a copy of the forbidden *Blasphemy*.

"We should begin making arrangements, my sky," Ximena says. "We could leave—"

I hold up a hand to cut her off. It's crusted with Hector's dried blood. I say, "I'll think about it."

15

BUT I don't have time to think about it, for the day of the Deliverance Gala dawns hot and bright and busy. Everyone hurries through preparations sheened with a layer of sweat. I spend the morning approving last-minute changes to the menu and guest lists and practicing the blessing I will recite at the ball. That afternoon, I tell Mara and Ximena about healing Hector, though I leave out the most pertinent detail. Ximena is beside herself with excitement that I have found a way to tap into the Godstone's power.

"God has a great destiny for you, my sky," she says, her eyes shining.

If she realizes I'm keeping something to myself, she does not press. Still, I'm relieved when it's finally time to dress for the gala, for it means I'll have something to do besides avoid her zealous gaze.

I can't stop thinking about Hector. I can't wait to see him again, for Doctor Enzo has declared him well enough to escort me tonight.

Because of the attempts on my life, my own personal guard will be on my arm, soldiers will be stationed at every entrance and crossbowmen in the high cupolas overlooking the audience hall, and every guest will be thoroughly searched for weapons. Still Ximena insists on one further precaution.

She holds up a corset of leather nearly as stiff as rawhide. "I had it specially made," she says with a pleased look. She knocks it with a fist, and I wince at the hollow sound. "It should repulse a dagger, or at least minimize damage. And it's fitted, just flexible enough to wear under a gown."

I gaze at it in despair, already feeling suffocated. "All right," I say, resigned. When she fits it around me and begins to lace it, I try to convince myself it's not much worse than my regular corset with its thick stays.

Mara looks on with amused interest. "It looks like Hector's informal armor," she says. "Except with space for breasts."

"Funny," I say with a glare. But my glare dies when I see my reflection. I hardly recognize the girl looking back at me. She seems so strong in her corset armor. I throw my shoulders back and hold my head high.

My gown—made of aquamarine satin—slides over it with surprising ease. It's a bolder color than I usually prefer, but I like the way my skin glows next to it, the contrast of my dark skin and black hair. The gown is sleeveless but has two impossibly long chiffon ties that form a halter behind my neck and float down my back, all the way to the floor.

Ximena sweeps my hair up, leaving a few curls to trail down my neck. Mara lines my eyes with kohl and adds a little sweep at the corners, which enhances their cat shape and makes them look huge. She steps back, grinning smugly, and says, "I've been practicing on the laundress."

Tears fill Ximena's eyes. "You look like a queen, my sky."

Mara says, "You look like the most eligible marriage prospect in the country."

The face staring back is strange. More chiseled, less pudgy than it used to be. And the eyes—so dark and dramatic and large! They are the eyes of someone who has seen and lost much.

Softly I say, "I look like a widow."

They shift a bit closer, as if forming a protective hedge, and Mara settles an arm across my shoulder. I'm grateful for their sympathy, their understanding.

Mara squeezes my shoulder. "You'll find love again," she says.

I catch my breath. *But I already have. And I don't know that it matters.* Carefully I say, "Love is not for me. I'll marry for the good of my kingdom." But my words seem too hard and sharp. "Probably a northern lord," I continue, forcing nonchalance into my voice. "Approved by the Quorum."

Ximena regards me thoughtfully—she knows me too well. But she doesn't press the matter, just arranges the ties of my dress to drape more fluidly and says, "You're ready to go as soon as Hector gets here."

My heart does a little flip at the sound of his name, but I ignore it, saying, "First I have something for you." I gesture for them to follow me into my bedchamber. I reach into my nightstand to retrieve the gifts I've hidden there and hand each of them a packet wrapped in supple leather.

Mara beams as she opens hers but then gasps with astonishment. "A spice satchel. With marjoram, cinnamon—oh, Elisa. Saffron! How did you procure saffron?"

I'm so glad to have surprised her. "There are advantages to being queen. Now you, Ximena."

My nurse peels back the leather wrapping to reveal a bound book with a painted cover and gilded pages. *"The Common Man's Guide to Service,"* she breathes. "It must be two hundred years old."

"Look at the pages."

She opens it. "Oh, my sky."

I laugh, delighted with her reaction. "They're illuminated!"

Ximena runs a finger across the elaborate lettering, caresses the border painted in shimmering sacrament roses. Tears fill her eyes. "I've never owned something so valuable."

It takes so little to please my ladies, and my heart fills to see the happiness shining in their faces. I reach my arms out, and then the three of us are elbowing one another in an awkward hug. "Happy Deliverance Day," I whisper, and they respond in kind.

Someone's throat clears, and we separate. Mara moves from my field of vision to reveal Hector standing in the doorway.

My mouth goes dry.

For the first time since I have known him, he is dressed as a Quorum lord. He still wears the red cloak of the Royal Guard, but instead of combing back his black hair, he has let it curl naturally at his forehead, at the nape of his neck. In lieu of a breastplate and thigh guards, he wears a loose white blouse tucked into tight black breeches. A sword belt slings across narrow hips, but it's a smaller gentleman's sword. Without the bulk of his armor, I see how very broad his shoulders are, how tanned the skin of his neck and collarbone is.

He looks vulnerable. Exposed.

And yet he looks stronger than I've ever seen him. He's not beautiful like Alejandro, for there is nothing of delicacy about Hector. And he is not wild and unpolished like Humberto. Hector's jaw is too smooth and solid, his eyebrows too full and well shaped, his neck and shoulders hard with sculpted muscle. Everything about him speaks of elegant power.

I realize the silence has stretched forever. How long have I stood here gaping?

His pupils are huge, his gaze on me steady. He has watched me study him, and more than anything, I wish I could read his thoughts.

I find my voice at last. "Happy Deliverance Day."

"You are beautiful," he says simply.

Warmth floods my neck, and I swallow hard. "Thank you. You look very nice too."

"I brought something for you."

"Oh?" For the first time, I notice the package in his hand. It's box shaped, large enough that I will need two hands to hold it. "You didn't have to get me anything." Earlier, I had a page deliver a silver brooch for his cloak—the same gift I gave all my guards. I didn't know what else to do. There is still so

much I don't know about him—about his childhood, his interests—and I couldn't think of a gift that felt personal enough
for someone so important to me. Staring at the box in his hand,
I wish I'd given it more effort.

"It's from all of us," he says. "The Royal Guard, Ximena,
and Mara."

I whip my head around to stare at my ladies. Mara grins
like a child about to eat naming-day pie. "Go ahead," Ximena
says. "Open it."

Hector hands the box to me, and our fingers brush as I take
it. I pull at the twine until it unravels, then peel away the dec-
orative wrapping to reveal a hinged jewelry box of polished
mahogany. The de Vega seal is burn etched onto the cover. My
heart is in my throat as I tip the lid back.

Inside, resting on blue velvet, is a crown made of white gold
with swirls and loops as intricate as lace. It's dainty enough to
be light on my head, and yet so much more substantial than the
tiaras I wore as a princess. Indeed, it is fit for a queen.

But what makes me draw breath sharply, what fills my eyes
with tears, are the shattered Godstones set into the gold. They
range from dark blue to black; some are no more than shards.
In the center is the largest, the one Godstone that survived
mostly intact, though a large spiderweb crack bursts across its
surface just left of center.

Whoever designed the crown was inspired by the broken
jewels and carried the theme through the whorls and spikes
of gold. Though delicate, the overall impression is one of bold
strength and jagged shimmering.

It's the crown of a warrior. Of someone who has faced destruction.

Because I am frozen in place, Ximena lifts it from the box and settles it on my head. It feels perfect. I step into the atrium to view my reflection in the vanity mirror. Tiny motes of untouched sapphire spark under the skylight.

"No one," I breathe, "in the history of all the world has worn a crown such as this."

"No one else could," Hector says over my shoulder. Our eyes meet in the mirror. I'm the first to look away.

"Thank you," I say. "Thank you all. But how——"

"All those gifts from your suitors," Ximena says. "When you were convalescing. We sold several items, melted the jewelry down. It was Hector's idea. Mara helped the jeweler design it. Each of the guards chipped in a few coins."

"It's amazing," I say. "It's magnificent."

"Go show it off, my sky," Ximena says with a soft smile.

I find I'm eager to do so. I look to Hector, and he holds out his arm.

The audience hall is transformed for the Deliverance Gala. Rose garlands swoop from crystal chandeliers, filling the hall with their heady scent. The casement of each high window holds a lighted candelabra, so that the room seems surrounded by stars. Low tables line the walls. They are covered with silk cloth and brimming with appetizers and drink served in silver dishes, all surrounded by sitting cushions for easy chatting.

Musicians play vihuelas and dulciáns from a wooden stage near the entry, and hundreds of people mill about, smiling and laughing, dressed in their yearly best. More trickle in through the entrance after being thoroughly searched for weapons, but even this does not damper the mood. They're as bright as a flower garden in their Deliverance colors—coral hibiscus and yellow night bloomers and sky-blue vine snaps. Women wear their hair up in jeweled nets; men wear long stoles trimmed in gold embroidery. It's a night for shimmering, for catching the light just so.

No one dances yet. It's up to me to begin the festivities.

The moment I enter, the hall goes silent. Hector pauses in the threshold, giving them a chance to size up their queen. I hold lightly to his arm, and he reaches with his other hand and gives mine a quick squeeze.

Everyone bows, but their collective gaze fixes on my new crown. I give them a defiant smile in return and wait the space of a few beats for them to fully understand what they see.

I gesture for everyone to rise, and Hector and I resume our procession. The crowd breaks into a flurry of low-voiced conversations. I catch the words "Godstone" and "sorcery." I hold my smile easily, knowing the crown has had its intended effect.

At the end of the hall, my throne dais has been rolled away to reveal the massive Hand of God, a masterwork of marble sculpture we gaze upon only once each year. My Godstone leaps in rapturous response. I calm it with my fingertips, mumbling, "Stop that."

The man who carved the hand, Lutián of the Rocks, spent his whole short life working on it. They say he was overcome with God's spirit, that he carved with fevered frenzy, stopping only for occasional food and drink and sleep. When he finished at the age of twenty-one, he pronounced it good and promptly collapsed of a burst heart. He bore a living Godstone, like me, and carving this giant hand was his great service.

With Hector's help, I climb the steps leading to God's cupped fingers. I step across them carefully, for they are as rounded and ridged as real fingers. I spread the skirt of my aquamarine gown around me, and lower myself so that I sit cross-legged in the giant palm.

The crowd hushes in expectation.

I close my eyes, lift my hands to the sky, and intone the Deliverance blessing.

In you our ancestors put their trust,
they cried out and you delivered them.
Yea, from the dying world they were saved;
in you they trusted and were not put to shame.
Bless us, O God, as we remember your hand;
your righteous right hand endures forever.

"Selah!" the crowd thunders.

The musicians resume, dancers float onto the center floor, and the Deliverance Gala has officially begun.

From below, Hector gestures for me to come down. Normally, the monarch would sit in the Hand of God for several dances, absorbing luck and blessing. But it is too dangerous for me to be exposed for so long.

Holding tight to his hand for support, I navigate the steps, mindful of my full skirt. My foot has barely reached the floor when I am accosted by my first partner.

"May I have this dance, Your Majesty?" asks Prince Rosario. He bows with the ease of long practice, his small fingers outstretched in gentlemanly supplication.

"Of course!" I say with genuine enthusiasm, taking the offered hand.

His head does not even reach my chest, and I'm tempted to lead him, but he seems determined to do the job credibly, so I let him.

"Did your nurse put you up to this?" I ask.

He peers up at me from beneath thick lashes—his cinnamon eyes are so like his father's—and says, "No, but Carilla wants to dance with me." With a quick tip of his chin, he indicates a young girl with wild curls and satin ruffles standing at the edge of the crowd, no more than nine years old. Rosario wrinkles his nose. "She tries to kiss me. It's awful."

I laugh. "So you told her you had to dance with me instead."

He nods solemnly. "Even though you are a terrible dancer. Dancing with you is better than dancing with Carilla."

With equal solemnity, I say, "Excellent decision. You will be a wise king one day."

"Yes," he agrees. "Wiser than Papá. Everyone says so."

My heart breaks for him a little. "We should drift across the hall so that you are far away from Carilla when the song ends."

He brightens. "Good idea!"

As we dance, I ask him about his studies, which he loathes, and his swordsmanship lessons with Hector, which he loves.

By the time our dance ends, we are laughing together over his favorite pony, who can nose his way to a syrupy date even through three layers of clothing. I don't step on Rosario's feet even once.

When we separate, he bows. "I thank you for the dance, Your Majesty," he intones.

"It was a pleasure, Your Highness," I respond. Several people around us applaud lightly, as if we have put on a bit of theater. And I suppose we have. I hope it has cheered them to see their queen and her heir having a good time together.

A hand grasps my elbow. I look up into Hector's worried face. He whispers, "*Please*. Do not drift through the crowd while dancing. Stay close to the edge, where I can see you."

The music changes to a slow, rhythmic bolero.

"I didn't realize . . . I'm sorry." He is very close, and my heart starts to pound. I remember our last lesson, the way his hands stroked up my bare forearm, showing me proper form, guiding my movements. The way the world dropped away as we moved effortlessly together, lost in the drill that was more like a dance.

I whisper, "Dance with me."

He pauses, as if considering. Then, "Yes, Your Majesty." And my heart sinks to think that dancing with me may be yet another *duty* for him. But then I can't think of anything at all, for his hand has slipped around my waist to pull me toward him. Holding my gaze, his left hand slides gently down my forearm to my fingers. He entwines them with his own and spins me into the center of the floor.

We are not close enough as we dance. I imagine myself pressed against him, my face buried in his neck. But this particular dance demands a certain choreographed distance, and we comply. I focus instead on the hand at the small of my back. The leather of my hidden corset protects me from daggers, but it protects me from Hector's touch too, and I find myself hating it. I can feel the pressure of his hand but no more. I want to feel his fingers, his warmth. I want to feel *everything*.

"How is your injury?" I ask, to distract myself.

"I have forgotten to notice it."

I have no idea how to respond. After a moment of my stunned silence, he says, "Of all your suitors, has any one caught your particular attention yet?"

His question startles me. It feels out of place. Forced.

I consider making a joke but abandon the idea. Instead I say, "I haven't encountered many yet, but Conde Tristán seems nice. He's intelligent and charming. And . . . and I think he likes me, too."

"You think he could be a good friend, then?"

"Maybe. I don't . . ." *I don't love him.* "I don't know that the Quorum will approve. He's southern, after all. But I think he's a good man."

I hear him sigh, and his arm squeezes my waist, pulling me a little closer. He says, "I'm glad. You could do much worse. And I'll always be grateful to him for coming to our aid."

I nod agreement, trying to keep the disappointment from my face. It's wrong of me, I know, but I don't want Hector to be glad about a potential suitor.

The dance floor is full now, and Hector is careful to keep us from brushing against anyone else. He leans down and whispers, "I'm not sure it's proper for a queen to dance with her guard."

My heart sinks a little more. Always the dutiful commander. I lift my head to whisper back at him, and my lips accidentally brush his jaw when I say, "I don't care."

"May I cut in, Your Majesty?"

I turn toward the intruder, angry.

It's Conde Tristán. He is so wide-eyed with nervousness that I soften at once.

Hector says, "Of course, Your Grace. Her Majesty and I were just discussing some of the finer points of security, but our conversation is finished." He spins me toward the conde, and I catch one last glimpse of his unreadable face before Tristán traps me in his arms and Hector drifts back into shadow.

The bolero is picking up speed now. "I can't imagine that anyone would risk God's wrath by trying to harm you during his own holiday," the conde says.

I don't care to discuss my safety anymore. "How is Iladro?"

He brightens. "Much better, thank you. He can only eat small portions, and he remains weak, but he's better every day. I pray for a full recovery. If God can heal Lord Hector so thoroughly, surely he has some mercy to spare for my herald."

"You are very devout then?" I crane my neck, looking for Hector, but I can't find him. I know he watches me, though. I can feel it.

"Only in recent years. Since my father's death, I've taken

great comfort in weekly services, most especially the holy sacrament of pain. The slight discomfort of a thorn prick is very meditative and calming. It helps me exist in the present moment, helps me forget the stresses of ruling a countship."

He could not have answered more perfectly if I had coached him myself, and I stare at him in suspicion.

"Does Selvarica have its own monastery?"

"No. But it would be my life's greatest legacy to establish a Monastery-at-Selvarica. I've been working on it. So far, we've been unable to attract a head priest to our tiny countship."

"Why not?"

"Honestly, I can't imagine. We're remote, I suppose. But Selvarica is the most beautiful place in the world. A lush green island, surrounded by sea the color of blue quartz. Never too warm, never too cold. The mountain peaks trap enough rain-clouds to provide water year-round. Waterfalls tumble from verdant cliffs into icy pools. Flowers grow everywhere. Truly, Selvarica is God's own garden."

"It sounds lovely."

His voice grows husky. "I would love to show it to you someday."

I return his intent gaze without flinching. We are the same height, which is a nice change. Hector and Mara and Ximena are all unusually tall, and it seems as though I'm always cran-ing my neck.

I say, "I may pay a state visit. The Quorum has suggested I tour the country after hurricane season. They would like to make a very big deal of it. Lots of fanfare."

He laughs. "You sound as though you despise the idea."

I grin. "I've considered making unreasonable demands. Just to punish them for the thought. Like refusing to ride in a mere carriage. Only a litter will do!"

"And trumpets. A queen should be heralded for the entirety of her journey."

"And chilled fruit, which would be near impossible to provide during a long journey. Imagine the fit I could have."

"Also, a change of clothes every two hours. A queen should stay fresh at all times."

The song ends, and I'm surprised to realize that I enjoyed our dance.

Conde Tristán raises my fingers to his lips and kisses them. "Thank you, Your Majesty." Before dropping my hand, his gaze turns mischievous. "You are not as terrible a dancer as your reputation indicates."

I laugh. "Just a little bit terrible, then."

He has a wonderful smile, with eyes that shine. "A little bit," he agrees. "But you forgot to step on my feet." With that, he whirls away and disappears into the crowd.

I look around for Hector again and spot him near a drink table. He chats easily with a young woman I don't recognize. She wears a soft green gown, and her clear skin sparkles with metallic powder. A long black lock drapes from the mound of luxuriant hair piled on her head, across her bare shoulder.

I stare at her with dejection. I'll never be so lovely.

Lord Liano claims me next. He is oafish and wide gazed, his sweaty lip as protuberant as ever, which makes him appear stunningly stupid. I listen with heroic patience as he regales me with the tale of an epic hunt for wild javelinas, which he lovingly describes as piglike creatures that roam the scrub desert of his brother's countship. When he attempts to mimic the chattering noise that javelinas make by rubbing their tusks together, I am forced to conclude that, indeed, sometimes the impression of a man's look and bearing holds true.

I hope Conde Tristán will claim me next—he asked me for two dances, after all—but Conde Eduardo finds me first. He is rough and jerky, and his hand on mine is too tight, his beard oil too pungent. I plaster a game smile on my face, but it wavers when I notice Hector dancing beside us, the lovely green-gowned creature in his arms. They seem to have an easy conversation interspersed with much laughing, though he looks over her head occasionally to check on me, always the devoted guard. I can't mask my relief when the song ends.

After thanking Eduardo, I catch Hector's eye and gesture toward the nearest refreshment table to let him know where I'm headed. Though it lies only a few steps away, I decline three offers to dance during the short journey, saying that I'm still healing from my ordeal and need to pace myself, but thank you so very much for the invitation.

A servant offers a glass of chilled wine, and I accept with grateful despair, knowing that a new taster now risks his life for me. Everything at the gala has been thoroughly tasted, hours earlier, and then again right before bringing it out.

As I sip, I glimpse Mara between dancing pairs. She twirls, laughing, and I smile to see her having such a good time. She is beautiful in a light yellow gown that sweeps into a slight train behind her. It's the plainest gown in the hall, without a stitch of embroidery or even a tiny pearl. But the simplicity suits her well, and the women around her seem gaudy by comparison.

"Mara seems to be enjoying herself," says Hector in my ear, and I hope he doesn't notice my tiny jump.

"She deserves to have a good time. As do you." I gesture toward the floor. "You should dance. Have fun. If your injury allows it, I mean." I can't deny him a little celebration. He works so tirelessly on my behalf.

He starts to protest, but I cut him off. "Don't worry," I say. "I'll protect you from harm. I stand ready to jump to your defense."

He laughs, and I love the sound. "I'm very content to enjoy the festivities from here," he says. "Is that Belén dancing with Mara?"

I crane my neck just as the pair shifts, revealing the face of her partner. Even from a distance, there can be no mistaking the patch over his eye. "Yes, that's him." I have a sudden urge to march over there and throw my wine in his face for what he did to my friend years ago.

"Well, they seem to be familiar," Hector says. "They're easy with each other."

His words check me. Hector is right. Mara chatters, and Belén laughs in response. Then the two glide behind a wall of dancers, obscuring my view.

"They are very old friends," I tell him. I suppose that if Mara can forgive Belén so thoroughly, maybe I can too.

I catch a movement in the corner of my eye and turn to see Lord Liano bearing down on me, his purposed stride a stark contrast to his vacuous gaze. Again I look around for Tristán, hoping he can save me from another disastrous turn with Liano, but he is nowhere to be found. "Oh, God," I mutter.

"What is it?" Hector asks.

"Please walk with me. I need some air. The gardens, maybe?"

16

HECTOR offers an arm, and I accept gratefully. We turn at the same moment Lord Liano calls out, "Your Majesty!"

"Keep walking," I say under my breath.

Hector snickers. "I take it your first dance together did not go well?"

"I learned that the best place to spear a javelina is in the throat, just above its chest."

"Aahh. Well, if you ever find yourself needing to ignore him, ask him about the time he stumbled upon a mother puma in her den. He's good for half an hour, uninterrupted."

"I'll remember that. Thank you."

The double doors to the gardens stand open for fresh air. As we step into the night, onto the winding paver path, I breathe deep of the sweet scent of yellow night bloomers. They are like a weed, the way they twine around trellises and ferns. Unchecked, they'd choke everything around them. But we tolerate them, cultivate them even, because at night they spread their weblike petals wide, proudly showing off stamens that glow brighter than fireflies.

"Hector, would you mind . . . that is, do you think it's safe for me to walk alone for a bit?"

"I think so, yes," he says with obvious reluctance. "It's an interior garden, and I have guards stationed around its perimeter. It's also best for propriety's sake that I stand guard where everyone can see me. But promise you'll remain within yelling range?"

"Of course."

He squeezes my arm and lets me go. And as I meander through the garden of tiny stars, I feel heady—from my glass of wine, from the cool breeze on my skin, from the touch and scent of the man I just left behind. A fountain tinkles nearby. Dimmed laughter and music curl around me.

The palm beside me rustles unnaturally. I hear hurried whispers, heavy breathing.

Surely there is no danger. Everyone was searched for weapons, and guards watch every entrance. But my mouth is dry and a slight tremor sets my fingers twitching as I check my Godstone for telltale cold. Nothing.

I reach out, and with the tip of my finger I move the palm fronds aside.

A man stands in a cavern of star-pricked foliage, his back to me. He is locked in a passionate embrace with someone else, someone smaller whose delicate arms ring his neck.

I can't help the giggle that bubbles from my mouth.

They whirl at the sound, and their faces are pale and stark among the dark greenery. I gasp with recognition.

It's Conde Tristán. Encircled in his arms is the herald, Iladro.

They stare at me, horrified. I want more than anything to run away, but shock freezes my feet.

The conde's features soften into resignation. Without breaking my gaze, he says, "Iladro, dear, why don't you go calm your stomach with a glass of water?"

The herald disengages himself, manages a panicked half bow in my direction, and flees toward the audience hall.

We are silent for what seems like an eternity. Finally Conde Tristán says, "Your Majesty, I swear on the *Scriptura Sancta* that everything I have told you is true."

Indignation helps me find my voice. "That I am stunningly beautiful? That you intend to court me?"

"Yes."

"Do you even *like* women?"

"Not in that way, no. But one doesn't have to be a lover of women to understand your quality."

I'm shaking my head. "Everything you said is a lie. Maybe not the words themselves, but your intent has been to deceive me." And deceive me he has. I'm so naive.

The conde lowers his head, whispering, "I'm sorry, Your Majesty. Truly." He sighs hugely. "Iladro is the love of my life. But Conde Eduardo has been gradually annexing my land, and my countship is in desperate need—"

"I suggest you retire for the evening."

The conde starts to protest but changes his mind. He nods instead. Then he slips out of the grotto and disappears.

Suddenly I'm not just alone but lonely. I stand there a long time, swallowing against tears, taking deep breaths to calm the fluttering humiliation in my breast. I don't blame Tristán for wanting to help his people during hard times. But it does sting to know that a man can't find me desirable. Maybe no one will. Maybe not ever.

Certainly not Hector.

I wipe under my eyes to make sure my kohl has not smeared. Then I throw my shoulders back and lift my head high. Thus collected, I return to the entrance and to my personal guard.

He makes no effort to disguise his relief at seeing me. "I saw Conde Tristán," he says. "He left in quite a hurry. Didn't even notice I stood here."

"We . . . we quarreled."

"I'm so sorry."

I can't bear to be pitiable before him, so I wave it off. "It was nothing."

But he is not fooled. When I take his offered arm, his free hand settles atop mine and squeezes gently. "Go back inside and dance," he insists.

"What?"

"Have a good time. Dance with as many suitors as possible. Let them flatter you outrageously." He's so intent, his voice urgent.

"But none of it will be real. None of them will want *me*. My throne, yes. Prestige. A conquest. But not me."

Silence stretches between us, and I realize I could not have given him a better opening to pay me ridiculous compliments.

It probably sounded like I was begging for them.

"Elisa . . . I—"

"You're right. I'll go back inside and do my queenly duty." I force brightness into my voice. "Who knows? Maybe Lord Liano has hidden depth of character."

He sighs. "I hear he once chose a short spear for the hunt instead of the crossbow, just to give the javelina a fighting chance."

"A man of true compassion!"

"He'd be glad to tell you about it."

For the rest of the evening, I play the role of queen. I down another glass of wine to dull the sharpness in my chest, fix a smile on my face, and work hard to not step on anyone's toes. I dance with everyone who asks, and I never lack partners. I'm told that I am radiant, that I have a beautiful smile, that I am a gifted dancer. They compliment me on my choice of gown, my speedy recovery, my political savvy. They extend condolences on my recent ordeal. They offer their personal services, suggest trade policy, beg me to raise taxes further, beg me to lower taxes.

Later, when I am finally back in my suite, Ximena helps me out of my gown. "How was it?" she asks. "Did you have a good time?"

I have run out of banalities and niceness. I have nothing to spare. "Fine," I snap. "It was *fine*."

"Will it cheer you up to know you have a letter from home?" She pulls a tiny leather canister from her apron pocket and waves it at me. "Just delivered from the dovecote."

She drops it into my palm, and my heart does a little flip when I recognize the de Riqueza sunburst stamped into the leather. From Papá. Or maybe my sister. I haven't spoken to either in over a year, except for a few brief messages like this one, via pigeon. I'm eager for news of home.

No, I correct myself. Joya d'Arena is my home now. My time in Orovalle feels like it happened to another girl, a different Elisa.

I open the canister, break the wax seal with a fingernail, and unroll the parchment. I'm glad to see my sister's careful and lovely script.

> *Dearest Elisa,*
>
> *Word reached me of your grave injuries. I'm glad to know you are recovering well. I pray for you every day.*
>
> *I write because Papá's council has asked that I begin seeking a husband in earnest. They suggest I choose from among Joya d'Arena's most influential nobility to further strengthen ties between us. Ximena has written to me about Lord-Commander Hector of the Royal Guard and has suggested I consider him. There is no opinion I trust more than yours. Please tell me: What kind of man is he? Would I do well to open negotiations with him? Your earliest reply is most appreciated.*
>
> *Papá sends his love.*
>
> *Alodia*

It feels as though someone is standing on my chest.

"Elisa?"

I look up from the parchment now crushed in my fist. Ximena studies me carefully while the guards exchange worried glances.

I can't force the proper platitudes to my lips.

You knew this was coming, Elisa. Of course he will marry, and marry well. It is right and good that he become a prince consort. Would you rather Alodia marry someone who does not feel like family already?

"I need parchment," I whisper. "And quill and ink." I can't seem to remember where I put them.

Fernando rushes to fetch the items from my writing desk. Ximena takes a step toward me, but I back into the atrium, shaking my head. I can't even bear to look at her for wondering if she knew all along that I was falling in love with him.

By the time Fernando enters with the writing implements, my fist is to my lips, as if it can tramp down the nausea roiling in my belly. *Get control of yourself.* I take a deep breath. Then another. I force my jaw to unclench. Then I grab the ink and parchment and set them on the vanity.

But my fingers tremble and my script is jerky as I write.

Dearest Alodia,
Hector is the best man I know. You could not do better.
Elisa

I roll it tight and slide it inside Alodia's canister. I hand the canister to Fernando with instructions to send it immediately.

As he leaves, Ximena says, "Do you need to lie down for a moment? Maybe a glass of wine?"

"I'd like to be alone, Ximena," I say in the deadliest whisper, and she lowers her head and backs away.

But alone is such a nebulous state when one is queen. Knowing the guards surround me, I pull the canopy closed and cry as softly as I can manage it.

It is near morning when an idea finally dams the flood of tears.

17

I scoot off the bed and throw a robe around my shoulders. Ximena is already awake, though her long gray braid is sleep mussed. She sits near the balcony, taking advantage of the morning light to work on a tapestry. She looks up at me. "Is everything all right now?"

"I need to dress quickly. No time for a bath."

"We need to wash your face. With luck, people will think you had too much to drink and will not guess you spent the night crying."

At least she doesn't ask me why. "Fine. Is Mara awake yet?"

"She didn't get back until very late." She gathers the material in her lap and plops it into a basket near her chair.

"Let her sleep a few more minutes, but we'll have to wake her soon."

"Are you going to tell me—"

"Soon." I don't even want my own Royal Guard to know what will transpire next. My idea hinges on secrecy.

I send a guard to fetch the mayordomo while Ximena

begins sifting through my wardrobe. She holds up a riding gown; it has a split skirt and a tight black vest. I never ride, but I sometimes wear it when I need to feel strong.

I nod approval. Ximena has read my mood well.

I have just finished dressing, and Ximena is combing my hair in the atrium, when the mayordomo arrives. His dressing robe hangs crooked, and the left side of his head is sleep plastered into a solid wall of hair.

"Your Majesty?" he says, out of breath. "The guard said your summons was urgent."

"Thank you for coming so quickly. Tell me, is Conde Tristán of Selvarica still here in the palace?" Ximena's face in the vanity mirror shows perfect composure, but I sense increasing tension in her brushstrokes.

"He filed a departure notice very late last night." He shakes his head with disgust. "Who departs during Deliverance week? And on the night of the gala! It was most untoward, and I—"

"But Tristán is still here? He hasn't left yet?" I realize I'm wringing my skirt in my right fist. I release it and flex my fingers.

"I don't know."

"Find out. *Now*. If he hasn't yet departed, tell him I require his presence immediately in my chambers."

"Yes, Your Majesty." He executes a quick bow and hurries away on slippered feet.

Ximena puts her hands on my shoulders and makes eye contact with me in the mirror.

"I'll explain soon," I whisper. I just hope the conde has not had time to gather his entourage and flee from last night's encounter.

Fortunately, I do not wait long.

When a guard escorts the conde into the atrium, Tristán drops to one knee and bows his head, refusing to meet my eyes.

"Rise."

He does, and I note his traveling clothes: leather breeches, a loose blouse, a utility belt.

"Going somewhere so soon?"

He focuses on a point just above my head. "Yes, Your Majesty. I thought it prudent."

"You were going to leave without saying good-bye."

He looks sharply at me, really looks, not bothering to hide his confused suspicion.

I press on. "I had thought . . . or maybe just *hoped* that we had found a sort of connection, you and I."

"Your Majesty, I . . . I'm sorry, but I thought . . . last night . . ."

"Your Grace." I stand from my stool and offer him my arm. "Let's go somewhere private where we can talk." To Ximena, I say, "Wake Mara. I need that room."

She hurries away. The conde and I follow at a slower pace.

When we enter the austere attendant's room, Mara is sitting up in bed, rubbing bleary eyes. She and Ximena start to leave, but I hold up a hand. "Stay." I close the door behind me.

"Keep your voices low," I say. "My Royal Guard listens close for danger, and I do not care for them to know about this."

"About what, Your Majesty?" the conde says wearily, looking at the floor. "Why am I here? If you're going to punish me, or exact some kind of revenge, please get it over with."

Ximena and Mara exchange a puzzled look.

Something about his frankness pleases me. I say, "Conde, I need your help."

His gaze snaps to mine. "Oh?"

"How many people know about you and Iladro?"

"Not many. My mother. A few attendants."

"Good. I need a reason to . . ." I almost say "escape." "To leave the city and go south. I also need the Quorum—no, the whole country—to believe I am very serious about selecting a husband."

His eyes flash with understanding. "You want to pretend we are betrothed."

"Or at least pretend to begin negotiations. Which, of course, would require that I visit Selvarica and inspect your holdings."

"Of course. I assume that, after an acceptable period of time, we would regretfully conclude that we are not as compatible as we had hoped?"

"It might be a long period of time. But yes."

"And if I don't agree to this? Will you expose me for the liar I am?"

"No."

He stares at me.

"I'm not interested in that. If you don't want to help me, you are free to go." I shrug nonchalantly. "Though if you tell any-one about this conversation, I will destroy you."

He cracks a relieved smile in response to my threat, which also pleases me. But then he leans against the frame of Mara's bunk, and his eyes turn thoughtful. "You do realize that a broken betrothal would be a huge blow to my countship's status? Everyone would assume the worst, that you found me lacking in some way."

"I am prepared to offer something in exchange."

"I'm listening."

"Despite our incompatibility in marriage, you and I will discover a deep mutual respect and affection. I will be so taken with the good people of Selvarica, with their character, their potential to evolve into a great countship, that immediately upon returning to Brisadulce I will nominate your house to the open Quorum position."

He gapes at me. "I . . . I hardly know what to say."

"I also want two votes once you are a Quorum lord. Two separate occasions of my choosing when you *must* vote with me on an issue, regardless of your own feeling on the matter."

He begins to pace. I force myself to remain silent and still, giving him time to consider. I glance at my ladies. Mara is wide-eyed, whether from surprise or alarm I cannot tell. But Ximena wears a soft, approving smile, and when I catch her eye, she gives me a barely perceptible nod.

At last he says, "This seat on the Quorum. It will be permanent, yes?"

I nod. "To be passed down through your heirs. Only the military seats are not inherited."

"You think you can get the votes to approve my nomination?"

"I have one vote assured. I only need one more, and I have a few ideas on how to get it."

"So you can't guarantee that I will have a seat on the Quorum."

"I guarantee that I will try my best. Even if my nomination does not pass—which is unlikely—you will be forever marked as one who has the queen's favor."

He stops pacing, runs a hand through his hair, looking suddenly sheepish. "We could marry in truth, you know," he says. "You needn't offer me the concession of a Quorum position. I think . . . I think we could be good friends, you and I. Marriages are built on less."

Softly I ask, "Could you give me another heir?"

"Probably?"

I stare at him.

He sighs. "So, a fake betrothal in exchange for a Quorum nomination. And two votes if I take office."

"That is my bargain."

"Done."

I reach out and clasp his offered hand. He returns my smile with a delighted grin that lights up his whole face, and I think, briefly, what a tragedy it is for women everywhere that he cannot love them.

Then I add, "This is a secret bargain, witnessed only by my two ladies. It's fair that you be allowed two witnesses as well. Would you like me to repeat my offer in front of anyone?"

He doesn't even think about it. "I trust you."

"Then we are agreed. Would you mind postponing your departure? I would like to inform the Quorum of our imminent betrothal and give the nobility the opportunity to fawn over you."

He bows. "Of course, Your Majesty."

"Please. Call me Elisa."

We make preparations quickly. Tristán's people and mine will travel together in state. But there are certain precautions we must take, and Hector and Tristán spend long hours together, going over routes and formations and personnel.

Hector alone of the Royal Guard knows our betrothal to be a pretense.

We have a heated discussion about whether Storm the Invierno should accompany us. Ximena insists that he is too easily recognizable. But Father Alentín believes his knowledge could be useful. I point out that I would rather have him where we can keep an eye on him. When Hector promises to keep him cowled and hidden in a carriage, and Tristán vouches for the discretion of everyone in his entourage, we agree that Storm will come.

He is only too willing. He knows the truth of it: that I go in search of the *zafira*.

I cancel the Quorum meeting, the one I would have used to explain my foray into the prison tower, pleading eagerness to spend time with my potential husband. I tell Conde Eduardo that Tristán and I used the prison tower to begin negotiations, that with so many visiting the palace for Deliverance week, we both preferred privacy. It's a weak lie, and by the narrowing of his black eyes, I know the conde does not believe me.

But he does not press. He merely says, "It's not too late to change your mind and do what is best for our kingdom. I'm confident you'll come to understand that one of the northern lords would be more suitable."

I thank him for his counsel and assure him that I will make a considered choice.

The night before our journey, I am grateful for the darkness and solitude. I lie awake a long time, thinking of Alejandro. Though I've no intention of marrying Tristán, everyone *thinks* I do. A tear trickles down my cheek to think how easily displaced my late husband is. His presence touches everything around me. I see him in the dark woods and jeweled tones of his chamber, in the newly commissioned portrait in the Hall of Kings, in the face of his son. But the court gives him up so easily. When I do finally marry, it feels as though even the phantom memory will be well and truly gone.

"Elisa?" I feel the mattress dip as a tiny form crawls toward me on the bed.

I lift the blankets to let Rosario slip underneath. He worms close, and I wrap an arm around him.

"Does your nurse know you're here?"

He shrugs against me, which means she does not. I press my lips to his forehead.

"You're going away again," he accuses.

"Yes."

"I want to come."

Excuses run through my head. But I settle on the truth, as I always seem to, with him. "Bad people are trying to hurt me. So I can't have my heir travel with me. I need you to stay here and be safe."

"Are they going to kill you?"

"I hope not. I'm going to try my hardest to live."

"Hector will protect you."

I smile. "Yes, he definitely will."

"Will you come back?"

"I'll try my hardest to do that too. I promise."

He shifts, and his cold bare feet knock my leg, but I know better than to pull away. He says, "You always keep your promises."

I catch my breath. It's something I told him long ago. Little did I know at the time how important it would be to him, a boy to whom promises had never been kept. "I do."

He is quiet for such a long time that I think he must be sleeping, but then he whispers, so softly that I have to strain to hear, "I don't want to be king."

It's like a dagger in my chest, because if feels like failure. Of course he doesn't. Of course he's terrified. I know how hard it is to be frightened for so long. *I'm so sorry, Rosario.*

After a moment spent collecting myself, I say, "I think that if you decide you want to be king, you will be the greatest king in the history of Joya d'Arena. But I won't make you. You don't have to." My court would have collective apoplexy if they heard me say this, but I could never force the boy.

He sniffs. "Promise."

"I promise. But you have to promise me something too."

"What?"

"Promise me you won't discuss this with anyone until I get back." The last thing I need is for the country to start rumbling about an abdication. "Not a word. Also, if anything goes wrong, or if anything scares you while I'm gone, I want you to find Captain Lucio, Hector's second-in-command, and do exactly what he says. He will help you. If you can't find Lucio, go to Matteo. He's with Queen Cosmé's delegation in the dignitaries' suite."

His wide eyes gleam in the dark. "I promise."

I don't want to frighten him, but this is important. So I ask, "Who did I just say to find if something goes wrong?"

"Captain Lucio or Matteo."

"That's my boy." I pull the quilt up over his small shoulders. "How about you sleep here tonight?"

"Oh, all right," he says, as if it wasn't his grand plan all along.

The entire palace sees us off—servants, resident nobles, the city garrison. Conde Tristán's carriage leads the procession, followed by several guards on horseback, another carriage for my servants and supplies, and finally the queen's carriage, larger and more elaborate than the others, surrounded by even more guards on foot. The royal crest streams behind on pennants, and almost-sheer curtains hang in the gilt-framed windows.

But I am not in the queen's carriage.

I walk just behind it, surrounded by the conde's servants. I wear a rough cotton skirt and a shapeless blouse, a maid's cap pulled low on my brow. My skin is powdered to appear lighter, and my hair—my most distinctive trait—is plaited tight against my head and hidden under my cap.

General Luz-Manuel and Conde Eduardo stand on a balcony overlooking the main gate. The general is as cold and unreadable as always, but the conde seethes blackly. His eyes are narrowed, his jaw taut, his arms crossed. It's obvious that my last-minute excursion to Selvarica is not part of his plan, whatever it is. As we pass beneath him, under the palace portcullis, I force myself to look straight ahead lest I catch his eye.

Hector walks nearby, and from the crowd's perspective, I hope it appears as though he guards the queen's carriage. Through the almost-sheer curtains is the shape of a young woman sitting inside, a large crown on her head—my ruby crown, not my new one. The one made of shattered Godstones rides comfortably in my pack beneath the carriage bench.

Hector hired her. I don't know who she is or where he found her. And I don't want to know. She waves enthusiastically at the crowd, and I'm terrified for her, this decoy Elisa. I scan the onlookers for danger, thinking of all the ways to kill a person. It would be so easy.

Just like the day of my ill-fated birthday parade, we make our way down the Colonnade toward the city gate. To my left, a townhome towers above us, its high windows sparkling in the sunshine. An archer could hide up there, send an arrow spearing into the carriage, and then slip away in the chaos. And though the crowd is not as thick as it was for my birthday parade, enough strangers press close that I find myself flinching away. Any one of them could be carrying a dagger.

This is what it's like to be Hector and Ximena, I realize. Always terrified for someone else, always distrusting, imagining weapons and foul intentions where there are none. Is that why Hector is so stoic and hard? Why Ximena keeps so many thoughts to herself? Because it's the only way to deal with existing forever on the cusp of disaster?

My guard and my guardian.

Hector said that damage is the price of royalty, but maybe my price is so high that others will be forced to pay it. Maybe he and Ximena are the damaged ones. And Mara. And Rosario, who is afraid to be king.

It's a very long walk.

But when the gate and the desert beyond come into view, my heart starts to pound, not with terror but with excitement, maybe even happiness. I'm desperate to get beyond these walls, into open air and sunshine. I can't wait to feel the crush of sand beneath my boots, for the dry air to whip my hair against my cheeks. I hope we trade our horses for camels somewhere along the way. I miss their soft, long-lashed gazes and their resolute plodding. I even miss the scent of camel-dung campfires.

At last we pass through the shadow of the great wall and into the light. Our road leads south along the coastline, but to our left stretches my desert, vast and golden and shimmering with heat. Looking at it, my heart is so full I can hardly stand it. I feel freer, lighter, with each step we take away from the city. I want to skip or run or reach my arms wide to the openness of the sky and breathe it all in. I settle for kicking at bits of sand and gravel on the highway.

Hector sidles over and peers down, an odd look on his face. "I've never seen you smile like that before," he says.

I hadn't realized I was smiling. "Just glad to be outside, I guess. And look at that desert! Isn't it beautiful?"

"Yes," he says softly. "Beautiful."

"Did you know that some nights, if you time it just right, you can glimpse the Sierra Sangre at sunset? As the sun dips below the ocean, the eastern horizon flashes red, bright as blood. It's amazing."

"No, I didn't know that."

"You should look for it tonight. And in the afternoon, when it's the hottest, all the colors of the world coalesce where the sand edges up against the sky. Like a ripple of light."

"You don't say."

I look up at him sharply, wary of the amusement in his voice. Is he mocking me? "Surely there's a place you love too? Somewhere you're always happy to go back to? Where you feel more yourself than anywhere else?"

As Hector considers, our procession shifts to the right to allow the steady stream of oncoming traffic—a few dusty riders, both on camelback and horseback, one small merchant caravan. They view the queen's carriage with wide eyes and keep their distance. Up ahead, Mara swings out of the servants' carriage to walk beside it. I don't blame her; I wouldn't want to be ensconced with Storm for any length of time either.

"Yes, there is such a place," Hector says at last.

"As your queen, I command you to tell me about it." I want to whip off my maid's cap, to expose my head to the sun and sky, but I don't dare. Everyone in our group knows who I am—their participation in the plan is crucial—

but the highway is too busy this close to the city.

"Well, since you command it," Hector says wryly, "I'll tell you about Ventierra, my father's countship."

For some reason, I'm feeling the need to tease. "Oh? Surely that tiny patch of dirt is nothing compared to this." I gesture toward the dunes.

He takes it in stride. "'That tiny patch of dirt' is made up of rolling hills, bright green during the rainy season, golden when dry. The grass is like an ocean, so long that it ripples on a windy day. From a distance, it shimmers like velvet." His eyes grow distant as he speaks, and the planes of his face soften. "Waves crash against the coastal cliffs, spewing geysers of white water into the air. Near the mouth of the river are tide pools—I spent hours and hours playing there as a boy. But nothing is more beautiful than a vineyard ready for harvest. Rows and rows of grapevines, dripping with frosty purple . . ."

"Ah," I say. "That painting in your quarters."

"Yes. I used to steal grapes off the vine when my father wasn't looking. I felt sorry for them, getting beaten and pressed, rotting into something that smelled bad. It seemed to me that grapes would rather be grapes than wine."

I laugh.

"What did I say?"

"Nothing. It's just that I've never seen *you* smile like that before."

Our gazes lock. The rest of the world drops away, and all I can think is, *God, I love his smile.* It melts the last few years off of his face, and I see the boy underneath, the one who scampered among tide pools and rescued helpless grapes. What happened to that boy? Alejandro, I suppose. And war. And me.

I say, "I'd like to see Ventierra someday."

His smile fades. "I would too."

"You miss it, then?"

He just shrugs.

I stare at his profile, which has gone flinty. It's his way, when he's trying not to feel too much.

"I didn't realize you were so homesick."

He whips his head around. "I didn't say—"

"You didn't have to."

He shrugs sheepishly. "I like my home in Brisadulce too."

"I'm glad."

Up ahead, the curtains of the queen's carriage part, and Ximena peeks out. I smile and wink. She starts to smile back, but then she sees Hector beside me and her smile fades. The curtain swishes back into place. I frown at the spot her head just vacated, wondering what she is thinking.

As evening burnishes the sand to copper, we bypass a busy way station of scattered adobe huts and palm-roofed stables in favor of making camp alone, well off the road and in the sand.

I peer into the queen's carriage for my pack and tent. Ximena sits beside decoy Elisa, looking stiff and out of sorts. The girl herself has wilted beneath her veil and crown, and pools of sweat collect under her arms. I wince in sympathy. "I don't think the crown is still necessary," I tell her. "Or the veil. This far from the road, why don't you open the curtains and cool off?" She and Ximena will sleep in the carriage, presenting a tempting target for any would-be assassin.

"Thank you, Your Majesty," she says in a shy voice. I haven't bothered to learn her name. I don't want her to become too real to me.

I spot my pack and tent beneath the bench and grab them. I call out to Hector, "Where do you want me to set up?"

He gestures toward a flat spot, saying, "We'll make a perimeter around you."

I flip open the tent roll, pull out the poles, and get to work. My fingers fly with motion memory, and I revel in the feel of it, the crunch of sand as I bear down with my poles, the sound of fabric flapping in the wind. I leave the entrance open, tied up at the side with loops for that purpose. I rummage through my pack for flint and steel, then toss the rest of the pack inside my tent. Time to get a cook fire started, if Mara hasn't already.

A shape looms before me, and I nearly drop my flint and steel.

Conde Tristán is staring at me, his eyes wide. "I don't think I've ever seen someone set up a tent so fast. I didn't know you could do that." Other tents are going up around mine, including a larger one to be shared by Belén and Alentín.

My grin is smug. "Did you think I spent my days as leader of the Malficio embroidering? Composing odes to the desert sunset, maybe?"

He runs his hand through his hair. "No. I guess I just imagined more . . . administrative tasks."

"I can also start a fire, skin a rabbit, forage for edible plants, tend minor wounds." It feels good to brag shamelessly. "Oh, and I can definitely scare something off by flinging a rock in its general direction with a sling."

Several paces away, Hector has removed the saddle from an antsy bay gelding and is toweling him down. He looks up from his work and catches my eye, a smug look on his face. Hector, at least, is unsurprised to find me so capable. He might even be a bit proud. It makes me feel warm all over.

Later as we sit around the campfire sipping Mara's soup—not jerboa, but a light broth made with lentils and dried vegetables—the sun dips into the distant sea. I'm not paying attention to see if the sky flashes red on the opposite horizon because I'm staring north instead. Though we are too far from Brisadulce to see its walls, a soft sphere of radiance against the black sky marks the spot. I think of the thousands of lanterns and candles now brightening my capital city. And I think, with a twist of despair, how I feel so much happier, safer, *abler* away from it.

But we haven't gone far the next day when Hector mutters, "I think we're being followed."

I snap my head up to look at him, then force myself to stare straight ahead. If indeed we are being followed, then it wouldn't do for the queen's Guard to be seen talking to a maid who looks uncannily like the queen.

I say, "Are you sure? This road is highly traveled."

"No. Just something to watch for now. But a group of riders has kept a steady distance behind us since we set off. They don't have carriages, and no one is on foot. So they should be traveling much faster than we are."

"Everyone knows I journey south. Maybe someone is curious. In fact we may attract quite a caravan along the way."

"Maybe." But his tone is unconvinced.

"Would it help for me to walk in front of the queen's carriage instead of behind it?" I say hopefully. I'm choking on dust, and I've had to tie my shawl across my nose on several occasions.

"It might," he says. "Though I hate to give up the advantage of having you covered in filth. No one would recognize you like that."

I can't help turning to glare at him. His lips twitch, but the amusement fades quickly. "We'll keep an eye on them," he says.

"No." I'm in the desert now. I know exactly what to do. "We'll do better than that."

"Oh?"

"If they're still behind us when we camp tonight, I'll send Belén to scout them."

"You've decided to trust him, then?"

"I trust his ability to scout." I think back to the day of Iladro's poisoning. It felt so natural to call on Belén for help. The moment required it, and we slipped back into our old roles as if nothing had happened. "And I dare hope the other kind of trust will come in time."

When we make camp, the riding party Hector spotted is still there, tiny black figures near the horizon. Other travelers come and go, but these riders stop when we do, make camp when we do. Their campfire glows as dusk fades to night.

I order everyone to forego campfires tonight, and we dine on jerky, dried dates, and flatbread. I don't want anyone to see us from a distance, to know that we hold council.

We sit in a rough circle with only the moon and stars for light. There are almost thirty of us, including Tristán's people, all of whom were personally vouched for. Even Storm dares exit the carriage to join us. The others eye him warily but make a space for him. He does not remove his cowl.

I stand and say, "Belén, come here."

He approaches without hesitation and drops to one knee.

I ask, "Do you still wish to swear fealty to me?"

His soft indrawn breath is the only indication that I've taken him by surprise. "I do," he says evenly.

"Then I would accept you into my service."

He reaches up with both hands and clutches the fabric at my waist, quickly, as if he's afraid I'll change my mind. It's intimate and unnerving, especially when the side of his thumb brushes across my Godstone, and I hear the whisper of drawn daggers somewhere nearby. But it's the traditional gesture of a newly sworn vassal, and it must be allowed.

Belén intones, "I swear my life and service unto you. I swear to protect you and to honor you. I am yours to command in all things. For as long as I live, your people shall be my people, your ways my ways, your God my God."

I take his hands and pull him to his feet while everyone in the group mutters, "Selah."

He towers over me. I can't help but stare at his eye patch. He was tortured. For me. Because he refused to give me up once he realized his mistake. On impulse, I pull him close and hug him tight.

He whispers, "Thank you, Elisa."

Behind him, I glimpse Mara's face. Her cheeks shine with moonlit tears.

I pull away, hoping I have not forgiven too easily. But it feels right to do it. "I need your help," I tell him. "Tonight."

"Anything."

When I explain about the riders following us, he nods, unsurprised. I don't even have to tell him what to do. He simply says, "I'll be back by morning." And he slips away into the darkness.

"Who do you think it is?" Mara asks, once he is gone.

I sit back down and cross my legs. "I suspect Conde Eduardo. He was displeased to hear of this journey and its purpose. He is set on me marrying a northern lord. And he knows I've been keeping things from him."

"He does not know about me, yes?" Storm says in his sibilant voice.

"That is one of the things I've been keeping from him."

"If they are the conde's people," Ximena says, "we might be able to use them to our advantage. Set a false trail, maybe."

"Exactly what I was thinking," I say.

"What if they're thieves?" says a female voice I don't recognize.

Hector barks a laugh. "Then they are poor thieves indeed," he says. "Five against all of us?"

He is right to be amused. He and Tristán could probably defeat five common thieves alone. What I worry about, what I don't say, is that they might be assassins. They might be observing, patient and cold, waiting for the right moment to creep into our camp.

Perhaps Hector is thinking the same thing, because he says, "Until we know for sure, we're doubling our watch. Elisa, will you ride in the servants' carriage tomorrow, out of sight?"

I open my mouth to protest, to say that I prefer my own two feet to a hot, bumpy carriage, but then I remember that I've decided to trust his judgment in these matters. "All right," I say. And it really is.

18

I'M awakened by a hand pressing across my mouth. I arch away from the intruder, pulse pounding, drawing breath through my nose. It's happening at last, what I have feared—

"Elisa!" comes Belén's whispered voice. "It's me."

I go limp with relief. He removes his hand, saying, "Shh!"

"What do you think you're doing?" I whisper furiously.

"I wanted to see if I could sneak past Tristán's sentries and the Royal Guard and into your tent."

"Oh." I push back my bedroll and sit up, then rub warmth into my arms. My guard is the most elite force in the country. Surely not just anyone could slip by them. Weakly I say, "Well, you *are* one of the sneakiest people I've ever known."

"I don't deny it." I can't see him in the dark, but I hear the smile in his voice.

"What did you find?"

My tent tilts precariously as he knocks the wall crossing his legs. "Five men trying to pass as desert nomads. By their clothing, you'd think they came from my own village. But the hair isn't right. It's too . . . careful. Coifed, even. And their horses are stout and sea bred. No colors, no markings, but their tack is high quality. Even the weave of their saddle blankets testifies to wealth."

"So they might be Conde Eduardo's men after all. Or the general's."

"I recognized one. I don't know his name, but I've seen him at the conde's shoulder. A very tall man, taller than me. Fine, straight hair slicked back with oil. He seems young at first glance, but I'd wager not. He has the look of experience about him."

I search my memory, cataloging the conde's advisers and attendants. There is only one I've never encountered. "You may be describing Franco," I say. "An elusive man. I don't know that I've ever spoken to him."

He pauses, shifts in his rear. "Elisa . . . you should know. If Humberto were alive, he would be very proud of you."

The hurt that wells up is so unexpected that it's a moment before I can speak. "Thank you," I manage. I have to redirect the subject. I'm not sure I want to talk about Humberto. "Did you overhear anything?"

"A tasteless observation about one of their mothers and her goat, which I will not repeat. One suggested they allow themselves to drop farther behind tomorrow. 'Out of sight,' he said. But the tall one—Franco?—said, 'We have to keep her in view. She'll make a move soon enough.'"

I loose a breath I didn't realize I'd been holding. "So we can reasonably conclude that they follow us, most likely on the conde's orders."

"I think so, yes."

I lie back down and pull the blanket up over my shoulders. "Go get some sleep. We'll let the others know in the morning."

"Yes, Your Majesty." He turns over on his knees, no longer bothering with stealth.

"And Belén?"

"Yes, Your Majesty?"

Maybe I *do* want to talk about him. A little. "Humberto would be proud of you, too. He always believed you'd come back to us." Saying his name aloud doesn't hurt as much as I thought it would. *Humberto*, I practice silently. *Humberto*.

A soft catch of breath. Then: "He had a way of believing in people long before they believed in themselves, didn't he?"

The entrance to my tent flaps closes, and he is gone.

As we breakfast on corn cakes fried in olive oil, Ximena and Hector argue about whether or not to split the group apart. Everyone else listens to their discussion, shifting awkwardly in the sand, trying to be invisible.

Only Storm has not joined us for breakfast; he does not dare leave the carriage in daylight.

"There is safety in numbers," Ximena insists. "Five men against our guard and Conde Tristán's warriors? It's no contest. And I'm not convinced they're out to cause trouble. It's likely the conde just sent them to keep an eye on Elisa. This journey does not play into his plans, and he's desperate to feel like he has some sort of control over the situation. The best thing we can do is stick together. Go to Selvarica as planned.

The more expectations we meet, the less suspicious we become to observers. But if we separate, Elisa is even more vulnerable."

Conde Eduardo is not the only one desperate to feel some sort of control, I muse as I chew on my corn cake. Ximena seethes with the frustration of being stuck in the carriage with the decoy queen, unable to keep close watch over me. She hates ceding complete responsibility to Hector.

"I hope you're right, Lady Ximena," Hector says. "But if he merely wanted to keep an eye on the queen, why didn't he insist on letting his own delegation travel with us? It doesn't make sense. And the presence of Franco has me concerned. He's a shadow adviser. No one knows anything about him. My instincts say all is not as it seems."

"We should have traveled with a larger party," Ximena says.

Hector shakes his head. "I don't trust enough people to form a larger party. Better the enemy out there than here among us."

Tristán has been listening quietly, sipping from a waterskin at regular intervals. He ties it off, sets it in the sand, and gains his feet. He does it gracefully, in such a way that all our eyes are drawn to him. His beautiful face is grave when he says, "My father was killed on a journey such as this. It's the perfect opportunity, you see. Anyone can be blamed. So no one ever really is. I still don't know who killed my father."

Everyone is silent. I say, "What do *you* advise?"

He shrugs. "I don't know. Caution, I guess. I think the Lady Ximena is overly optimistic to hope the conde merely wants you observed. But I'm also not convinced that splitting off would be safer for you."

I take a deep breath. I have to make a decision. And it's one that could lead to someone's death. Mine, or decoy Elisa's, or someone I care about. I used to make these kinds of decisions all the time, when I was only a desert rebel. I would have expected to become accustomed to it.

"We have a plan for splitting the group if necessary, right?" I say.

Hector nods. "We do. But we can't do it in open desert. We need to reach a village or trading post. Better yet, a large port like Puerto Verde."

"Then we continue on as we are for now. Belén, you will observe them every night, so long as you feel you can get there and back undetected."

He ducks his head obediently. "I can do it."

"I'll reevaluate when we reach a trading post."

We break off to pack up camp. Ximena glowers as she returns to the decoy carriage.

As I'm rolling up my tent, Hector comes up beside me. "Tonight," he says, "I'll sleep outside your door. We'll see if Belén can get by *me*."

I freeze, and my fingers dig into the tent fabric. Humberto used to do the same thing, to protect me from the others. I look into Hector's eyes. They're steady and fierce, but I can't tell what he's thinking. I could always tell what Humberto was thinking.

Hector is so much more complicated, and though he is less a mystery to me than he used to be, it feels like I could spend years peeling back the layers, trying to learn his whole person.

When I don't answer right away, he says, "Please let me do this."

One thing I am certain of: I trust him utterly. "Thank you," I say at last. "I'll sleep easier knowing you're there." And it's the truth.

Riding in the servants' carriage is as awful as I anticipated. In no time, my back and rear ache from being jostled against the wooden bench, and I am crazy with heat, for we deliberately chose carriages with only small, curtained windows. Sweat pools between my breasts and soaks my hairline, curling wisps of hair that have escaped my plaits.

There are two nice things about the arrangement, though. One is that Hector sits beside me, and our thighs brush with every jolt of the carriage. When one wheel hits a large stone, the carriage lurches to the side and I slide along the bench until our hips collide. The carriage rights itself quickly, but neither of us bothers to move away.

The second nice thing is that it gives me a chance to talk with Storm for the first time in days. He sits on the bench across from us, and he is so tall his head nearly brushes the roof. He has pushed back his cowl, and sweat glistens on his near-perfect skin. He fans himself with a dried palm frond.

"Are you enjoying our journey so far?" I ask with no small amount of amusement.

He hisses, and his green eyes spark with fury, or maybe loathing. I feel Hector's body go taut.

But I am no longer afraid of the Invierno. Logic tells me to consider him a threat, to remember that he might even be the assassin who stabbed me in the catacombs. But my instincts say otherwise. Perhaps it's his transparency that makes me feel safe with him. He is one of the few who never bothers to hide his true thoughts from me. Maybe the only.

"This desert is God cursed," he says.

"Your people do not seem well suited to it," I observe.

"Indeed not. Our skin cracks and dries; our feet blister. There are days it feels like my blood is boiling. I found much relief from the wretched climate in my cavern hideout."

I scowl at him. "And yet you marched an army of thousands across the desert to try to overrun us."

"Well, we skirted it to the north and south, but yes. It was a difficult journey. Hundreds perished from the heat alone."

"Your own country is much cooler by comparison?"

"Cooler. Wetter. Lovelier. Better, really, in every possible way than this forsaken blight that you rule."

I surprise myself by laughing.

I'm further surprised to see his lips twitch with a hint of a smile. He says, "So tell me, Your Majesty. Why do I have the displeasure of your company today?"

"I yearned to bask in the light of your empathy and good cheer."

"Sarcasm again. I thought you would tell me you had decided to hide like a frightened rabbit from the group following us."

"I'm hiding like a wise rabbit."

"Do you think they are the conde's men?"

"I do, though I can't be sure. One of them, a tall, quiet

man, has been seen with the conde before."

He starts forward so abruptly that our knees collide.

Hector's dagger is at his throat in an instant. "Back. Away."

Storm edges back, resumes fanning himself with the palm frond. His face becomes a mask of calm, even as he keeps a careful eye on Hector's dagger. He says, "Describe this person to me."

So I do, trying to remember Belén's description exactly: Tall, hair slicked back, young looking, a close adviser. Storm coils in on himself, growing tighter and tighter with the telling until he looks like a cornered cat.

"What is it? Do you know this man?"

"I have to get away," he says. "At the soonest opportunity. Leave me at the next trading post. No, leave me when we get to a large port. I'll need a place big enough to disappear in. I can make my way back—"

"Storm! Do you know this man?"

He inhales deeply, and the mask of calm settles over his uncanny features once again. "I do know him. Franco, right? That's not his real name. His real name, in God's language, is Listen to the Falling Water, for Her Secrets Carve Canyons into Hearts of Stone."

I gasp. "An Invierno!"

"A spy," Hector says.

Storm says, "If Franco learns I am here, he will kill me."

"Conde Eduardo has an Invierne spy working for him," I say, as though sending the words aloud into the world will help me believe them. "Does the conde know that Franco is an Invierno?"

Storm shrugs. "I don't know."

"Why didn't you tell me there was an Invierne spy in the employ of one of my own Quorum lords?"

"You didn't ask. Also, I've been underground for more than a year. I didn't know he had worked his way into the conde's inner circle."

"Have any others infiltrated my court?"

"Not that I know of. Your Majesty, you *must* let me go at the nearest port."

The carriage lurches again, and I grab Hector's knee instinctively. Storm's gaze drops to my hand, and he allows himself a secret smile. I draw my hand back, curl it into a fist in my lap.

"If I let you go," I tell him, "you would miss your chance to accompany us to the *zafira*. You won't get another. Only someone who bears a living Godstone can navigate there, remember?"

He runs a hand through his golden hair, considering. Now that I've become a bit used to the odd color, I find it more beautiful than alarming. "You make a good point," he admits.

"We could leave Storm behind," Hector suggests, and his gaze on our companion is unwavering. "It might distract Franco, give us a chance to put some distance between us."

That will never happen. I don't care to show my hand to Eduardo or the Invierne spy by revealing that I'm harboring the former ambassador. But the alarm on the Invierno's face is so satisfying that I pretend to consider it.

"If we left you behind, do you think you could get away?"

"No! Not if Franco sees me and recognizes me. He would stop at nothing to have me killed."

"So it *would* be sufficient distraction. They would abandon us for a while to chase after you."

He opens his mouth, closes it. I see the exact instant he recognizes that I've trapped him on purpose.

"This Franco. He must be very capable for you to be so frightened of him."

Fury rolls off him in waves. He says, "Your Majesty, he is a trained assassin."

I gasp. An Invierne assassin in my own palace all this time. In the employ of a Quorum lord. I never even suspected. What if he's the one responsible for the attempts on my life? If so, he will surely try again.

I say to Storm, "I suppose you ought to stay hidden in the carriage. Like a frightened rabbit."

He scowls.

"Don't worry," I add. "I'm sure I can find someone to keep you company."

"I'd rather be alone."

I turn my lips into what I hope is a decent approximation of his own smug grin. "I know."

"You would do well to hide, too," he says. "Franco is cunning and skilled. He is to murder what an animagus is to magic."

"Oh." I let my face fall into my hands, not caring that Storm will see and be amused. "Hector, we have to tell everyone about this."

He reaches over and gives my knee a squeeze. "Yes," he

murmurs, and I close my eyes to savor the sensation.

When we break for the noon meal, I tell everyone else what I learned from Storm. No one is more surprised and terrified than decoy Elisa, who clings to Ximena's arm with a white-knuckled grip. Her veil blurs her eyes and nose, and I'm relieved that I can't see the fear sparking there, even more relieved that we cannot make eye contact. Because I'm terrified for her, too.

"I can take care of him," Belén says. "Tonight. I'll slip into his camp and put a dagger to his throat."

"Storm said Franco is specially trained," I remind him. "He might be your match."

"I can take care of him," Belén repeats.

I know what Belén can do. Cosmé once told me the story of how she watched from a ridge as he snuck into an Invierno scout camp, slit the throats of three of their warriors, and disappeared like fog. Should I send an assassin to kill an assassin? I know so little about Invierne. Is this Franco an anomaly of their world? Or does he come from a long tradition of elite selection and training, like my own Royal Guard? I must ask Storm about it before deciding.

Tristán says, "I'd like to change my vote."

"Vote? What do you mean?" I ask.

"I think our company should split up," he says. "At the next port, you and a few others should go off in search of the *zafira* without the rest of us. We'll try to draw the assassin away. It's an opportunity you shouldn't pass up. They'll eventually figure out what happened, but you could buy yourself days, even weeks, of safety."

I nod, considering.

Ximena says, "I agree. It was one thing to be followed by the servants of a pouting Quorum lord. An assassin is another thing entirely." She looks down pityingly at the creature clinging to her.

"Hector, when is the soonest we could split off?" I ask.

"If we can make Puerto Verde, a few days south of here, I might be able to commission a ship. I know a captain who's scheduled to be in port soon with a batch of early-harvest wine."

Probably wine from his home in Ventierra. "Someone you trust, then?" I ask.

He nods. "With my life and honor."

"Then we continue on to Puerto Verde and split off there. We'll keep a close eye on Franco and his group until then and adapt as necessary." I look around at everyone. "Unless I hear convincing counsel otherwise?"

No one has anything to add.

"Then let's get moving."

As Hector and I climb back into the carriage, I glance northward, along the shimmering highway. It's strangely devoid of travelers, except for the small group following us. They are barely more than motes on the horizon. So there is no reason, I tell myself, no reason at all, to feel as if the assassin's gaze is boring holes into my back.

19

AFTER an evening meal of dried tilapia and dates, I sit cross-legged just inside the threshold of my tent while Ximena unpins my hair to let it down into a more comfortable sleeping braid. While she works, Hector comes over and flips out his bedroll in front of my door. He sets his pack beside it, shoving it down into the sand so that it doesn't tip over. I watch him carefully, fascinated by the way he moves. Every motion is so strong and sure.

When he pulls off his overshirt, my heart speeds up. His bare shoulders flex as he reaches beneath one arm to unlace his breastplate, and I swallow hard against the sudden moisture in my mouth as he lifts his breastplate over his head and sets it on top of his pack. His back is broad and taut with muscle, his waist trim. His sun-darkened skin shimmers faintly, and even though our camp is dimly lit, I see his scars, several of them. Most are tiny white lines, but one is larger and jagged, running diagonally across his lower back. I have an overwhelming urge to trace its length.

Instead I place my fingertips to my own mark, just left of the Godstone. Both of us, scarred. I wonder how he got his? I want to know about it more than anything. I want him to share that part of himself with me. I want—

Ximena's fingers grip my chin. She forces my gaze to hers and regards me sternly for a long moment. "It is a hard thing to be queen, my sky," she says.

I blink up at her. She's warning me. She wants him for Alodia, after all. And she's right. It would be a smart match.

But the very thought hollows out my chest, leaving me empty and aching.

Not trusting my voice, I just nod. She kisses my forehead, then goes off to attend her fake queen.

Ignoring Hector, I crawl into my tent and lie down on my bedroll with my head at the door. I lie there a long time, listening to him breathe.

Minutes later, or maybe an hour, I raise my head and whisper, "Hector?"

"Yes?" he whispers back.

His face is so near. Just the space of a breath away. I swallow hard. "My sister. Alodia. She has . . ." Oh, God, it's so hard to say, but I can't bear to pretend away such a huge thing. I inhale through my nose and try again. "My sister has made inquiries about you. In regards to a potential marriage agreement."

A long pause. Then, "Well, that would explain why she opened correspondence with me."

"Oh!" Pain, sharp and hard, squeezes my chest. Alodia already made her move then, before writing to me.

"She's like you, you know," he says. "Intelligent. Beautiful. But . . ."

"And will you . . . that is, are you considering . . ." I can't finish. I'm not sure I want to know.

He looses a shuddering breath. Then he says, "I will do whatever my queen commands."

Of course he will.

Something overtakes me, desperation maybe, and before I know it I'm slipping my hand past the tent flap. My fingers find his wrist. It shifts, and suddenly my hand is wrapped in one of Hector's much larger ones. Something about his gentle strength brings tears to my eyes.

It's on the tip of my tongue to tell him I love him. Instead I say, waveringly, "I told Alodia that you are the best man I know."

He gives my hand a squeeze. "Thank you," he whispers.

I fall asleep like that, my fingers woven with Hector's. Belén does not visit me. Or if he does, he chooses not to intrude.

Two days later, the desert cedes to rolling coastal hills. The sand still stretches east as far as the eye can see, but the hills along the coast mark the beginning of the southern holdings, the most temperate part of my kingdom. As we climb, the land beside the road turns from sand to hard dirt that is dotted with dry grass and the occasional scrub tree.

A day after that, we reach Puerto Verde. We crest a hill and there it is, laid out before us, a deep crescent bay the color of turquoise, carved into cliffs that protect the port from heavy surf. Cargo ships dot the water; I stop counting at twenty. There are even more small boats; dinghies and fishing vessels predominate, with a handful of flat pleasure barges.

A medium-size city hugs the cliffs, spills into the water on stilted buildings and docks. It seems that docks are everywhere, sending crooked fingers well into the bay. It's such a boisterous place, and from this distance, it takes a few moments for me to make sense of the bustle. Traders haggle and yell. Sailors load and unload ships. Clerks catalog piles of items. Everyone is busy, fast moving, loud. It's so different from the easy rhythm of Brisadulce.

My people, I think. I rule this city as surely as any other, and yet this will be my first time setting foot in it.

The road zags down the cliffs, and we hug the walls tight as we travel. I've never been afraid of heights, but I still can't bring myself to peer out the carriage window and over the edge to the bay far below. I gaze out the opposite window instead, and I catch glimpses of wooden platforms jutting out over our heads, of elaborate pulleys and winches used to haul cargo up the cliff face.

By the time we reach the bottom, word has gone out that the queen's carriage approaches, and the city goes still with reverent silence. We made no secret of our journey. Wasn't that the whole point of this excursion? To be openly courted by Conde Tristán? To explore a remote part of my kingdom in search of the *zafira* without raising unwanted questions? But my teeth clench and my neck and shoulders ache with strain. Everyone stares as we pass.

We reach an inn called the Sailor's Knot. A small crowd gathers on the porch to greet us—the inn staff, no doubt. I see smiles and nervous shifting and a few flags hastily embroidered with my royal crest. Our official itinerary declares a two-day recess here.

But our official itinerary, like my decoy queen, is meant to throw off potential ambushes. I'm glad. The place looks creaky, with a porch made of poorly joined driftwood and sandstone walls that drip random stains. As we pass by, though, I twinge with self-reproach, for the faces in the crowd deflate, then gaze after us with confusion and disappointment.

A block farther, we turn a corner and arrive at our actual destination, the King's Inn. Conde Tristán chose it specifically because its high third-story provides a good view of the surrounding buildings, and because its location one block from the main street makes the entrances less visible.

Our caravan noses into an alley that leads to a wide, dark stable. Hector and I jump from the carriage—Storm will stay inside until nightfall—and my guard moves quickly to establish a perimeter at our rear while Tristán's men unhitch the horses and begin unloading. When decoy Elisa steps from the queen's carriage, a cry of greeting goes up, from the few stubborn souls have followed us here. "Queen Elisa!" a voice calls. "Your Majesty!" yells another. Someone jostles my guard for a better view, but my men hold firm.

Decoy Elisa doesn't react, except to clutch her veil close to her throat. Led by Belén and Alentín, my ladies hustle her through the stables and into the back entrance of the inn.

I sling my pack over my shoulder, then grab a trunk from the queen's carriage, just like a real maid. I follow my decoy into the inn, feeling darkly wrong about leaving my people outside, ignored and unacknowledged. "I'll make it up to you," I whisper. Someday, I'll come back when I can be *me*.

The innkeeper, a gnarled man with a bald patch and a nervous smile, falls all over himself to accommodate us, arranging for hot baths and meals in our rooms. Decoy Elisa smiles vaguely at him and manages a few thank yous. When he finally leaves, she lies down for a nap, and I have my first bath in days.

"I do love baths," I say with a luxuriant sigh.

Mara laughs. "I know. Though truly, Elisa, you hardly need pampering out here. You seem perfectly happy to tramp about the desert in your nomad clothes, sweaty and dusty and sun darkened."

My smile dies on my face before fully formed. "I would be, if I weren't terrified for my life and the lives of those around me."

She doesn't say anything to that, just grabs my hand and squeezes.

Ximena approaches armed with a brush and several hairpins, but I put up a hand to ward her off. "Can we leave my hair down, please? Just for tonight? It's been tightly plaited the last few days, and my head *aches* from it."

She frowns and puts the hairpins and brush away with obvious reluctance. I stare at my nurse while Mara towels my hair dry and finger brushes it. Ximena has always been unperturbedly calm and stoic—I suppose she and Hector have that in common. But lately she seems downright surly.

Awhile later, my hair has dried in waves down to my waist, and I am dressed in a clean linen tunic belted over soft leather pants when the rest of our group files quietly into my suite. Two guards will remain outside to watch the door, but everyone else squeezes inside and finds a spot on the rugs or the beds to sit.

Hector is the last to arrive, and when he sees me, he freezes, then moves quickly to an empty space at the foot of decoy Elisa's bed, where he plunks down and stretches out his long legs.

Mara leans over and whispers in my ear, "I know you're charmingly naive when it comes to matters of the heart, but you just stopped him in his tracks."

I bring my knees to my chest, reach down to finger the hem of my pants. I whisper back, "I was about to tell myself I had imagined it."

She rolls her eyes at me.

Tristán moves to the center of the room to address everyone. "We're scheduled to be in town for two days," he says. "I'll meet officially with Puerto Verde's mayor tomorrow. The dowager queen, Rosario's grandmother, is also in residence here, on an estate in the hills, but reportedly in failing health and unable to offer us hospitality. I'll make an attempt to see her, for appearances' sake. Her Majesty Queen Elisa has unfortunately taken ill from a bad batch of oysters and will be unable to make any appointments."

Everyone titters with amusement.

"But we need to be prepared for contingencies, which

means lengthening our stay, or even cutting it short. I expect everyone to be alert at all times for changes in plan. Understood?"

I find myself nodding along with everyone else. Tristán has such a nice presence about him. Commanding, intelligent, worthy of my trust.

"Hector?" Tristán cedes the floor to the commander of my guard and sits down beside Iladro, who gazes at him with unabashed admiration. Now that I know they're lovers, it's so painfully obvious to me that I wonder how I didn't notice before.

Hector stands, saying, "I've confirmed that a ship is scheduled to dock here this week. It could be tomorrow or a week from now, depending on weather. The ship is well known to me, and I trust its captain and crew to protect the queen with their lives. So I suggest we wait for it before splitting off. Alternately, we could hire a different ship, or even a caravan."

As one, everyone turns to me for the ultimate decision. I say, "Belén, can you scout again tonight? I'd like to know if our new friends have followed us into the city and whether they take lodgings nearby."

"I can," he says.

"Then we will wait for Hector's ship, unless Franco makes a move."

"Or if he disappears entirely," Hector adds.

I nod. "If he is able to slip Belén's careful eye, I will consider that making a move."

"My offer to kill him stands," Belén says. "Just say the word."

"Thank you," I say, and it gives me a strange, twisty feeling to know I'm grateful for someone's willingness to kill for me. "But focusing Conde Eduaro's efforts in the wrong direction is too good an opportunity to pass up."

Tristán says, "Majesty, have you decided who goes with you when we split off?"

I take a deep breath. I have been dreading this moment. "Tristán, you and Iladro will of course continue with the caravan."

He bows his head. "Of course."

I need people who are used to rough travel, people I trust with my life. "There will be five of us, the holy number of perfection," I say. "Mara, you will come with me. And Belén. I confess I'm not sure what to do about you, Father Alentín. I'd like to have a priest with me as we track down the *zafira*. Your knowledge, your ability to sense the Godstone, could be crucial. But as Cosmé's ambassador, your absence would be noted."

The priest nods wearily, rubbing at his stumped shoulder as if aching with phantom pain. "I want to help you find the *zafira* more than anything," he says. "But I'm an old man now. And Her Majesty Queen Cosmé will be disappointed if I do not travel in state with false you and your soon-to-be betrothed. My ultimate loyalty must be to Basajuan now, you see."

I manage a sad smile. This is it, then, for us. Truly, he will never again be *my* priest. "Then I insist you go with the caravan," I tell him.

"I will pray for you every day," he says softly.

I swallow the lump in my throat. "Thank you."

"What about Storm?" Ximena asks.

"His knowledge may be useful. And he'll behave, so long as he's on the track of the *zafira*. He comes with me."

Ximena's eyes narrow. "He is nothing if not noticeable."

I nod. "I'll order him to cut and dye his hair tonight. That should help him pass cursory glances, at least." It will also give him something harmless to focus his fury on. I smile just thinking about it.

"I will go with you, of course," she says. "As your guardian—"

"No." There. I've said it.

Her black eyes fly wide. Not with surprise, I note carefully, but frustration and anger. She knew it was coming as much as I did.

"You are the queen's most visible attendant," I explain. "Mara has been my lady-in-waiting for less than a year. But you've been with me my whole life, and everyone knows it. You *must* be seen with my decoy."

"I have to go with you," she whispers. "Always. It is my duty. I was ordained for it by the Monastery-at-Amalur. Elisa, *it is God's will.*"

And that is exactly the wrong thing to say to me, because anger boils up in my throat, so thick I almost choke on it. "You will attend my decoy as if she were me." I enunciate each word, my voice sharp and hard. "You will protect her with your life."

Her chest rises as she draws breath to argue further, but Tristán wisely interjects. "So, you, Mara, Belén, and Storm. Lord Commander Hector too, I presume?"

"Yes. Hector. He's the one with the plan." I meet Hector's eye and note the slightest softening of his features. "The five of us."

Hector says, "We'll slip away at dusk disguised as highway traders. A small wagon waits for us in the stables, packed with a few odds and ends. We'll take it to the docks, ostensibly to trade with one of the ships there, but of course, we will never disembark. If something goes wrong, I have an alternate escape prepared through the sewer beneath the inn."

"Ugh," Mara says.

"We'll hope it doesn't come to that," Hector says. "And a few weeks from now, we'll rendezvous in Selvarica after finding the *zafira*."

"That's it, then," I say. "Everyone get a good night's sleep. Except Belén."

Belén's answering grin is as quick and bright as lightning. He is the first to slip out the door. Everyone else follows at a more leisurely pace.

I overhear Ximena saying, "Hector, a word with you, please?"

His face is expressionless as he follows her to a dark corner of my suite. She speaks softly to him, but her gaze is intent, her fists clenched at her sides.

Mara whispers, "You made the right decision."

"Yes." But I press my fingertips to the Godstone and pray. *Oh, God*, did *I make the right decision?* Ximena is the closest thing I've ever had to a mother. She has always wanted what is best for me. It feels strange to have pushed her away, like pushing away an extra limb or a small part of my soul.

It also feels a little bit like freedom.

"What do you think she's telling him?" I ask.

Mara covers her mouth to mute soft laughter, and I look at her, startled. "I'd bet all the saffron in my spice satchel," she says, "that she's threatening to hang him upside down by his toes if he ever takes your clothes off."

"Oh!" Mara talks about these matters with such casual ease, and I'm not sure I'm ready to hear it. Still, I study Hector's reaction very, very carefully. He has drawn himself to full height, chin raised, eyes hard.

"You could order her to tell you," Mara suggests.

"She would lie if she thought it necessary." As the words leave my mouth, their truth hits me full force. She has not always wanted what is best for me. She has always wanted what *she thinks* is best for me. And she has never hesitated to work around me or anyone else to accomplish it.

Hector is shaking his head. Ximena sticks a finger in his chest and hisses something at him. His eyes narrow, and he spits something in response. Then he turns his back on her, sweeps past Mara and me, and exits the chamber.

Ximena's cheeks are flushed, and her breath comes fast. I've never seen her so angry, so lacking composure.

A year ago, this would have terrified me. I stand and approach her.

Her gaze on me turns soft with longing, and I wish there was a way to convince her that separating myself from her doesn't mean I love her less. I give her the only peace offering I know. "Ximena, I'm ready for you to braid my hair now, if you don't mind."

She nods, swallowing. "Yes, my sky."

I wake to someone jostling my shoulder. My eyes fly open. A forefinger presses against my lips, and I hear, "Shh, Elisa."

"Belén?"

"Franco is coming here," he whispers. "Now."

Oh, God.

"The others accompany him, but at a distance," he adds. "He'll slip inside the inn, and his companions will block the entrances to prevent escape. Majesty, it's a siege."

I fling the covers away and sit up. "Where is Storm?"

"He came in not long after our meeting."

"And how long until sunrise?"

"About three hours."

My heart thumps in my chest. This is it. We have to make it happen now, or never. I glance at decoy Elisa, sleeping in the narrow bed against the opposite wall. She could die tonight. *I* could die tonight. *Please, God, keep us all safe.* The Godstone responds to my wispy prayer by sending dry heat up my spine. At least it has not yet gone cold. "Get Hector. I'll wake the ladies."

"Stay away from the windows." And then he's gone, as quickly and easily as a breeze.

I shake Ximena awake first and explain. She dives into her pack and pulls out a gleaming stiletto. I gulp back a wave of nausea. A stiletto is useless for cutting; its only purpose is to stab, hard and deep, even through armor. She grips the hilt with the ease of long familiarity.

"Wake Mara," she says. "And get into the corner beside the dresser."

"The girl?" I indicate decoy Elisa, who is softly snoring.

"Let her sleep." *Let her be a target*, she means.

"How . . . will you be able . . ."

"Rope ladder out the window, but we have to draw them toward this room first, and you must be gone by then."

I'm shaking Mara awake when the doorknob twists. Ximena strides unerringly toward the door, elbow bent to plunge her stiletto. But it is only Hector, followed close behind by Tristán.

Hector says, "Storm and Belén will meet us in the cellar. Do you have your things?"

"At the door beside you." I indicate Mara's and my packs propped against the wall. They are always ready to go, a habit from our time as desert rebels.

Tristán pushes past Hector and heads toward my sleeping decoy. To my shock, he crawls into bed with her. She startles awake, but he shushes her, drapes an arm around her shoulders, says, "I'm here to protect you, my lady."

But I realize the truth of it: They've brought an extra warrior to protect her, yes, and who would be surprised to learn that the queen's betrothed is sneaking into her bed?

"Tristán," I say. "Thank you. And please be careful. Eduardo opposes our match; I'm sure of it. If he can't kill me, he may go after you." And with those words, I fully embrace the staggering possibility that I am at war with my own Quorum lord.

"Just find the *zafira*," Tristán responds. "Joya d'Arena needs it."

Ximena hugs me close. "Be safe, my sky. Be wise. Remember God's words from the *Common Man's Guide to Service*: 'Blessed is he who puts the sake of others before his own desires.'"

Even now she can't help but warn me away from Hector. I pitch my voice low so that only she can hear. "I know you want him for Alodia."

Ximena goes rigid in my arms. "It's a good match," she whispers back.

"Elisa!" Hector hisses from the doorway. "We must go *now*!"

"Yes. A good match. Ximena, be well." I push her away. "Protect the girl."

Then Mara and I grab our packs and hurry out the door.

20

WE are met outside by four of my Royal Guard. "Go with God, Your Majesty," one says, and I barely have a chance to nod before Hector is hustling me down the corridor.

"Wait." I freeze in my tracks.

"Elisa, we must go!"

But it's not right. Too much depends on sleight of hand, on stealth, on chance.

I turn back up the corridor toward the guards. "You!" I say to the one who addressed me. "Find the mayor of Puerto Verde. Rouse him from sleep. Tell him his queen demands his presence right now. Tell him to bring his entire household. Tell him I expect him here within minutes."

"Yes, Your Majesty." He flees.

"And you, rouse every single person in this inn. Make noise. We want chaos. Lots of it. You two, stay and guard this door with your lives. Where are Tristán's guards?"

"One floor below," Hector says.

"Let's go." I jog down the hallway toward the stair, my pack bouncing at my back. Hector and Mara hurry after me. When we reach the floor below, I bang on doors and walls as we pass. Hector follows my lead, pounding with the pommel of his sword, producing a shocking, hollow boom that no one could possibly sleep through.

Belén intercepts us, gliding up like a wraith. "I lost track of Franco," he says. "He may be inside." Doors swing open, people spill into the hallway, sleep mussed and startled. "Is this your doing?" he asks, looking around in alarm.

"We need chaos. A reason to be in the corridor, more obstacles for an assassin."

He nods. Then he bangs on the nearest door and yells, "Fire!"

I take up the cry. "The stable is on fire!" Then, softer, to Belén, "Go light the stable on fire. Bring the whole city down on us."

His answering grin gives me shivers. "Meet you in the cellar," he says, and then he's gone.

We rush down the stairs, through another corridor, into the kitchens. We duck to avoid hanging brassware, skirt a huge stone bread oven, and find the trapdoor leading to the cellar. Hector grabs the iron ring and heaves it open, revealing steps that lead into dank gloom. It smells of pickled fish and spilled wine.

"Mara, you first," he says, and as she descends my heart is in my throat, for he has ordered her to go first in case danger lies in wait at the bottom.

After a moment comes her clear whisper: "No one here but Storm!"

Hector nudges me down and follows after, closing the trap-door over our heads. We are left in utter darkness. I step carefully, feeling with my toes for the edge of each step.

I hear the strike of flint and steel, and brightness sears my vision. It dies, then light flares again, softer and surer. Storm stands at the bottom of the stair holding a torch aloft, Mara beside him. His cowled head nearly brushes the ceiling.

He scowls. "You made me cut and dye my hair."

Surely he understands that we face greater problems? "I thought it would greatly improve your looks," I snap.

"Shorn hair is a sign of shame. You humiliate me greatly."

"I'll light a candle tonight in honor of your dead tresses."

His frown deepens. "Where is Belén?"

"Causing chaos. We wait for him."

It seems that we wait forever, and the space grows tight and hot. Food stores surround us—a few wine barrels, hundreds of tightly sealed ceramic jars, slabs of raw meat hanging from ceiling hooks. Opposite the stair is a low, dark hole in the wall, a trash chute, I presume, that leads to the sewer and the sea.

"Hector, has the ship you were expecting made port yet?"

"No. But her colors were seen yesterday evening. As soon as the wind picks up, she'll be here."

"So we row out there and hope for the best?" It seems like too tenuous a plan to me. One of the hardest things about being queen is determining when to trust someone to take care of things for you and when to take charge yourself. I have trusted Hector and Tristán to handle all the arrangements and contingencies for this journey. They are good men, natural leaders. I hope they have thought of everything.

"I can signal them from a distance," he says cryptically. "We'll head out to sea and keep going until we intercept them. It will be fine so long as the waters are calm."

I study his face. "You must know this ship and crew *very* well. To be able to exchange signals. To know their exact route."

"Yes." This time I'm looking for it, so I catch the twitch in his jaw that tells me he is being taciturn in order to keep from feeling something too much.

The trapdoor above us groans open.

"Snuff the torch!" Hector says.

The cellar goes black. Hector fills the space before me, backs me up with the press of his body. "Back," he whispers in my ear. "Behind the stair." I catch a glint of light along his sword edge, held at the ready.

I hear no footsteps, not even a breath of movement, but the trapdoor shuts with a soft *clunk*, and Belén says, "The inn is in an uproar, but I haven't been able to find Franco. We must assume he will follow."

Storm relights his torch. "He may be able to sense Her Majesty's Godstone," he says.

A panicked prayer flies unbidden to my lips, and as my belly warms in response, I realize that praying is the last thing I should do. I slam my mouth closed.

Activity has always made the Godstone easier for others to sense. Prayer comes so naturally to me, and I will need to focus hard to keep from doing it.

Hector gestures toward the barrels along the wall. "Belén, roll them in front of the trash chute while I get everyone down into the sewer. It might buy us a few seconds."

"Trash chute?" Mara asks quaveringly.

"You first, my lady," he says. "You'll slide a bit, then drop into the water. It's about waist deep. If you go under, don't panic. You'll be able to stand up. Now go!"

She closes her eyes a moment, then, holding her precious spice satchel above her head, she slides neatly inside, feet first.

Belén rolls a barrel up to obscure the view of the entrance to the chute as Hector takes the torch from Storm. "Now you. Go!"

Storm growls, low and deep, but he follows Mara's lead and plunges into the hole. His disappearance is quickly followed by a distant, echoing splash.

"Elisa? Your turn."

Oh, God.

The Godstone leaps, and I curse myself for stupidity. I dangle my legs into the hole. It reeks of dead fish and rotting vegetables. I place my hands beneath my thighs and push off.

I slide, but not quickly. My pants catch in muck, slowing me down. I reach out for the walls of the tight tunnel to push myself forward. My fingertips sink into sludge. I refuse to think about what I am touching.

I slither a bit farther, and suddenly I'm surrounded by air, and falling. I've no time to be surprised before my heels hit the water, then my rear. My feet hit bottom but slip out from under me, and ice-cold water closes over my head. I gather my feet and shoot to the surface, sputtering. "Mara?" I call.

"Here."

I wade toward her voice, wiping water from my eyes and nose. The surface reaches just past my Godstone. It's cold, but not as bad as I feared. Wading is going to be difficult in my boots and thick desert garb. I hope we reach a boat soon.

A splash behind me brings light with it. Another splash sounds quickly after.

"All here and uninjured?" Hector asks. He looks everyone over quickly.

"My cloak is ruined," Storm says. His cowl has fallen back, and in the torchlight, I finally glimpse his new hair. It's cropped close and inky black. It makes his cheeks appear even more gaunt, like a feral cat's.

"You'll live," I tell him. "And when we get back to—" I gasp as my Godstone becomes ice.

"We must go!" I whisper. "Now. He is very near."

"Belén, guard the queen's back," Hector says, grabbing the torch from him and starting down the sewer tunnel at an impossible pace. There is a slight hiss as he dunks the torch in the water. The tunnel goes black.

Pushing through waist-deep water at a near run while fully clothed and booted is one of the hardest things I've ever done. It's as hard as wading through sand, as hard as climbing cliffs. My lungs burn with effort and my limbs become leaden with cold, for the Godstone continues to pulse icy warnings through my veins. But I don't dare pray myself warm. I imagine Franco searching the cellar above, hoping to feel the tickle of warmth that tells him the Godstone is near.

I take comfort in the fact that if Franco is following us, it means he is not following Ximena. Maybe they'll get away. Maybe they'll be safe. I hope the entire city has descended upon the inn by now.

The arching ceiling of the tunnel begins to appear, dark and blurred as a ghost; we must be approaching the exit to the bay and open sky. But I don't know how I'll make it that far. My teeth chatter and my lips have gone numb. My limbs move too slowly. Hector's form grows distant.

"Hec . . ." My mouth can hardly form words. "Hec . . . tor."

He spins, and water laps against the sides of the tunnel as he rushes toward me. "What is it?" His whisper is frantic. "Are you . . ." His hand reaches blindly for me, connects with my cheek. "Your skin is ice." He grabs my shoulders and pulls me against him, saying, "Belén. Do it now."

In my peripheral vision, I catch a faint gleam as Belén clamps the blade of his dagger between his teeth, breathes deep through his nose, and then slips below the surface of the water.

I bury my face in Hector's neck, seeking his heat. He rubs up and down along my arms. "Is it the Godstone?" he whispers.

"Can't. Pray."

Storm and Mara are silent in the space beside us as we wait for Belén. What if more than one person pursues us? How will Belén be able to see what to do?

Hector's grip on me tightens, and my soaked body molds to his. Warmth sparks in the pit of my stomach, something wholly separate from the Godstone. Of their own volition, my arms snake around him, slide beneath his pack. My hands splay against his broad back, and I pull him close, closer. It would be the easiest thing in the world to press my lips to his throat, the line of his jaw. It would almost be like an accident.

A grunt. A splash.

Hector releases me and pulls fighting daggers from the vambraces at his forearms.

But the ice is fading from my blood. "It's all right," I say, laying a hand on his wrist. "The cold is gone." I send out a quick prayer, just enough for a smidge of warmth and a bit of gratitude.

A moment later, Belén's shape appears. Something dark and glittering streams across his face. "There was only one," he says. "Not Franco, but definitely one of his men." Beside me, Storm looses a ragged sigh. "If we are very lucky," Belén continues, "they'll never find the body. But only if we are very lucky. I suggest we go quickly."

"Elisa, can you move?" Hector asks.

In answer, I push forward through the black water. Behind me, I hear Mara whisper, "Are you hurt?"

"No," Belén says, and she breathes soft relief.

The tunnel stinks more and more, like a rotting privy or meat gone sour. Odds and ends float in the water beside us, and I try to avoid touching anything. My inner thighs chafe from the wet fabric of my pants, and my boots sink into sludge with each step. I feel like I'll never be clean again.

The details of my companions' faces are beginning to show

when we reach an iron grate. I glimpse a shimmer of moon-light on the water beyond.

"We have to swim under," Hector says. "There's a hole on the bottom left. Mara?"

Looking resigned, she says, "Hand the satchel to me through the grate?"

He takes it from her, saying, "There's room enough if you dive low."

Mara gulps air, then sinks below the surface. She kicks hard, connecting with my shin underwater, and then nothing. I count. *One, two, three, four, five, six . . .*

Her head breaks the surface on the other side. "Easy," she says, gasping. Hector pokes her satchel through the grate, and she grabs it.

Storm goes next, then Belén. Hector and I are alone. He hooks me around the waist and pulls me back, into the dark.

"Hector? What—"

"Quickly," he whispers, and his face is very close. "This may be our last chance to speak alone for a long time." I'm acutely aware of the pressure of his hand on the small of my back. The buzzing warmth returns to the pit of my stomach. "Last night Ximena warned me that you have a tendency to form strong attachments to people in close proximity to you."

"People like you," I say flatly.

"I told her you were stronger and smarter than she real-ized," he says, and his gaze drops to my lips. "She wanted me to promise that I would be wary of getting too close."

Did you? I want to ask. *Did you promise?*

"We argued right in front of you. It was a terrible breach, and I'm sorry."

"Hector? Your Majesty?" comes a whispering voice.

I can't stop staring at his lips. "Ximena's right, you know. Do you think it weakens me? To care so much?"

"No," he says without hesitation. "I don't think that at all." Our bodies are a hand's breadth apart, separated only by a cushion of heat.

"Me neither," I whisper. "It just hurts more."

Suddenly, he yanks me against him and bends his head to kiss me.

I melt into him as his fingers tangle in my wet hair. My mouth opens to his, and our tongues meet for the briefest instance before he pulls away.

We stare at each other. I read dismay in his face, as if he can't believe he did such a thing.

"Elisa?" It's Mara's worried voice.

Before I can think about anything else, before the pain of his regret can bloom in my own chest, I take a deep breath and sink. Water closes over my head, and I reach blindly for the grate. My fingers grasp slick algae. I leverage myself down, down . . . there! I find the gap and kick through. My pack snags on a jagged end, and I have a moment of panic and struggle, and then I'm free. I shoot to the surface.

I wipe water from my eyes and note that we are in a narrow inlet, sheltered by stone breakwalls on each side. The ocean lies just beyond. The water is as calm as a mirror, and the low moon paints a stream of light across its surface. To our right looms the dark shape of a long, high dock meant for mooring large ships. The water must drop off quickly, to accommodate their deep hulls.

Hector surfaces beside me. He shakes the water from his eyes and points toward the dock. "A boat there," he whispers. "Tied to the pilings beneath. We must go quietly; every sound carries on a calm night such as this."

He sets off and we follow, edging along the breakwall toward the dock. It's getting easier to see, as though all the candles and lamps in Puerto Verde illuminate the water. Maybe they do, after the ruckus we caused. I hope Ximena is safe. And Tristán. And the girl pretending to be me.

The end of the breakwall crumbles with disrepair. As we skirt it, I stub my toes on chunks of rock or mortar or brick that have fallen into the water. I step carefully, wary of a twisted ankle.

We slip beneath the shelter of the dock. Sure enough, the plunge of the ground is precipitous; it feels like walking along the side of a very steep hill. I clutch the pilings for support, and barnacles slice at my fingertips.

We weave through the pilings into chest-deep water. At last a shape manifests in the gloom. It looks like a small fishing boat—or maybe a large rowboat—with enough benched seating for eight people.

Hector lifts Mara over the edge, and the boat tips treacherously as she topples over the bench before gaining her seat. Hector pulls me in front of him.

"Hands on the side," he says in my ear, gripping my hips.

"When I lift, push up and swing your legs over."

He lifts; I scramble. My left knee knocks hard against the edge, but I make it in. I slide over on the bench to make room for Storm, who grumbles as Hector gives him a boost. Then Hector and Belén vault over the side.

Hector unties the thick rope holding us to the piling and coils it into the prow. He pulls one oar from the floor; Belén grabs the other. With a dip and a swish, Hector maneuvers us away. Belén follows his lead, using his oar as a pole against the pilings. Together they weave us out from under the dock and into open sea.

I take a deep breath, relieved to have gotten this far. The night is warm, and I know my chill will be gone soon, even wet as I am. Before us, the moonlit harbor is dotted with ships and smaller boats. Surely one more won't cause a second glance?

At my feet is a rolled-up sailcloth, a large net, a floppy wide-brimmed hat, and a wooden crate filled with fishing supplies: a dagger, bone hooks, twine, weights. We've commandeered a trawling boat.

I whisper, "Should we pretend to fish or something?"

"In deeper water, maybe," Hector says. "If we're out here for a long time."

I'm about to ask him just how long he thinks we'll be trapped in this boat when my nose pricks with something sharp and my neck itches, as if I'm being watched. I twist around to look at the city we leave behind. My hand flies to my mouth.

It's in flames. Clouds of grungy smoke roll into the sky, their bottom edges glowing red-orange.

No wonder the sky was so bright. No wonder we got away so easily. My plan to create chaos worked too well. "What have I done?" I whisper. Mara turns to see what has caught my attention and lets out a little "Oh!" of dismay.

"We did what we had to do to get away," Belén says. "It's just a few buildings."

Looking closer, it seems that only three, maybe four, structures are on fire. Still, I worry for the people who lived and worked there. Are they burning in the flames? Choking on smoke? Even if they did get out safely, I have destroyed their livelihoods. The King's Inn has stood on that spot for over a century.

Is it really worth it, to destroy someone's life to save my own? Even if I am the queen?

I turn my back to the flames and squeeze my eyes closed. Now that we are away from the shelter of the breakwall and the dock, I hear shouting, maybe screaming. What if they can't contain the blaze?

I consider ordering Hector to turn us around, to face this thing I've done, to make it right. But now is not the time. I must find the way that leads to life and the *zafira*; my country depends on it. I just hope that once we've found it, my list of wrongs to right is not too long.

We row through the bay, weaving between hulking ships. Figures move around on decks and climb through the rigging, even though it is not yet dawn. Shadowy shapes stand at the rails, gazing toward the conflagration. Surely they will turn toward us at any moment, notice that we don't belong.

But they don't. As we leave the bay and aim south along the shore, the sky brightens to dark indigo, still fading to deepest black along the watery horizon. Shadowy but glorious estates dot the rolling hills and cliffs above us, with vined trellises and marble statues and sandstone terraces. Soon we pass beyond even these. The waters are calm, and not a single ship goes by. We are alone, and very small.

Hector's breathing grows labored. As the sun peeks over the hills, its light catches on the sweat of his brow and shoulders. He closes his eyes, hardens his jaw, and keeps rowing.

Belén struggles too. Sweat runs from his hairline, mixes with dried blood and dirt, coating his face in a gruesome patina of red and black. There must have been a lot of blood. Cauldrons of it, for some to remain even after his dip under the sewer grate.

I wonder when they last slept? Certainly not last night; Belén was tracking an Invierne spy, and Hector was making arrangements for an escape that came too soon.

"Hector." I lean forward and put a hand on his wrist.

He looks up, startled, blinking sweat from his eyes.

"Rest," I say. "Both of you. We are alone and safe for now."

"We have to keep going," he says. "Felix's ship will—"

"On my order, you will rest. I need you sharp. Mara and I will row for a bit. And if a ship comes into view, we'll rouse you."

He lifts his shirt to wipe his eyes, and I can't help notice his stomach, taut and tanned from the training yard. I swallow hard.

Hector rests the oar on his lap and rolls his shoulders to loosen them. "Have you rowed before?"

"No."

"Mara?"

"Me neither," she says.

"I refuse to row," Storm says.

I say, "We'll figure it out. Close your eyes so you don't see how embarrassingly awkward we are at it." I'm gratified to see his glimmer of a smile.

"Trade places with me," Hector says.

We both stand, and the boat lurches. He grabs me to keep me steady, and we manage to squeeze past each other. I settle on the bench and grab the oar, saying, "There's plenty of water in my pack. Help yourself. You should probably rinse the water skin first, though; it's covered in sewage."

He does exactly that while Mara and Belén trade places; then, using my pack as a pillow, he slides under the bench and closes his eyes. Belén stretches out beside him. Mara takes up her oar, and after some useless splashing and a few hard knocks against the side of the boat, we slowly push south.

As the sun rises, the surface of the water becomes so bright hot as to be blinding. How will we ever find a single ship out here? What if it takes us days? Will our drinking water last that long? Though surrounded by water, we are as alone and barren as if we traveled the deep desert.

In no time, everything burns with effort; my back, my shoulders, my wrists. My palms and fingertips are rubbed raw. Every stroke makes me gasp for breath. Mara and I switch sides so we can abuse a different set of muscles, but even that mild reprieve does not last long.

To keep my mind off the pain, I gaze at Hector. He sleeps soundly, his chest rising and falling with deep, even breaths. His features have softened, and the hair at his temples curls loosely as it dries. His mouth is slightly parted.

My lips tingle to remember his kiss. It was desperate and tender and wholly unexpected—and as easy as breathing.

Later, when we've found this mysterious ship of Hector's and are safely away, when I have time to rest and worry and a quiet corner to hide in, I will coldly remember that being a queen means being strategic. And I will imagine sending off the man I love to marry my sister. I'll rehearse it in my head, maybe. Get used to the feeling.

But not now. Now, as I row toward an uncertain destination, his kiss still throbbing on my lips, I luxuriate in watching him sleep.

21

STORM is the one who spots the ship. "There!" He points.

I twist and shade my face to peer through the brightness. The coast curls southeast, hiding the bulk of the ship, but I can see a long bowsprit, a beak head painted red, and what might be a foresail, hanging limply in the windless morning. I'm caught between hope and alarm.

Please, God, let it be the right ship.

I lean forward to shake Hector. He startles awake, whipping his hand to his scabbard.

"Watch your head," I tell him, putting my hand between his forehead and the bench above. "There's a ship, just south of us. I doubt they've seen us."

He blinks sleep from his eyes and frowns at the blisters on my hand.

I pull my hand back. "Is it the right ship?"

Still frowning, he slides out from under the bench to peer southward. He is quiet a long time. "I think so," he says, and for some reason the raw hope on his face is hard to look at.

"We'll have to get a little closer to be sure."

I grab the floppy, wide-brimmed hat and toss it to Storm. "Put that on."

He shoves it onto his head and hunches over. I don't blame him for being afraid; in the close quarters of a ship, anyone would recognize him for an Invierno, even with his falsely darkened hair.

Hector and Belén take up the oars again, and we cut through the water with relative ease and speed. Mara and I exchange a scowl.

Gradually the ship comes into view. It's a gorgeous *caravela* with three masts and wickedly curved lines of burnished mahogany and bright red trim. Painted sacrament roses twist along the bow, and it seems as though their petals fall, become drops of blood, before disappearing into the sea.

"That's her," Hector says. "The *Aracely.*"

My heart thumps. I have a feeling I'm going to learn something very important about Hector. "Should we signal?" I ask.

He throws back his head and laughs. As we all gape at him, he explains, "I had this system all worked out to signal them from afar. But with the sea so calm, all we have to do is row right alongside."

Storm mutters, "It's about time *something* on this accursed journey proved easier than expected."

"The captain and the crew," I say. "Are they to know who I am?"

"The captain, yes," Hector says. "We'll speak to him first and then decide."

As we approach, Storm crouches lower and lower on the bench. My own misgivings swirl in my thoughts, but I'm also a little bit excited. I've studied about ships and seafaring, but I've never been on a ship before.

Figures appear on deck as we close the distance. Two others hang fearlessly from the rigging; another watches us from the top castle above the main sail. I shudder to think of him so high up, tossed this way and that by wind and water.

The curving bow looms over us when Hector waves his hands. "Ho, *Aracely*!" he calls.

A bell rings across the water, letting the crew know they've been hailed, and they respond with a flurry of footsteps. More heads peek over the rails. They're a ragged, weathered bunch, with long hair tied back, two-week beard growth, and suspicious eyes.

"Ho, trawler!" The speaker's voice races across the water. "We're short on supplies and have little to trade. Best to be rowing back toward Puerto Verde."

"We wish to treat with Captain Felix," Hector yells.

Some of the heads disappear. The others exchange wary glances. A moment later, another man appears, more finely dressed than the rest in a clean linen blouse and thick black vest tight across his barrel chest. The whites of his eyes are uncannily bright next to his sun-dark skin. Beads are woven into his enormous beard; they catch the sunlight and return sparks of amethyst and aquamarine. His neck is thick and corded. He places huge hands on the rail above us; he's missing the first two joints of his right pinky.

He scowls deeply when he sees us. "I was afraid that would be you," he growls in a voice black as night. He turns to the crew. "Winch them up onto the quarterdeck!"

Hector is grinning like a little boy as he and Belén maneuver us to the front of the ship. The crew lowers thick hemp ropes. Hector grabs one and dives neatly into the sea, which sets us to rocking wildly. A moment later, he comes up on the other side, rope in hand.

They wrap the boat three times and tie off in a flurry of twisting knots. Hector gives the signal, and after a loud count and a "Heave!" we are sucked out of the water and left swinging in the air.

When we are halfway up, Hector leaps from the boat to the netting hanging over the side and climbs up. Belén follows, and the lightened load allows us to be hauled up more quickly. When we are close enough to touch the gunwale, Hector is already there, looking down at me, his hand outstretched. His hand clasped in mine feels relaxed, which surprises me. With his help, I pull myself over the rail and land on the quarterdeck.

As he reaches to help Mara and Storm, I look around. Most of the crew are busy hauling up the boat, their forearms veined and straining at the knotted ropes. But the others eye me with obvious interest. Some warily, some hungrily, as if I am a delicate cream puff with honey glaze. Instinct forces me to back away, but my rear hits the rail and I realize I've nowhere to go.

"A lady!" one whispers loudly.

"Two ladies," says another as Mara clambers over the side.

"I don't see any ladies here," the captain bellows. "And nei-ther do you. Get back to work."

The crewmen on the ropes flip the boat onto the stern and tie it down through iron loops that I realize are for that exact purpose.

The others stare unabashedly at Mara and me, even as they resume their tasks. I stare right back, trying to seem unafraid. At least they're staring at us rather than Storm. Maybe they won't notice his uncanny height or that his eyes shine like emeralds.

The dark captain herds us with his vast arms. "This way. To my quarters *now*." His urgent voice rumbles, like empty barrels rolled across cobblestone.

We take the steep steps to the main deck at a near run, then twist under the quarterdeck and through double doors hung with real glass. He closes the doors behind us and swings the latch closed.

The chamber is low ceilinged and made entirely of polished mahogany. Light pours in from portholes, two on each side. A large desk rife with paper and ink and small metal instruments I don't begin to understand takes up most of one wall. Jutting out from the other is a huge bed covered in silk the shade of pomegranate fruit. A thick rug covers the floor, woven to show a cluster of purple grapes in a circle of green vines—the seal of Ventierra.

The captain turns to us, and a huge smile lights his face. I gasp in recognition. I know that smile. I've seen another ver-sion of it many times.

"Hector!" he says, opening his arms wide, and the commander of my Royal Guard rushes into the embrace and endures a fierce back thumping.

The captain grabs Hector's upper arms and pushes him back to study him while Hector grins like a little boy. "Look at you," the captain mutters. "A Quorum lord."

I say, "You're Hector's brother."

His gaze whips to me, and his eyes narrow. He studies every part of me: my dirty face, my unraveling braid, my breasts, legs, and feet. Something sparks in his black eyes, as if he has learned something. My face grows hot, but I refuse to flinch.

Softly he says, "And you are his young queen." And he drops to one knee with more grace than a man his size ought to have. "Welcome aboard the *Aracely*, Your Majesty."

"Thank you. Please rise."

He stands and turns an accusing look toward Hector. "This is a very dangerous thing you ask me to do, little brother. Our hold is full and we sit low in the water. We should not be so near the coast. I trust you have a good reason?"

Hector nods. "You may have heard that Her Majesty is on her way south to negotiate a betrothal with Selvarica?"

"Yes, the whole country speaks of nothing else."

"It's a fabrication."

Captain Felix raises his eyebrows.

"We were heading south, it's true," Hector continues. "But we were followed by an Invierne spy, a trained assassin. Given the recent attempts on Her Majesty's life, we thought it prudent to slip away."

I gape at Hector. He must trust his brother indeed to share all these details with him. Mara shifts uncomfortably in the space beside me.

The captain steps out of Hector's reach and crosses his arms. "You want me to take you south," he says.

"Yes."

"I can't." He turns to me. "I'm so sorry, Your Majesty, but I have a hold full of early harvest wine, the first decent harvest since the hurricane three years ago. I *must* get it to port so I can pay my men and bring home much-needed supplies."

At first, Hector's face is cast in stone and unreadable. But I see the exact moment he resigns himself to his next course of action. He's going to commandeer his own brother's ship. He has the right, as a Quorum lord. But not even brotherly affection could survive something like that. And I can't bear to see it happen. Not because of me.

He opens his mouth to give the order, but I jump in. "Can you sell your cargo at Puerto Verde?"

Hector slams his mouth closed and stares at me. I give my head what I hope is a near-imperceptible shake. *Please don't do it.*

"Yes," the captain says. "But we'd only get half price. It's the Orovalleños who pay top coin."

I smile with remembrance. "I don't doubt it. Ventierra wine was a favorite in my father's court. Do you mind if we sit down?"

"Please," he gestures with a flip of his hand. "Anywhere."

I plunk down on the nearest cushion and say, "It's a long

journey to Orovalle and back. You'll overlap with hurricane season."

He grins with the understanding that we are about to haggle. "It's one of the many reasons I love the life of a sailor," he says. "Don't you find, Your Majesty, that when you and death are bedmates, *that* is when you feel most alive?"

"I wouldn't know."

His eyes widen. He expected to put me off balance by referring to the attempts on my life.

"I'm always in bed with death. Since the moment I left my father's palace. I've nearly died more times than I can count. And I'm a bearer, which means I'm likely to die very young. So, you see"—I shrug with purposed nonchalance—"I wouldn't know the difference."

His beard hides any turning of his lips, but his eyes crinkle with amusement. "What do you propose?"

I have a hunch about him, about the person he is. What kind of man leaves the soft life of a conde's son to embrace the open water? Sacrifices his youth to endless sun and wind, his fingers to the sea? Someone who loves open space and danger, I'd bet my Godstone crown. Someone who can't wait to see what lies just over the horizon.

"My honor compels me to warn you," I say, "that our journey is dangerous and our destination uncertain."

Sure enough, one eyebrow raises high, and the expression is so familiar, so endearing, that it's hard not to smile. "Oh?" he says.

"I need a captain and crew I can trust absolutely. For it is a secret journey. Outside this room, only a small handful of people know its purpose."

He raises his chin and looks down at me through lidded eyes. "Seems to me that someone would pay top price for such a venture."

"Seems to me that the kind of discretion I need cannot be bought for any price. I hardly know where to start."

His eyes glow, and he's practically salivating over what I'm about to offer. Good. "Let's start with my lost cargo. I'll need to be compensated for the difference in price."

I nod. "That's fair."

"And I'll need extra supplies."

"You'll need the same supplies as if you were traveling to Orovalle," I point out. "You'll just be going in a different direction."

"I'll need compensation for this *danger* you speak of, and to ensure crew loyalty."

"So the crew is loyal to coin but not to you?"

"They're loyal to me because I make good on my word to give them coin. Did you bring any to give me?"

I hesitate.

He glances at Hector, then throws up his hands in a show of frustration that may be a bit exaggerated.

I've intrigued him, certainly, but here I am at a loss. I'd hoped to trade on royal credit. But I have no coin on hand, no horses or—

"I have saffron," Mara says. "Enough to line the pockets of your crew and then some."

I twist to face her, remembering how carefully she has pre-served her satchel throughout our journey so far. "Mara, are you sure?"

In answer, she pulls a small porcelain phial from her satchel and hands it to Felix for inspection. He feigns disinterest, but his eyes light up when he raises it to his nose.

"I suggest you sell your cargo in Puerto Verde," I say. "Get what you can for it. The saffron will more than make up for the rest."

But how do I compensate the captain for risking his ship and his crew? I purse my lips, thinking hard, while Captain Felix unstoppers the phial and examines the contents carefully.

I get an idea. Though I don't have money to bargain with, as queen I possess something much more valuable. I add, "And for the service of taking us where we need to go, fear-lessly and loyally, I'll write a letter to my kitchen master and stamp it with my own seal, declaring Ventierra the official Royal Vintner."

His mouth drops open before he can school his expression, and his breathless voice belies his nonchalant demeanor as he turns to Hector and says, "We'd have to pull out all our stores to meet demand. We'd have to sell the oldest barrels at pre-mium prices to keep from running out. We'd have to replant the southern vineyard."

"Yes," Hector says. "We would have to do all that." But he's staring at me, a little perplexed.

"Do we have a bargain?" I ask. "Because if not, your men

should lower our boat before we're too far from shore."

The captain crouches down to take my hands in his huge ones. He pauses, noticing the burst blisters from my disastrous attempt at rowing. I'm determined not to wince. Instead, I squeeze his hand hard, and the expression on his face takes on a measure of respect.

"Your Majesty, we have a bargain." His beard tickles my knuckles as he kisses them.

"You haven't even asked where we're going!"

"Later," he says, his nose wrinkling in disgust. "First, baths for everyone. I can only offer seawater for baths, but I must insist. You all reek of something terrible."

"I can't smell anything except the fish oil in your beard," Hector says, straight-faced.

Felix laughs free and easy, so unlike his younger brother. On his way out the door, he clasps Hector's shoulder and says, "That queen of yours played me like a *vihuela*, didn't she?"

"Yes," Hector agrees, and though his face is solemn, his eyes shine.

"Please stay here while I make arrangements," the captain says to the rest of us. "I need to evaluate my crew and see if anyone should be quietly disembarked before you start making regular appearances on deck."

As the doors close behind him, Hector says, "Thank you, Elisa."

"You're welcome."

"I don't think he noticed Storm," Mara says.

The Invierno is huddled on a cushion behind me, partly

hidden by the corner of Captain Felix's enormous desk.

"Oh, he noticed," Belén murmurs. He is using a small knife to clean under his fingernails.

"Felix trusts me," Hector explains. But the look he gives Storm is one of suspicion. Or maybe regret that he brought the Invierno onto his brother's ship.

22

AFTER baths and a quick meal of salted pork with too-hard bread dipped in onion broth, we agree that Felix will give up the captain's quarters for me and Mara. He and the men will share the largest passenger cabin below deck.

The next day at midmorning, I'm trying to make sense of the captain's navigation charts when the crew sends up a raucous cheer, followed by much pattering across the decks. The ship lurches. I rush to the nearest porthole and am delighted to see choppy water pass by. We have caught a wind.

It takes two whole days to unload and sell the wine cargo and acquire a new batch of supplies. I spend the time pacing in the captain's quarters, trapped and antsy, frustrated at having to backtrack, even for a short distance.

When Felix returns from his final negotiation, he brings back news.

"The queen and the conde are safely on their way to Selvarica," he says, his eyes dancing. "Apparently it is the city's greatest shame that the inn she was staying in burned down around her, but no amount of apologies could convince her to stay. They're already calling it The Great Embarrassment."

The relief is so overwhelming that I have to sit down. "They're safe, then. No word about an assassin?"

"Nothing."

"Good. That's good." *Thank you, God.*

"So, where to, Majesty?"

I look up at him and return his grin. "South, toward the island countships. I'll know more . . . eventually."

But as he takes his leave, I wonder, *Will I?* If God's holy scripture has thus far proved unreliable in matters pertaining to the Godstone, how much less should I trust the apocryphal writings?

I pinch the bridge of my nose and whisper experimentally: *"Zafira."*

My Godstone vibrates joyfully in response.

I'm standing in the prow, gripping the rail, fascinated by the way the *Aracely* slices the water below. Wind has whipped my braid into a tangled mess. Spray stings my eyes and chaps my lips. The foresail above me bulges with air.

The crewmen have accepted Hector and Belén easily enough, and they gawk at Mara whenever she passes. Storm stays hidden in the passenger cabin. But they give me wide berth, too frightened or shy to approach their queen. Or maybe the captain has warned them off. I don't mind. It's nice to feel a little bit alone on this tiny ship.

I sense a dark presence and look up to find Captain Felix

studying me thoughtfully. "You've found your sea legs," he observes.

"Not really," I say. "It seems like they were always there, not needing to be found." It's been nice to have something come naturally for once. Storm, on the other hand, can barely get out of bed without vomiting, though we've been assured it will pass eventually.

"It's like that sometimes," he says. "It was like that for me."

"Is that why you became a sea captain?"

"Partly."

"I'm quite interested in the other part. You gave up the life of a conde's son in favor of a dangerous career running cargo. But from what little I know of Hector's family, I doubt they threw you out in the street. I'm guessing you ran away."

He laughs. "Hector warned me that you are the cleverest girl I would ever meet." My face flushes at the praise. "I understand now," he adds.

"Understand what?"

"Why Hector stayed with you."

I stare at him blankly as my grip on the wet rail tightens.

"You really don't know, do you?"

I force myself to relax my hold. If I squeeze any tighter, I'll hurt my healing blisters. Wearily, I say, "Please explain."

He leans over and rests his forearms on the edge, gazes out to sea as if soaking up the sight of a lover. "I was set to inherit the countship of Ventierra," he says, his voice distant with remembering. "But I hated it. The pageantry, the polite warring between houses, and sweet holy sacraments, the paperwork. One day, when I was seventeen, my father and I fought. I don't even remember why, but yes, you're right. I ran away to the shipyards. Offered my services as a deckhand on a merchant ship for no pay except food to eat and a hammock to sleep in."

"And you fell in love with the sea."

"Among other things."

I don't know what this has to do with Hector. "Why not go back? You could still inherit, couldn't you?"

"Well, no. You see, I also fell in love with a lady of the docks and had a son with her."

It takes me a split second to realize that a "lady of the docks" must be a prostitute, a split second more to remember how the crewmen referred to Mara and me as "ladies" when we first boarded.

"When my father heard," he continues, oblivious to my flushing face, "he journeyed to Brisadulce to rescue me from what he was certain were monumentally bad decisions." His smile breaks wide. "So when I heard my father was in town, I rushed Aracely to the nearest priest and married her."

"You named the ship after her!"

He nods. "Well, yes. When you tell your wife you're going to be gone sailing for several months, and by the way, have fun with our screaming newborn, it helps to make a grand gesture."

I chuckle. "You are a wise man."

"Funny, I tell my wife that exact thing all the time!"

"What does this have to do with Hector?"

He sobers. "When I married Aracely, my father gave up

trying to groom me to be a conde and turned instead to his next son, my brother Ronin." Pain flashes across his features, so aching and fresh that I almost recoil. Softly he says, "Ronin died in the war with Invierne. On the day you defeated their sorcerers. He went with Conde Eduardo to defend the southern front and was cut down with an arrow to the chest."

"Oh." Hector lost a brother in the war. Barely seven months ago. And I never knew. *Why didn't he tell me?* "I'm so sorry," I choke out.

"So that left Hector," he said. "To inherit Ventierra."

I gape at him.

Felix says, "My parents wrote to him, begging him to come home. *I* wrote to him. His king was dead, after all, and Hector has always been the best of us. Born to lead, to rule. He wrote back. Said he would come home as soon as possible. That he missed Ventierra more than words could say, that he would resign his position as commander of the Royal Guard and give up his seat on the Quorum. But something happened."

It feels like someone is standing on my shoulders, and I'm frozen with the weight of it.

I happened. I changed his mind. I remember the day well. He came into my office and laid a letter of resignation on my desk. I asked him to reconsider, to become my own personal guard.

"I had no idea," I whisper. "None at all." And more recently, after visiting Storm in the tower, he asked me to dismiss him. He thought he had failed me. But maybe, just maybe, he also wanted desperately to go home.

"He gave up a countship for you, Majesty. And the home he loves. I've always wondered why. But now I understand."

I open my mouth to protest but change my mind.

Is it possible? Could Hector love me as much as I love him? Is it cruel of me to wish that he would, when there is no chance for us? *Something* made him kiss me in the sewer tunnel, at a time when we should have been fleeing.

After too long a silence, I say, "Hector is naturally loyal, with a strong sense of duty. He'll stay in whatever position he feels will be in best service to his country." Would he, though? If I gave him the choice, would he stay with me?

"You know him well," he says.

"No one knows Hector well."

He says something else, but I don't hear because my Godstone leaps. I gasp.

"Your Majesty?"

"I'm not sure . . ." The stone tingles, and then I feel the slightest brush across my belly, like butterfly wings. "My Godstone! It . . ." The butterfly wings coalesce into something more solid, poking, prodding, and like ghost fingers, they reach painlessly into my stomach, wrap around my Godstone, and *pull*. "Oh," I breathe. "Oh, my."

"Should I fetch Hector?"

"No. It's all right." The sensation eases, but it's still there, tugging gently. Tugging in a very specific direction. "I think I've found it. The way." I turn to him. "I know which way to go."

He gives me a skeptical look. I don't blame him. It seems ridiculous. Maybe I've imagined it.

But I close my eyes, let the tugging sensation guide me. It's faint but sure. I pivot slightly to my right, lining up my toes with the exact direction. I raise my arm and point into the endless watery horizon.

"That way."

He shakes his head, resigned. "Of course it's that way. Right into the wind." He turns toward his crew, cupping his hands to his mouth. "Beat to windward!"

I return to quarters, knowing it's best to keep out of the way as they work to adjust our course. The *Aracely* is a warren of ropes and hooks and beams and swinging things, but I seem to have an instinct for it all, and I navigate it with ease. And so much glorious wood! Always kept in polish. Never have I seen so much wood in one place, for it is hard to come by in my desert.

Mara is alone, sitting on the huge bed, her satchel opened and spread out before her. She looks up when I enter.

"I found it, Mara. The *zafira*. My Godstone sensed it."

"That's wonderful news!" she says, closing up the satchel. "I felt us shift course, but I didn't know why."

"I'm sorry we had to sell your saffron," I say, eyeing the leather in her hands. "You took such care to keep it from getting wet, even in the sewer."

She laughs. "It wasn't the saffron I was worried about. Something much more valuable."

"Oh?"

Hector bursts in, and we look up, surprised.

"Felix said you gave him a new course," he says.

"Yes! Hector, I sensed the way. It called to me. Just like the *Blasphemy* said."

He takes a deep breath, whether from relief or trepidation I cannot tell. "That's good," he says.

"It's good," I agree. I turn to Mara and say, "There's something I'd like to discuss with Hector—"

"I'll go visit Storm," she says. "He'll hate that." She gathers up her satchel, and at my curious look, she mouths, "Later."

After she shuts the door behind her, I turn to face my guard. Neither of us moves to close the distance.

He leans against his brother's desk and crosses his ankles. His fingers thrum against the beveled edge. It's the tiniest break in his usual composure, but it's enough to make me study him closely. He stares wide-eyed at his brother's rug as if it contains all the wisdom of the world. He's nervous, I realize. Why?

Ah. Our kiss. He thinks I want to talk about it.

I clear my throat. "Felix told me . . ." This is going to be harder than I thought. But I can't bear to think that he might be with me against his will. I plop onto the bed, lean my head against the bed post, and try again. "After Alejandro died, you could have inherited Ventierra."

The words come out wrong, like I'm accusing him of something. They hang in the air between us, and he is silent for so long that I worry I've offended him.

At last he says, "I chose not to."

My fingers dig into the silk bedspread as I softly ask, "And do you regret that choice?"

He hesitates, which tells me all I need to know. "It was the right choice," he says.

"That's not what I asked."

"No," he agrees, "it's not."

I steel myself, force steadiness into my voice. "Hector, I'm so glad you stayed. There is no one I trust the way I trust you. And . . . and whose company I enjoy as much." Surely my heart is in my eyes, saying all the things I really shouldn't. "But when this is over, after we've found the *zafira*, I'm going to give you the option to go home. To be free of me. So think about it."

His mouth parts and his eyebrows lift. After a long moment, he says, "I thought you might marry me to your sister and pack me off to Orovalle. I'm quite the bargaining piece, or so Ximena tells me." I'm certain I don't imagine the edge of bitterness in his voice.

I sigh, too loudly. When I see Ximena next, we will have a very long talk about . . . a lot of things. Carefully I say, "It *is* important that we find a good match for you." Now my hands are clenched so tightly in my lap that my knuckles hurt. "But only in consultation with your own feelings on the matter. I know what it's like to not be consulted. I could never do that to you."

He nods, though he looks everywhere but at me. "It would be very nice to see home again," he muses, staring out one of the starboard-side portholes. Toward Ventierra.

I smile sadly. "So you already know, then, what your choice will be?"

"No. But I thank you for giving it to me."

The sun drops below the horizon. Mara and I are alone in Captain Felix's quarters.

"Storm said something you should know about," she says as she unravels my braid.

"Oh?" I say, feeling my muscles slacken as she works.

"He said that the gatekeeper would sense you coming. That he would test you."

The relaxation disappears and I sit straight up. "What does that mean?"

"I don't know. But it makes sense that the gate would have a gatekeeper, yes?"

"Maybe so." I frown, wishing I had thought to bring my own copy of the *Blasphemy* to study. Ximena was the one who packed it into the queen's carriage. I never even saw it. Perhaps she *meant* for me never to see it.

"Father Alentín said something about a test, about proving myself worthy, but nothing about a gatekeeper."

She pulls the brush through my hair. "Maybe you should pay Storm a visit. Ask him about it."

"I will, yes. But right now I want to know what's in that spice satchel. Mara, what could you possibly be carrying that is more valuable than saffron?"

She moves around to face me. Her eyes sparkle. "Just a little something I brought for us."

I watch, wildly curious, as she retrieves it and lays it out on the bed. She reaches into a pocket and pulls out a clay figurine. It's ochre-colored, shaped like a naked woman from the knees up. She's voluptuous, and she crosses her arms over her stomach, as if protecting it.

Mara pulls off its head; it comes uncorked with a popping sound. She tips it, and a few tiny grains spill into her palm.

"Lady's shroud," she says. "I have two bottles, one for each of us. Had to sneak it past Ximena. I knew she wouldn't look in my spice satchel."

At my confused look, she sighs. "Ximena never told you about lady's shroud, did she?"

"No." There are many things Ximena never told me about.

"Take eight to ten of these seeds once per day. No more. Chew them well and swallow." She pours them back inside the bottle and stoppers it, then shoves it into my hand. "It will keep you from getting pregnant."

My hand closes around the bottle like a fist. "Oh," I breathe.

"You don't have to take it, of course. But I just thought, well, we were going on this journey, and there was so much talk of splitting off, and I knew Hector would be with us, and sometimes the look you two share could liquefy sand, and . . . I wasn't too presumptuous, was I?"

"No. Well, I don't know." I stare at the figurine. She is lush in my hands. Naked. Shameless.

Mara's voice is softer when she says, "You could have a first time with someone you trust and love."

I look up at her, startled. So she knows how I feel. If she knows, then Ximena assuredly does too. "He might not have me," I admit.

"Elisa, he wants you desperately."

Warmth floods my neck. "I think he regrets staying on as my guard. He may leave after we find the *zafira*. To go home. And my sister, Crown Princess Alodia, has expressed an interest in betrothal with him. So, you see, it would go nowhere. There is no future for us."

She moves the satchel aside and sits next to me on the bed. "But you love him," she says, and at her simple acceptance, the last of my barriers crumbles away.

"Oh, Mara, I do. I love everything about him. I love that he cares so much about honor and duty. I love how, when he's working hardest to mask his feelings, they're actually leaking out all over the place. I love the way his hair curls when it gets wet, his slightly crooked smile, the way he smells. When he laughs, I feel it in my toes." I let my forehead drop onto her shoulder. "I sound like an idiot."

"Yes," she says, and I hear the smile in her voice. "You do."

"He kissed me. In the sewer."

"Holy God," she says. "That was very bad timing."

"The worst."

"And very unlike Hector."

"Very unlike him, yes."

"I really think you should start taking the lady's shroud. Just in case."

I straighten, take a deep breath, look calculatingly at the figurine in my hand. "Ximena wanted him to promise not to form an attachment with me."

She wraps an arm around me and hugs me tight. "Ximena

is a wonderful woman, and she loves you very much, but she is a meddlesome fishwife."

I choke on surprise and laughter.

"You have to be the one to decide, Elisa. Not Ximena. What do *you* want?"

"I want Hector." There. I've said it.

"Even if it means you can only have him for a short time?"

"I don't know."

"Fair enough." She scoots behind me and reaches for my hair to put it in its sleeping braid. We sway a little as the wind picks up and rocks the ship. It's comforting, like being rocked in a cradle.

"You said you brought two," I say. "One for each of us."

Her fingers on my hair still. "Yes. Belén and I . . . He is so handsome. And capable. Quiet and fiery, both at once." She sighs. "We've both changed a lot. He's scarred too, now. So maybe he won't mind that I . . . even after everything that happened between us, I thought . . . maybe . . ."

"Just in case," I say.

"Just in case," she agrees.

Tonight, I decide not to take the lady's shroud. But I wrap it carefully in my spare blouse and stash it in my pack. I lie awake a long time, wondering which would be more foolish, to prepare for something that may never happen, or not to prepare for something that might.

23

THE waves grow playful. They toss the *Aracely* about, and I clutch the rail as I descend the stair on my way to the passenger cabin to visit Storm.

I knock, and I hear what might be permission to enter, but I can't be sure. I open the door anyway.

The scent of stale vomit makes me gag.

"You really need to let some fresh air in here."

"Go away," he mutters. He lies on the bottom bunk, one long leg dangling over the side, his arm over his eyes. Footsteps patter across the deck above us. A single fly executes lazy circles around the slop bucket near the head of his bed.

"Maybe you should go up on deck. At least you'd be able to throw up over the side instead of in that bucket."

The ship tilts on a sudden wave, and he groans.

"I sensed the *zafira*," I tell him. "We're heading toward it now."

He lurches to a sitting position. "You're sure?"

"It feels like it's calling—"

He heaves into the bucket. It hasn't been dumped in a while, and a bit splashes over the side. I jerk my feet away just in time. "Ugh," I say. "I could get someone to clean that up."

He wipes his mouth with a sleeve. "No. It keeps Hector and the captain out of my room. They've been sleeping in the hold."

I'm torn between laughter and disgust.

"You'll be tested," he says. "The closer we get, the harder it will be."

"That's what I came to talk to you about. You said something to Mara about a gatekeeper."

He nods. "I did, yes."

I sigh, exasperated at how he makes me work for every bit of information. "Tell me everything you know about the gatekeeper."

He lies back down. "Fetch me some water. Throwing up is thirsty work."

"Information first, water later."

I catch the faint hint of a smile before he says, "It's an ancient Invierne legend. The gatekeeper was selected from among the animagi. Only the most powerful applied. There was a contest of sorts, and the winner was sent to watch over and protect the *zafira*."

I frown. "You've never mentioned any of this before."

"You never asked. Also, I'm not sure he really exists. But I *am* certain that my people would have erected some kind of defense around their greatest resource. Why not use the most powerful animagus in our nation to do it? And since the *zafira* conveys life and power, someone in close proximity could live a very long time."

I stare at him in disbelief. "But your people have been cut off from the *zafira* for so long. He'd have to be hundreds of years old."

"More like thousands."

I laugh. "Not that old. After God brought humans to this world, it was a long time before we split off into separate nations."

He gapes at me. "You're a very stupid girl," he says.

"What? Why?"

The ship lurches, and he covers his mouth as he gags. I ease away from the bucket before repeating my question. "Why do you think I'm—"

The ship's bells peal, starting high and faint at the top castle, gaining strength as the other bells pick up the signal. A voice booms down the hallway. "All hands! All hands!"

Crewmen hurry past Storm's doorway. "I'll be back!" I say to the Invierno before rushing out after them. Have we been hailed? Have we sighted land already? Has someone gone overboard?

I burst onto the main deck and into blinding daylight. Sailors mill about with tasks I hardly understand. Two scurry up the rigging, daggers in their teeth. Why would we be preparing to cut the sails?

"Elisa!" It's Hector. He stands at the bottom of the stair leading to the beakhead, gesturing for me to hurry.

I jog across the main deck. He grabs my hand and yanks me up the stairs. Captain Felix is already there, staring southeast. I follow his gaze.

A blue-black cloud bank curls along the horizon, a rolling

darkness in an otherwise crystal sky.

"It's a huge storm," Hector says. "Maybe even a hurricane. We'll know more in a few hours."

The air feels different. Charged. Like it holds its breath.

"It's too early in the year for hurricanes," I protest, even as the storm bank flashes, turning the clouds a sickly green. *Please, God, not a hurricane.*

"By a month at least," Felix agrees, staring out to sea. A gust of wind lifts his hair from his temples. "And from the wrong direction. In all my years on the water, I've never seen one come from the south. It's unnatural."

His words chill me. "Can we make for land?" I ask, even as I realize that we've been sailing away from the coast. We'd never make it back in time.

He shakes his head. "There's no port for days. The *Aracely* has ridden out some rough storms, but a hurricane would swamp us. If we can last long enough, we may be able to harness it, get it to push us onto the reefs. We'd wreck her for sure, but some of us might be able to get to shore." He skims his hand along the railing, caressing it like a lover. "She's been a good ship," he says quietly. "The best ship."

I squeeze my eyes closed, unable to face his brave resignation. As I do, the *zafira* lurches into focus, pulling me forward like I'm a fish on the line. I have a sudden urge to dive off the prow and swim in the direction it bids me, straight into the roiling storm.

I open my eyes to find the clouds bearing down on us, already larger and darker than moments ago. And as the rising wind presses my garments against the shape of my body and my Godstone begins to twitch with telltale cold, I decide that Captain Felix is absolutely right. The swelling storm is unnatural.

To no one in particular, I mutter, "Storm said I would be tested."

Hector raises an eyebrow. "You think God is sending a tempest to test your mettle? Surely he knows you better than that by now."

I appreciate his attempt at humor, but I can't bring a smile to my lips. "Not God. The gatekeeper." The most powerful animagus in the world. Someone who has lived maybe thousands of years. "And Father Nicandro said I would have to prove my determination. He said there would be a test of faith."

"What exactly are you saying, Your Majesty?" says Felix in a cold voice.

I loose a breath that is nearly a sob. It's one thing to be God's chosen, to be put in danger at every turn, made to fulfill some nebulous destiny. It's another thing entirely to endanger a ship full of good people to do it.

I do my best to explain, even though I know it won't be good enough for Felix. "I am the champion, according to Homer's *Afflatus*. And I must not waver. I'm sure you've heard it? 'He could not know what awaited at the gates of the enemy, and he was led, like a pig to the slaughter, into the realm of sorcery.' The passage promises that if the champion stays the course, he will be victorious by the power of God's righteous right hand."

Hector pinches the bridge of his nose and groans.

"What?" Felix says, looking back and forth between us. "What am I missing?"

I point toward the storm. "We need to go through that. Straight through. No wavering in our resolve."

The captain gawks at me. "You can't be serious."

Instead of answering, I place my fingertips to the Godstone and allow its warm pulse to comfort me. It's so familiar. I can't imagine being without it.

My faith has been greatly shaken in the last year, but not broken. I have this conduit, after all, this constant reminder that someone or something listens to my prayers, grants me strange power in trying circumstances, warns me of danger. So I know to trust where it leads.

Hector turns to Felix and says, "Not two weeks ago, I was hit with an assassin's arrow." Hector pulls up his shirt and twists around to reveal a thin white scar just beneath his shoulder blade. It looks like the injury happened years ago. Felix studies it with interest. "The arrowhead nicked my lung," Hector says before letting the hem drop. "I had to fight through it, so I bled everywhere. By the time I got help, it was too late. I was a dead man."

Though I know how the story goes, I'm intent on his every word, hoping for a glimpse into his mind.

"Elisa healed me," Hector says. "With the power of her Godstone. It was sore for a few days"—he curls his arm and straightens it again—"but it's fine now. Not even a twinge."

Now he looks at *me*, dead-on. "She saved my life," he says. "It took a lot out of her, more than she'll tell me, but she did it. So if she says we must steer into the storm, I believe her."

I could almost forget about the storm, about my Godstone, about everything, when he looks at me like this, like I'm the only thing in the world.

Felix says, "You're asking me to risk more than twenty lives. Not to mention my ship. If we ran aground on the reef, I could at least salvage part of her. Maybe a lot of her. I don't know if you've noticed, Majesty, but your country is in shambles. Good work is hard to come by. This ship means life for a lot of families—not just my sailors, but the coopers who make our wine barrels, the seamstress who mends our sails every year, the pig farmer who sells salted meat for our long hauls."

I tear my eyes from Hector's with reluctance. "Oh, I know," I say to Felix. "I know all that and more. There were four riots in Brisadulce during the last month alone, thanks to a tax increase I was maneuvered into. The people are right to be angry. The Wallows is in more desperate condition than ever, mostly because the blue marlin ran so poorly last season. And did you know the output of the tanners' guild was reduced by thirty-one percent? My fault, you see. I let Basajuan secede, and now we don't have access to their sheep hides until we work out a trade agreement with Cosmé." I turn my back on the storm and lean against the railing. Felix regards me with undisguised alarm. Maybe he's worried I'll commandeer his ship after all. Maybe I will.

But I'd rather convince him. "Joya d'Arena needs to heal. And we could. We're in desperate need of timber for rebuilding, for instance. Someone could make a fortune hauling mangrove and cypress from the southern islands. But no one will take on the venture. Because of the recent war, because of the animagus' threat, and because"—it hurts to say it, but I'm going to anyway—"and because I have been a weak ruler. Everyone is frightened. They're holed up in their homes, the curtains closed, growing hungrier and more desperate.

"I *need* the *zafira*. It's the only way I know to neutralize the Invierne threat once and for all and consolidate my own power. So while I appreciate the sentiment you feel for your crew and the livelihoods of those connected with the *Aracely*'s commerce, please understand that I have a whole kingdom on my shoulders. And yes, your ship is worth the risk."

He sighs, fingering one of the beads in his beard. "You really think we should steer straight into a hurricane."

"I do."

"Can you guarantee that no one will be harmed? That God will see us through?"

I shake my head. "I won't lie to you. There is always a cost. All I can guarantee is that it will be the right thing."

"It's insane," he says, but without vehemence.

"It's faith," I say.

He caresses the gunwale with his fingertips. "If we do this, I insist on telling the crew everything, about the *zafira*, about your Invierno refugee. They should know why we risk so much."

I hesitate only a moment. "Agreed."

He bows from the waist. "By your leave, Your Majesty." And he hurries down to the main deck to speak with his men.

Hector leans forward onto the rail, and we gaze out to sea

together, our shoulders not quite brushing. "I won't let any-thing happen to you," he says. "You'll survive this."

"You will too," I tell him, and my voice is fierce. "I order you to. I didn't go to so much trouble to heal you only to let you die."

He traces a whorled pattern in the wood with his fingertip. "What trouble exactly, Elisa? What happened that day?"

"I . . ." It's on the tip of my tongue to tell him everything, to tell him how I feel. "I wasn't harmed in any way, if that's what you're worried about."

"You thought you were going to die to save me, so yes, I'm worried about that."

I hate keeping something from him. I've trusted him with everything, always. But I couldn't bear it if he didn't return the sentiment. Or maybe I couldn't bear it if he did.

Thunder rumbles in the distance as I slide my hand along the rail toward him. I find his fingers and clutch them tight. He squeezes back.

I say, "I hope that I am . . ." Foolish enough? Courageous enough? ". . . *able* to tell you someday."

He sweeps his thumb across my knuckles. "I shouldn't press the matter. You're not obligated to tell me anything. You're my queen."

For some reason his words sting, and I find myself fighting tears. I pull my hand away. Lightning spears the horizon as I say, "I need to tell Mara what's happening."

I feel his watchful eyes on me as I descend the stair. Ever the dutiful guard.

24

Night comes early with the mounting clouds. Crewmen light the ship's lanterns and quietly go about the tasks of tying down cargo and checking and rechecking the rigging. I marvel at their brave acceptance. They continue to avoid me, but after watching them at work for a bit, I can't help it: I have to seek them out. Accompanied by Hector, I pat each one on the shoulder, ask his name, tell him "Thank you." Up close, it's easier to see the fear in their weathered faces. But they still manage to duck their heads and mutter a few clumsy "Your Majesty"s.

There can be no doubt that we face a hurricane. Already the lanterns swing violently as we dip and plunge through the sea. White water gushes over the prow at irregular intervals, soaking everything. We've shortened the sails to take less wind, and several crewmen have lashed themselves to the rigging, ready to cut the sails completely if the masts start to give way.

I stand with Felix and Hector near the ship's wheel, for we are sure to go off course. No ship can sail directly into a storm.

The best we can do is tack through the water, pushing directly into the waves whenever possible to avoid being capsized. My Godstone and I will be the ship's compass, pointing us in the right direction as we do our best to make corrections. Hector holds thickly coiled rope in his hands, ready to tie me down if the waves threaten to wash us overboard.

I have trouble keeping my feet as we climb and dive. In the night, the waves are a huge black darkness tipped in foamy white, swelling higher than the gunwale, but always, at the last moment, our prow breaks through and my stomach drops as we slip down the other side.

Felix tells me it's too early to be afraid, that they've survived harsher weather than this. "We are barely at the edge of the storm, Your Majesty," he says with a grin that holds more mania than humor. "The worst is yet to come."

An older man with a gray beard and a missing earlobe rushes up to the captain and yells, "Bilge is halfway to the first mark."

"What does that mean?" I holler through the wind.

"Some of the water coming over the side filters down to the bilge," Hector yells back. The wind has whipped his hair into a wild, curly mess. "Someone mans the pump at all times, but if the water gets high enough, we'll have to use buckets too. If it goes past the third mark, the ship is lost."

And then it begins to rain in great stinging sheets.

The deck is slick and chilled. I cling to a bit of rail stretching across middeck that seems to be made for that purpose. The sky flashes brighter than daylight a split second before thunder crashes around us.

God, please show us the way and keep us safe.

A smidge of warmth snakes through me, bringing the sensation, stronger than ever, of tugging at my navel.

Hector bends close. "You just prayed, didn't you?"

I look up at him, surprised.

"I can always tell," he says. "Your face changes." He wears a slight smile, as if we're sharing a secret. Lamplight shines against the planes of his sea-soaked face.

The ship rolls sideways, flinging me against him. He wraps one arm around me, braces us against the railing with the other. "Maybe having you on deck is not such a good idea," he says in my ear. "You heard what Felix said. Things are going to get worse."

"I have to help navigate!"

"There will come a point when it doesn't matter anymore, when we just have to survive."

I stare up at him, acutely aware in spite of everything of the way our bodies are pressed together. What if I *don't* survive? It would surprise no one if I died young, like most of the bearers before me.

Or worse, what if *he* doesn't survive? I lost Humberto before I could tell him how I felt. I can't bear to do it again.

"Hector, I need to tell you—"

"Oh, no, you don't," he says, putting a finger to my lips. "No good-byes, no confessions. Because we are going to live. Both of us. It's faith, right?"

Lightning streaks the sky behind him, as if in punctuation.

"Yes," I say. "Faith." He's right. I need to prepare to *live*, not to die.

Maybe I've been preparing to die for too long—ever since that day in the desert when I decided it would be better to die in service to God than to live uselessly. And maybe I will. Maybe tonight.

But I'm suddenly frantic to do something—anything—to prove to myself that I won't, to feel some kind of power over my predestined future. Hector's face is very close. It would be so easy to wrap my arms around his neck, force his lips to mine, and kiss him until we are both breathless.

I want more from Hector than a single ill-timed kiss. No, I want more from life. I clench my fists, and my nails bite into my palms as I think, *My supposed* destiny *can drown itself in the deepest part of the sea. Along with everyone else's plans for me.*

"Elisa?"

"I'll be right back!" I yell, and dash across the deck to Captain Felix's quarters.

I bang open the doors, and Mara looks up, startled. She's huddled on the floor at the foot of the bed, knees to chest, and her cheeks are streaked with tears. "Elisa?" she says waveringly.

I shed water everywhere as I grab my pack and drop down beside her. The ship rolls while I reach inside for the naked figurine that holds the lady's shroud.

"What are you doing?" she asks.

"Preparing to live." I put my hand to the stopper.

Mara grabs my wrist. "Wait." She reaches for her satchel

and retrieves a matching figurine. "Me too," she says with a shaky grin. "Ready?"

In answer, I pull the stopper and upend a few seeds into my palm. She does the same. In unison, we toss them back and start chewing. They're bitter and hard and taste faintly of lemon rind.

The ship rolls again, and I almost choke on the seeds. The captain's chair slides across the planking and tips over at our feet. Mara whimpers. I wrap my arms around her, and she does the same right back, mindless of my soaked state. I shouldn't linger, but I revel in the luxury of stealing these precious moments with my friend.

"You should go," she says, disengaging.

I rise to my feet, and though the floor sways beneath me, I feel steadier than I have in a while. "Stay here. I won't risk you getting washed overboard."

She nods. "Be safe, Elisa."

I open the doors to a dark deluge. Water pours from the frame, soaking the entrance. Hector is there already, as if standing watch, and he helps me fight the wind to pull the doors closed.

My thanks are whipped away as we lurch and slide across the deck. Captain Felix mans the wheel himself. "I need a bearing, Majesty," he shouts.

I grab the rail and close my eyes. Wind sends rain stinging into my face, and it's a moment before I can focus enough to feel the tug, but it's there, steady and sure. I point toward starboard. "That way."

What I don't tell him is that the Godstone has gone ice cold.

Felix gives the order and swings the wheel while others adjust the sails, and slowly, gradually, we fight through wind and waves toward a new heading.

During the next hour, the waves grow higher. The deck tips precariously as we climb and plunge. My hands become stiff with cold, and my grip on the rail slips. I slide to the deck and wrap a leg around the rail instead. Hector takes it as a cue to tie me down. He wraps the rope once around my waist and ties off with a quick but sturdy knot.

Then he pulls a long dagger from one of his vambraces and plunges it into the planking beside my knee. "If something happens to me," he yells, "you may need to cut yourself free."

I nod, praying, *Please don't let anything happen to Hector.*

Lightning streaks the sky ahead, illuminating the strangest cloud I've ever seen. It's a long, crooked finger poking at the ocean's writhing surface, sending spray in all directions.

I tug on Hector's pants and point. But there is only darkness, and he looks at me, confused. "Wait for the lightning. Watch!"

The next time lightning cracks the sky, the finger cloud is even closer, close enough for me to understand its Godlike power, how even the mighty sea tossing us about like driftwood is helpless against it.

"Tornado!" Hector yells, and others take up the cry, but their syllables are washed away by driving wind and stinging rain.

The ship rolls, so hard and fast that Hector falls hard to the deck. He slips across the planking, toward the edge.

"Hector!" I reach for him, but the rope at my waist holds me fast.

He grapples against the planking, finds purchase with his fingertips, but the *Aracely* continues to tip. Water pours by him, and I know he can't hold on for long.

"Felix, help!" I scream, but thunder booms all around us, and he does not hear. He fights with the wheel, straining to turn the ship into the wave before we capsize.

I grab for the knife at my knee. It takes both hands to pry it from the deck. I start to saw at the rope around my waist, but then I get a better idea.

"Hector!" I wave the knife to make sure I have his attention, then pantomime what I plan to do. He nods once, his face veined with strain.

I aim carefully, then let the knife slide toward him. He hangs by one hand as he reaches out to catch it, flips it around, slams the blade hard into the deck.

I breathe easier, knowing he'll last longer holding to a knife grip. Hopefully long enough to crest this wave.

All available deckhands are at the opposite side of the boat, clinging to the rail, trying to use the weight of their bodies to keep the *Aracely* from going over. Felix continues to battle with the wheel, gesturing wildly to adjust the sails.

I look toward the masts and see the problem: the mizzen sail has not turned like the others. Something must have broken; it's dragging us, keeping us from steering into the wave. Two figures hang like spiders from the rigging, sawing at the ropes to cut the sail free.

Hector has begun a stomach crawl toward me, using the dagger to pull himself up, which means that for the split second it takes to reposition the dagger, he must hang by the fingertips of one hand. I shout at him to stop, but a blast of seawater fills my mouth and chokes me.

Something claps, like a drumbeat, and the mizzen sail drops for a split second before being snatched away by the wind. Only one man remains in the tattered rigging near the mast. Where is the other?

Realization dawns. *Oh, God. He's gone.*

But now the ship turns, with agonizing slowness. The prow rises. Water gushes over my face, up my nostrils. I'm hacking and gasping for air as the bowsprit pierces the wave's crest.

And then we're falling, falling into the trough. I feel Hector's arms wrap around me as we level off at last.

Thank you, God. Thank you. Hector leans against my shoulder in exhaustion, and his chest lurches against me as he coughs water from his lungs. He clings to me, taking strength instead of giving it for once.

"Majesty!" Captain Felix yells. "A bearing!"

The tug is stronger than ever. I point, to port this time, as lightning flashes a portrait of the sky.

I am pointing directly at the tornado, which is nearly upon us.

The captain gapes at me, frozen with shock. His beard is plastered to his face, and it seems as though I stare down a darker, wilder version of Hector. He starts to protest, but a deckhand plunges across the deck to the wheel. "Bilge is to the third mark," he yells. "We cannot bail fast enough."

Felix's features soften as he nods acknowledgment, and the deckhand disappears as quickly as he came. The captain closes his eyes, caresses a spoke of the wheel. His lips move with prayer, and I know he is preparing to die.

One arm still wrapped around Hector, I put my free hand to my stomach. The rope at my waist is in the way. I wrestle it downward to reveal my Godstone, and the effort scrapes my skin through my saltwater-soaked blouse.

I place my fingertips to the stone. *What am I supposed to do? I know I should have faith, but this, God, this is impossible.*

The boat is suddenly steady, though spray comes at us from all sides. It's the tornado, more powerful than even the waves, forcing calm to the nearby water before sucking it up.

Hector shifts so that I sit between his legs. He wraps one arm around the railing, the other around me, as if he can protect me from the monster bearing down on us.

I lean back and lift my lips toward his ear. "Pray with me," I say.

"I have been."

I find his hand, guide it toward my navel, press his fingertips over my blouse to my Godstone. I hold it there as I intone, "Blessed is he who walks the path of God. He shall stray neither to the left nor the right, for the righteous right hand guides him for all his days."

Hector is muttering too, urgently, though I can't make out the words. There's power in this, something about the two of us praying together; it builds inside me.

"The champion must not waver," I say, as warmth floods

me until my body sings with it, until I am a goblet about to overflow. "The champion must stay the course. Yea, though he pass through the shadows of darkness he shall not fear, for God's righteous—"

A crack, even louder than the storm. I open my eyes to see that the tornado has snapped the bowsprit in two. Needles of water sting my cheeks and eyes. In moments, we'll be ripped apart and washed away.

Hector's hand slips beneath my soaked blouse, his fingers slide across my skin, find the Godstone. He presses down gently. I cover his hand with my own. "The champion must not waver," he says in my ear. "Yea, though *she* pass through the shadow of darkness, *she* shall not fear, for God's righteous right hand shall sustain her and give her new life triumphant."

The warmth inside me becomes an inferno. My body blazes with heat, with desire, with desperation. The Godstone is riotous with it, pulsing with unused power. *God, I want to live. I want all of us to live. What should I do? Why did you lead us here?*

Another snap, a sail ripped asunder. The ship begins to pivot.

And then I sense it, tiny tendrils curling into me. I can't see them, but I feel them, like will-o'-the-wisps on the wind, coming from every direction. I know them well, for I've been living with them my whole life.

Prayers.

Everyone on this ship is praying right now, I'm sure of it. And their broken, desperate thoughts flit toward me and feed my stone with even more power.

The tornado rips into the side of the ship. Planking and splinters fly everywhere.

Hector's prayer falters. His grip on me freezes for an instant before tightening, even more fiercely than before. Then his cold, wet lips press against my cheek, just in front of my earlobe.

He says, "I love you, Elisa."

Something breaks inside me. The world flashes brighter than daylight for the briefest moment—debris from the ship spins in the air, and beyond it, the largest wave I've ever known looms wicked and black—and then there is nothing but darkness and calm and a stillness like death.

I can't see. I can't feel my limbs. I can't hear. It's as though I've ceased to exist, save for my thoughts in a vast emptiness.

And then a heartbeat, true and steady. No, it's two heartbeats, mine and Hector's, beating almost as one.

And then nothing at all.

25

I'M lying on my side, my cheek mashed into the planking. Hector's body curls protectively around me.

Everything is still and bright, so bright that I blink against the pain of it. A soft breeze caresses my face, bringing the scent of hibiscus. A gull cries, a slide of sound from low to high.

A gull!

Gasping, I sit up.

Crewmen lie prone all around me. I worry they might be dead, but then my eye catches movement at the wheel. It's Felix. His great beard twitches as he mutters and stirs from the place he fell. Others stir around us.

Alive. All of us, alive.

I look down at Hector. Sleep has softened his features. He seems so peaceful. So young. Before I realize what I'm doing, I'm tracing the line of his eyebrow with my fingertips, trailing down his cheek, to the shadow of his cheekbone, where a drop of blood has welled. It's caused by a splinter; it must have speared into him when the tornado hit.

Alarmed, I look closer to make sure he breathes. Where there is one splinter, there could be more. There could be a whole plank, impaled in . . .

His eyelids flutter.

"Hector?"

When he sees me, he shudders with relief. "We're alive," he whispers.

"I did order you to live, after all."

He sits up and looks around. "How?"

"I have no idea. Something to do with everyone's prayers, I think, channeled by my Godstone. Be still. I have to pull this out." I brace his chin with one hand and reach for the splinter with the other. Just enough protrudes for me to grip it with my fingertips. I pull gently but steadily, trying to keep to the exact angle of entry.

He gazes at me without flinching.

The splinter is longer than I thought—the length of the first joint of my forefinger—and a good bit of blood wells up after it. I toss it to the deck.

I'm about to wipe the blood away with my fingers but he traps them, lifts them to his mouth, kisses them. "I thought we were going to die after all," he says. "Right there at the end."

I think about the way he held me, the way we prayed. I remember his fingers on my Godstone, on my *skin*. And I remember what he said.

I blink hard against tears. "You might have saved me. Saved us all. I don't know how the Godstone's power works yet, or how we survived, but you kept me focused."

His gaze drops to my lips. "I shouldn't do this—"

"You really should." And I close the distance between us.

His lips on mine are so sweet, so gentle, like he's savoring me. Learning me. But he doesn't linger there. Instead he kisses the corner of my mouth, my cheek, the tip of my nose. Then he leans back to regard me. His eyes are steady and frank when he says, "I don't regret telling you what I did."

"That's good, because you did say it, and I can't unknow it."

He lifts an eyebrow, smugly amused, and I marvel that for all his usual stoicism, he seems unashamed to have exposed something so personal. "And I can't unfeel it," he says. "I won't let it interfere with my work. Even though I expect things will be . . . difficult."

"Oh, yes," I agree. "Very difficult."

"Land!" someone yells. "Dead ahead!"

We jump to our feet. People stir all around us. There is no sign of the storm. The sky is beautiful and clear, and the water dances lightly, teased by a breeze. I could almost convince myself I imagined the whole thing.

Except that the *Aracely* is a disaster, especially the port side, which has a huge, uneven gouge in the hull where planking was ripped away. Only one sail remains intact, and we sit much too low in the water. In the distance a bluish lump looms on the horizon, and the tug on my Godstone is stronger than ever, pulling me toward it. I just hope the ship holds together long enough to get there.

"We should check on everyone," I say.

He nods. "See to Mara. I'll look for Storm and Belén."

We part, reluctantly, me for the captain's quarters, Hector for the lower deck.

The quarters are in shambles. Paintings and bits of furniture litter the floor, water streaks the walls, and the glass in one of the portholes is shattered, its jagged edges sparking in the sunlight.

Mara huddles on her side in the middle of the bed, her knees curled to her chest.

She looks up when I enter but does not move. "You're alive," she says, and it's almost like a sob.

Something is wrong. I rush over to her. "What is it, Mara? Are you hurt?" I brush the hair away from her face. "We hit a tornado, and—"

"Belén? Is he all right?"

"Hector is checking on him. Mara, tell me."

"My scar. It split open again. The ship tipped so far that I had to hang from the side of the bed. . . ."

"Let me see."

"I'm afraid to move. Elisa, I think it's bad." She lifts the hand cradling her stomach and shows it to me. It's covered in blood.

My heart sinks. "I might be able to stitch it. I watched Cosmé do it often enough. Or Belén! He's done it lots of times. Did you bring your salve?"

She nods. "In the satchel."

I look around frantically for it. Who knows where it ended up after the storm, or if its contents are still intact? I note my own pack, lodged between the fallen chair and a broken shelf. I give a worried thought to the figurine, hoping it didn't break.

"Do you remember where you saw it last? I can't . . ." Then I get another idea.

I take a deep breath against the audacity of it. Could I heal her? The way I did Hector? That was sort of an accident. Actually, everything I've ever done with the Godstone has been sort of an accident. But I came here, put everyone to extraordinary risk, on the chance that I could figure out how to channel its power deliberately.

"Mara, give me your hands. I'm going to try something."

She does, her gaze trusting. I grab them, trying to ignore how cold and slick they are with her blood.

"Er . . . close your eyes and relax. Hector was unconscious when I did it to him."

She closes them.

Think, Elisa!

When I healed Hector, I felt the power stir inside me, sucked in from the world around us through my Godstone. I try to imagine it, the sensation of something flowing, filling me up. *Please, God. Help me.*

The power surges into me like a flood, and I gasp, delighted. So easy this time. So natural and right.

I say, "For the righteous right hand of God is a healing hand; blessed is he who seeks renewal, for he shall be restored."

Nothing.

Last time, it happened out of desperation and need. Out of love. Maybe love is the trick.

I focus hard, thinking about what Mara means to me. I consider her brave acceptance of the danger we share, her determination to learn everything she needs to be a good lady's maid. I've watched her edge away from the shy, broken girl whose village had just been destroyed to become a cheerful, laughing person, resolved to embrace her new life.

Mara is precious to me. I love her.

I whisper, "For love is more beautiful than rubies, sweeter than honey, finer than the king's wine. And no one has greater love than he who gives his own life for a friend."

The power is rushing out of me even before I finish. Mara stretches out her legs, arches her back as her face contorts in agony, and I lurch forward, worried that I've made things worse. But then her body goes limp. After a few panting breaths, her face relaxes into an easy smile.

"I think it worked," she says. Gently she probes her stomach with her fingertips. "It hurt, but it worked."

My breath catches with relief. So much easier this time. Maybe it's my proximity to the *zafira*. Or maybe I *am* finally learning to channel my stone's power. "That's good," I say. "That's very . . ." My head swims. "Just need to lie . . ." I collapse onto the bed.

I wake to a sea of faces. I blink up at them, recognizing Hector, Felix, Mara, Belén. "Stop hovering," I growl sleepily.

They lurch away, except for Hector, who says, "Are you all right?"

His hair is mussed, his eyes huge. He seems so young all of a sudden, so unsure. It's definitely not a good idea to wrap my arms around his neck and force him to kiss me in front of the others. "I'm fine. Tired but fine." I sit up and swing my legs over the side of the bed. "Mara?"

"The wound closed up perfectly," she says, her voice breathy with wonder. "And my scar . . . it's still there, but it's softer. Healthier, I think."

The relief is so powerful that my knees shake. Or maybe I'm just that fatigued.

The captain rubs at his beard and asks, "You think you could heal everyone on board? We have a broken leg, a few bad scrapes. One of my men can't get the water out of his lungs."

"Absolutely not," Hector says. "You've seen how it exhausts her."

"I'm not sure I could," I admit. "I think it only works when . . . for people I . . ." *For people I love.* I hesitate to say it straight out, because returning his sentiment would just make it worse, in the end. "It only works for people who are very dear to me," I finish lamely.

But hope flashes across Hector's face, so raw and exquisite. Maybe I ought to tell him anyway. I could lie to him, tell him that our future has a happy ending.

Instead, I scoot off the bed and step away, putting distance between us. "How is Storm?" I ask, refusing to look in Hector's direction.

"Uninjured," Belén says. "More interestingly, I haven't heard him complain in hours."

Hours. "How long was I—"

"Hours," Mara confirms. "We were very worried. We're almost to the island."

I rush out the double doors and take the steps to the beakhead two at a time.

The view makes my hands fly to my mouth in awe.

We approach a crescent harbor of aquamarine water, ringed with crystal-white sand. Beyond the sand is a forest of coconut palms, whipping in the breeze. And beyond them are impossibly steep mountains, or towers, or maybe the fingers of God, jutting into the sky, trapping clouds with their fingertips. They seem verdant and alive, smothered in green, veined by shimmering waterfalls. White birds with pointed wings dive and soar among them, giving scale to their vastness.

The tug at my navel is stronger than ever. I press my fingers to the Godstone, as if to keep it from leaping out of my body and into the sea.

"I've never seen this place before," says a voice beside me, and I jump. It's Felix. He rests his forearms on the rail. "No one has. It's not on any of my charts. My best guess is that we are somewhere south and slightly west of Selvarica, but I'm not sure I could navigate here a second time."

"Perhaps," I say, "the only way to get here is through a sorcerous hurricane."

"Perhaps. I just hope we don't have the same trouble when we leave."

I look down at the water, so clear and beautiful. Silvery fish dart away from the ship as we sail forward, and patches of dark green plants wave with the current. They seem to be just below the surface, but our draft is deep, so I know it is only an illusion.

"How is the *Aracely*?" I ask. "Can we repair her?"

"We're not taking on any more water, so the bilge will empty soon enough. I'll send divers down to inspect the hull when we anchor to be sure. The bowsprit is lost. We've only the main sail left. I've a small spare in the hold we could unroll and use as a mizzen. Looks like there's timber to be found on the island, enough to patch the port side. It will take a couple of weeks, but I expect we'll limp away from this place just fine, so long as the weather holds. Another storm and we're done for, so pray for sunshine."

A couple of weeks. That's far too long. Ximena and Tristán can't keep up a pretense with decoy Elisa forever. Our ruse is sure to be discovered, and a queen can only go missing for so long before everything degenerates into chaos, before ambitious condes—like Eduardo—begin wrestling for power in the wake of my disappearance.

"Our biggest problem," Felix says, "is supplies. Looks like we'll have plenty of fresh water, but we lost an entire barrel of salted pork, and one of the grain bins is soaked. We'll have to forage and fish, not just for our stay here, but for the return journey."

I'm about to ask after his wounded crewmen when Hector saunters up and leans against the railing. "It's beautiful, isn't it?" he says.

I nod, gazing at a sparkling stream pouring from the jungle and into the sea. From here it looks like a silver ribbon winding through green velvet. "All that water! The place looks *alive*. It's unnatural."

He laughs. "You've been in the desert too long."

I grin up at him. "I look at those waterfalls and see the wealth of a thousand nations."

"Maybe that's exactly what they are. Do you sense anything? Is it still guiding you?" He glances toward my navel, and my stomach does a little flip to remember his hands on my skin.

"It's very strong now," I tell him. "And when I healed Mara, it was a lot easier. The power was right there when I called it, even though . . . even though . . . I . . ."

He studies me, letting me struggle for words. Then, "Even though the need was not as great?" he offers softly. "She wasn't injured as badly."

I nod.

A crewman's head appears at the stair. "Captain!" he calls. "Eight and a half fathoms at last sounding."

"Drop anchor!" Felix booms.

"Ready to go ashore?" Hector asks.

I stare at the island; it's so wild and foreign and foreboding. "Ready," I lie.

26

I hurry back to the captain's quarters to grab my pack. I peek inside and find, to my immense relief, that my bottle of lady's shroud is intact. Mara holds up her satchel and nods, which I take to mean that hers survived too.

The *Aracely*'s dinghy was lost to the hurricane, but by some miracle our trawler stayed tied down on the quarterdeck. I'm eager to get to shore, but Hector insists on letting another group go first. "Let them scout around, make sure it's safe," he says, and I agree reluctantly.

I pace back and forth across the deck as a group of eight men with supplies rows toward the beach. Once they are close enough, they jump out and pull the boat onto shore, unload, and then disappear into the jungle. It seems like forever passes before they reemerge, waving with a signal that all is well. Finally two men push off and hop back into the boat, leaving the rest behind to start setting up a camp.

Mara, Belén, Storm, Hector, and I are in the second group to ferry over. As we settle in the boat, the tug on my Godstone is so insistent as to be nearly painful. To distract myself from the discomfort, I trail my fingers in the warm, clear water as we skim the bay. The fish astound me. I see brightest gold, flashes of red, even Godstone blue. I'm tempted to dive in for a swim.

Once we reach the shallows, I jump from the boat and splash through water, heedless of soaking my clothes. We drag the boat onto the sand, and I'm surprised when my legs waver, as if the land leaps and rolls like an ocean.

Hector notices my teetering and grins. "You'll adjust to solid ground soon enough."

The sailors who disembarked before us have begun setting up a haphazard camp. They've already lined a fire pit and erected one tent—but they're doing it all wrong. I suppose that, as seamen, they've had few opportunities to organize encampments on land. On the other hand, I've had plenty.

"You there," I call. "Haul the supplies farther into the trees. We need shelter from wind and surf. And you, would you move the fire pit, please? Find a spot where sparks won't catch on dried palm fronds overhead." I tap my fingers to my lips. If we're to be here for weeks, then we need a latrine pit, far away from our water source. "Belén, do you see a good spot for digging a—"

"Latrine? Against the cliff face, there," he says, pointing. "It's downwind and far enough from the stream."

"Yes, perfect." I gesture toward a man I've seen in Felix's confidence on several occasions. "Do you read and write?"

"Yes, Your Majesty."

"Compile an inventory of all our supplies—fishing gear, foodstuffs, tools, material we could use for repair, everything you can think of."

"Yes, Your Majesty."

I eye the stream critically. The silt has created a small sand-bar that protects it at low tide and keeps the mouth narrow. I mutter, mostly to myself, "We may have enough undamaged netting to stretch all the way across, which would take care of our fishing needs even if we come up short on other tackle."

I look up to find Hector staring at me thoughtfully.

"Anything I haven't thought of yet?" I ask him.

He closes the distance between us. My breath catches as he grasps my upper arm. In a low voice meant for my ears only, he says, "If you were like this, with this kind of confidence, this clarity of thought, while in Brisadulce, no one would dare challenge your rule."

My heart sinks a little. He means it as encouragement more than criticism, and the thumb sweeping across my shoulder attests to how much he cares. But it stings because he's right. A whole country is so much vaster, more complicated, more important, than a village of desert refugees or a temporary island camp. That's why I'm here, after all. Because I need something more than just me to do a good job of it. *I* haven't been enough.

"Perhaps I spoke out of turn," Hector says. "But I truly believe you have it in you to be a great queen."

I lift my chin. "Thank you for saying so."

"I'll get started on that latrine." He turns to go.

"Hector, wait."

He whirls. Sand clings to the bottom of his soaked breeches, and the moisture in the air has turned his hair into a mass of waves.

I say, "You have *never* said anything to me that is out of turn."

He knows I'm speaking of a different moment entirely, for he allows himself a slow, satisfied smile that turns my insides to date pudding.

I add, "I expect honesty and truth from you always."

He nods once, firmly. "And you shall have it."

We end up making camp in a small clearing well back from shore, where the coconut palms are interspersed with rambling pink bougainvillea bushes and thick banyan trees with sprawling roots. Morning-glory vines wind up their trunks, dripping purple flowers. Their close cousins, the yellow night bloomers, twine in sync with them, and it's hard to see where one ends and the other begins. But when evening falls, the morning glories will twist closed as the night bloomers unfurl, bathing our campsite in soft light.

After a late-afternoon meal of dried jerky, pistachios, and fresh mango, I announce that I will begin searching for the *zafira* first thing in the morning, while Felix's men make repairs to the ship.

"You know which direction to go?" Hector asks.

"Oh, yes," I say, pressing my fingertips to the Godstone. "It's very . . . compelling."

"I'd rather explore a bit first," he says. "The island seems to be deserted, but I'd like to be sure."

I sigh. Of course he would. "The day after tomorrow, then?"

"I think it would be best."

I nod, but I avoid his gaze as I come to a decision.

The hurricane is not the only test I will face; I'm certain of it. Storm said it will get harder as I get closer, and I've put everyone else at risk enough as it is. We have lost two men overboard already. I could not bear to lose Mara or Belén. Or Hector.

I have demanded his honesty but not given him mine, for tomorrow I will deceive him. While he's out exploring, I will slip away—alone.

When I finally dare glance at him, he is studying me through narrowed eyes.

Beside me, Mara wipes her fingers on her pants and says, with a mouth still full of mango, "I need a bath. And to wash my clothes. Maybe we could find a good place upstream?"

I'm glad for the excuse to turn away from Hector. "That sounds lovely. My boots still stink of sewer."

"Belén and I will scout first," Hector says. "We'll need to sweep the area."

Mara and I make no effort to disguise our shared eye roll.

We tell Captain Felix where we're going, and then the four of us make our way upstream. It's a rough hike through thick jungle and slippery mud. The farther inland we go, the rockier and steeper it gets, and I step carefully.

At last the stream widens into a pool, hemmed in by black boulders and curving palms. In the middle of the pool, just slightly off center, is a large bean-shaped rock with a flat top. "It's perfect!" Mara exclaims.

While Hector and Belén scout around, we empty our packs and rinse everything—spare clothes, knives, water skins—of any leftover sewage. I even pull out my crown box. The wood is warped and streaked with salt, the cushion a soggy mess. But the Godstone crown is as pristine as ever. I dunk it in the pool, wipe it down carefully with my spare blouse, and then set it atop my pack to dry.

When they are out of sight, when we can't even hear them rustling through the jungle, we pull out our bottles of lady's shroud and quickly down the appropriate dose. Mara grins all the while, delighted with our little intrigue. But I feel awkward and strange. I'm still not sure what I'm going to do. And Hector feels far too important to be merely the object of two giggling girls playing at love.

But maybe that's how it's supposed to be. Perhaps by forcing smallness onto this thing that is so huge in my heart, I'll be able to manage it.

They return and declare the area safe. "We'll be within earshot," Hector says as he and Belén retreat downstream.

"I just bet you will," Mara mutters.

I look at her, startled. "You really think they would . . . peek?"

She sighs. "Just wishing. Neither of them would. Too honorable." She waggles a finger at me. "But don't think it hasn't crossed their minds."

I manage a wan smile in return. The thought of being so exposed fills me with a little excitement and a lot of dismay. I don't despair of my body the way I used to. But it's still worrying.

Being naked before Mara, however, is another matter; she's my lady-in-waiting, after all. "Race you," I say.

Together we struggle with the laces of our blouses, shuck our boots and our pants, and jump in. It's deep, and when I break the surface, I gasp from the cold shock. But it's clean and clear and wonderful, and soon Mara and I are splashing and laughing and forgetting to wash anything.

We swim for a long time before Mara finally grabs soap from her pack and we lather everything—our skin, our hair, our clothes. We hang the clothes to dry, then lie side by side on the flat rock, soaking up the warmth of late afternoon.

"Your scar," I say. "It really is better." It's less angry, less puckered.

"Yours too," she says, and then she laughs. "We're an oddly matched pair, aren't we?"

The sun is dipping behind the giant peaks and tree frogs are beginning to chorus by the time we swim to shore and don our still-damp clothes. We find Hector and Belén downstream a ways, and it's obvious they did some washing up of their own, for they are scrubbed clean and smell faintly of soap.

"Sorry to keep you waiting so long," I say to Hector as we begin the trek back. "We lost track of time."

"It's not a problem," he says, but his voice is curt. I glance up to find his face has gone flinty cold.

I look away, feeling vaguely hurt. But I won't ask if I've done something to anger him in front of the others. The four of us hike through the jungle in silence.

The night bloomers have unfurled by the time we return

to camp. Our tents float in a garden of stars, reflecting palest blue in their soft light. A breeze rustles the palm fronds above us.

After a quick meal of whitefish baked on sticks over the fire pit, I unravel the hasty braid Mara did for me after our swim. I'm beginning to loose the laces of my blouse when the import of what I'll do tomorrow hits me. My fingers pause on the ties.

I know so little about the *zafira*. I have no idea what will happen or what I'll find. I don't even know if I'll make it back. What if I never see him again?

I crawl from my tent and go in search of Hector.

I find him on the beach, just outside the line of palm trees. He sits on a hollowed-out log, one knee bent, the other long leg stretched out in the sand. He grips a tall stick, which he whittles with his dagger. It takes me a moment to realize he's making a spear.

He looks up as I approach, his face unreadable.

"Do you mind company?" I ask.

With a lift of his chin, he indicates the space on the log next to him. I settle beside him, careful to avoid the end of his stick, and lean forward to rest my elbows on my knees. The sea glows with the light of a half moon. I lift my face to the breeze and listen to the gentle lap and suck of the surf and the *whisk-whisk* sound of Hector's knife against the wood.

"What are you doing here, Elisa?" he asks in a weary voice.

I flinch away. "I . . . I didn't mean to intrude. If you'd rather be al—"

"Did you come to torment me?"

"What?" Well, yes, maybe a little. "I know you're angry at me, but I'm not sure why."

He's gripping his dagger too tightly, and his next stroke lops off the tip of his spear. He sighs. Dagger still in hand, he wipes his brow with his wrist. He says, "I'm not angry at you. Mostly at myself."

"Oh?"

He opens his mouth to say something but changes his mind. Instead he whittles at his ruined stick, and I recognize the expression as the one he wears when chewing on a particularly tough problem.

Finally he says, "Honesty in all things, right?"

"Yes, please." But I'm coiling in on myself, trying to make my heart a stone, because I have no idea what he's going to say.

He stares out across the moon-glass bay. "It was difficult for me today," he says, "to stand guard for you. To hear you laughing and splashing with Mara, knowing you were . . . bathing. Very . . ."

"Oh," I breathe. "I see."

"The most important thing I do is protect you. I would die to keep you safe." He's gripping his dagger so tightly his knuckles are turning white. "But you make it very difficult. Sometimes you can't help it, of course. But sometimes you can."

"I don't understand." I don't know why, but my chest tightens with shame. "I've been taking your advice. I'm taking fewer risks. . . ."

He lets the dagger and spear drop into the sand and twists

to straddle the log. His eyes are very close when he says, "I can't defend against *you*."

My heart is a drum in my chest.

His forefinger reaches toward me, to my cheek, gently sweeps a strand of hair behind my ear. From there his finger trails along my jawline, up to my mouth.

My lips part. My whole body buzzes.

"I told you I wouldn't let it interfere with my work. But every time you smile at me, and especially when you look at me the way you're looking at me right now, everything disappears." His thumb sweeps across my bottom lip, down my chin. His voice is low and dark as he says, "When it happens, I'm not guarding you anymore. Your enemy could come up behind me, and I would never know, because all I'm thinking about is how badly I want you."

My heart sings. I stare at his mouth. It's beautiful, with full pale lips set off by his sun-darkened skin. I would only have to lean the tiniest bit to close the distance between us.

He starts to back away.

In desperation, I blurt, "Mara says I should take you as my lover."

His indrawn breath is as sharp and hard as if I've wounded him. My face fills with heat, and I can't bear to look at his face. I'm embarrassed at my own weakness, unable to say such an important thing straight out. *I want you as my lover*, I should have said. But I can't bring the words to my lips, because if he says no, he'll be saying no to me, instead of merely to Mara's idea.

But he'll have none of that. "Elisa. Are you asking?"

Panic and hope war inside me. It's up to me, as it has always been. I can ask him or not. Asking him is terrifying. But not asking would be so much worse.

"Yes, I'm asking. Hector, I—"

With a swift motion, he cups the back of my head and presses his warm lips to mine. The pit of my stomach drops away as I open my mouth to his.

He groans, wrapping his other arm around my waist, pulling me toward him until I am almost in his lap. I arch against him; my breath comes fast as he explores my mouth. Before, his kisses were patient and sweet. But there is nothing of sweetness in him now, just heat and desperate need.

He tangles his fingers in my hair and yanks my head back, breaking our kiss. I let out a little "Oh!" of disappointment, but then he's sliding his mouth along my jaw, to the pulse at my throat. "Elisa," he murmurs. "I've wanted to do this for a long, long time."

His words send me spiraling with dizzy gladness. I clutch at his hair—it's even softer than I imagined—and press my lips to the top of his head. I close my eyes, wanting to memorize this perfect moment, and I breathe deeply of leather oil and fresh-washed jungle and something a little sharper, something distinctly Hector.

His lips brush my collarbone and then dip lower, toward my breasts. I slide my hands to the hem of his shirt and start to pull, desperate for more, more skin, more *him*.

He freezes. Then he pushes me away.

"Hector?" I gasp out, suddenly aching and bereft.

He closes his eyes tight, takes a deep breath. Opens them. They are huge and warm and . . . wet? as he whispers, "Elisa . . . I . . ."

Why did he stop? Did I do something wrong?

He tries again. "I can't. I won't." He slides back, putting cold hard space between us.

I pull my knees to my chest, curl into a tight ball. This is what I've feared, why it was so hard to ask. I find myself shaking my head against whatever comes next.

"I need to explain," he says.

I find a tatter of pride and say, "No, you don't owe me an—"

"I said I need to explain."

I rest my chin on my knee to steady myself. "All right."

He says, "You have every possible power over me."

"What?"

"You have the power of a dear friend, you have all the power that a beautiful woman has over a man who loves her, and most importantly, you are my sovereign. You have the power to command me in everything."

Something about his choice of words makes me angry. "You have plenty of power over me too," I say.

But it's like a dam of control has burst, and he hardly hears me for needing to get out all the thoughts that have been spinning in his head.

"Have I told you about my parents?" he asks. "They're best friends. Partners in everything." His eyes grow distant as he talks, and his mouth curves into a sad smile. "I've watched them my whole life, the way they are with each other. So easy and natural. They finish each other's sentences. They can exchange a look across the dining table and instantly know what the other is thinking."

The gaze he turns on me is fierce, like he's desperate for me to understand. "Neither is subject to the other; they're more like two halves of a whole. And that intertwining of lives, of *being*, it's amazing to see. Being lovers . . . it feels like it would be such a big thing, yes?"

God, yes.

"But it's only the littlest bit of who they are together. And theirs is the only kind of love I could have with you. Anything else makes me *less*." He takes a deep breath, as if steeling himself. "I won't become a helpless marionette or a temporary diversion for my queen."

Pain blooms beneath my breastbone, because I'm starting to understand.

He grabs my hands. I lower my knees and let him draw me toward him until our foreheads touch. "I understand how careful you have to be with your alliances right now. So when we get back from this, you'll marry someone else. I will too. Maybe your sister. We might be able to arrange a tryst on occasion, and God, part of me thinks I should do anything, *anything*, if it means having you once in a while. But it wouldn't be enough." His thumbs caress my knuckles. "Don't you see, Elisa? I love you the way a drowning man loves air. And it would destroy me to have you just a little."

I choke on a sob, and tears leak from my eyes. It's the cruelest of cruelties, for him to love me so deeply but refuse to have me.

He lifts his fingers toward my face and gently, so gently, wipes a tear from my cheek. He says, "I'm glad to know, though, that you think of me that way. I'll always remember that."

Grief threatens to strangle me. I have to push it away before I dissolve into a puddle of despair.

I blurt, "I just started taking lady's shroud. Isn't that silly of me?" I mean to sound cavalier, like I'm ready to laugh at myself and move on. But my face flames as soon as the words are in the air.

He grasps my hands and rises, pulling me to my feet. "You've been thinking about this a lot," he says, a touch of wonder in his voice.

I nod, swallowing against further tears. "At least as much as you have."

"Oh, I doubt that very much." And suddenly he's kissing me again, a deeper, longer kiss, and it's a good thing our arms are wrapped around each other, because I don't think I could stand on my own.

I want the moment to last forever, but of course it can't. This time, when he pushes me away, I'm ready for it. I slide my arms from his shoulders, let them fall to my sides.

He takes a step back. We regard each other solemnly.

He says, "I won't kiss you again."

My vision wavers and the world tilts beneath my feet. *I won't kiss you again.* Humberto said that to me once. It proved prophetic, for he died not long after.

Hector is turning his back, walking away from me. How

can he, when my head still swims with his words and my skin still hums with his touch? When my heart feels as jagged as Godstone shards?

Something wells up inside me. Desperation, maybe, that I have loved and lost yet again. Or terror; people have a tendency to die after kissing me.

But no, neither of those. It's rage.

I clench my hands into fists and yell, "Hector!"

He whips around.

"You were never, *never*, going to be just a diversion to me."

He sighs, nodding. "That was unfair of me," he says. "I'm sorr—"

"And you *will* kiss me again. That and *more*. Count on it."

His mouth slams closed, and his eyes flare like a starving man's.

I whirl and stride away.

27

MORNING brings a light shower, but the skies clear quickly, and our tents steam with the scent of wet goat hair in the rising sun. Hector scurries easily up a nearby palm, using both feet and hands for leverage. He twists off several coconuts, which he drops to the ground. Mara bores holes in them and spices them with cinnamon and honey, and we sit around our too-damp fire pits and drink coconut milk for breakfast.

A group of sailors laden with axes sets off for a grove of acacia trees to cut timber for repairs, while Hector and Belén organize others to explore the island. Hector is shoving a water skin inside his pack when he says to me, "Stay within sight of someone at all times. Don't go anywhere alone. If you sense danger, have someone row you out to the ship. I'll be back by nightfall."

I nod up at him helplessly, knowing I'm going to do the exact opposite of all those things, wishing I could kiss him one last time, or at least tell him how I feel. He deserves to know.

"Hector, I . . ." I'm not sure what stills my tongue. Guilt, maybe. "Be safe," I finish lamely.

"You too." His gaze drops to my lips. And then he hurries away, slinging his pack over his shoulder.

I sense Storm's impossibly tall form at my back. He whispers, "Take me with you."

I whirl on him, glaring.

"Please." For once, his face is devoid of mockery or smugness. "I can sense it too, you know. Not like you can, I'm sure. But it's close. We could find it by nightfall."

"What makes you think I'm—"

"You love your people too much, little queen," he says. "You won't risk them. This is your only opportunity to slip away. He always watches you, you know. Like he's a man dying of thirst in the desert and you're his wavering mirage that stays just out of reach."

"Storm!" I hate hearing it from him. He makes it sound so cheap and ridiculous.

"It must be hard for you. To do what you're planning, knowing he may never forgive you when he finds out."

I'm torn between the desire to strangle him and gratitude that there is at least one person I needn't deceive. "Haven't you ever loved someone, Storm? Besides yourself, I mean."

His head lowers with something that might be regret. "Yes. Oh, yes."

Something about his tone makes me soften toward him. "Then maybe you do know how hard this will be."

"Does this mean you'll take me with you?"

"Hector doesn't trust you."

"But you do."

I sigh. It's true, mostly. And if he can sense the *zafira*, nothing would stop him from sneaking away without me. "Yes, you can come." At least this way, if one of us slips and breaks an ankle, the other can go get help. "No packs," I tell him. "Gather as much food as you can carry in your pockets. I'll meet you upstream in a bit. Try not to let anyone see you."

I have as much right to walk through our campsite as anyone, but it feels as though every eye is on me as I return to my tent. From my pack, I grab my water skin, which I hook through the loop in my utility belt; pouches of dried jerky and dates, which go into the pocket of my pants; and my knife, which I shove down into my boot. I grab my crown too. It's made of Godstones, after all. Maybe it will prove useful. No place to hide it, though. Reluctantly I put it back into my pack.

I feel bulgy and obvious as I make my way to the stream.

Mara sits on the edge atop a rocky outcropping. She holds a smooth gray stone in one hand and is grinding away at a thick brown root. Something spicy-sweet pricks at my nose. She looks up at me and says, "Ginger! A whole patch of it across the stream. I'm going to dry it out and take some home with us."

"It will be a wonderful addition to your satchel," I say.

Something about my tone sobers her. "Is something wrong?"

"No," I'm quick to say. "But I haven't spent much time praying lately, so I'm going upstream a ways for privacy. I'll keep the camp in sight."

"I'll come find you when lunch is ready."

"No! I mean, I might be longer than that. I have a lot on my mind." Truly, I am the worst liar in all of Joya d'Arena.

But she just shrugs. "In that case, I'll save some for you."

"Thank you." I wish I could lean down and hug her, but I dare not arouse suspicion by making a big deal out of what should be a very small good-bye. As I turn my back, I hear the *scrape-scrape* of her grinding stone.

I'm barely out of sight of the camp when Storm melts from the trees to join me. Wordlessly we clamber upstream, and we navigate the jungle trash with agonizing slowness because of our need for stealth. Eventually we pass the pool where Mara and I bathed, and the terrain grows rocky and steep until we are scrambling over moss-covered boulders, using palm trees for leverage that have found stubborn rootholds in deep crevices and patches of mud.

The *zafira* calls to me; I feel it as surely as a lasso around the waist, pulling tighter and more agonizingly with every step. I pray as I walk, and soothing warmth spreads through my abdomen to take the edge off the pain.

The stream dead-ends at a small lake shadowed at the base of one of the mountains. A waterfall rushes down the side of the mountain and crashes into the lake, a faint rainbow shimmering in its white spray. I look up, up, up—but the source of the waterfall is hidden in the clouds.

I stare at the cliffs ahead of us, dismayed, for there is nowhere to go. Yet the *zafira* continues to tug at me.

"Another test," Storm says.

"I've climbed cliffs before, but those are impossible. Too slick and steep. Too high."

"Don't be stupid," he says.

I open my mouth to insult him right back, but hesitate. He's right. I need to think differently.

I take a deep breath and focus hard on the tug. It leads straight across the lake to the cliffs. The base is blurred by mist. Just maybe, a ledge lurks behind the water fog. Or boulders. Something we can use to get a better look.

"We need to go around the lake," I say. "Get to the other side."

"Yes," he says, his eyes distant. "I think so too." Surrounded by jungle foliage, his eyes are greener than ever, like the sun shining through emeralds. I shudder as I turn to lead the way.

The boulders edging the lake are black and porous and sharp, and as I use my hands to climb, the soft pads of my fingers are scraped raw. Movement catches my eye. I peer into the crystal water—it's deep and shadowy, but something swims down there, something large.

I lean closer. It darts away and disappears beneath an underwater overhang. I stare at the spot it vacated, puzzled, as the silt it churned up diffuses to the bottom. The creature was larger than a tuna, but I could have sworn I saw stubby legs and a long, whipping tail. Maybe I imagined it.

"Something wrong?" Storm asks.

"This is a very strange place," I say as I continue on. But I keep a close eye on the water's edge.

Mist from the waterfall settles in my hair, on my clothes, on

my skin. As we approach, the mist turns to spray, then stinging needles of water, and the air is so drenched that I can't
see but a few hand spans in front of me. The waterfall booms
around us, whipping up a fierce wind. I'm careful to place my
hands and feet just so on the slippery rocks, testing each step,
each handhold, before taking another.

And finally we can go no farther. We stand on a slight lip
between the cliff and the lake, the waterfall before us. There
are not enough handholds. No way to climb. Storm yells something, but his voice is whisked away by the merciless water.

Think, Elisa.

I gaze at the cliff face, blinking through water. It's black
with wetness, save for a few mossy outcroppings. Stubborn
ferns curl out of rocky grooves, straining for sunshine. Vines,
choking in parasitic night bloomers, drip down the side and
swish back and forth in the water-churned wind, brushing the
surface of the lake.

The vines. I peer closer. A darkness lies behind them—
something darker than wet rock. I push the vines aside.

It's a cave, or maybe a tunnel, curving behind the waterfall
into utter blackness. The tugging at my Godstone leaves no
doubt that we must go inside.

I curse myself for not bringing my tinderbox, but then I
realize that in this wetness, nothing would catch fire anyway.
We'll have to feel our way along in the dark and trust my stone
to guide us. It's a test, after all. It's supposed to be difficult.

But no, we *do* have a source of light. I grab a handful of
vines and yank hard until they pull free. I wrap them several

times around my forearm. Storm understands instantly and does the same. Then we step into the cave.

The noise of the waterfall becomes echoing and hollow and so, so much louder. A few more steps take us behind a wall of white water. Soft daylight barely penetrates, giving the fall a crystal sheen, and I'm suddenly thinking of Hector, wishing he was here to see something so beautiful.

I clench my jaw and turn away from the waterfall, into the tunnel. The light grows dimmer as we walk. The tunnel is just high enough for me to stand upright, which means Storm has to stoop. Gradually, though, the night bloomers wrapped around my arms unfurl and begin to glow, faintly at first but with increasing determination, until we can see several paces in every direction.

The tunnel is obviously unnatural. The walls are too perfect, too polished, the floor too even. It slopes slightly upward, and rivulets of water trickle past us to empty into the lake.

Our path curves to the left. We round the corner, and the light from our vines catches on a bit of unevenness in the wall. My heart hammers with a sense of familiarity.

Lichen grows over the unevenness, fanning out in rings of yellow and brown. I reach up with my fingers and scrape it away to reveal script carved into the wall. The Lengua Classica. An ancient style of writing. *The gate that leads to life is narrow and small so that few find it.*

"It's the same," I say to Storm, and my voice echoes. "The same as the tunnel leading to your cavern in the Wallows."

"Yes," he says. "That holy passage has long been associated

with the *zafira*. I used to climb up to the tunnel and look at it. I would sit there for hours, hoping God would reveal something to me."

I look at him sharply. He just admitted that he climbed up into the tunnel.

He returns my gaze, his eyes wide with wonder, and I notice, unaccountably, how the roots of his falsely dark hair shimmer gold in the soft light. "Yes, I know the tunnel leads up to the catacombs," he says. "But no, I'm not the one who tried to kill you that day. Truly, I am Your Majesty's loyal subject."

"Do you know who did?"

"No."

"But you've been pursuing the *zafira* for a long time. Even in your exile, you thought about it."

"Yes."

Something clicks into place. "Is this your redemption, Storm? Do you hope that by finding the *zafira*, you can be reconciled to your people? Hailed as a hero? Your death sentence commuted?"

He turns away. "I don't know," he whispers. "Maybe."

"And would you betray me for the same purpose? If you handed over the only living Godstone, would you receive a hero's welcome?"

He shoves me aside and continues down the tunnel. But I understand him a little now, and I've observed he avoids answering to keep from telling a lie.

Chilled—and maybe a little relieved to finally know for sure—I hurry after him:

Our path grows steep, steep, steeper. The smooth floor gives way to perfectly sculpted steps and sudden switchbacks. My thighs burn, my heart pounds, and my breath comes fast as we climb ever upward. It's drier now, and creatures scuttle away at irregular intervals as we approach. I imagine crabs. Or cave scorpions. Or maybe rats with nails long enough to scrape the stone. Whatever they are, they disappear before the arc of our fading light can reach them.

It seems that hours pass, or days. I find myself stepping in time to my heartbeat, which is huge in my chest and throat. My lungs burn, and the tug on my Godstone has become a fire in my belly. Surely we are near the top of the spire by now. Surely we are at the top of the world.

We round another switchback to find the vaguest hint of light. As one, we hurry forward, desperate to lose these walls. The light strengthens. One more corner, and light explodes full in our faces. I blink and raise my forearm against it.

The night bloomers snap closed. Gradually my eyes adjust, and I lower my arm.

We look out over a high mountain valley, green and gently rolling, hemmed in by summits that catch the clouds. They are the same mountains I saw from the ship, I'm sure of it. But now I view them from the other side, and from so much higher up.

Exactly five narrow peaks jut into the sky—the holy number of perfection. One is a little shorter and squatter than the others, like a thumb, and with a start I realize that from a certain angle, I could almost imagine I'm staring at God's righteous right hand, and the streams cutting through the valley are the creases of his cupped palm.

It's a huger, greener version of Lutián's Hand of God sculpture in Brisadulce.

Storm clutches at his chest, and his breathing comes hard, but not, I think, from exertion. The astonishment in his face is stunning to see; it shifts his angled lines into something a little wilder and nearly beautiful.

"You're sensing it very strongly now," I observe.

"Oh, yes. It's almost painful. We're supposed to go down into that valley."

I peer down at the incline in dismay. It's too steep to descend safely. Maybe by using the vines and ferns that hug the slope, we can lower ourselves gradually.

"There," Storm says. "Steps cut into the rock."

I look in the direction he's pointing and decide that calling them "steps" is generous. They are more like handholds, overgrown with moss. After scraping the dying night-bloomer vines from my forearms, I scoot down, lodging my heels into the indentions, clutching plants for support.

Sharp pain pierces my finger, and I yank my hand back. A drop of blood wells on my forefinger. With my other hand, I push aside a fern frond to see what pricked me.

A rose vine, not quite blooming. Deepest red peeks from budding green tips. Thorns wrap around the stems, much longer and harder than those of common roses.

Tears spring to my eyes, for I feel like God has given me a gift.

I have no priest to guide my prayer, no sizzling altar to

accept my blood, no acolyte to bathe my wound with witch hazel. But I can't help but feel that this moment was meant to be, somehow, and so I decide to do what I always do when I am pricked by a sacrament rose: pray and ask a blessing.

In the past, I have asked for courage. Or wisdom. This time, I close my eyes and mutter, "Please, God. Give me *power*."

I open my eyes, turn my finger over, and let the drop of blood fall to the earth.

Something rumbles—whether it is the world around me or the prayer inside me I cannot tell—and the earth tilts. The air shifts, like a desert mirage, and for the briefest instance, I see lines of shimmering light, Godstone blue and thin as threads. They race from all directions through the mountain peaks, across the valley, to meet at a central point where they are sucked into the ground.

I blink, and the vision is gone, leaving me breathless and puzzled and frightened.

"What just happened?" Storm demands. "You fed the earth a bit of your blood. I felt it move."

"I'm not sure. I saw something strange. Lines of power. But they're gone now."

He stares at me suspiciously. "Let's go. I become impatient."

It doesn't take long to reach the valley floor, which is a good thing given how my legs are shaking from exertion. There are no palm trees here, just sprawling cypress and towering euca-lyptus and a tree I've never seen before, with such huge broad leaves that a single leaf would cover my whole body. Birds flit among the branches; dappled light catches on them and shoots away in prismatic facets. It's so startlingly odd that I peer closer.

No, not birds. They're giant insects, as large as ospreys, with downy white abdomens and gossamer wings.

Misgiving thumps in my chest. This valley has a wrongness to it. It is alien. *Other.*

And there is something about it that inspires silence. We move quietly, as if in expectation, or perhaps reverence. Piles of stone like crumbling altars litter the forest floor, some as tall as I am, covered in green lichen and dust. A cypress tree clings stubbornly to the side of one, its roots prying open cracks in stone.

We round a bend and find another pile, but this one is as tall as a tree and square shaped, with arched openings for windows. A ruined building. I look around in awe at the other piles. Ruins, all of them. This was once a city of stone, its shape now worn down by sun and wind and tree roots and time.

"This must be centuries old," I breathe.

"Several millennia," Storm says, and there is a quiet sadness in his voice I've never heard before.

I regard him sharply. "That's impossible. God brought people to this world—"

"Yes, yes, he rescued you from the dying world with his righteous right hand less than two thousand years ago. I've heard you tell it." The anger in his voice is palpable. "Little queen, don't you realize? We Inviernos have *always* been here."

I stare at him agape, even as the rightness of his words spark inside me. Behind him, one of the insect birds flits through the branches of a eucalyptus, alights atop the ruined building, and begins to groom its rainbow wing with a spindly black leg.

"Your people came, bearing magic we'd never seen," he continues. "They changed us, made us less than we were. Changed themselves too, the legend goes, though I don't know how or why. They scattered across the land now called Joya d'Arena, and we fled before them into the mountains. After that, *they changed the whole world.* Your country wasn't always a desert, you know."

I'm shaking my head, with uneasiness rather than denial. If what he says is true, then my ancestors were interlopers. No, thieves. But surely one cannot be considered a thief when one is taking only what God gives? God offered us this world. All the scriptures say so.

My old tutor did tell me our great desert was an inland sea before a mysterious cataclysm forced the water deep below ground. So maybe what Storm says is partly true. Maybe we *created* the desert somehow. But how? "That makes no sense," I say aloud. "God wouldn't—"

My Godstone leaps, and the tugging on my navel becomes a dagger in my gut.

Storms gasps. "I don't like pain."

I bend over, clutching at my stomach with one hand, even as I grab Storm's shoulder with the other and push him forward down our path. "Just . . . keep . . . moving." I can hardly put one foot in front of the other. All I want to do is drop to the ground and curl up, knees to chest. Maybe this is what Father Nicandro meant when he said my determination would be tested.

I have a lot of determination.

But a few steps farther and the vise on my abdomen twists suddenly, and I tumble to my knees, panting. I will crawl if I have to. I will—

"It's worse for you, isn't it?" Storm says, looking down at me with irritation.

I nod, unable to speak.

He stares at me a moment. Then he sighs, squats down, grabs one of my arms, and loops it over his shoulder. He stands, pulling me to my feet. "Just a bit farther, Your Majesty."

I swallow my surprise and concentrate on moving my feet as he drags me down the path.

Just when I think the pain can't get any worse, when my body wavers between vomiting and passing out, we break into a small clearing. In the center is another ruined building, as perfectly round as a tower. But its summit has long since crumbled, leaving it merely the height of a man.

Chains rattle.

A pale face with eyes the color of a hazy sky peeks out from behind the tower. White hair streams from a middle part on his sunburned scalp, all the way to the ground. It's the gatekeeper.

28

HE has the flawless face of an animagus, but his stooped shoulders and rheumy eyes make him seem as old as the mountains themselves.

"Two!" he squeals. "Two apprentices!" His Lengua Classica is thick and muddled, like he has a mouthful of pebbles. "I must be one of God's favorites," he says, "to be so blessed." He steps from behind the tower to reveal tattered clothes of indeterminate color and filthy bare feet in rusty manacles. The skin of his ankles bulges up around the manacles so that it is impossible to see where iron ends and flesh begins. I have to look away.

"Who are you?" he asks. "I've felt you coming for hours now. Or years?"

I try to speak, but I can't. I am nothing but pain and that awful tugging.

"Oh, yes, that," he says. He flicks his fingers, and the pain disappears.

Relief floods me, and desperate gratitude starts to bubble

on my lips, but I bite it back. I straighten cautiously.

"Are you the gatekeeper?" I ask.

"You first!" he says, clapping. "Tell me who you are. And come here, come here. Let me get a better look at you."

I edge forward. He lunges toward me, and I recoil, but his manacles have caught him. He is chained, I see now, to the tower. He cries out in frustration, stomping on the ground like a child throwing a tantrum. Then he collects himself, and the frustration melts from his face as quickly as it came. "I believe you were about to tell me who you are?" he says with preternatural calm.

I'm careful to stay just beyond the reach of his chains when I say, "I am the bearer." And after a moment of silence: "And a queen."

He taps his lip with a crooked, dirty finger. "Not very good at either, are you? Your heart screams your inadequacy." He turns to Storm. "And you?"

Storm draws himself up to full height. "A prince of the realm," he says.

I gape at him.

He shrugs. "You never asked."

The strange man leans toward us conspiratorially. "But not much of a prince anymore, yes? A shadow of what you were." He grins, like it is all a great game, and I shudder to see his teeth, pointed like canines and brown with rot. "Would you like to see the *zafira*? I can show it to you, yes, I can. It will have a bit of your blood, and then it will decide whether you live or die."

Storm and I exchange an alarmed look.

I say, "So you *are* the gatekeeper? What's your name?"

His teeth snap in the air. "I've told you a thousand times and you never listen! I am Heed the Fallen Leaf That Grows Dank with Rot, for It Shall Feed Spring Tulips."

"Of course. Apologies." He is insane. Totally and completely insane. "I think I'll just call you . . ." *Rot.* "Er, Leaf."

"Leaf! Yes, I'll be Leaf. Let me see your stones." When I hesitate, he barks, "Now! I must see them to let you inside."

Reluctantly I lift the edge of my blouse to reveal my stomach and its resident jewel.

And then Storm reaches beneath his shirt and pulls out a leather cord that dangles a Godstone of his very own, in a tiny iron cage.

I gape at him. "How did you . . . When did you . . . ?"

"I've always had it. Since birth."

Too many possibilities compete for attention in my head. Was it given to him? Was he born with it? "My Godstone never warmed to it," I protest. "Never reacted. It always senses another Godstone nearby. *Always.*"

Storm wilts a little. "It's quite dead. It fell out at the age of four. I trained to be an animagus, to learn to eke some power out of it. But I never could. I failed."

Understanding hits like a rock in the gut. "The Inviernos are born with Godstones."

Storm shakes his head. "Only a few of us. They fall out very early. And we've been separated from the source of their power for so long that they are mostly useless."

"The animagi burned my city, burned my husband. That's hardly useless."

Storm shrugs. "That's destruction magic. Easy, for an animagus. It's creation magic, like barrier shields or growing plants or healing, that's difficult."

"*I* can heal." The words are out of my mouth before I think to censor them.

"What? You can?" His green eyes narrow. "You never said."

I stick a finger in his chest. "You. Never. Asked."

His brief moment of startlement dissolves into desperate laughter. "And yet you can't even call your stone's fire, which is the easiest, most basic power. You might be a worse failure than even me."

Leaf has been looking back and forth between us, grinning all the while. "You are enemies!" he says, clapping with delight. "So much fun. Look, here's mine." He parts the rags hanging from his shoulders to reveal petal-white skin and protruding ribs.

A Godstone is sewn into his navel. Threads of hemp or dried grass crisscross over the top, holding it in place. The skin around the edges is puckered and scarred from so many piercings. One thread dangles, wisping back and forth in the breeze. I avert my gaze, sickened.

"Will you take us now?" Storm asks. He leans forward and his face twitches, as if he's about to crawl out of his own skin in anticipation.

"This way," Leaf says, and disappears behind the tower, his chains clattering with each step. After exchanging a troubled look, Storm and I follow.

An archway on the opposite side leads into darkness. Leaf reaches down and grabs his chain, which seems to have a little slack now, and hoists it over his shoulder. "Ready?" And he steps inside.

I remember the way he lunged at me. I debate the wisdom of following. I put my fingertips to my Godstone and whisper a quick prayer for safety. It nearly scalds my fingers with its sudden heat, and I gasp with the sensation of power flowing into me.

So much! It's what brought me here, after all. I take a deep breath and step inside the ruined tower.

My eyes adjust quickly to the gloom. A spiral stairway bores into the earth. It smells of wet earth and mold. A few twists down, and our path begins to glow faintly, bluely, as if from night bloomers. The glow brightens as we descend, until the colorless walls have taken on its tint, until my skin is bathed in it. My Godstone thrums softly, as if crooning to a lover.

When the stair opens into a vast cavern, I fall to my knees, gasping in amazement.

The walls are lined with Godstones. Thousands. Tens of thousands. A river flows against the far wall, but not of water. It's a slow-moving course of light and fog and power, glowing blue, as nebulous as a cloud. Its light reflects off the Godstone walls so that the cavern seems under a barrage of sapphire sparks.

My own Godstone sings in greeting. A finger of glowing fog creeps from the river, slithers across the damp ground like a searching tentacle, glides over my knee and up to the Godstone, where it presses gently.

There is an audible *click*, like pieces of a puzzle coming together. The energy inside me flares joyously, and suddenly I feel connected to the whole world as the *zafira* feeds me life and energy through the siphon of my Godstone. My head swims, my limbs tingle, and I'm a little bit delighted, a little bit horrified.

"Oh, it loves you, yes, it does," murmurs Leaf. "Have you fed the earth a bit of your blood already, then?"

"I . . . yes. On the way down. I found a sacrament rose bush, and prayed for . . ." Power. I prayed for power. And here I am, connected to the source of all magic, but I feel no closer to my goal than before. My body buzzes with energy, certainly, like I could do anything. I could heal a thousand people. Bring down a hurricane. But can I take that power with me to help me rule a kingdom? Or does it only work here, in this cavern?

Storm is gazing at the walls, his mouth agape. "It's a grave," he says. "A catacomb of animagi."

"Oh, yes," Leaf says. "They used to come here to die. Or if they died too soon, they would have their bodies brought here. But only their stones remain. No one has come here to die in a very long time. Until now!" He claps, showing his rotting teeth.

Fear shoots through me. I jump to my feet, eyeing the opening to the stairway, wondering if Storm and I could outrun him if he turned on us. But no, I won't run. I can't. "We came to learn about the *zafira*," I say firmly. "Not to die."

"Oh, no one minds being dead!" he assures us. "But some people mind being alive. Like me. I've lived far too long." He rattles his chains, which now lie coiled like a snake at his feet. The opposite end drops over the lip of the riverbank, into the vast blueness. "One of you will take my place as the *zafira*'s gatekeeper, its living sacrifice. God is so kind; he gave me two to choose from!"

The wonder on Storm's face cedes to misgiving.

"One of you, *if* you survive, will leave here a true sorcerer," Leaf explains, "having made the pilgrimage and tasted of the *zafira*. And oh, she is fickle. It's fun to guess if someone will live or die. I only get it right some of the time. But the other . . ." He dances a joyful jig, blood oozing around his swollen ankles. "The other must stay so that I can sleep. Oh, I am so tired. Let's begin, shall we?" He lifts his arms above his head and mutters something unintelligible. A stream of light rises from the river of fog and rushes to the space between his hands, where it grows, coalesces, begins to spin.

I gasp with recognition. I know what this is, for I've done it myself, when I destroyed the animagi with my Godstone amulet. He is drawing the power to himself, storing it up, readying it to explode into a wave of energy.

Panic builds in my throat. I have to do something. But what? The force he gathers brightens. It illuminates the whole cavern, showing a roof gnarled with the roots of trees from the valley above.

Storm sprints for the doorway.

"Trying to get away, little mouse?" says Leaf. A tendril of blue fire whips from the river, shoots toward Storm, wraps his torso like a snake, and yanks him to the ground. He lands hard on his back, where he gasps like a beached fish, the wind knocked out of him.

Think, Elisa! I have channeled this power before. I've won a war with it. I've healed people. I pushed the *Aracely*, somehow, through a massive hurricane. I can *do* this.

I close my eyes, place my fingertips to the Godstone, and imagine the *zafira*'s power pouring into me.

It does, like a flood, like a hurricane, until I'm spinning with it, mad with it. My hair lifts from the nape of my neck, and my fingers tingle with power that feels so natural, so easy. The earth beneath me disappears.

I open my eyes to discover that I float several inches above the ground and the *zafira*'s soothing flame has wrapped around me like a lover's arms. But what to do with all this power?

"Interesting," Leaf says as his ball of blue fire begins to shoot white sparks. "You may be a worthy opponent, with your living stone." And from his spinning sun, he sends a bolt of blue fire spearing toward me.

I imagine Hector's forearm shield, the way it sheltered me when arrows flew down the hallway of my palace. A shimmering barrier materializes out of thin air before me, and the bolt of fire bounces harmlessly against it. So easy! The power, drawn directly from its source. Exactly what I've been looking for. Exactly what I need.

Leaf giggles with delight. He sends more bolts, so fast they are blurs of streaking light, but I continue to pull the *zafira*'s energy into me, and they bounce away from my barrier.

"And now I try to kill your enemy!" he yells, and he turns toward Storm, who lies defenseless on the ground, still gasping for air.

"No!" I send my barrier flying toward him, but it is too late—a bolt of energy plunges into his leg. He screams as the fabric of his robe sears away in a widening, blackening circle, and I catch the agonizingly familiar scent of burning flesh.

I clench my fists with frustration. I have all this power, but I lack the skill, the finesse, to channel it properly. I can't defend both of us. I close my eyes, racking my brain for an idea.

I've never been able to destroy, save for the one time. But I can create. I can knit flesh and renew life. I focus on the tree roots over our heads. I think about their bark, their soft insides. I imagine them growing.

Another bolt shoots toward Storm, but he rolls away just in time. Leaf bends his elbows behind his head, readying to fling the ball of light at Storm. I know what will happen next—it will explode in a wave so powerful that nothing can stand in its way.

Grow. Please grow.

Light tendrils whisk up my arms toward the ceiling. They wrap around the roots, untwisting them, pulling them down. And suddenly I *am* the roots, reaching as if with massive fingers. I grasp for Leaf, coil around him, yank him from the ground and dangle him in the air.

His light ball blinks out. He gapes at me for a moment, then kicks his legs in the air, which sets his chain rattling.

"Well, all right, then," he says. "Your apprenticeship is

complete. You're a sorcerer now. I declare it so." He closes his eyes and mutters intelligibly. Something jerks in my chest as my roots release him. He falls to the ground, lands with a great *crack* beside Storm. I drop to the ground a moment later. My knees buckle, but I keep my feet.

Leaf sprawls, his knee bent at an unnatural angle. "Ah, broke that leg again," he says, as if it's hardly worth his notice. "But no healing for me this time." He cocks his head at me. "Would you like to be my replacement?"

I take a step back. "Er, no thank you."

"I thought as much. You are a queen, after all. Things to do, things to do, yes? Also, I probably could not make you, living stone that you have. No matter. I'll take this little mouse, weak as he is." Leaf reaches out with a spindly hand and splays his fingers across Storm's horrified face. "And now, my weak prince, all the power you've ever wanted is yours."

"No!" I shout, grasping for more of the *zafira*. I sling tendrils of light toward Storm to pull him away, even as the manacles around Leaf's ankles dissipate into fog.

Storm begins sliding toward me, but it doesn't matter. Shadows form around his ankles, darkening until they are as hard and true as iron.

Leaf sways; then his cheek hits the ground, hard. He gasps in the dirt, a smile on his face. "Free!" he whispers. "You'll put my stone into the wall, yes? With the others?"

His face caves in on itself until he is little more than a grinning skeleton. His hair turns black as he shrinks, dissolving into a cloud of dust. The dust coalesces in the air, then rains to the ground, forming an ashy pile. A single glittering Godstone winks from the pile's center.

"I'll be here forever," Storm whispers. "Forever."

I tear my gaze from the pile of dust that used to be Leaf and say, "No. We'll find a way to free you. Maybe an ax? I'm sure Captain Felix has a blacksmith in his crew."

Storm's face falls into his hands. "The chains are formed by magic. No blacksmith can break them."

"Maybe I can—"

"You can only do creation magic, remember? You can't destroy these chains."

"I'm very good at figuring things out."

He clambers to his feet, and his features suddenly calm with resignation. "Majesty, go. Leave me here. Even if you could figure out a way to free me, you won't do it. The *zafira* connected with you. I saw it. You'll be able to call on its power forevermore. No matter where in the world you are. Just like the animagi of old, when we had our full strength. You truly are the chosen one."

He's right. Even now, I hum with strength, like I can do anything. It's wonderful to feel such breathtaking power. I'm almost dizzy with it.

"But the *zafira* needs a living sacrifice, a conduit," he says. "Without a gatekeeper, it's useless to you."

All I do is walk away from this place, and I become the most powerful sovereign who ever lived. "Storm, I never meant—"

"You told me you would choose your own life over mine, remember? So do it. Choose now and leave me alone. You know I prefer to be alone than in your miserable company."

Tears prick at my eyes, and I suck in air through my nose to keep steady. "Will you . . . How will you . . . ?"

"The *zafira* will sustain me. Even now it heals my burns. Just promise me that when you face Invierne—and you will face them—that you'll tell them about me."

"What do you want me to say?" I ask in a small voice.

"Tell them that the man who failed as an animagi, who failed as a prince, and who failed as an ambassador, found the *zafira* and restored his honor by becoming its living sacrifice. Will you do that?"

"You never cared about honor! You've been content to live without it, so long as it meant you could *live*."

"It's all that's left to me. Please?"

I nod, voiceless.

He lowers himself to the ground, crosses his legs, and closes his eyes. "Go now, Elisa. Go be the queen you couldn't be on your own."

I turn away, even as his words bore into my chest, twisting like barbs. *Go be the queen you couldn't be on your own.* I have what I came for. Power beyond imagining.

Why then, with it coursing though me, filling me to overflowing, do I feel like a hollow shell of a girl?

I have passed through the doorway, and my foot is on the first step leading out of the cavern when I freeze.

Channeling all the magic of the world is no different from choosing a regent or making a desperate marriage alliance. It's just an instrument. A crutch.

Hector's voice, low and intimate, echoes in my head. *If you were like this, with this kind of confidence, this clarity of thought, no one would dare challenge your rule.*

The *zafira* is not what I need.

What I need is to be a better queen.

29

I turn back around. My heart flutters and my knees tremble at what I might do. *Is this the right choice?* But there is no response, or if there is, it is so overwhelmed by the rush of the *zafira* that I can't detect it. I must make a choice wholly independent from God's voice, from his stone, from his power.

I take a deep breath. "Storm."

His head whips up.

"Come with me."

"What?"

"To the surface. Now, before I change my mind."

He bolts to his feet and hobbles toward me as quickly as his manacles will allow. "How will you get the chains off? And if you do, the *zafira* will be lost to you forever. To all of us. What if—"

"Do you *want* to stay here for thousands of years?"

"No."

"Then shut up and follow me."

Before we enter the archway, I cast my gaze around for one

last look at this catacomb of Godstones. So beautiful. So much history and remembrance and even worship, so much magic.

Think like a sorcerer, Storm said. But what I need to do is think like a queen.

And as the stones shine brighter than the brightest sapphire, I think: *so much* value.

Quickly I pry a Godstone out of the wall. It comes loose with a soft *plink*, and I shove it into my pocket. I grab a few more, until my pocket bulges.

"Let's go." Together, chains clanking behind us, we spiral up the steps and into the sunshine.

"Now what?" he asks, gasping for breath.

I look around the tiny clearing. The trees are very close.

"Keep still," I order.

I gather power into myself until my muscles thrum with it. I cast my awareness into the earth, to everything growing there—tiny grass roots, a colony of ants milling about in oddly organized industry, a worm. I feel them all, as if they're an extension of myself. With the *zafira* coursing through me, perhaps they are.

There. A mass of cypress roots, twisting together like a nest of snakes, perfectly sized.

I coax them toward us. They writhe through the ground, poke out of the grass, weave through the links of Storm's chains. I shove them hard, and their widening girths strain the links. Something groans like a dying animal as I torque them mercilessly.

The links snap.

"Run!" I yell. I have no idea if the chains will reform, if the *zafira* will grab him back with a relentless light tentacle.

Storm sprints away, and I dash to keep up. His manacles rattle with each step, dangling lengths of broken chain that threaten to catch in the foliage and yank him down.

For the first time since entering this valley, my Godstone turns to ice. The earth begins to rumble, and Storm freezes, but I shove him on. "Just go!" I hope I have not broken the world.

We scramble up the footholds toward the entrance to the cavern, chased by the sounds of grinding rocks and splitting earth. I tell myself not to look back, to concentrate on moving forward, but when we gain the top, I can't help it. I turn around and gasp.

Trees slowly lean toward the center of the valley like they're bowing to God. Then a series of massive *pop*s echoes all around as roots rip from their moorings and the trees topple over. Clouds of dust explode into the air.

The valley is caving in on itself, forming a giant sinkhole where Leaf's tower used to be.

I press shaking fingers to my lips. *What have I done?*

A stream diverts, collides with another in a thunderous spray of water and mud. Their joined force is relentless as it sweeps boulders and uprooted trees into the gaping sinkhole.

My teeth rattle in my jaw as the valley booms, again and again. No, it's not just the valley. The sound comes from above too. The mountain is about to tumble down on us.

"We need to move," Storm says. "Fast."

His words spur me to action, and I sprint toward the cavern. It gapes darkly before us. "We need light!" We don't have time to feel our way down the dark stairs. But by traveling in haste, we will surely fall to our deaths. "Do you see night bloomers? Anywhere?"

"Just the ones we discarded. Nearly dead."

"They'll do." I grab the wilting vines from where I dropped them. Drawing on the *zafira*, I reach inside their stems and coax them to life. But the power bleeds away from me even as their leaves straighten with health, as the petals unfurl. By the time their stamens have brightened into a steady glow, the power is gone.

I allow myself the tiniest moment of grief. I brush the night bloomers against my cheeks, breathing in their honeysuckle-like scent. Then I step into the booming mountain.

Dust and pebbles rain down on us, urging us on as we descend. Our way becomes slick with mud. Twice I slip on my heel, but Storm is quick at my elbow, shoring me up with a strength that belies his delicate frame.

We dare not stop when we reach the waterfall, for we are still too close to the shaking mountain. Dusk has fallen, and as we clamber across the boulders lining the lake I find it nearly impossible to distinguish between cracks and sinkholes and shadows.

It is nearly full dark when we reach the stream, and living night bloomers unfurl in the trees all around us. The noise of the collapsing valley fades, and I dare to hope that we are safe.

We stop to catch our breath. Storm bends over, hands on his

knees, heaving for air. His face and robe are covered in drying mud, tinged gruesomely blue in the night bloomers' light. I imagine I look the same. "Why?" he manages between gasps. "Why did you save me? My own people would not have done so much. Stupid queen. You are powerless now."

"You are my loyal subject."

He stares at me.

"But I'm not powerless." I continue. "I've always had my Godstone and its minor magic. I healed Hector in Brisadulce, you know, so there are things I can still do just by reaching through the skin of the earth." It would be useless to tell him that I'm done sacrificing other people for my own gain. I won't whip innocent kitchen workers, I won't burn down buildings, I won't ask anyone to give up an inheritance for me, and I certainly won't leave a friend at the mercy of a mysterious magical force—merely for the sake of my own power. I press my fingers to the stone at my navel, taking comfort in its familiar pulsing. What I tell him is, "And I have me. *I* will be enough."

The camp is silent and somber and half emptied when Storm and I step from the trees. Mara sits alone near the fire pit. She holds up a steaming fish speared on a stick and is about to take a bite, but she sees us and lets it drop into the embers, jumping to her feet. "Elisa?" she whispers, and then she's running toward me, wrapping me in her arms. "Oh, God, I knew you had probably gone off alone, that you weren't *taken*, but when I heard all that rumbling a bit ago, I thought that . . . I thought maybe . . ."

I return her hug fiercely. "I'm sorry," I say.

She steps back. "Did you find it?"

"Yes."

"And what happened? Did you . . ." she makes a vague gesture with her hand.

"Can I tell you about that a little later, maybe? I need to . . . think."

Her eyes drift to Storm's shackles, then back to my face. "All right," she says, but her gaze is troubled, maybe a little bit wounded.

"Where is everyone?" I ask, though I think I know.

"Looking for you. Hector is sick with worry."

I wince, dreading the moment I will face him. I say, "I need to walk. I'll be at the beach."

"Do you want something to eat first?"

"No, thank you." I feel her puzzled gaze at my back as I step away.

The half moon sends ripples of gold across the water. In the distance floats the black, battered shape of the *Aracely*, her main sail hanging limp in the windless night. The air is hot, the water calm.

On impulse, I shuck my filthy boots and blouse. Wearing nothing but my linen pants and a sleeveless undershirt, I wade out into the warm water.

A strange thing happens. Where the water touches me, it glows, Godstone blue. I lie back and float, waving my arms experimentally. The glow is like a shield wrapping around my body, a clinging aura of power. I laugh, delighted, thinking about all the things I've seen lately that glow in this way: my Godstone, when I'm about to release its power. The river of energy. The night bloomers. And now this luminescing bay.

And I realize that the *zafira* is everywhere. I may have destroyed access to its purest form, but it leaks out all over the world.

I see movement along the shore. A dark shape materializes out of the trees, and I catch my breath. I know him from so far away, just by the way he walks. I'm suddenly desperate to see him up close, to look into his eyes, to hear his low, soft voice, even though I know whatever we say to each other next cannot end well.

I swim toward shore until my feet touch bottom; then I walk from the glowing water to meet him.

He stares at me as I approach, his face unreadable to me again, the way it used to be. When he is only an arm's length away, I say, "Hector, I'm sorry."

He studies me thoughtfully. Then my whole body goes hot as his gaze travels—slowly, deliberately—from my neck, to my breasts, my hips, down to my feet, and all the way up again. My clothes cling to me like a second skin, leaving little to the imagination.

At last he says, "Sorry for what, exactly?" and his voice is cold, cold, cold.

I swallow hard. "For leaving without telling you."

"A queen need never apologize to a mere guard." He makes it sound like an insult, and I gasp from the pain of it.

"Still, I should have—"

"You're my queen, Elisa. You can do whatever you want. You never owe me an explanation."

He is reminding me, with patient and lethal efficiency, of how much power I have over him, of why we could never be together.

"Now, if we were *lovers*," he says, "I might feel angry that you demanded my honesty but refused me yours. I might feel insulted that you slinked away to do something dangerous knowing full well that the most important thing I do is protect you. And I might feel perplexed that you lacked the courage to face me, when all you had to do was give the order."

I've never felt so contemptible and small. Part of me wants to flee, to escape his ruthless gaze. Another part wants to wrap my arms around him and beg forgiveness, for there can be no doubt that I have hurt him deeply.

He can't help adding, "It's a good thing, then, that we are not lovers, yes?"

It's like a dagger to the gut. He means it to be his final rejection. He means to hurt me, and maybe to grasp on to some power of his own. It's cruel of him, and unworthy of the Hector I've come to know. And yet the anger melts out of me as quickly as it forms.

I reach up and cup his face with one hand. It shocks some feeling into his eyes, and I watch carefully as he considers whether or not to recoil from my touch. He doesn't.

I say, "What I did was weak. Cowardly. Unqueenly. But I learned some things about power when I went to the *zafira*, and you were right. About everything." I brush across his cheek, memorizing the texture of his skin, the feel of slight stubble against the pad of my thumb. "I do have power. Enough that I don't need you. But I will miss you awfully."

He lurches away, and my heart aches to see the torment on his face. He looks everywhere but at me, running his hands through his hair as if to keep them busy. He says, "How do you *do* that? You always disarm me. You have from the day I . . . And I hate it. I truly hate it."

From a place of knowledge as old as the *zafira* itself, from the depths of a feminine power I'm only beginning to understand, I say with conviction: "No, you don't."

I want to tell him how much I love him. He deserves to know. But it would be too perilous in this moment. It would sound like I was begging, or saying what he wanted to hear just to diffuse his anger.

So I leave him alone with his thoughts. I return to camp, resolved to face Mara and tell her everything, hoping I can salvage at least one friendship.

30

WE spend the next week repairing the ship and gathering foodstuffs. We make a rack of mangrove roots and set it in the sun to dry fish. A pile of coconuts becomes a mountain as we forage. I've always been handy with a needle, so I volunteer to repair a rip in one of the smaller sails. All the while, we are surrounded by the sounds of ax and mallet.

Hector is unfailingly polite to me, but I miss the way his warm gaze used to linger on my face, the way his lips would quirk when I said something that amused him. We renew our lessons in self-defense, carving out a space on the beach to work. He demonstrates the places on the human body that are most subject to pain. He shows me how to use my own body weight to throw an opponent to the ground. He explains how to shove a man's nose into his brain with the base of my palm to kill him instantly and has me practice the motion on an unlucky coconut.

He does all this while managing to never touch me.

And though he says nothing, I'm certain he has decided

to leave my service and go home to Ventierra. There's a desperate focus to his teaching, as if he's shoring me up with as much knowledge as possible before we part ways.

I dread leaving this place, for it means returning to all the problems I left behind, problems that have inevitably worsened. Our ruse has certainly been discovered by now. I hope decoy Elisa has survived and that Ximena is well. I worry for Rosario and his safety. And I cannot doubt that Conde Eduardo has maneuvered in my absence, that he has found a way to turn the situation to his advantage.

Too soon, Captain Felix declares us prepped and ready, and we weigh anchor and set sail for our rendezvous point in Selvarica. I stand on the quarterdeck, the wind whipping hair into my eyes, watching the island grow small. From this vantage, I can see that one of the mountains is shorter now, with a jagged peak, its zenith a crumbling ruin in the valley I destroyed.

During the voyage, we try to remove the manacles from Storm's ankles. But the blacksmith cannot forge them open, the cooper cannot pry them open, and though I can make them glow warmly, I cannot force them open by magic. Storm grumbles at our efforts and finally snaps at us to leave well enough alone. "To all my other failures, I must add my failure as gatekeeper to the *zafira*." He sighs dramatically.

"I don't believe you mind so much," I point out.

He cracks a rare grin. "Truly, I do not." He pulls himself up to full height. "In fact, I will wear these chains proudly. However, I require salve and a bit of cloth to use as cushioning around my ankles. Silk, of course."

"I think it's an improvement," I tell him. "I'll never again worry about you sneaking up on me."

"I hate you."

I reach up to squeeze his shoulder. "I know."

The wind holds, and it takes less than two weeks to make port in Selvarica. The land is as Tristán described it: lush and green and gorgeous, not unlike the island we come from.

As soon as we dock, we are greeted by a large complement of solemn-looking soldiers in full armor.

"What's going on?" I demand.

"Conde Tristán sent us to escort you, Your Majesty," says one. "This way, please. Quickly."

Hector and Belén flank me as we hurry down the dock. Mara and Storm, who is cowled once again, follow behind, and Storm's clattering steps cause dockworkers and fishermen to pause and stare. We reach a waiting carriage, and a soldier assures us our belongings will be collected and sent to us. Then he smacks the horse's flank and waves the driver off.

A group of soldiers jogs alongside as we travel up a steep drive. I peer out the window and notice fortifications along the road. Temporary walls with arrow slits. A blockade on the side that could be moved quickly to block traffic.

"Tristán is preparing for war," I say to no one in particular, and my heart thuds. I thought I was done with war. Forever done.

"I see Conde Eduardo's colors too," Hector says in a grave voice. "Tristán may no longer be in command of his own garrison."

We reach a carriage house, where we are quickly unloaded and ushered through a servants' wing, across an inner courtyard with marble fountains and tiled pathways and hanging plants, and into a long dining hall with an enormous low table, much like the one in my own council chamber where the Quorum meets.

A handful of people already sit on cushions around the table, and they look up when we enter. I am so very glad to see Tristán, Iladro, a few of my own Royal Guard, and . . . my eyes sweep the room looking for her. There! Ximena leaps to her feet and barrels toward me, arms outstretched for an embrace. I fall into the hug easily and gratefully.

She pushes me back to arm's length, and her eyes are wet with tears when she says, "I'm so glad you're safe and well, my sky."

A puckered redness slashes across her cheekbone—a clumsily stitched wound that will leave a large scar. I point to my own cheek. "Ximena, what happened?"

"Later." She guides me by the shoulders toward the table.

"And the girl?"

"Dead." She sighs. "I'm sorry."

I swallow hard against the sudden knot in my throat. Another innocent person added to my wake of bodies. I'm torn between writhing guilt, and gladness that Ximena survived.

Hector and his men greet one another in a fierce demonstration of backslapping. Then Hector and Tristán clasp forearms while Mara and Ximena embrace. Finally we all settle onto our cushions.

I lean forward, elbows on the table. "Tell me at once what is going on."

Tristán rubs wearily at his temples. "Franco came after the girl," he says. "It happened very publicly, with an arrow to the neck. We had no choice but to reveal that she was not you, that the queen still lived. As planned, Father Alentín began circulating the rumor among the priests that you were on a mission from God himself."

"And Franco?" I ask.

"Disappeared."

"Was he working alone or on Eduardo's orders?"

"We don't know."

Ximena says, "Conde Eduardo came south not long after we left Brisadulce. He began asking, in the politest way possible, of course, if you had abandoned Joya d'Arena. He claimed distress over your choice to pretend to court a southern lord, only to disappear. Without ever saying it straight out, he convinced a lot of people that the south had been dealt an insulting blow."

All the decisions of the last few months are like a millstone about my neck. I don't need them to explain the rest, because it all clicks together in my head until I am sick with it.

"The southern holdings were already in tumult," I say. "They blame the arid north for draining the country's resources. There has been talk of seceding, like the eastern holdings did."

"Yes," Tristán says.

"Eduardo wants a civil war." I hide my hands under the table so no one can see how much they tremble. "He wants to be king of his own nation. It's what he wanted all along. He tried to have me killed. When that didn't work, he did everything he could to weaken me, especially in the eyes of the southern holdings. That's why he was so set on me marrying a northern lord—to keep my southern alliances thin. That's why General Luz-Manuel had Martín executed—to weaken and dispirit my guard. The two of them must be working together." My heart pounds with certainty and dismay. "The general is the one who has ordered these fortifications, yes?"

The ensuing silence is heavy and thick.

I whisper, "What about Rosario? Is he all right?"

"We don't know, Your Majesty," Tristán says.

I'll never forgive myself if something happens to the boy.

"Captain Lucio will have gotten him to safety," Hector says. "At the first sign of trouble."

Even as I meet his gaze and nod my thanks, I pray to God that he is right.

"So, Your Majesty, what do we do?" Tristán asks.

This is it, then. The moment I must think like the girl who led a desert rebellion and won a war for her husband. Like a queen.

I rise to my feet and begin pacing, worrying at my thumbnail with my teeth. I need allies. Resources. I must turn sentiment in my favor, at least long enough to stall the conde's inciting efforts, long enough to prepare my own fortifications.

My pacing quickens. The first thing I'll do is announce Conde Tristán's nomination to the Quorum. Maybe it will bury the "insult" a little, bely Eduardo's claim that I have abandoned the south. But that will only go so far.

Then what, Elisa? You need a demonstration of your commitment to the south. Something permanent. You need . . .

My head whips up.

I need . . .

I almost choke on grief and gladness and terror as my gaze snaps to Hector's.

I need to marry Hector.

Inheritor of a southern holding much more powerful than Tristán's. A war hero. The best leader I know. Before, marrying him would have been foolish, for he was already my staunchest supporter. But now that my kingdom is about to split apart, a very public alliance with him could be the thing that holds it together.

"Elisa?" he says softly. "What is it?"

I stare at him, at his precious face. I love his dark eyes, the way his hair curls slightly around his ears, his strong jaw, his beautiful lips. I know exactly what those lips feel like against mine.

I could ask him. Right now. But he might say no. Or I could command, and he would obey, but he would never forgive me.

But maybe, just maybe, I will ask and he will say yes.

How, exactly, does a queen propose? Is there an etiquette to observe? A document to sign? I look around the room in panic. Everyone gazes back, puzzled.

I hear shouting. Stomping footsteps, the ring of steel on steel.

Soldiers pour into the dining hall from all three entrances. They are dressed in the crimson and gold of Conde Eduardo's countship.

Everyone at the table shoots to their feet, drawing their weapons, even as a strong arm wraps around my shoulders and the cold point of a dagger presses against my throat.

Eduardo's soldiers ring the room. We are outnumbered three to one.

"Drop your weapons," says a sibilant voice in my ear.

Hector looks to me for instruction, and more than the arm holding me captive, more even than the dagger at my throat, the desperation in his face sends terror shooting through me. Never have I seen him so frightened and helpless.

If they defend me, we will all die. But if the assassin kills me without a fight, maybe he'll let them live. "Do what he says," I say calmly. "Lower your weapons."

They do, reluctantly, plunking them onto the dining table.

Without turning to face my captor, I say, "Hello, Franco."

"Well met, Your Majesty," he says with equal calm. "You have given me an enjoyable and challenging chase. Thank you for that."

"How did you find me?"

"We followed the old lady." Ximena's mouth drops open. "We knew you'd rendezvous eventually."

"Are you going to kill me, then?" I ask, preparing to send my heel into his instep, the way Hector taught me.

"Possibly not." He steps back and lets me go.

I turn to face him. Up close, I don't know why no one saw him for an Invierno. He is too tall, too preternaturally beautiful, to be anything else. His slicked-back hair is a shade or two lighter at the roots, and his eyes are a startling gold—a rare color among Joyans.

But maybe that's why we never met, why he conveniently absented himself when I summoned him. Because more than anyone, I was likely to recognize an Invierno among us.

"Then what *do* you want?" I ask, even as I pray silently, drawing power through the earth, into the Godstone. It comes slowly, a mere trickle, but it comes.

"Don't you dare," says Franco. "If you try to work the magic of your stone, I'll kill every single person in this room."

And just like that, the power dribbles away, leaving me empty and hollow.

"Better. Now, if you want your people to live, you must come with me."

"Come where?"

"Invierne, of course. As a willing sacrifice. It is very important that you come willingly, in accordance with God's will. Failing that, my secondary objective has always been to kill you, which I did attempt, but you have proved wily."

I don't understand what my willingness has to do with anything, though I can't help but note the eerie similarity to Leaf's words about the gatekeeper. *A living sacrifice.* I'll have to think about it later.

"You've been pulling the strings the whole time, haven't you?" I ask. "Invierne meant to weaken me with a very public martyr and set the stage for a civil war. You want us to tear ourselves apart so you don't have to."

His edged grin gives me shivers. "We did say we would come at you like a ghost in a dream."

"Does Eduardo know you're an Invierne spy? Does he know he's being manipulated?"

He shrugs. "He knows. But his ambition allows it. I have promised to rid him of you, another weak ruler in a long line of them. The rank fool thinks he betrays you in service to his country. So, Your Majesty, will you come?"

Ximena rises to her feet. Swords ring her neck instantly, but she puts her hands out, palms up, to show that she means no harm. "I have a better idea," she says.

"Ximena? What are you—"

"The queen still has supporters. If you take her now, Joya d'Arena will rise up against Invierne. So take him instead," she says, pointing to Hector. "If you let everyone go and take him, she will follow. Willingly. She loves him."

I stare at my nurse, shocked and sick. What is she doing? What is she thinking?

"Is it true, little queen?" Franco asks eagerly. "Do you love that man? Such a thing would be even more pleasing to God— for you to follow, intending to give yourself up for him. *No one has greater love than he who gives his own life.*"

I hate Franco for quoting that verse, the one I used to heal Hector. Swords ring Hector's neck now. His eyes on mine are steady but dark with fear—for me, not himself. He nods once, almost imperceptibly. He wants me to say yes. He hopes they'll take him away, leaving me alone and safe. *Don't ever give your life for mine,* he once told me.

Without breaking his gaze, I whisper, "Yes. I love him. Enough to follow him anywhere."

And then Hector realizes his mistake because he gasps like a dying man and closes his eyes against the pain of it.

I turn to Franco, and my voice is clear and cutting when I say, "Hector is a Quorum lord. Taking him hostage is an act of war."

Franco grins. "Stupid queen. We never stopped being at war, your country and mine. Invierne merely retreated." He gestures to the men surrounding Hector, and they grab his arms and haul him roughly away from the table. Hector does not resist.

"You have two months," Franco says. "I expect to see you in our capital by then. Come with no thought to returning, for this is pleasing to God. You may bring a very small escort, but no soldiers. Otherwise, he dies."

"If you kill him, I'll destroy you." Actually, I think I'll destroy him anyway. Yes, I most definitely will.

But Franco ignores me. "Let's go," he says to his men. To Tristán he says, "If your soldiers follow, he dies."

They are halfway out the door when I cry out, "Wait!"

Franco whirls.

My anger, my resolve . . . it has melted into anguish, and all I can do is beg. "Let me say good-bye? Please?"

Franco looks back and forth between us, amused. He shrugs permission, and the soldiers loosen their grip on Hector.

I fly into his arms. He holds me close, stroking my hair, pressing his lips to my temples, murmuring words I can't take in.

"I'll come for you," I whisper.

"Elisa, no." He pushes me away, holds me at arm's length. "Let me do my job this one last time. Take my advice."

"I need you to survive this. Stay alive for me, Hector. Please? *And be ready.*"

And then they're dragging him away, and it feels like I've been gut punched, for I can't force my lungs to draw breath. I fall to my knees, clutching my stomach. *God, how did everything turn out so wrong?*

A hand squeezes my shoulder. It snakes around my neck, pulls me close. "I'm so sorry, my sky," says Ximena. She draws me against her breast, the way she did when I was a little girl. I clutch at her bodice, taking in her familiar scent as she strokes my hair.

"I hope you find comfort in the fact that he sacrificed himself for you," she murmurs. "As I always knew he would. He loved you very much."

I lurch away from her and stare, puzzled, my skin crawling.

"Oh, my sky, the pain will fade. I promise. Just like it did with that boy from the desert. I know it's hard to understand now, but your destiny is so glorious, Elisa. You are a bearer *and* a sovereign. Twice chosen by God. And someday, all this will pale in your memory." She holds her arms out for another embrace.

I rise to my feet, wiping at tears I don't remember shedding. I look down at my nurse. My guardian. The closest thing I've ever had to a mother. It seems as though she kneels at my feet.

"Ximena," I say with imperturbable calm. "You have killed

for me. You have kept things from me. You have sacrificed one of my dearest friends. You did all this without consideration for my will."

Her black eyes are hot with conviction. "I have only ever done what is best. You're just seventeen! You need—"

"I am a grown woman and a queen. And *you* are dismissed."

She gapes at me.

"Go home, Ximena. To Orovalle. I'm sure Papá and Alodia can find a post for you."

"No! I'm your guardian! Elisa, my sky, I love—"

"Tristán, would you please have my former nurse escorted to the nearest passenger ship?"

"At once, Your Majesty," he says coolly, and he gestures toward a handful of men.

Ximena rises, smooths her skirt, then folds her hands together in perfect composure. As they lead her away, she glances over her shoulder at me and says, "I'll always be your guardian. No matter what. It is God's will."

I turn my back on her, sickened and sad, but well and truly ready to be the queen my people need.

"Tristán. Are you still willing to take a position as Quorum lord?"

"Yes, Your Majesty."

I fish one of the Godstones from my pocket. It glitters more deeply than any jewel, in spite of its lifelessness. "Take it. It should fetch a high enough price for a whole garrison. I'll validate it as an authentic Godstone from my personal collection, with a document bearing my royal seal."

His fingers pause in the air above my hand for a moment before he takes it. "Thank you."

I gesture for Fernando to approach, and then I pull out another Godstone and lay it in his palm. "Take this to Captain Lucio. Recruit more guards to defend the palace, if it is not overrun already. If it is, you must go into hiding and rebuild the Guard in secret." I close his fingers around the stone. "Fernando, make me an army of my very own."

"Yes, Your Majesty." He stares at his fisted hand.

"Belén!"

He approaches, his face dark.

"You are now my personal guard. You will see to my safety above all else."

He nods acceptance, then peers down into my eyes. "You're planning something dangerous and brilliant again."

In spite of everything, I smile up at him. Indeed, the threads of a strategy are patterning together in my mind, and I'm heady with the power of it. The kind of power I really need.

"I want messages sent to Crown Princess Alodia and Queen Cosmé," I say to no one in particular. "Multiple copies, to be safe. See if they'll agree to meet me in exactly three months' time in Basajuan, for the world's first parliament of queens."

I resume pacing, right where I left off when Franco's men barged in. "I'll send a message to Ventierra, to Hector's father, commanding that he reinstate Hector as his sole heir. And I need a proclamation—Mara, did my wax and seal survive our journey?" When she nods, I say, "A proclamation announcing my betrothal to Lord-Commander Hector, heir to the countship of Ventierra." That should stall Conde Eduardo's efforts to discredit me with the southern lords. All I need is a little time.

Mara hurries over and takes my hands. "Er, congratulations on your pending nuptials?"

I whisper, "He'll be so angry when he learns I have engaged us without his knowledge."

"Yes," she says. "Definitely. But you'll convince him."

Belén says, "When do we all leave?"

"We all?"

"We're going to Invierne with you, of course," Mara says.

Of course, she says. As if journeying deep into enemy territory is no more than a quick jaunt through the market. I blink against tears. "I need a few days to make arrangements and set things in motion. Then we go."

Clanking chains echo through the dining hall as Storm rises to his feet. "I'm going, too," he says. He has been near invisible the whole time, huddled beneath his cowl. "You need a guide. And it's time I stopped hiding like a frightened rabbit."

I nod, knowing he offers in friendship this time, that he truly is my loyal subject. "The four of us, then."

"You should have five!" Tristán protests. "For blessing and protection. It's the holy number."

I draw myself to full height, and my voice rings clear when I say, "The fifth place is for Hector."